The Second-Last Woman in England

Also by Maggie Joel

The Past and Other Lies

The Second-Last Woman in England

Maggie Joel

Constable & Robinson Ltd
55–56 Russell Square
London WC1B 4HP
www.constablerobinson.com

First published in Australia by Pier 9,
an imprint of Murdoch Books Pty Ltd, 2010

First published in the UK by Corsair,
an imprint of Constable & Robinson Ltd., 2013

A copy of the British Library Cataloguing in Publication
Data is available from the British Library

ISBN 978-1-47210-193-8 (hardback)
ISBN 978-1-47210-498-4 (ebook)

Printed and bound by CPI Group (UK) Ltd, Croydon, CR0 4YY

1 3 5 7 9 10 8 6 4 2

For my mother, Sheila

Acknowledgements

Thanks to Colette Vella, Kay Scarlett, Ali Lavau, Rhiannon Kellie, Tricia Dearborn, Louise Godley, Sheila Joel, Anne Benson, Liz Brigden, Sharon Mathews and all the wonderful people at Murdoch Books for your continued assistance, support, expertise and encouragement during the writing and publication of this book.

The Second-Last Woman in England

Prologue
JUNE 1953

Towards the end of May 1953, Mr Cecil Condor Wallis made the decision to watch the Coronation on a newly purchased television set rather than give in to his children's wishes to join the hundreds of thousands lining the streets less than a mile from his South Kensington home. It was an odd decision for a man who had, on a number of occasions, expressed his loathing for the new medium—and one that probably cost him his life.

There were, of course, other factors, aside from the decision to purchase the television set, that contributed to Mr Wallis's death.

On the day in question—that disappointingly wet Tuesday on the second day of June—the Wallises, their two young children and a number of close family and friends gathered in the Wallises' home at number 83 Athelstan Gardens to watch the broadcast. A party had been organised. Not just tea and lemonade, but champagne!

Ordered from Harrods and delivered the day before by a liveried man in a large green and gold van. The silver had been polished. A Scottish smoked salmon, plump Spanish olives and tiny wafers of French toast had been laid out on silver trays in the kitchen downstairs. A pale-pink crab soufflé steamed gently in the oven. (How all this had been achieved on the extra ration of one pound of sugar and four ounces of margarine provided by the Government over the Coronation month remained a mystery.) And a television set had been purchased for the occasion from Peter Jones of Sloane Square and set up in the upstairs drawing room.

On that day Mr Wallis wore a navy blazer, beige flannel trousers, a white linen shirt, a cricket club tie, navy socks (wool) and black loafers (leather, Italian). He had eaten two kippers and some buttered toast for his breakfast and at some point during the morning he drank one cup of tea and one of coffee, both with milk but not sugar—so noted the coroner's report the following week.

How long Mr Wallis took to consider his wardrobe that morning (should he wear the cricket club tie rather than the rowing club?) or his breakfast half an hour later (ought he to risk that second kipper? Should he butter his toast but perhaps not spread marmalade on it?) was undoubtedly less time than the coroner took to record all these facts and to present them, first at the inquest and later at the trial. And it was certainly less time than the prosecuting counsel and the jury took to mull, at length, over each and every item.

On the morning of her Coronation, Queen Elizabeth, travelling in her Gold State Coach drawn by eight handsome Windsor Greys and surrounded by sundry gloriously liveried and uniformed escorts, left Westminster Abbey after her crowning and returned along Whitehall and The Mall, arriving in triumph at Buckingham Palace at a little before one o'clock in the afternoon. At a few minutes past one, according to those present, Mr Wallis left his drawing room to ask the housekeeper, Mrs Thompson, to bring another bottle of champagne up from the kitchen. He re-entered the room at 1.20 pm, having not (according to Mrs Thompson) spoken to her.

He returned to his seat and picked up a glass of champagne at the exact moment that his wife, Mrs Harriet Wallis, entered the room and shot her husband six times in the chest, abdomen and left leg with a double action Webley Mk VI revolver. Two bullets, the second and third, entered his heart and he died instantly.

All of the witnesses later recalled that at the precise moment Mrs Wallis had entered the room, the newly crowned Queen Elizabeth had stepped out onto the balcony of Buckingham Palace with her family. The thousands waiting outside the Palace, their faces pressed against the railings, had burst into a spontaneous rendition of 'God Save the Queen'. It represented not simply the culmination of a magnificent day, but the beginning of a glorious new era.

And perhaps it was the breathtakingly unpatriotic timing of Mrs Wallis's crime that caused the jury to take a mere 45 minutes to find her guilty of murder.

By the time the new Queen and the Duke of Edinburgh had departed on their tour of the Commonwealth in November, Harriet Wallis had been tried, convicted and hanged and lay in an unmarked grave in West London.

Which was a pity, for had Mrs Wallis waited just twelve years to murder her husband—capital punishment by then having been abolished—she would merely have received a life sentence; might, indeed, still be alive today, paroled and living quietly under an assumed name in a provincial town. But it was 1953 and on that grey November morning Harriet Wallis became the second-last woman in England to be hanged.

Chapter One

The settee was lop-sided—high at one end and low at the other and with an arm only at the high end so that you felt as though you were going to slide off it. It was made of a dark, highly polished wood that gleamed importantly and was upholstered in a rich crimson velvet that resisted any attempt to render it simply a piece of furniture on which to place your bottom.

Jean Corbett attempted, unsuccessfully, to hover about an inch above the rich crimson velvet. She knew that if she so much as came into contact with it she would mark it—indelibly, and for all time.

And worse, that she wouldn't get the job. She swallowed and hoped her thigh muscles were up to it.

'You don't appear to have any qualifications, Miss Corbett.'

Jean's heart sank and the settee sighed contemptuously beneath her.

13

Opposite her in a chair of such slender proportions, with such spindly legs and narrow back it hardly seemed designed to hold an actual person, sat her prospective employer. It was a modern chair— a chair that thumbed its nose at wartime utility furniture. A chair whose sole purpose it was to hold someone like Mrs Harriet Wallis.

For Mrs Wallis, too, seemed bizarrely out of proportion. She sat, one leg crossed over the other, the sheen of her nylons giving her shins a metallic quality, the toe of her black court shoe pointing directly at Jean. Her legs, from knee to foot, seemed impossibly long but instead of appearing deformed, Mrs Wallis appeared to be some higher being, some superior species of female that instantly rendered the remainder of her sex stunted and obscene. Once Jean had accepted the distressing reality of such legs, she took in the suit—smart, elegant, cream-coloured and probably Dior (Jean had no idea if it was Dior; this was the only designer whose name she knew)—she noticed the hands (slender, manicured), the lips (brightly lipsticked) and the hair (fair without being blonde and if it came from a bottle you would never have spotted it) piled high on her head. As for Mrs Wallis's eyes, they appeared to look straight through her and yet not see her at all.

Jean clutched her handbag and then released her grip lest Mrs Wallis see how tightly she was holding it. Her palms were damp.

She needed this job.

They were seated in a sort of upstairs living room. Around her, Jean had an impression of gaily coloured wallpaper. Of paintings on the wall showing randomly daubed paint. Of hectic patterns on the carpet—narrow, curved lines on a background of burnt orange. It was all Very Modern. Only the lop-sided settee seemed strangely out of place. The settee—and herself. The room was situated on the first floor of a four-storey town house. Jean had never been to a house where the living room was on the first floor before. What was the ground floor for, she wondered? Was there another family that lived downstairs? She knew there wasn't, of course, but her head swam with the thought of so much space for just four people.

Mrs Wallis's eyes rested a moment on Jean's face, flickered for less than a second the length of her body then returned to her face. Jean felt herself being appraised and one part of her flinched and another part hardened. She sat silent, and very still. It seemed important not to draw attention to herself. Difficult when she was being interviewed for a job.

Some moments passed. She had not yet answered Mrs Wallis's question. Perhaps it did not require an answer, for Mrs Wallis had abruptly returned to her silent contemplation of Jean's credentials.

Jean pulled her grey knitted jacket more firmly across her chest and tucked her feet further out of sight beneath the settee. (No matter how much you polished an old pair of shoes it was still an old pair of shoes: heavy, ugly, functional—the kind of shoes, in fact, that a nanny might wear.) No doubt she ought to have worn gloves but she had no gloves—or not the sort you wore in a house like this, in a street like this one. She slid her hands beneath her handbag and waited. Besides, for all she knew nannies didn't wear gloves. She didn't really know what nannies wore—or, in truth, what they did. It made applying for this position something of a challenge.

Mrs Wallis continued to study Jean's papers, holding them at arm's length, her head held back like a long-sighted person who refused to wear their glasses. Or like someone reading something distasteful and rather beneath her.

Jean turned her face towards the window and the street outside. Athelstan Gardens was in South Kensington, situated in a confusing maze of streets wedged in between Fulham Road and Old Brompton Road. Except the streets weren't streets at all—they were gardens and terraces and crescents. In Stepney a street was a street. Here, elegant white-painted four-storey villas lined the west side of the road, each with black painted railings, four steps leading up to a buttercup-yellow front door, a number picked out in polished brass, a perfectly symmetrical orange tree in a little red tub on the front step and, as often as not, a car parked outside. And not just an old black Ford either—on her way here she had counted a Daimler,

15

two Bentleys and three Rolls-Royces, cars scattered casually about like toys in a nursery—well, how she imagined a nursery might like look, had she ever seen one. The east side of the street was bordered by black railings and a newly painted wrought iron gate, securely padlocked, and beyond by a very dense privet hedge tall enough to prevent passers-by from seeing over it—though not tall enough to prevent someone in a first-floor room in a house opposite from seeing what lay beyond. Jean could see a large, leafy private garden with a wide lawn recently mowed, beds of rose bushes and dahlias and four wooden benches, one on each side of the lawn. She had a brief view of a young man in a hat seated on a bench on the far side of the park. The young man stood up agitatedly then at once sat down again.

A park—but a park that was padlocked and only for people who lived in this street.

Jean turned away to concentrate on the room and the interview. She had been advised that the agency had vacancies for a nanny—indeed, it had turned out that the agency had eleven such vacancies. In these post-war days nannies, it appeared, were as much in short supply as eggs and sugar. A girl could take her pick, even a girl with somewhat limited experience.

'I am a product of the Norland Nursery Training College, myself,' Miss Anderson of the agency had explained that morning, passing Jean's letter of application back to her. 'Nowadays, of course ...'

Miss Anderson had not completed her sentence though from her tone it had been clear that things were no longer as they had once been and that if the young woman sitting opposite her was the very best that the world could now offer, well, one would simply have to make the best of it.

From the eleven vacancies offered to her, Jean had selected this one, the Wallises in Athelstan Gardens. There were two children, and Mr Wallis, explained Miss Anderson at the agency, was Something Important in Shipping. Jean understood she was to infer from this that Mr Wallis was not a sea captain or anything in that line, but instead was the owner of a ship or perhaps of a whole fleet of ships. Yet a glance around the room presented no miniature ships cleverly mounted in glass bottles or oil paintings of three-masted sailing ships tossed by turbulent seas—or any evidence at all of maritime endeavours.

'The agency implied you had a certain amount of prior experience, Miss Corbett,' Mrs Wallis was saying. She handed Jean's papers back and reached over to the silver cigarette case which lay on an occasional table beside her, opening the lid and selecting a cigarette. The lid snapped shut and she placed the cigarette in her mouth.

Jean watched and knew that this brief interlude provided her with time to present a good response. She knew that she had prepared a good response to this question, that Miss Anderson from the agency had raised this very question herself at their interview that morning, had even provided her with that very response. And yet for the life of her she couldn't recall what the response was.

Opposite her, Mrs Wallis produced a slim gold cigarette lighter and flicked the lever with a sharp rasping sound. A blue flame shot out and a second later a thin wisp of smoke slowly rose ceiling-ward. The lighter was then laid carefully on the table beside the cigarette case and still the question of Miss Corbett's prior experience remained unresolved.

'Yes,' said Jean, nodding to give her reply added emphasis. 'I mean, that would be correct. I have a great deal of experience, one way or another.'

('Remember, Miss Corbett,' Miss Anderson at the agency had said, with a shrewd glance over the top of her half-lens glasses, 'there is a chronic shortage of nannies—or indeed any sort of domestic staff—in these austere times. The ball, one might say, is entirely in our court. Your court, Miss Corbett.' There had been a delicate pause before she had resumed: 'Naturally, this agency would only wish to supply the absolute cream of suitable personnel to its clients; however, it must be said that when demand outstrips supply our duty to supply must take precedence over our need to excel.')

All of which was intended to inform this most recent addition to their books that they were scraping the bottom of the barrel with her but that they could, in all probability, get away with it if they all played their parts correctly. Jean tried to remember her part.

'I come from—came from,' she corrected herself quickly, 'a large family and I was the eldest child, you see. Well, naturally it fell to me to look after the other children, particularly the elder ones. Mum— my mother—had the little ones to see to, you see.'

She paused. Somehow she did not think Mrs Wallis did see.

No one said anything for a moment. Mrs Wallis drew on her cigarette and another wisp of smoke joined the first somewhere above their heads. The cigarette was a du Maurier. At home people smoked Craven A's or Players or Woodbines. Jean waited.

Mrs Wallis tapped the cigarette on a small silver ashtray with a sharp rap.

'And this was in ...?' she said.

'Oh, before the war. And during.'

'I meant, where was this? What place?' Mrs Wallis asked as if inquiring after some distant land one had heard of only in fairytales or in newspaper reports.

'Stepney,' said Jean.

Mrs Wallis nodded slowly. No doubt she had heard of Stepney.

'And afterwards I cared for Mrs McIlwraith's two little ones. Mrs McIlwraith was our neighbour. Her husband having left.'

('Be precise, Miss Corbett. And at all times stick to the point in hand,' advised Miss Anderson from the distance of their interview that morning.)

'Mrs McIlwraith's children were a boy aged seven and a girl aged five. I looked after them for some years, provided their meals and made sure they got to school.'

'I see. My own children are, of course, a little older than that.'

'Oh, of course,' said Jean, understanding that by 'older' Mrs Wallis was only partly referring to their ages and was in large part referring to their social standing.

'Therefore I require someone who is able to provide general home-help duties as well as nannying. The agency will have explained that?'

The agency had not explained that.

Jean nodded vigorously.

'And your own family have no further need of you, Miss Corbett?'

'I'm afraid my family were all killed by a V2 rocket that landed on our house, in 1945. February. I was out, you see, that day so—'

Jean made herself stop.

There was a pause. She ought not to have said that. A flicker of panic began to rise in her stomach. Stupid, *stupid* to say that.

'Oh, my dear, how simply ghastly for you,' said Mrs Wallis and she leant forward, gave a slight frown and flashed a quick smile of sympathy in Jean's direction.

It was so unexpected, such a complete reversal of her earlier detached coolness, that Jean replied with a somewhat stiff smile of her own.

She hadn't intended to mention the bomb. Had told herself she wouldn't under any circumstances—well, you didn't, did you, not to a prospective employer? And not if you intended to present yourself as a calm and emotionally unencumbered person capable of taking charge of some stranger's precious offspring. But there, now she *had* mentioned it, it had just popped out and perhaps, if Mrs Wallis's smile was anything to go by, it was all for the best.

There was a silence that began to stretch for longer than was entirely comfortable.

('Your credentials, Miss Corbett—do not forget to present your credentials. They are your passport to employment.')

Jean held out the two sheets of paper, one typed, one handwritten, that contained her reference from Mrs McIlwraith and another from the head teacher of the small local school she had attended during the war.

'My references,' she explained as Mrs Wallis merely stared at the outstretched pages as though they contained lewd pictures.

'Ah. Quite.' Mrs Wallis took them and leant back in her chair. A moment passed as she read first one page and then the second. She took a sharp pull on her cigarette and her eyes narrowed dramatically as she read and Jean felt herself slowly tensing. What could she see? What error had Mrs McIlwraith made in her reference? Were the dates wrong? Was her name misspelt? Did they, perhaps, look fake?

Just as the moment seemed stretched to breaking point, Mrs Wallis looked up.

'And you are how old, Miss Corbett?'

'Twenty. Last birthday. April.'

'And have you a young man?'

('Your prospective employer will no doubt enquire as to your status vis-à-vis a young man, Miss Corbett.' Miss Anderson had paused significantly at this point. 'Naturally she will wish to be reassured regarding your long-term loyalty, and, of course, as to the welfare of the children she places in your care.')

'Oh no, no young man. Nothing like that.'

Mrs Wallis made no response other than to smoke silently for some moments. Had she got her heart set on employing someone who was twenty-one? Or nineteen? Someone respectably betrothed to a steady young chap instead of dangerously unattached and flighty?

Mrs Wallis smiled with alarming suddenness. 'Well. No doubt you will wish to meet the children?'

'Yes, indeed!' said Jean smiling brightly in reply.

Did this mean she had got the position? Or was it part of the interview? A test to see how she got on with the children?

'Good. I shall fetch them. Please wait there, Miss Corbett,' and Mrs Wallis uncrossed her legs and arose from the chair in one fluid movement. Hastily Jean half rose, then gingerly lowered herself down again on to the rich crimson velvet, realising just how tired her thighs were becoming.

There were voices outside the door. A man's voice, quite deep and speaking from a distance, but becoming more distinct as he approached.

'...*devil's* going on? We're supposed to be at Leo's at twelve.'

'Don't be tedious, Cecil. He's hardly going to miss us for half an hour. And if you care to cast your mind back approximately two hours you may recall my mentioning to you that I intended to interview a new nanny this morning.'

The man now moved away from the door so that Jean could not make out his reply, only the tone, which was cross.

Mrs Wallis, however, was evidently still standing beside the closed door:

'Oh heavens, Cecil, I really haven't the faintest idea who she is. Some wretched orphan from Stockwell. Family wiped out en masse in the war—no danger of this one running off home to nurse an elderly parent, at least.'

In the drawing room, where Jean sat, a chrome-plated clock on the mantelpiece chimed the quarter-hour then fell silent. On the small occasional table Jean's credentials and the letter of introduction from the agency lay discarded. One of the references had slipped down between the chair and the table and lay on the thick pile carpet.

Jean released her aching thighs and sank down into the crimson velvet of the settee waiting for something to break or rip, but nothing happened.

Stepney, she thought, not Stockwell.

She looked down at her feet. Her shoes had been Mum's shoes once. A new pair of wartime shoes when new shoes in wartime were as scarce as good news. They had survived the blast. It had been surprising what had survived, considering so much of the house, so much of the people in it, had been destroyed. But Mum's shoes had survived. Navy, they were. Stout, practical. Low-heeled. Not fashionable, even when new, but built to last. Built to withstand a V2, at any rate.

Against the chaotic pattern of the Wallises' drawing room carpet and the rich crimson velvet of the lop-sided settee they looked indecent. Jean stared silently at her feet and on the mantelpiece the chrome-plated clock ticked discreetly.

The door opened and a girl came in.

She was, if Miss Anderson's information was correct, a child of nine though she had a smallish frame and the rounded face and nose of a younger child. She was neatly dressed in a tartan pinafore that was tied with a bow at the waist and beneath which she wore a pressed white blouse. Her hair was tied in a ponytail with a matching tartan ribbon and she wore knee-length white socks and highly polished navy shoes fastened with a buckle. They were the exact same shade of navy as Jean's own shoes but they looked as though they had never ventured beyond the front door of number 83 Athelstan Gardens, let alone survived a V2.

The girl stopped about a foot inside the door and put her head on one side, narrowed her eyes and surveyed the stranger on the lop-sided settee with a scrutiny that belied her youth.

'I'm Anne,' she announced loudly and decisively as though to scotch a nasty rumour. 'I suppose you are going to be our nanny.' It wasn't a question. 'Of course, we don't need a nanny, you know. We're far too old.'

Jean got to her feet and offered a smile, one that was intended to project authority and competency with a hint of warmth and the possibility of friendship.

'Well, your mother seems to think that you do,' she replied.

Anne appeared to consider this for a moment. 'Oh, I doubt it,' she replied airily, though she did not then go on to explain why she doubted it. Instead she announced: 'Julius will be here in a minute.'

Julius was presumably the older child.

'He's doing his Latin prep, so he can't be disturbed.'

Jean had a sense that she had somehow lost the initiative in this meeting, and meetings—*first impressions, Miss Corbett*—were crucial.

'How do you do, Anne? My name is Miss Corbett, Miss Jean Corbett. I'm very pleased to meet you.'

Anne dismissed this and went across the room to the large sash window, which was wide open. Clearly unimpressed by the arrival of a potential new nanny, she leant precariously out until her feet left the ground. Alarmed, Jean took a step towards her, ready to spring into action should the child decide to tip right over and fall out.

'I had a kitten,' Anne announced, placing her feet back on the floor and turning to face Jean. 'Perhaps Mummy told you? A darling little ginger kitten it was. Called Nellie after our last nanny—'

'Oh, how adorable!' said Jean obligingly, glad that the girl had left the window and now appeared keen to establish some sort of rapport.

'—but she died. The kitten, I mean, not nanny. I drowned her one Sunday afternoon in the kitchen sink because she had made a puddle in my bedroom when I had expressly told her not to.'

The girl laughed, a high-pitched laugh that seemed devoid of the usual things that laughter was meant to contain—like humour.

'What absolute *rot*! Anne, you are an utter bore.'

Jean spun round as a second child stalked into the room. In contrast to his sister, Julius looked older than his thirteen years. Perhaps it was the open-necked white shirt he sported or the long grey flannels when most children his age and in the sunshine of a warm September morning would still be going about in short trousers. His hair was razor short at the back and around his prominent ears and remarkably long at the front so that he stood with a sideways stance to keep it from falling into his eyes. He smiled in a business-like fashion and thrust out his hand.

'I'm Julius. You *are* the nanny, aren't you?' he said as Jean hesitated.

'Yes. That is—if your mother—'

'Oh Mother's hardly going to send you away, not in the current climate,' he said blithely and, as Jean had nothing to add to this, she took his hand and shook it.

'I expect you want to hear that the last nanny had such a rotten time of it here that she was eventually wheeled away in a straitjacket and locked up in a loony bin, don't you? Well, you're quite safe. Actually she left to administer to an aged parent. All very dull.'

'She returned to Leicester,' announced Anne, darkly, from her position by the window. 'Have you been to Leicester?' she enquired, rounding on Jean abruptly, her eyes suddenly very bright and vivid.

'No, Anne, I can't say that I have.'

'Where are you from, then?' the girl demanded, and both children eyed her with sudden curiosity as though a nanny who did not herald from Leicester should be viewed with some suspicion.

'Well, I'm from here. From London.'

Julius dismissed this with a wave of his hand. 'Yes, but obviously not from *here*. Where exactly?'

'From East London. From a place called Stepney.'

Jean paused. No, it was no good. No matter how you dressed it up, Stepney still sounded exactly like what it was. 'Have you heard of Stepney?' she added, just for something to say rather than out of any expectation that the Wallis children undertook regular field trips to the East End.

But Anne had returned to her death-defying stance on the window sill and Julius had picked up a copy of *The Times* and neither showed much interest in the far-flung reaches of Britain's Empire beyond the City of London.

The clock on the mantelpiece chimed the half-hour. No one moved. Outside in the street a car pulled up and a door slammed. In the distance a small dog yapped and a child laughed. Anne began to kick the wall beneath the window with her foot with a thud, thud, thud.

'Well. Perhaps I ought to just speak to your mother to make sure everything is in order,' Jean suggested, getting up briskly from the settee. (Briskness was the key! She had an idea that nannies should do most things briskly.)

Through the open window she could hear the latch of the gate being lifted and footsteps coming up the front steps.

'It's the police,' observed Anne, matter-of-factly. 'I expect they've come to make an arrest.'

Chapter Two

SEPTEMBER 1952

'It's the police,' announced Mrs Thompson, standing in the doorway of the upstairs drawing room and rubbing her hands on her apron in a manner that suggested she had known it would come to this and, frankly, she was washing her hands of the whole lot of them. 'An Inspector 'Arris and another gentleman,' she added and stood awaiting further instruction.

Harriet knew very well it was the police. She had observed the black Maria as it had cruised along Athelstan Gardens and glided ominously to a halt outside number 83. She had taken a step sideways away from the window as the two gentlemen, one in uniform, the other in a cheap grey suit and hat, had emerged from the car and consulted their notes. She had held her breath while they had exchanged a brief word and there still remained the slim, ever-diminishing, possibility that they would go up to number 85 instead. And finally she had ducked out of sight and leaned, for a moment, with her eyes closed against the wall to take a deep breath as the policemen had turned towards the gate of number 83 and lifted the latch.

Now Mrs Thompson was standing in the doorway holding out an inspector's card and two policemen were waiting in the hallway.

'They're here to see Mr Wallis,' added Mrs Thompson and for a disorienting moment Harriet could make no sense of these words.

Then she felt her jaw fall slack and instantly snap shut again loudly: they were here to see *Cecil*! She closed her eyes for a moment. No doubt Mrs Thompson found it amusing to withhold this vital piece of information until the very last moment.

'Well, what are you waiting for, Mrs Thompson? Kindly show the gentlemen into the reception room.'

And then, belatedly, she thought, What could the police possibly want with *Cecil*?

Inspector Harris turned out to be a very young man for such a senior rank—late thirties perhaps, not much more. One heard often of young men who had acquitted themselves well in the war, who had risen rapidly through the ranks and who, consequently, found themselves in civilian life at a rank much higher and much sooner than such men might have achieved before the war.

The war had changed, and continued to change, many things.

'Inspector. How do you do? I am Mrs Harriet Wallis.'

Standing just inside the doorway was a young constable, a boy, really, in a uniform that didn't fit him, and she smiled at him. He blushed and ducked his head then hastily removed his helmet. And that was a good sign, surely? If they were here to do anything too official surely the constable would not have taken off his helmet?

On the other hand, you didn't send an inspector round to deal with 'a motoring offence'.

'Good morning, madam,' said the inspector tipping his hat but maintaining his position in the centre of room rather than coming forward to offer his hand. 'Sorry to barge in on your Saturday morning.'

'Oh dear, I do trust something *dreadful* hasn't happened,' Harriet replied. After all, this was the sort of question one was expected to ask, wasn't it? This was the way one was expected to react to a visit from the police? She produced a handkerchief and crushed it anxiously between her fingers.

The inspector regarded her expressionlessly.

'No, madam, nothing like that, I can assure you,' he replied. 'But I would be obliged if I could have a word with your husband. Is he at home?'

Indeed, he was at home but what did the police want with him?

'Certainly, Inspector. Mrs Thompson, perhaps you would be so kind as to ask Mr Wallis to join us?'

'No need to bother yourself, madam. We can go up to his study and talk there. Mr Wallis has a study, does he?'

Harriet smiled pleasantly. He needn't think he was going to get away with questioning Cecil alone in his study.

'It's no trouble, Inspector. Please take a seat.'

Harriet sat down on the edge of a chair and produced a cigarette.

'Inspector?'

'No, thank you all the same, Mrs Wallis.'

The inspector took the chair opposite and the constable remained in his position by the doorway, his eyes flickering around the room and settling on the Graham Sutherland print above the fireplace.

As she lit her cigarette Harriet could feel the inspector's eyes watching her, and continuing to watch as she put down the lighter and sent a thin stream of cigarette smoke upwards. It was warm in this room. The French doors at the end of the room opened onto the back garden and sunlight flooded in. A shaft struck the carpeted floor and dust motes floated upwards, caught in its glare. Harriet felt a prickle of moisture on her upper lip, behind her knees and beneath her arms. She wanted to dab her handkerchief to her face but that would draw attention to it.

'Really! This heat is intolerable.' She stood up. 'I must get Mrs Thompson to open these doors up and let in some fresh air.'

No one replied to this.

She went to the windows and looked out. It was quite likely no one had opened the French doors since the garden party late last summer. A thick layer of dust coated the door handle—what *was* Mrs Thompson being paid for?

The clock on the mantelpiece indicated that it was approaching noon. The woman from the nanny agency had rung during breakfast and Harriet had agreed to an interview at very short notice. But somehow it had taken the girl two hours to get here from Kensington High Street when the woman from the agency had said she would be there in half an hour. The girl was upstairs—what was her name? Corbett, yes. Not particularly good references. Easy enough to fake—though why would someone fake a reference to get a job as a nanny? The girl would do, she would have to. There were more important things to think about at present. And they were supposed be at Leo's at twelve. Would they go, now that the police were here?

What *were* the police here for?

Harriet closed her eyes for a brief second and felt a pressure at her temples.

'This is a very pleasant neighbourhood, Mrs Wallis,' remarked the inspector, settling back in his chair.

Harriet observed him silently over her cigarette. No doubt Scotland Yard found themselves more often than not in unsavoury places. The remark had been fatuous and there was no need to reply to it. Though she had an idea that this young inspector did not just make conversation.

There were footsteps outside in the hall, then Cecil's voice.

'Thank you, Mrs Thompson,' and in another moment the door opened and Cecil came in. Or rather he stood in the doorway as if this wasn't his house and he hadn't the right to simply come walking in and where, a week ago—two days ago—Harriet might have smiled at this, now she felt a rush of irritation.

Cecil was in his Saturday uniform, which meant grey flannels of a fractionally lighter grey than the grey trousers he wore to the office, a white shirt, a striped club tie and a blazer. His shoes were brown loafers and in deference to the unseasonable September heat he wore beige socks rather than the usual dark grey. His hair was neatly flattened and precisely parted. It was only when the inspector got hurriedly to his feet that Cecil took a step forward into his own room and held out his hand. Reticent, that was Cecil. But there nothing on his face to indicate guilt. Surprise, yes; confusion, possibly; but certainly not guilt.

'Inspector,' he said. 'How do you do? What can I do for you?' and he shot a quizzical look at his wife, perhaps weighing up whether she already knew or not. Harriet returned his look calmly through a haze of cigarette smoke.

Was he remembering the last time two policemen had come to the house? But that was in 1944 and there had still been a war on. He had no reason to think that this was in any way connected.

'Perhaps we might go somewhere private, Mr Wallis?'

Good *God*! Had Cecil visited a prostitute or something?

But Harriet banished that thought almost at once. Cecil still did not look even vaguely guilty—although he was now beginning to look somewhat alarmed. Besides, Cecil with a prostitute! No, it was something the inspector wanted to inform Cecil about, not something he wanted to charge him with—and Harriet felt the pressure at her temples again.

'No need, Inspector,' she said getting up. 'I'll leave you gentleman to your business,' and she left the room so abruptly that Cecil had to sidestep rapidly to avoid being bowled over.

Harriet closed the door behind her. Outside in the street a milk cart rattled past returning empties to the depot. Upstairs she could hear the children's voices:

'Unfortunately he lost an ear and his nose last Christmas, which is rather sad, don't you think?'

Anne's voice floated down the stairs quite distinctly and Harriet presumed her youngest child was introducing nanny to her teddy bear. Downstairs in the kitchen Mrs Thompson had the Light Programme on—*Housewives' Choice* or something equally edifying— though all one could make out was a background whine of popular music and a steady stream of crackling interference. The radio abruptly went silent and a moment later Mrs Thompson herself emerged from the kitchen below, her face red and shiny with the effort of ascending the short flight of stairs.

'Everything all right, is it?' she enquired, without even the grace to look abashed at asking such a question.

'Mrs Thompson, it's stifling in here and the gentlemen are finding it quite unpleasant. Please open up the French doors so they can get some air. And see if they'd like coffee. I expect Mr Wallis will want some as it's approaching noon. And some biscuits, of course. But do see about that door at once.'

Mrs Thompson reached the top of the stairs, paused, then opened her mouth to reply. Mrs Thompson would, of course, have her own thoughts about the opening of doors—French or otherwise.

'Oh, and open the doors in the dining room too,' Harriet added.

She went through into the dining room and walked over to the bay window that looked over Athelstan Gardens. The milk float had gone. Two small boys walked past carrying fishing nets and glass jars with string handles, heading south towards the river. A nanny and a small child emerged from a house further up the street, crossed over the road and walked towards the garden opposite. She couldn't see into the enclosed garden from here, the privet hedge was too high. It was possible to see in from the upstairs rooms, though, if one was looking.

After a short delay Mrs Thompson bustled in, her face a little redder, a little more indignant.

'Weren't too pleased about being interrupted, those gentlemen,' she observed, casting a malevolent look at her employer. 'Said they didn't wish for coffee, thank you very much,' she added, going down to the far end of the room and attacking, with pointed vigour, the doors that opened onto the back garden.

It was possible these doors had not been opened since before the war, but Mrs Thompson had located a key and was already shooting back the bolts at top and bottom and throwing open both doors with a gesture dramatic enough to rival Elsie Morison in last year's production of *The Marriage of Figaro*.

'Will *you* be wanting coffee?' asked Mrs Thompson, rounding on her employer suspiciously.

'No thank you, Mrs Thompson. And we shall be lunching at the Mumfords', so we shan't be wanting anything till teatime.'

She had informed Mrs Thompson of this fact two days earlier, and again last night, but it seemed important to restate it now— Mrs Thompson did not cope well with changes to the household routine.

'I see!' replied Mrs Thompson, her nostrils flaring as though this was the first she had heard of any luncheon at the Mumfords' and frankly she'd have preferred a little notice, thank you very much, and she swept from the room.

Surely there had been a time (before the war) when domestic staff had said, Very good, madam, and did one's bidding without comment?

Would they be lunching at the Mumfords'?

Harriet walked down to the garden end of the room and took in a deep breath of fresh air. Outside sparrows swooped and dived noisily, observed by next door's tom cat. A wasp buzzed in through the open door, followed a moment later by a large fly. In the distance a child in a neighbouring garden laughed, a car backfired, distant traffic rumbled on Fulham Road. A burst of birdsong—a thrush, a chaffinch?—filled the air for a moment and when it ended an abrupt silence fell.

'Rocastle? Dear God. But it's … I simply can't believe it of him.'

Mrs Thompson had evidently opened the French doors in the reception room as instructed. Harriet stood on the step facing the garden, blowing her cigarette smoke carefully in the other direction. It wouldn't do for her smoke to drift into the room next door.

It was Cecil who had spoken. Rocastle worked at Cecil's firm. He had dined with them here in this very room, he and his wife, though the man was quite junior in the firm. He had some connection—an uncle who held a senior post at the F.O.—which explained the man's presence at the dinner. She remembered him as being a rather bland man, a little over-eager perhaps, and his wife a bit not-quite-the-thing. But pretty.

'There doesn't seem to be much room for doubt, I'm afraid, Mr Wallis.'

The inspector said these words as though he were reading the lines from a detective novel. Perhaps that was how it was if one worked for Scotland Yard—one said the same things over and over again so that eventually everything sounded like a cliché.

'I see. You are aware, Inspector, the fellow's an Etonian? A Cambridge man? He went to my old college. Damn it, his uncle is in the F.O.! Really, Inspector, I find it impossible to believe—'

'Facts speak for themselves, I'm afraid, sir. The safe has been opened, it's empty—well, barring some documents which I'm hoping you'll look over for me, sir? And a sum of money has gone. A Mr Pickering noticed the safe this morning—'

'Yes, Pickering is the nightwatchman but—'

'Quite, sir. And the safe, as I can myself verify having just come from there, was opened using the combination.'

'But surely a safecracker—'

'Quite so, sir. However this same Mr Pickering has made a statement to the fact that Mr Rocastle was working late in his office last night, very late indeed, it would appear. And now he is gone and so too are the contents of the safe.'

'Then he has been kidnapped! Or he is at home right now. I mean, really, Inspector. Pickering is a decent enough man, but he's not—'

'No, indeed, sir. But you'll be interested to learn that Mr Rocastle is not, in fact, at home—number …'

There was a pause while presumably the inspector consulted his notebook.

'Flat 9, Leinster Mansions, Hammersmith. I took the liberty of going straight there, you see, sir, where I discovered the household in question to be in some …'—he cast about for an appropriate word— 'uproar. The man of the house had, it soon became apparent, not returned from the office the previous evening and furthermore—'

'Then surely—'

'And *furthermore*, his passport had been taken. So too his ration book, chequebook, various items of clothing, one, or possibly two, pairs of shoes—the lady of the house was uncertain as to the exact number—and a large suitcase. Dark green in colour, I believe it was.'

'Well, but—'

'Now, sir, if Mr Rocastle had indeed been kidnapped as per your hypothesis, then might I venture to say that it would be a very thorough, not to mention fortunate, kidnapper who had endeavoured to spirit away not only Mr Rocastle himself but Mr Rocastle's passport, his ration book, his cheque book, plus sundry other items previously mentioned, in a large, dark-green suitcase, and all under the nose of Mrs Rocastle.'

There was a silence.

Harriet pulled on her cigarette which had been burning slowly away unsmoked as she had listened. Intolerable little man, she thought, picturing the inspector observing Cecil with his placid gaze. He was thoroughly enjoying himself at Cecil's expense.

A footstep at the doorway of the neighbouring room suggested someone—Cecil?—had walked over and was standing on the step. Harriet took a precautionary step backwards. Her cigarette had gone out but she held off relighting it.

Jeremy, that was his name. Jeremy Rocastle. So, he had gone bad, had he? She would never have spotted it and it went without saying Cecil hadn't. Perhaps what she had taken for eagerness was really ambition, greed. Or perhaps the man had got himself into some difficulty—a woman, gambling, a debt, some indiscretion, a business venture gone sour. The poor wife.

The exact details hardly mattered. The point was: what was going to come out? How much would the firm—would Cecil—be affected? He hadn't even enquired, of course. That would have been the very first thing *she* would have asked.

'There is no absolutely no question, Inspector, that any one of us could have seen this coming,' said Cecil, his voice much louder and closer than she had expected so that she took another step backwards. 'He was a model employee, excellent war record. Really I ... But his poor wife. Poor Jenny. He was so ... so ordinary, really. What *can* have happened?'

There was no reply to this and the inspector did not attempt to offer one.

'Have you spoken to Standforth or MacIntosh or to Sir Maurice, Inspector? They're the other directors of Empire and Colonial. Sir Maurice Debden is the chairman.'

'Not yet, sir. Yours was the first name Mr Pickering gave us.' There was a silence, then: 'We'll need you to go through the books, sir, of course.'

'But good *God*, man, you can't suspect him of embezzling company funds? Surely this is just a one-off thing?'

'In my experience it rarely is a one-off, sir,' replied the inspector in his tiresome, world-weary way.

But how typical of Cecil not to even think of it!

'My God, the firm!' he said.

And that was it. That summed up Cecil. The firm. Never mind he himself might be implicated, or that the family may very well be exposed to Lord knew what sort of unsavoury publicity.

And today, of all days.

Harriet turned and paced the length of the dining room.

What was to be done? Nothing until the policemen had gone. Would they take Cecil with them? That would set tongues wagging. No, Cecil wouldn't put up with that—he'd surely insist it wait till Monday morning. The policemen, then, must be made to leave.

She looked at the clock on the wall and saw that the half-hour was about to strike. If they were going to make it to Leo and Felicity's at all they needed to leave at once. Well, it was probably best to assume they were going. To do everything as normal.

And the nanny! What a day for her to turn up.

Harriet went quickly up the two flights of stairs to the second floor, following the sound of the children's voices. They were in Anne's bedroom.

'Don't pay any attention. It's generally rubbish,' observed Julius from behind the half-open door, no doubt dashing some extravagant claim of Anne's.

Harriet pushed open the door to see Anne sitting on the floor at one end of an extensive line of stuffed animals, stretching from Panda to what looked like a headless elephant. Anne looked up and, seeing her mother, jumped to her feet excitedly.

'What do the police want, Mummy?' she demanded.

'Don't be vulgar, Anne,' Harriet countered, then she regarded the toy parade lined up on the carpet. One of the animals, a small brown bear, was minus an eye and in places its fur had worn completely away. They had purchased the little bear themselves, she and Cecil, at Harrods the week before Anne was born. When they had returned from the hospital Cecil had placed it in the cot and Anne's tiny hands had clung to the thing, curling tightly around it.

Something caught at the back of Harriet's throat at the memory and she bent down and reached for the little bear. From behind the door there was a scuffle of feet and the rustle of cheap clothing as the nanny leapt to her feet.

Harriet stood up abruptly. 'Anne, aren't you a little old for all these?' and she indicated the menagerie on the floor.

'Oh, but I asked to see them,' said the nanny.

And so it had begun already: the conspiracy of nanny and child against parent.

'Miss Corbett. I didn't see you down there.'

'That's because she was behind you and you don't have eyes in the back of your head,' observed Julius, who was standing, leaning against the window, hands in pockets so that you didn't know if he was being clever in an irritating way or deliberately rude.

'We shall be leaving for Uncle Leo and Aunt Felicity's very soon, so please both be ready.'

'Mrs Wallis—'

'But why *are* the police here, Mummy?' said Anne, interrupting the nanny. At Anne's question the nanny turned pale and looked as though she wished she were anywhere else but here.

'I'm sure it's none of our business, Anne,' said the girl, kneeling down to pick up Panda. 'Now why don't we put these away and get you ready to go out.'

She really did look as if the very last thing she wanted to know was why on earth two policemen had turned up at the doorstep of a prospective new employer's house. Perhaps the nanny was used to the police turning up? No doubt when the police arrived at one's house in Stockwell one assumed the very worse and was rarely disappointed.

'Thank you, nanny. We'll let Anne clear up. May I have a word with you outside?'

She went back out, not waiting for the girl's reply.

The girl followed her. She was tall, taller than one expected so that her eyes were at the same level as Harriet's own—or perhaps even an inch higher. She was thin-faced and pale—a childhood of slum tenements, dark alleyways and air raid shelters, presumably. But her nails were clean and her clothes and shoes sensible (though what dreadful shoes!) and her hair tightly crimped in a ghastly home permanent wave which was, after all, what one wanted from a nanny. And the children seemed to have taken to her. Not that one could imagine the children not taking to someone—they seemed amazingly indiscriminating.

'I do apologise, Miss Corbett, for not concluding our interview.'

'Oh, that's all right, I understand—' and the girl stopped because that was leading her perilously close to matters which did not concern her. At this point she seemed to realise she was still holding Panda and she dropped her arms down to her sides as though to hide him.

'Quite. Well, I am satisfied that you have proved yourself adequate to the position, so if you are happy with the conditions outlined by the agency you may commence employment with us at once.'

The girl seemed to take a deep breath, but whether this was because she was relieved or because she was having second thoughts—or simply because she was short of breath—it was impossible to ascertain.

'Thank you. That would be wonderful,' she said.

Would it? Were the girl's ambitions so stunted that working as a child-minder for some other woman's children on two pounds a week plus board seemed wonderful? Apparently so. And thank God for it, Harriet reasoned, otherwise one would be forced to look after one's children oneself. At least during the school hols anyway.

Two floors below, voices could be heard in the hallway.

She turned back to the nanny. 'Now, perhaps if you'll see that the children are ready, Miss Corbett? We are having lunch at my brother-in-law's house, Mr Leo Mumford's at Hampstead, so we shall be away till teatime, I would think. I suggest you move in tomorrow morning around nine o'clock when Mrs Thompson will show you your room and give you a tour of the house.'

'On a Sunday?' said the girl blankly.

'Yes. Unless, of course, that arrangement does not suit you?'

The girl said nothing, as there was nothing one could say to such a question, and Harriet forestalled any further discussion by ushering her back into Anne's bedroom and closing the door behind her.

Downstairs the front door opened and the policemen at last appeared to be taking their leave.

'That would probably be for the best, Mr Wallis. Until we know the full extent of the situation it's very hard to ascertain.'

The inspector's voice got louder as he crossed the hallway then less distinct as he neared the front door.

'Well, I am usually at my desk by nine o'clock, Inspector, should you or your men need to speak to me. And naturally we shall be going through our books with a fine-toothed comb—though I must say it seems like ...'

Cecil's voice trailed off so that she never heard what exactly it seemed like to him.

Downstairs the front door closed and there was silence. Harriet went over to the window and looked out at the street below. She watched the hat and the helmet of the two policemen go down the steps, the constable hold open the gate and the two of them climb into the police car. After a long moment (to compare notes? To weigh up the various suspects? But no, she doubted the inspector would do that with his constable. Perhaps they were deciding where to go for a cup of tea?) the car moved off. The street was deserted, the only presence a solitary figure in a hat seated on a bench in the garden opposite.

Harriet leaned, for a moment, against the wall. They were going to Leo's. Would Simon be there? And, if he was, what would she tell him? Everything? Or nothing?

Chapter Three

SEPTEMBER 1952

The two policemen had gone and Cecil Wallis stood in the hallway for a moment, half listening for the sound of the police car's engine—which came after an intolerable delay—and half wondering what exactly to do. Harriet would need to know what had happened, of course. He must tell her at once.

A noise upstairs from the children's rooms—a thump followed by a child's plaintive voice—distracted him and instead of going in search of Harriet he went quickly and silently upstairs to his study and closed the door firmly behind him.

Silence. Peace. Calm. Here everything was in order. His desk, solid and immovable, standing where it had always stood, its polished walnut veneer gleaming satisfyingly in the midday sunlight. It was a kneehole flat-top desk, late Victorian, and one of the few items he had decided to keep from Father's estate. His leather writing pad rested at a gentle angle on the desk top, his ink pen sat in its holder. Beside it was the wooden paperweight in the shape of a ship's wheel, carved from the mast of an eighteenth century clipper. He had picked it up for a shilling in a shop in Cornwall twenty or more years ago, brought it home and placed it on his desk, where it had sat ever since, and as far as he could recall it had never weighted down a single sheet of paper in all that time. He reached out and traced its smooth weather-worn surface. There was something satisfying, almost comforting, about old timber, especially timber infused with the sea and the thrill of maritime history.

Rocastle.

He placed both hands on the edge of his desk and closed his eyes for a moment. He had made a bad error of judgement. He had compromised the firm. He had compromised himself. *Damn* Rocastle!

Harriet would need some kind of explanation, of course; no way he could keep this quiet. Perhaps he should talk to Leo this afternoon? Good God, no, not Leo of all people. But it was bound to be in the press soon enough.

Well, so be it! It was surely no reflection on him? To what extent was a firm, a director of a firm, responsible for the actions of his employees? Liability, yes, if an accident occurred in the workplace, but if an employee stole from the firm, then surely the firm, the directors, were not liable at all?

Unless of course one had suspected.

He pulled out the chair and sat down at his desk. The fleet of Empire and Colonial Lines was displayed in large format black and white photographs, expensively framed, on all four walls of the study from the 300-ton steam packet *Tilbury* in 1860 to the 80,000-ton *Swane*, head of the current fleet, in pride of place on the wall opposite his desk. The old girl had 16 steam turbines, ten decks and a cruising speed of 30 knots—at her launch she had been the largest and fastest ship in the world. The photograph showed her on her Blue Riband run in '38. He had been on board for that trip. There had been a buzz of excitement aboard the majestic three-funnel liner, a thrill that had swept through the decks so that every crewmember, every passenger had felt it at Southampton. And when she had sailed into New York a mere four days later! The press, he remembered, had been camped at the dockside to welcome them! Five times the *Swane* had won the Blue Riband.

But that voyage in '38 had been the last time. Last week the *United States* had won the Blue Riband for doing the journey in a little over three days! That would have seemed inconceivable a few short years ago.

A few short years that had contained the war. And now nothing was the same.

There was dust on the glass that covered the photograph, a film of dust that turned the *Swane*'s clean white flanks a dull shade of grey and obscured the smiling faces of the crew. He was in that photograph, a small white face cheering as loudly as anyone, standing right beside the captain. What was the man's name?

But he found he could no longer recall it.

It was the war. Nothing was the same. One did one's bit for the war effort, endured it so that things *would* remain the same, could return to how they had been. But now the war had been over for seven years and nothing was the same. And what did three days to cross the Atlantic mean when the Comet could fly the same distance in ten-and-a-half hours? Nothing was the same. The *Swane* needed a refit but how could you justify such an expense when the rest of the fleet was heading for the breaker's yard?

And now this.

Damn and blast Rocastle! How much damage would it do? Theft by an employee could be covered up—that is, it could be dealt with discreetly. But embezzlement … That was bad. That was the kind of thing that affected public confidence, caused share prices to plummet, brought companies down. Resulted in directors being prosecuted.

Ought he to telephone Clarendon? Did one call in a solicitor in such circumstances or did that look like guilt? Or, at the very least, panic?

Somewhere above him a door slammed and footsteps tumbled down the stairs followed sharply by Harriet's voice.

'Anne. We do not slam doors in this house.'

There was a new nanny, he remembered. The children must be getting ready to go out. Oh Lord, they were lunching at Mumford's and—

There was a knock on the door and he felt the colour drain from his face. He got up and called out, 'Yes. Who is it?'

'It's me, Cecil. I'm assuming everything is all right and that we shall be going to Leo's?'

He hesitated. He would tell her, of course; after all, there was no actual shame in it, not for himself at any rate. But perhaps not quite yet. And no need to mention what had happened in August.

'Yes, indeed. Nothing to worry about,' he called out. His voice sounded strained, unnatural. He cleared his throat and tried to speak more normally. 'A minor matter, my dear. I shall be along directly.'

He sank back down into his chair and heard the reassuring creak of the leather. The old chair emitted a musty, almost antiquated, odour. He breathed it in hungrily.

Rocastle was an Etonian. They had been to the same Cambridge college, albeit fifteen or more years apart. The man and his wife had dined here, at this very house.

But it would seem that, in the end, these things counted for little.

There had been an irregularity in Rocastle's bookkeeping. Cecil had discovered it quite by accident three weeks ago, on the last Friday in August. The directors had shared a traditional Friday afternoon glass of sherry in Sir Maurice's office at the end of the day—not that there had been much to toast but Sir Maurice's sherry was always first class—and afterwards Cecil had returned to his own office to lock up. There had been a light on in Rocastle's office and on an impulse he had popped his head around the door to wish him a good weekend.

Rocastle had not been in his office, though he had clearly been intending to work late as a ledger had been open on his desk. It was part of Rocastle's duties to authorise the weekly wages of the head office staff.

Cecil might so easily have turned and left and noticed nothing at all—had he not seen a name on the ledger that caught his eye: Arthur Laurelstone. It was an unusual surname and a name that one tended to remember. The man, Laurelstone, had worked briefly in the shipping clerks' office down on the ground floor but had been dismissed for drunkenness. He had returned to the office a day later and there had been some unpleasantness—a brick thrown through a window or something along those lines—and a constable had been called to remove the man from the premises. It had caused quite a stir at the time.

The incident had been in June. And now here was Laurelstone's name on the ledger of employees receiving their weekly pay packet even though he was no longer employed by the firm. It seemed hard to imagine Rocastle would make a mistake of such magnitude. So what was the explanation? He ought to confront Rocastle, of course; that was obvious. But to accuse a man of such a mistake? Or worse, to hint at … irregularities. Nevertheless, one's first loyalty was to the company.

He had waited in Rocastle's office until he returned.

'Ah, Rocastle, glad I've caught you. That fellow Laurelstone—chap that was dismissed some weeks ago. Noticed he was still on the payroll. Wondered why?'

And Rocastle had provided a plausible explanation—there had been some overtime owing, that was all. Somehow it had been overlooked at the time of the man's dismissal. No harm done. The man had since got himself a position elsewhere.

And that had been that. A simple explanation. Rocastle had made an error but he had admitted the error, had rectified it and there was surely little reason to report it. Yet Cecil had gone back to his desk and noted the incident, written down the details on a sheet of paper and kept it, not at the office, but here at his desk at home.

He reached for the sheet of paper now and glanced again at the dates and names and figures. The thing was, there had been no overtime since the December rush. It was only necessary when things were excessively busy and Lord knew it had been months since they had been even remotely busy. Not only that, but usually overtime was paid from the overtime ledger, not the weekly staff wages ledger. He had realised it at once. He had resolved to report it to Standforth first thing the following Monday morning.

There were more footsteps outside his study door.

'Cecil, are you coming?'

'Yes, almost ready.'

He didn't move from the desk.

He had resolved to report it to Standforth—and yet, in the end, he had not done so.

Cecil stood up and went to the door and opened it. His family were assembling outside, Harriet marshalling them. Anne came tearing past with all the hysterical urgency of youth, clutching a hat, then stopped and twirled in a bizarre pirouette, suddenly and for no obvious reason, in the middle of the landing.

On an impulse he turned and went back to his desk and put the sheet of dates and names and figures inside the large cabinet that stood behind it.

'Are you coming, Daddy?' called Anne from the hallway.

'Yes, just a moment, Anne,' and he turned the key in the lock and stowed it safely in the bottom drawer of the desk.

Outside, the unseasonal September day was continuing to heat up, the air muggy so that Cecil's shirt stuck unpleasantly to his back and his collar clung to his neck.

Harriet was outside already, winding down the windows of the Morris Oxford. The old car had been standing in direct sunlight all morning and inside she would now be as hot as the engine room of an 80-ton liner.

Cecil came down the steps with a cheery wave which Harriet chose to ignore.

'Jolly hot in here, I expect,' he observed, opening the car door and standing back to let a rush of hot air come out. He considered removing his blazer for the journey, but decided against it. They could always drive with the windows wound down.

The children appeared in the doorway and made their way down the front steps, Anne in a gaily coloured tartan pinafore, Julius rather surprisingly in a large knitted Fair Isle sweater. Behind them stood a tall and rather gaunt-looking girl, cheaply dressed, who watched their departure with a mixture of curiosity and something else that he couldn't quite read. The new nanny, presumably. Cecil gave an encouraging smile which caused her to frown.

'What ho, Pops,' remarked Julius in that ultra-informal manner he had recently adopted, the sole purpose of which appeared to be to irritate.

'Where on earth did you get that ghastly sweater, Julius? Please remove it and put on your blazer. You resemble some sort of grammar school jazz fan.'

'Right-ho,' said Julius, turning obligingly and going back into the house.

'Do *I* resemble a grammar school jazz fan, too, Daddy?' asked Anne very seriously as she paused beside the car to study her reflection in the car window.

'Thankfully, no, you do not, Anne. You resemble a nice little girl who is about to go and lunch at her uncle and aunt's. Now, hop to it, we are going to be rather late.'

The reason for the lateness was not mentioned but, as Anne climbed in to the back seat, yelping as her bare thighs touched the hot seat leather, he caught Harriet's eye over the roof of the Oxford.

She raised both eyebrows, a gesture that meant: I presume you intend to tell me what's going on, and in the meantime is there anything I ought to be worried about?

He nodded briefly which meant: As head of the household I have the situation well in hand and there is nothing you need be concerned about.

Julius returned, having discarded the Fair Isle sweater and now sporting a navy blazer, and got wordlessly into the car.

Once they were all seated Cecil pressed the Oxford's starter button. She was a 1930 Morris Oxford Saloon, practically vintage now, of course, but she started first time. He studied the view in the rear mirror, signalled his intention to pull out and moved out from the kerbside.

Harriet and the children sat motionless and silent, staring straight ahead.

Cecil settled back into his seat determined not to let the interview with the policemen spoil the drive. The roads were pocked and cratered still from the bombing, and the congestion nowadays was atrocious (every man and his dog appeared to have a motor car since the war had ended) yet it was a pleasant enough run to Mumford's once past the Edgware Road.

'Crater,' remarked Harriet.

There was indeed a crater, stretching halfway across the road and so choked with rosebay willowherb one wondered if the road had simply been abandoned as a bad job. And in St John's Wood too! Cecil negotiated the obstacle with some aplomb, followed, a little further on, by a second, and then an annoying new roundabout at the Finchley Road turn-off. He sailed through Swiss Cottage without further incident and before long they were approaching the outskirts of the Heath.

The Mumfords lived in All Saints Crescent, a tree-lined semi-circular avenue on the south side of Hampstead Heath. Their house, a sprawling Victorian mansion, was designed for a nineteenth century family with an average of eight children plus sundry servants.

Consequently Leo and Felicity rattled around in it like spectators at a Test match in winter.

The driveway already contained four cars including Leo's silver 1950 Jaguar Roadster which was parked loudly and showily outside the house and had obviously been polished that morning. Cecil squeezed the Oxford in between a Vanguard and another, somewhat newer, Morris, crunching to a noisy stop on the gravel. The engine spluttered for a moment then fell satisfyingly silent. They had arrived.

'We have arrived, safe and sound,' Cecil announced, because this was expected. It was by way of being a family joke after so many years, and there was an unspoken rule that no one moved, no one opened the car door or gathered their belongings together until the ignition had been turned off and these immortal words spoken. It was the same with 'Homeward bound!' on the homeward journey.

Really, it was like any other day; a normal trip on a normal day.

Cecil climbed out of the Oxford and smoothed down his trousers. As the rest of his family sorted themselves out he strode up to the front door and rapped on the giant brass knocker that was shaped, in somewhat vulgar fashion, like an elephant with a ring in its mouth. The boom of the knocker had hardly had time to resonate around the big old house when the door was flung open and Leo Mumford stood there brandishing a cocktail.

'Cecil, old man! How the devil are you?' he said by way of greeting.

'Mumford. How are you?' Cecil replied.

It was impossible to call him 'Leo' even though Mumford had been his brother-in-law for the best part of seven years. Today Mumford was in a crisp, white linen shirt. He and Cecil had the same shirt-maker and yet on Leo the self-same shirt—open at the neck, tucked into loose-fitting cream-coloured flannels—took on an entirely different air. It made Cecil think of that summer in St Tropez in '38. An air of foreignness, then? But Mumford was as English as the Queen. He was more English than the Queen's husband, at any rate. And besides, Mumford worked at the BBC.

'Bit early for that, isn't it?' Cecil said, indicating the transparent liquid in Leo's glass, an olive bobbing decadently on its surface.

'A martini? Never too early for one of those, old man.'

Mumford, as usual, was trying just a little too hard but, when all was said and done, the fellow had married one's little sister. Cecil softened a little.

'Oh well, I expect you're right,' he agreed and, as he suspected Mumford intended to clap him on the shoulder, he side-stepped neatly.

'Go on through, Ceece. The gang's out in the back garden,' said Leo, waving his martini in that general direction.

The gang! Did Mumford imagine himself on the film set of some American musical?

With a growing sense of foreboding, Cecil entered the hallway.

His brother-in-law's house was painted egg-yolk yellow and was stuffed with moulded, bakelite and laminated furniture—ghastly receptacles that Mumford called 'free-flow' chairs and hideous coffee tables which swept upwards at either end like meringue desserts and a piece he claimed was a genuine Barbara Hepworth— furniture one never felt inclined to actually sit on and artwork one never wanted to look at.

The French doors at the rear of the house were open and Cecil could hear voices beyond—a man laughing, a woman making some arch reply and a peal of laughter from several others—and he felt a shudder of dismay. Surely this wasn't going be one of those dreadful Continental affairs, everyone standing around in the garden juggling a plate and a fork in one hand and a glass in the other? Were they not going to sit down to lunch? What was it about a warm, sunny day that made otherwise rational people abandon a perfectly civilised lunch around a table in an elegant dining room just so they could stand about in the garden?

Beyond the French doors he could make out perhaps a dozen people in shirt sleeves and sleeveless summer dresses standing in a group on the lawn. The men all wore brightly coloured silk scarves tucked into their open-necked shirts like a badge that announced their BBC-ness. Everyone looked very young. Cecil paused a moment in the doorway.

'Cecil.'

One member of the circle broke free and came over to him.

'Felicity. How are you?'

Brother and sister greeted each other with a slight kiss on the cheek and a vague touch of hands then stepped apart.

Felicity looked unwell. The sunshine did not suit her. Her frame, always on the slim side, looked almost gaunt; her skin, always on the pale side, took on an unhealthy pallor in the sudden brightness of this September afternoon. And she had a knack for wearing something unflattering. Today it was a floral print frock with very short sleeves gathered at the shoulders and a hat of some undistinguished design in an unwise shade of mauve. One couldn't quite put one's finger on what exactly didn't work—no doubt Harriet could, that was very much her line of country—one simply knew that in a fashion sense Felicity rarely pulled it off.

She smiled at him now a trifle wearily. 'I'm quite well, thank you, Cecil. We're having a fork lunch in the garden. I know you'll hate it,' she said simply and resignedly as though such trials must be borne quietly and with the minimum of fuss.

'Ah well. Can't be helped.' No use denying his dislike of it. 'Leo's idea?'

'Naturally ... Harriet, my dear. How are you? Hello, Anne darling.'

When Felicity leant over to kiss her, Anne shied away in horror and ducked behind her mother. Clearly disconcerted, Felicity straightened up and smoothed down her skirt.

'Is Anne perhaps a little overwrought?'

'Oh, I dare say,' said Harriet, to whom Anne's behaviour had long ceased to be a subject for comment.

'And Julius. My! How you've grown!'

'I'm afraid it's inevitable, Aunt Felicity,' said Julius, thrusting his hands into his pockets in his man-of-the-world stance. 'At our age one never stays the same height.'

'It's really not our fault,' explained Anne, wiping a smear of scarlet lipstick from her cheek then studying her reddened fingertips thoughtfully.

Felicity laughed, her head back, her mouth slightly open, her lips remaining in a perfectly straight line and Anne and Julius observed her with polite interest. Cecil smiled. It really was a pity she and Mumford had no children of their own, Felicity was good with the youngsters. Most women were, of course, but Felicity had that something extra—an ability to get down to their level; yes, that was it in a nutshell.

And it no doubt explained the extraordinary success of the hippo.

'Would you like to help yourselves to lemonade, children?' she said. 'There's a lovely lot of strawberry ice-cream for afters, too,' she added and Anne and Julius smiled obligingly. They wandered off in the direction indicated by Felicity, where a long trestle table was set up, covered with a white cloth and a mountain of perfectly good food that was about to be spoiled by wasps and flies and falling leaves and pollen and, oh yes, if they were really lucky, a summer shower.

Julius was humming to himself. It was a familiar tune though for a moment Cecil couldn't quite place it.

'And you, Cecil? What would you like to drink? Leo will try to force a martini on you.'

It was the hippo song, of course, that Julius was humming. *Hip, hip, hip hooray! It's hip hip hippo day!* Or something like that. And there was a second line too though Cecil couldn't quite remember the words. Daft, really, but the children appeared to like it. He glanced at Felicity as she poured him a drink but she appeared not to have heard Julius's rendition of her theme song. Not Felicity's theme song really, the *Hippo and Friends* theme song.

'Bit early for martinis, isn't it?' he repeated, for something to say.

Hippo and Friends was a popular children's television program broadcast by the BBC at five o'clock on Mondays and Wednesdays, and Felicity was the presenter. It was a ludicrous sort of profession really, but there you were—not everyone could be, nor wished to be, a doctor or a policeman or to work in a law firm or a shipping firm. No doubt the war was largely to blame—Felicity had been in the ATS manning a battery in Victoria during much of it and, by all accounts, had acquitted herself awfully well. He had expected that once the war was over she would marry and have a family—most of those young girls did, eventually. Instead she had landed a job in radio—the announcer between programs. She had that sort of voice—more BBC than the BBC itself. And that was where she had met Leo. Now of course there was Television, which was purely for entertainment, and most people didn't even own, nor wished to own, a set, and yet here she was presenting a program about a hippo. And his friends.

Hip, hip, hip hooray. Damn catchy tune, though.

Harriet stepped into the garden and came over already carrying a martini. She moved gracefully in white shoes with a wicked stiletto heel that spiked the lawn as effectively as a golf tee would on the centre court at Wimbledon. But as the lawn was already pocked it was reasonable to assume every other lady had on similar shoes—except Felicity—and that Leo wasn't overly concerned. Or hadn't properly thought through his plan, which was more likely.

Harriet shot Cecil a glance (oh Lord, the Rocastle thing!) and for a moment it appeared certain she was going to come over to demand an explanation. He prepared to produce his nothing-to-worry-about smile. But she veered off at the last moment and he saw with surprise that Simon was here.

Relieved, he took a sip of lemonade. 'Certainly wasn't expecting to see Simon here,' he remarked to Felicity, who had remained standing beside him and looked in no hurry to return to her guests.

'Oh yes. He and Leo have become quite chummy,' she replied and it was hard to tell if she approved of this chumminess or not.

'The BBC is doing a program about Spitfires.'

'Good God, not another one? Haven't we heard enough about the war? Surely there can't be any more stories left to tell?'

'Apparently there are. At any rate, Leo has lined Simon up to be technical advisor.'

'Well,' was all Cecil could think of to say. What he wanted to say was, why in God's name would Simon Paget wish to get himself caught up in some ghastly Television program? Did Harriet know about this? Quite probably she did. She did have an unnerving habit of dropping some revelation into the conversation and then making one feel foolish for not having known it oneself: *Oh yes I've known that for simply ages—did you really not know?* It was unsettling. And Paget was Harriet's brother, after all. Yet Cecil had an idea she didn't know. He had another idea that she wouldn't actually care one way or the other.

Did he himself care? In light of what had happened this morning? *Damn* Rocastle for putting them—for putting *him*—in this frightful position.

'There you are, old man,' said Mumford, reappearing at his elbow and waving his martini glass before him like a divining rod. 'I hear things are not as one might hope on the work front?'

Cecil froze and felt an uncomfortable tightening of the chest. How the *devil* could Leo know about the Rocastle thing? Could Harriet have said something? He kept his expression blank and concentrated on making the tightness go away.

'I'm sorry, but I prefer not to discuss such things now, Mumford,' he replied, with an attempt at a smile to soften his words.

'But it's all over the papers, old man.'

Cecil blanched.

'The *United States*,' Mumford prompted. 'Made the Atlantic crossing in under four days! Extraordinary when you think about it. Think there's any way back for your lot?'

The Blue Riband. Of course. Cecil allowed various internal organs a moment or two to steady themselves.

'Certainly there's a way back,' he bristled. 'Do you really believe American engineering can defeat British?'

'Of course I do,' replied Mumford, with obvious surprise.

Cecil took a long sip of his lemonade.

'I see Simon Paget is here,' he remarked, choosing to pass over his brother-in-law's facetiousness.

'Oh yes.' Mumford gulped down his martini. Then he winked. 'Pompous old boy, just between you and I, Ceece, but he's proving very useful. We've made him technical advisor, you know, on this Spitfire drama.'

So it was true. Simon working for the BBC. And he a bone fide Battle of Britain hero.

'And how exactly does he square it with the Palace?' Cecil enquired. His brother-in-law worked in some sort of protocol capacity at Buckingham Palace, a position that entailed spending a great deal of time on the telephone to various obscure foreign embassies, consulates and trade missions.

'No idea,' said Mumford breezily. 'He does it in his spare time. Don't suppose they know—or care.'

Cecil frankly doubted this. A Palace employee assisting in the making of a fictional Television drama? Hardly appropriate, one would have thought.

'It's pretty exciting stuff, actually,' Mumford went on. 'Much of the action takes place in the air, well, in the cockpit really, and as we can't actually fly the things—none of them are airworthy nowadays— we do the entire thing in the studio. Camera peering in through the cockpit window, chap on a wind machine at the front, another chap on sound effects—roar of engines, radio static, ack-ack-ack of enemy machine guns, that sort of thing—and chaps three and four on either side of the cockpit rocking it back and forth to simulate flight. Ingenious, isn't it?'

Was it? Was a team of 'chaps' rocking a broken down old aircraft back and forth in a television studio the crowning achievement of human endeavour?

And meanwhile Rocastle had opened the safe in his office and absconded with who knew how many bonds and shares—not to mention the firm's reputation. Cecil said nothing.

'Have a martini, old boy,' said Mumford.

Cecil hesitated. Felicity, he noticed, had drifted off inside the house.

'May I ask you a question, Mumford?'

'Certainly, old boy. Fire away,' Mumford replied, reaching behind him for an olive.

But it was impossible. What on earth could one possible say to Mumford?

The silence was broken by an unpleasant squelch as Leo bit into the olive. Cecil felt slightly nauseated.

'Who on earth is that extraordinary creature in the hat?' he said instead.

They both looked over at a young woman in an enormous hat who was standing in a circle of Mumford's BBC-types blowing smoke rings and looking bored.

'Haven't the faintest idea,' Leo replied. 'Group Captain Paget brought her. Quite a girl, isn't she?'

Simon had brought a girl? First the BBC and now this! And she must be fifteen years his junior at least. But then one was led to believe the girls loved all that flying ace sort of thing. Cecil felt faintly disturbed by it all.

'I *had* thought this was to be a quiet family luncheon, old boy.'

'Had you? Yes, Felicity said you would detest it.'

Cecil felt a second flicker of annoyance at this betrayal.

'Well, better be the good host,' said Mumford, darting off.

I ought to go and say hello to Simon, Cecil thought. He could see his wife and her brother deep in conversation, Simon debonair in a smart dark-grey suit, all snow-white shirt collars and stiff creases. His Battle of Britain days were well behind him, but he still cut quite a figure. No doubt that was how one landed a job at the Palace.

At this moment he was frowning and looking across the garden, perhaps at the extraordinary girl in the hat, and Harriet was frowning too, though she was looking at Simon. She touched his arm to get his attention again, but when she noticed Julius making his way over to them she fell silent and looked away.

'Hello, Uncle Simes. How's it hanging?' called Julius, sauntering over.

'Julius. How are you, old man?' Simon pulled a pipe out of his jacket pocket and placed it in his mouth.

Harriet appeared irritated by the interruption, but she gave Julius a brief smile, pulled out a cigarette from her case and lit it.

'I suppose those policemen weren't here for anything serious, then?' Julius asked his mother.

Blast! thought Cecil. Why couldn't the boy learn some discretion? No chance now of forestalling the inevitable questions.

'Police?' Simon replied, raising an enquiring eyebrow.

'I expect it was serious to them, dear,' said Harriet, who was a master of deflection.

No one had yet answered Simon's question and Cecil moved out of ear-shot before he could ask it a second time. It was simpler to wander over to the food table, sip one's lemonade and pretend one was taking an awfully long time deciding between the tuna, the shrimp paste or the ham and tomato sandwiches. He studied the array of neatly cut sandwiches and was about to place his faith in the tuna when Julius sauntered past. The boy was munching on a sandwich himself, his shirt open at the neck, and, inexplicably, his shirt collar out over the collar of his blazer in a rather secondary-modern way.

They stood side by side at the long table, solemnly and silently regarding the plates of slowly curling sandwiches before them. There was, Cecil realised, something rather special in the bond one had with one's son. It was something to take pride in. It transcended other relationships, perhaps even the bond between man and wife.

He looked over to his wife who was studying the girl in the hat, over her sunglasses, the way women studied each other if they suspected the other one was more of a hit than they were. The marital bond was an enduring one—they had, after all, set up a home together, raised children together, gone through a war together—but once these things had been achieved, the relationship between a man and a wife naturally, perhaps even by necessity, tended to become more distant. One's interests, having once coincided, now drifted apart. Like a peace accord between distant nations.

He paused, his hand hovering over a plate of sandwiches. *Was* there still a peace accord? It occurred to him Harriet had barely spoken to him since Thursday. And it had taken him till Saturday lunchtime to realise it.

Beside him, Julius reached for a shrimp paste sandwich on the top of the pile.

'Oh, I should avoid that one, old man,' Cecil remarked, 'I saw a fly on it a moment ago.'

'Oh. Right-oh.'

Julius stuck out a hand and reached over for another sandwich, barely pausing to see what he had picked up from the plate.

'Having a good time?' Cecil asked.

'Rather,' replied Julius. The boy hesitated then he spoke, casually addressing the sandwiches. 'What did that Inspector want, Father?'

'Oh, procedural matters. Just procedure.'

'Procedure for what?'

'Police matters. Julius, do tuck your shirt collar inside your blazer, old boy. Don't want to look like an East End barrow-boy, do we.'

'No, we most certainly do not,' said Julius and he made a show of putting his sandwich down on the table and exaggeratedly carrying out this necessary adjustment to his appearance, then walked off.

Cecil selected a shrimp paste sandwich from some way lower down the pile and inspected it dubiously. He took a hesitant bite, then paused, unable to swallow.

Was he going to have to lie to the police?

Chapter Four

SEPTEMBER 1952

The following morning Jean Corbett travelled by bus rather than taking the tube, because this was a momentous journey and from a bus you could see where you were and you had time to think.

The number 11 took her from Liverpool Street into the city past bombsites and half-demolished office blocks and the remains of half a dozen churches. She changed buses at Trafalgar Square and there were no more bombsites. Hyde Park shone brilliantly in the morning sunlight and large, gleaming black cars cruised down Park Lane. In the distance a troop of Horseguards trotted silently through the park and a small crowd of smartly dressed women and small children with their nannies stood and watched.

This is not my London, she thought, clutching her small case tightly in her lap.

She arrived too early and had to sit in an ABC café on Old

Brompton Road sipping a cup of tea and watching the early risers on their Sunday morning strolls or walking their dogs. No one looked dressed for church.

At nine o'clock she presented herself at the Wallises' front door, but instead of pressing the doorbell her index finger paused, midair, refusing to go the last few inches and she found herself glancing to left and right down the length of the street waiting for someone to stop her, for a shout, running feet on the pavement, a policeman's whistle to pierce the serene Sunday morning stillness.

She took a deep breath. She had every right to be here, a God-given right. There could be—there *must* be—no turning back now. Too many years had already passed. She rang the doorbell.

The housekeeper, Mrs Thompson, opened the front door so rapidly she must have been standing right behind it.

'They've given you the job, then?' she enquired, peering at Jean with a raised eyebrow.

'Yes. Hello. It's Miss Corbett. Jean. I start today.'

'I dare say!' Mrs Thompson replied in a manner that suggested she had seen nannies come and go, and at this time in her life she didn't need to see any more. 'Well, I expect it's for the best,' she added cryptically. 'You're very early though,' and she peered at Jean as though the explanation for this early arrival could be read on her face. 'They aren't up yet.'

It was nine o'clock and hadn't she been told to be here at nine? But it seemed best not to argue.

'Well, you'd better come in,' Mrs Thompson announced, sounding as though she had weighed up various options and had arrived at this, the best one.

She was a stocky woman, short and broad, and Jean found herself regarding the top of Mrs Thompson's helmet of unlikely tight blonde curls as she stepped past her into the hallway. Yellow would be a more accurate description of the curls, the kind of brassy yellow that came out of a hairdresser's bottle. She wore a tight-fitting floral dress that looked at least one size too small with buttons that strained across an enormous bust, and a white apron double-tied around her waist.

Mrs Thompson led the way up a flight of stairs. Then they climbed a second flight and continued going up until Jean lost count of which floor they were on and Mrs Thompson turned purple and began to wheeze. At last she paused on a distant landing and opened a door on her right.

'This is the room,' she gasped. She didn't say: This is *your* room.

They stood in the doorway surveying the room, Mrs Thompson with an air of suspicion as though she half expected the now departed Nanny Peters to be hiding in the cupboard.

'That's the bed,' she said (Jean had already spotted the bed), 'the window—I don't think it opens or nothing, but they do say you can see right over to the hospital and beyond from there. There's a chest under the bed and the tallboy here for your clothes and what-not,' (she paused to regard Jean's meagre suitcase) 'and the bathroom's out here, second door on the left. I'm across the landing there.'

She finished up by reaching for a cigarette and appeared in no hurry to depart.

'Well, I must unpack,' Jean declared, going into the room. She placed her case on the pink, tasselled bedspread and hoped Mrs Thompson didn't intend to stand and watch. She slowly undid the clasps and surveyed the contents, aware that Mrs Thompson hadn't moved.

'You don't need to hide nothing from me,' Mrs Thompson declared huffily. 'I'm sure you've nothing I wish to take.'

Jean turned at once to face her. 'I'm sorry, Mrs Thompson, I certainly never meant to imply—'

Mrs Thompson had already turned and made her way, with some dignity, across the landing and down the narrow stairs. But she paused on the bend in the staircase. 'You can come down to the kitchen, if you want to, when you've finished unpacking. I daresay you'll be wanting a cuppa by then,' and she disappeared.

Unsure if this was an invitation or a challenge, Jean stood for a moment regarding the bedspread. It had a hole in its centre that had been inexpertly darned, she wondered for a moment about Nanny Peters, who had been here before her and who had left to tend to an elderly parent in Leicester. There was nothing of her here now, no trace at all.

She would leave something of herself here in the Wallis household, Jean resolved, something by which they would always remember Nanny Corbett.

The bed was pushed into the corner of the room. On the far wall was a window that faced east, across to the private garden opposite, and looking down the street she could see the roofs of the Royal Brompton and Marsden hospitals to the south. The room seemed quiet and empty and bare, but perhaps any room would seem quiet and empty and bare when compared with the room she'd shared with the children at Mrs McIlwraith's in Malacca Row, or with the room they had all slept in together at home. That had been four to a bed. Here you had a room to yourself—all to yourself!

And who did you talk to? Whose warmth did you share?

She stared for a moment into a gaping black void.

The walls were painted. And not just distemper but paint—a cream colour on three sides of the room—and wallpaper in a rose design on the fourth wall. Old wallpaper—she could see the corners peeling and some strips had been torn right off, but wallpaper, nevertheless. There was a single wooden chair and a rug on the floor, a wooden washstand in the corner with a tall chipped enamel washing jug on it and against the far wall stood a cupboard—a tallboy, Mrs Thompson had called it and Jean had spun around and half expected to see a lanky youth slouching in the corner but it was only a fancy name for a wardrobe. Its doors hung open and it stood empty as though no one had used it in years.

She went over to the window. The frame was old, the paint flaking, the wood rotting. It looked as though no one had ever opened it. Somehow she didn't want to be the first one to try.

How many girls had stood here at this window peering through this dusty glass at the street below? How many had placed their clothes in this cupboard? Had stood before this bed and thought about home? But those girls had been servants and the world had been a different place then. Jean was here because she had chosen to be. And she could leave any time she chose.

She surveyed the contents of her case. Everything was neatly folded and precisely packed. When you had little, you took good care of it. She carefully lifted out her three blouses and three skirts and placed them in the cupboard, hung her coat on the hanger and arranged both pairs of shoes beneath her bed. Her underthings, nylons and a pair of kid gloves that had once been rather smart but were now best kept out of sight went into the drawer and her Sunday-best hat, still in its protective tissue paper, she placed on top of the cupboard.

At the bottom of the case was the large and elderly copy of the Bible that she had purchased from a musty old bookshop near Liverpool Street. It had a burgundy leather cover, darkened by time and wrinkled and creased like an old man's hands, and the words on the front were picked out in gold that had turned black from the years and from the countless fingers that had traced its reassuring letters. It was the sort of Bible that must have been in a family for generations though not in the Corbett family. The Corbett family Bible, a green-covered one that had resided on the sideboard and was placed on the table each Sunday morning and on other important occasions, had perished along with the Corbett family on that fateful Sunday morning in 1945.

It was odd what had survived. Along with Mum's navy shoes, the small case contained a china horse that had once belonged to Gladys, Jean's younger sister. And wrapped around the horse was a length of yellow ribbon, tattered at one end, that her youngest sister, Nerys, had once worn in her hair. And beside that was a tobacco tin with a dented yellow lid showing a sailor in a jersey and a peaked cap and within which Dad had kept not tobacco, but quotations from the Bible. Now the tin contained two green buttons which Edward, aged six, had been wearing on his cardigan that far-off Sunday morning.

Of Bertie, five years old and last in the family, there was nothing to show that he had ever existed at all.

Jean lifted the items from the case and laid them ceremoniously side by side on the bed, then looking around she settled on a place on the floor beneath the window. She closed her case and laid it there, placing each item on it. Then she stood back to survey her arrangement. Yes, that was right. That was how things should be. Lastly she picked up the Bible and laid it on the pillow near where her head would lie.

There would be an apt quote for this moment, Dad could always find it, sometimes without even having to look it up, but Jean couldn't think of one. Eventually she settled on 'So we may boldly say: The Lord is my helper; I will not fear. What can man do to me?' which was from Hebrews 13 and was good if you felt lonely.

A bell tolled in the still morning air, an urgent single note over and over. And from further away, perhaps carried by a slight breeze, other bells were tolling, this time a peal competently rung in a steady rhythm. It was Sunday morning and the Wallises would be going to church. It was unlikely the family attended Chapel, more likely a Church of England church, but there would be a chapel of some kind in the district, she felt certain. Perhaps Mrs Wallis would let her go there sometimes instead of to their own church.

Casting caution to the wind she tackled the catch on the window and, with only a brief tussle, it loosened and she was able to ease the window open. It was warm outside, much warmer than when she had made her journey across London this morning from Mrs McIlwraith's.

Jean gazed out over the rooftops and at the silent and empty lawn of the private garden opposite. It looked so inviting, that large stretch of grass and the flower beds with their sprinkling of late-blooming yellow, pink and cream roses, and yet no one seemed to admire them. The whole street was silent and empty and, yes, it was a Sunday but even on a Sunday Malacca Row had been a bustle of activity, everyone in their Sunday best and Mum calling out not to dirty your clothes. But here no one called to anyone. No one even left their house.

Then a man did come down the street, a young man in a light-coloured and creased linen suit who walked with a long stride, not quite a swagger but close to it. He stopped at the padlocked gate and looked to left and right then hopped right over it and into the garden.

Good, thought Jean, because it was stupid having railings around a garden to stop folk getting in. Like having a lock on the church door.

The sun, which until that moment had bathed the whole street in glorious late-summer sunshine, was at that moment obscured by a solitary and very dark cloud. It was as though the day had abruptly ended and at the same moment Jean realised this was the young man she had seen in the garden yesterday, sitting on the bench. She stepped back from the window though it seemed unlikely the man would look up and notice her—and what did it matter if he did?

In another moment the cloud had passed and the sun came out again as brilliant, if not more brilliant, than before. But Jean remained where she was, in the shadows.

She could hear voices downstairs, a door opening and closing. The family were up, then, and she couldn't very well hide in her room any longer. She must present herself to Mrs Wallis. And get the children's breakfast. Or would Mrs Thompson do that? At Mrs McIlwraith's she had done everything from making the children's meals to queuing up for the meat ration. But Mrs McIlwraith was their neighbour, Jean had known her all her life. And that was Malacca Row, Stepney—there had been no housekeeper, no Mr McIlwraith and no Latin prep.

There had been nothing at all like this.

For a moment she couldn't quite catch her breath and she sat down heavily on the bed, a hand pressed against her chest. She had left Mrs McIlwraith's familiar four-room terrace, a house as familiar to her as her own. If she could go back—

But there was no going back. She had made her choice and she would stick to it. You couldn't avoid your responsibilities forever, not when God had finally shown you the way.

She stood up and smoothed down her skirt and blouse and patted her curls with a glance in the small hand mirror. Lipstick? No, that was the wrong look. Instead she straightened the seam of her nylons and left the room.

'Nanny! The new nanny is here!' shrieked Anne as Jean descended the stairs to the lower floor. The child stood rooted to the spot in the middle of the hallway, her arm stuck out before her, pointing a long, pale finger as though she were witnessing a supernatural phenomenon.

Jean arranged her features into a bright smile. 'Hello, Anne.'

'Nanny Peters used to come down those stairs *just like that*!' the girl exclaimed, dismay writ large on her pale face.

'What, one step at a time, you mean?' said Julius, appearing in a doorway. 'What would you have her do, Anne? Come down backwards? Or perhaps you'd prefer her to slide down the banister?'

Mrs Wallis appeared from another room wearing a cream silk dress that clung to her shoulders and bust and flared out over her hips.

'Miss Corbett. How delightful of you to join us.'

She was wearing scarlet lipstick and shoes that were so white they had surely never been worn before, and Jean felt a moment of dismay. Was this how she—how they—dressed for Sunday breakfast? For church? Mrs Wallis looked as though she was on her way to a Buckingham Palace garden party.

She came over and smiled and Jean's dismay slowly receded.

'I do hope you have settled in all right?'

'Yes, thank you, Mrs Wallis. I—'

'Good. Now here is your list of duties,' and she handed over three neatly typed sheets of paper. 'Please come to me directly if you have any queries. You'll find us quite informal on Sundays. Julius will complete his homework in the morning and Anne will need to practise her piano. The children ought to get some fresh air, so perhaps you'll take them to the park this afternoon? Mr Wallis and I have a luncheon engagement so Mrs Thompson will do you and the children something cold in the kitchen, then we generally have tea at five.' She turned to go back downstairs.

That didn't sound 'quite informal' to Jean.

'And will the children be attending church this morning?' she asked.

There was a moment when everything in the house fell quiet.

'Oh, I rather doubt it,' replied Mrs Wallis, pausing halfway down the stairs and producing a cigarette from the folds of her dress. She smiled suddenly, disarmingly. 'Not unless they stumble into one by accident, that is.'

After she had gone there was a silence and Jean realised both children were watching her. Their expressions quite clearly said: this is interesting; what will the new nanny do next?

Julius stuck his hands in his pockets and sauntered over. 'We are not a church-going family, you see, Nanny,' he explained. 'Not due to any deep-seated principles of atheism, you understand. No, it's more a sort of—' he paused to consider, '… general apathy, really.'

'I attend Chapel every Sunday,' Jean said.

'I should like to go too! Will you ask Mummy if we can come too?' begged Anne, her eyes bright as though someone were proposing a day at the seaside.

'Yes, Anne. I don't see why not. If Mrs Wallis thinks it's all right.'

'Oh, she won't mind,' said Julius. 'As long as Anne remains an interested observer. Mummy won't like it if she decides to sign up and become a nun, you know. And that's exactly the sort of thing she does do,' he added in a low voice, giving Jean a significant nod.

'I would make a beautiful nun,' said Anne dreamily, wasting little time in adopting this new role.

Jean had a sense of things getting away from her.

'Well, we don't really have nuns at Chapel, Anne.'

'Oh, what a shame,' said Anne, sinking down onto the floor under the weight of this devastating blow to her youthful ambitions.

'Now, have you both had your breakfast?' said Jean briskly and was rewarded for her briskness by Anne leaping up and running down the stairs.

'That means no,' explained Julius, leading the way downstairs. 'On Sundays Mrs Thompson usually has breakfast ready at nine-twenty. *Housewives' Choice* is on at nine so we get our breakfast at twenty past. We've tried writing to the BBC, but they refuse to move it,' and he went into a room at the rear of the house.

Through the half-open door Jean could see a large table at which Anne and Mrs Wallis were seated. She couldn't see the far side of the table, but she heard distinctly the voice of Mr Wallis.

'... go into the office this afternoon, Harriet. We'll go to the Swanbridges' for lunch as arranged, then I'll pop in afterwards. Anne, I am quite certain Nanny Peters did not encourage you to eat your egg in that manner. You are not dissecting a corpse.'

Jean turned away. She was fairly certain a nanny did not join the family for Sunday breakfast. Or indeed for any meal aside from tea with the children and the cold something in the kitchen to which Mrs Wallis had earlier alluded.

Instead she continued down to the ground floor, then down an uncarpeted flight of stairs to the only part of the house she had yet to visit, and found herself in the doorway of a large, white-tiled basement kitchen. A vast dresser filled one side of the room displaying an astonishing array of china plates and other crockery on its various hooks and shelves. Two huge chipped enamel sinks and a long wooden draining board stood on the opposite side and in the centre of the kitchen was a wide wooden table at which sat Mrs Thompson, cigarette in hand. Before her was a magazine, she had a cup of tea near her elbow and the radio set was switched on within reaching distance.

'...hymns from Kings College. And to start this morning's programme, here is the choir of St Martin-in-the-Fields singing "Jerusalem".'

'There you are, Miss Corbett,' said Mrs Thompson, putting down her cigarette. 'Let me pour you a nice cuppa.'

'That would be lovely, thank you,' said Jean, sitting down. 'Are you listening to the Sunday service, Mrs Thompson?' she asked, nodding hopefully towards the radio.

'Lord, no, there'll be some nice light music on in a minute. Can't abide all that hymn singing. But it'll be over soon enough. How d'you take your tea? Sugar?'

'Yes. Sugar, please,' Jean murmured and felt a rush of something—guilt?—swirl dizzyingly about her head. You never had sugar in your tea at home, you saved it for other things. Often you gave your whole ration so that a cake could be baked or a custard as a special treat if it was someone's birthday. 'Oh, I've brought my ration books,' she added and held them out.

Mrs Thompson nodded but seemed in no hurry to take them, being more concerned with the mass of tea leaves at the bottom of the teapot.

From her seat at the table Jean took in the boxes of eggs and the bread bins and the cake tins and the rows and rows of jars and tins and pots in the larder and the large tub of butter on the table. Was there no rationing in this part of London? Or were all the jars empty? Somehow she knew they weren't.

'Thanks ever so,' she said, taking the cup Mrs Thompson pushed over to her. Dipping a teaspoon into the tea she heard the scrape of the sugar at the bottom of the cup.

Mrs Thompson resumed her seat and reached for the cigarette.

'I'm glad you're here, Miss Corbett.' she said unexpectedly. She let out a puff of smoke from the side of her mouth, angling it away from Jean. 'You'll find us a friendly enough household. Mr Wallis is a well-respected gentleman and a good father and Mrs Wallis is ever such a nice lady—sophisticated, if you know what I mean.'

She raised an eyebrow significantly so that even though Jean had no idea what Mrs Thompson meant, she nodded wisely.

'The children are well brought up—though sometimes they're a bit too clever for their own good, if you get my meaning.' Mrs Thompson leaned closer over the table. 'Not like them delinquents you read about in the paper at least, going around in gangs with coshes and I don't know what else.'

Jean considered this. It seemed to her unlikely that there were many gangs of cosh-wielding delinquents roaming the back streets of South Kensington—but you could never tell.

'Yes,' she said, because she couldn't think what else to say. She took a sip of the tea and felt her tongue tingle and her teeth ache as the hot sweetness filled her mouth.

'Gotta fella, have you?' said Mrs Thompson, removing the cigarette from her mouth and tapping it on the ash tray.

Jean hesitated. It had been important to confirm her spinster status to Mrs Wallis—no employer wanted a nanny who was forever asking for evenings off to go dancing with her young man or, worse, running off after a month to get married—but the same question from Mrs Thompson required a different answer.

'Well, there was a young man, but we no longer have an understanding.' This wasn't lying, it was merely a different way of telling something.

'Shame,' said Mrs Thompson striking a second match to re-light her cigarette. 'Ditch you, did he?'

Jean sat up indignantly. 'No, he didn't. As a matter of fact *I* ditched *him*. Told him I wasn't ready for that sort of commitment.'

'Oh, he wanted a bit of the other and you wouldn't have it, eh?' said Mrs Thompson, the cigarette wedged once more in the side of her mouth, nodding in a 'what can you expect?' kind of way.

She eased herself to her feet, went over to the grill, and returned with a rack of toast. She selected a slice and proceeded to spread butter on it.

'You'll be wanting to know what the police were doing here yesterday morning,' said Mrs Thompson, wiping the knife on her apron and sticking it into a jar of strawberry jam.

Jean hesitated. She had almost forgotten about the two policemen but now a knot of something hard materialised in her stomach. Policemen meant bad things. Even those with an easy conscience felt that flicker of nerves when a policeman appeared in the street.

'I'm sure it's none of my business,' she replied tartly, taking a sip of her tea and feeling that shock of sweetness again. But it wasn't such a shock the second time.

'Are you?' said Mrs Thompson sharply and Jean started. 'Bit of a coincidence, isn't it? Your turning up and the police arriving not half an hour later.'

Jean stared at her, her heart thudding loudly in her chest, the blood rushing in her ears. She could feel heat rising up her neck and suffusing her cheeks.

Mrs Thompson suddenly burst out laughing, a laugh that quickly became a rasping cough, and for a moment she was bent double unable to speak. A bubble of spittle sprayed onto the table and glistened wetly. Jean gazed at it.

'Your face! It was a picture!' spluttered Mrs Thompson. 'I was only jokin', love.'

Jean arranged her mouth into a smile and her eyes went to the large radio set on the table. She saw someone pick up the radio set and smash it into the laughing Mrs Thompson's face and Mrs Thompson falling to the tiled floor in a mess of blood and mucus.

She blinked and the image disappeared.

'I think I might have some more sugar in my tea, Mrs Thompson.'

'You go right ahead, dear.' Mrs Thompson stood up, dabbing at her mouth. 'You mustn't mind me, dear; I've got what they call a wicked sense of humour. Your face!'

'So what did the police come here for, then?'

'It'll be those delinquents, you can bet your life on it.'

Jean said nothing. She helped herself to another spoonful of sugar and knew that the tea would be undrinkable.

'Will there be blood?' enquired Anne as she buckled up her shoes in preparation for the trip to church.

They were in the child's bedroom, which was on the second floor at the front of the house overlooking the quiet Sunday morning street. It was a smallish room, the walls lined with shelves and the shelves straining under the weight of dozens of books. Above the bed was another shelf, from which a row of teddy bears and other toys observed them indifferently.

They were off to church. Julius had toyed with the idea too, purely, he had been at pains to explain, out of academic interest. But in the end the pull of the Latin verbs had proved too strong and he had mooched off and shut himself in his bedroom.

'Blood? Certainly not! We're not the Catholics,' Jean replied, indignantly. 'And there won't be incense or candles or worshipping of idols either,' she added, in case Anne was expecting any or all of these. 'Come along, or we shall be late.'

The church, according to Julius, who seemed to be a mine of information on practically any subject, was five minutes' walk away and if there was a ten o'clock service they would just make it. If there wasn't, they would have a long wait.

They got as far as the first floor when a door opened and a man who could only be Mr Wallis came out. Jean almost walked right into him. She had an impression of a brown knitted cardigan over a white shirt, grey flannel trousers—neatly pressed—and loose brown slippers. His hair was greying and had receded a little at his temples. He was perhaps early or mid-forties, clean-shaven, a longish face, nose quite large and a little beaked. A normal, unassuming otherwise unmemorable face. She had seen a photograph of Mr Wallis once— he was something important in shipping, after all—but he looked less formal, somehow less like the director of a large firm, than she had expected. He wasn't wearing a suit, of course; that made all the difference. He was just a man, quite well-to-do, but normal looking, in his home on a Sunday morning in September.

He was also wearing a pair of reading glasses which he now took off in order to survey them with a curious frown.

'Oh, hello, I suppose you must be the new nanny?'

'Yes—Miss Corbett. How do you do?'

'Oh, quite well, quite well.' There was a silence. 'Off to the park, are we?'

'We're going to church,' explained Anne. 'But there won't be any blood.'

'Church, eh?' said Mr Wallis, somewhat astonished.

'It being Sunday,' explained Jean, because an explanation seemed necessary.

'Well. Very good. Carry on, Nanny,' and he turned and went back into his study.

He seemed just like a normal gentleman.

'*Ow!*' said Anne resentfully. 'You hold hands too tight, Nanny! It *hurts*.'

Chapter Five

SEPTEMBER 1952

'You've heard the rumour Princess Margaret might turn up? Of course, there's always a rumour Princess Margaret might turn up. She never does. Or rather, she turns up *every*where if *The Times* is to be believed, but never at the place that one actually happens to be. One always chooses the wrong party, visits the wrong the house, lunches at the restaurant a day too early. Of course, one pretends not to mind, but it is galling, there's no denying it. Pass me a cigarette, darling.'

Harriet opened her cigarette case and offered it to Valerie Swanbridge, who stood beside her at lunch.

'You really are the most terrific snob, Valerie,' she observed, snapping shut the case and producing a small flame from her lighter. Her hand, she realised, was shaking. She clenched it into a fist to stop it.

Valerie lit her cigarette and took an exploratory puff.

'Darling, what else is there?' she declared solemnly.

'I seem to recall at school you were full of all sorts of ideas and ambitions. What ever happened to you?'

'My sole ambition at school was to own a white pony. I got one for my thirteenth birthday,' replied Valerie, pausing to blow out a trail of smoke. 'It's a terrible thing, you know, Harri, to realise all of your ambitions at such a tender age. What does one do then?'

Harriet selected a cigarette herself and silently lit it. One threw a luncheon to celebrate one's husband's recent OBE and to which one invited royalty, that's what one did. Princess Margaret wouldn't turn up, of course, there was never any real danger of that, but it was impressive to be able to start such a rumour and have people speculate.

And a few days ago, Harriet realised, she herself might have joined in that speculation. Now her hand shook as she drew on her cigarette. It was the police, of course, coming to the house yesterday.

Beside her, Valerie sent a stream of smoke upwards, glancing sideways at Harriet's yellow dress as she did so.

'Norman Hartnell?'

Harriet nodded, not removing her own cigarette.

'Thought so. Unmistakeable.'

'Darling, you came with me when I went for the fitting.'

Valerie raised a single eyebrow. 'Did I?' Then she peered over Harriet's left shoulder. 'Don't look now. There's Daphne Goodfellow. She and Peter are getting a divorce.'

Harriet turned discreetly in time to see Daphne Goodfellow, in a Pierre Balmain bell-shaped skirt and a stole, followed a moment later by Peter Goodfellow in grey flannels, step into the garden, he smiling and shaking hands with everyone, she bestowing kisses and exclaiming. Peter was MP for Hertfordshire South and widely disliked. He had been tipped for a Cabinet post, yet the reshuffle had come and gone and no appointment had been forthcoming. Daphne, like Harriet and Valerie, was a Maldeville Old Girl, attending their old school briefly until her parents had transferred her to a more expensive establishment in Geneva.

One ran into the Maldeville Old Girls every now and then; it was inevitable. The Maud Maldeville College for Young Ladies, an antiquated establishment that had closed its doors forever just before the war, had once been populated with the daughters of the Empire, young girls whose parents resided—whose early childhood had been spent—in some pink-shaded area of the globe, far away from the pleasantly rolling hills of the South Downs where they had all, inexplicably, found themselves. Harriet did not dwell on that period of her life—couldn't, really, as much of that first year at school was a fog. Both her own and Valerie's parents had been in India; perhaps that was why they had become friends. A single bright flame in what was otherwise a dark time.

But today she had a role to play.

'Daphne, a *divorce*? Not really!' she exclaimed.

'Yes. *Ssh!* No one's supposed to know,' hissed Valerie. 'She told me in strictest confidence at the Hensons' last week.' She observed Daphne through narrowed eyes and a haze of cigarette smoke. 'Damned foolish, if you ask me.'

'The divorce? Why? What do you know?'

'No, silly. Her telling me in confidence. Surely she knows I'll blab to all and sundry?'

Daphne chose that moment to look over and smile and wave and they both smiled and waved back.

'Actually, I've been very good,' Valerie resumed. 'You're only the third person I've told—not including David, of course. Marjory! How *are* you? And Geoffrey. You both look *divine*.'

They kissed the Hensons, who had themselves just arrived. Marjory Henson was in some sort of fluffy white thing so that she resembled a giant meringue. Geoffrey was in his usual tweeds, though as it was seventy-five degrees outside, his face, normally a dull pink, was now the hue and shininess of a Royal Mail pillar box.

'Their eldest daughter has just debuted,' Valerie remarked in an aside, once the Hensons were out of earshot. 'I don't believe she was a great success.'

'Do you mean to tell me that you told two other people about the Goodfellows before you told me?' demanded Harriet.

'Darling, I haven't *seen* you.'

'There's such a thing as a telephone.'

'It's hardly the sort of thing one says over the telephone.'

'I would have thought it was *exactly* the sort of thing one would say over the telephone. What else is a telephone *for*?'

'I'm rather afraid the ice sculpture is melting!'

Valerie's husband David strode over, beaming cheerfully, as though a vast sculpture melting all over his expensive drawing room floor was part of the entertainment. 'Harri! It's marvellous to see you! You look radiant!'

'On the contrary. I look like someone whose glass is empty and who is wondering when they're going to get a refill.'

As David signalled to one of the hired waiters who was floating around balancing a tray of glasses, Harriet stole a glance at the clock on the mantelpiece. It was a little after three o'clock. Cecil had said he was going in to the office this afternoon. Surely they would have to leave soon?

What if the police returned while they were out?

Beside her, David drained the last of his champagne and reached for two fresh glasses.

'Harri, what the devil's going on over at Emp and Col?' and Harriet froze, a cigarette halfway to her lips. 'The share price is wobblier than a bowl of raspberry jelly. Is Cecil at all concerned?'

'He's not concerned, no,' Harriet replied. 'The share price always goes up and down. That's what share prices do.'

David had said that himself at some function or in some interview. But it seemed to Harriet that Empire and Colonial's share prices tended to go down while David's company's share price went up.

'Sounds like time to get out of the shipping business,' David remarked as casually as one's nanny might suggest it was time to get out of the bath.

And for someone like David it *was* as easy as getting out of the bath. But for Cecil—no. She could no more imagine Cecil working in some other office, in some other industry, than she could imagine Queen Elizabeth landing a job at a Lyons tea shop. She could see Cecil through the French doors, standing with the Hensons in the garden, making some point, putting his glass down to make the point better—some voyage he had been on, some new ship about to be built. Or not built. It seemed embarrassing suddenly to have a husband who was unable to get out of shipping.

'He likes shipping,' she said, because that was the truth. 'Oh, is that Princess Margaret?'

She hadn't spoken in a particularly loud voice yet at her words every conversation halted, every raised glass hung suspended in midair and hands in the act of reaching for a morsel of smoked salmon froze as a room full of people far too well bred to do anything as crude as stare, were, nonetheless, instantly alert.

Royalty was in their midst.

'Oh, no, my mistake,' murmured Harriet as a rather large young girl in a last-season Dior frock and clutching an ugly red handbag came into the room. There was a general sort of sigh and the talking and drinking and nibbling resumed.

'It's Stella,' said Valerie, obviously disappointed. 'David's niece. They live in Bromley.' She sighed and reached for another cigarette. 'Oh, how's that dashing brother of yours, Harri?'

There was a pause. Valerie frowned and leaned closer.

'What is it, darling? What have I said?'

'Nothing,' replied Harriet brightly. She took a mouthful of champagne. 'As a matter of fact I saw Simon yesterday. At Leo Mumford's. And he was with some deb fifteen years his junior!'

'Not really!'

'Yes. Can't say I conversed with her. Cecil did and reported that she seemed rather idiotic.'

'Oh well, one tends to be at that age. Lord knows, we were.' Valerie laughed.

Harriet was silent. She remembered her debutante year and the years immediately afterwards as being a constant, anxious round of parties and luncheons and balls that everyone had tried so hard to enjoy, but underneath it all there had been that constant, panic-stricken fear: *What if I don't find a husband? What if no one wants me?* Most of the girls had had their mothers, of course, to see them through it. She had had father once or twice until he had become too ill; Simon on occasion, when she had begged him. In the end she had learnt to do things on her own. Indeed, she had done so since she had come to England as a twelve-year-old. It had been a watershed. In India she had still been a child. If she had appeared idiotic after that it had, she realised, been a front.

'I'm rather afraid it looks as if Princess Margaret isn't coming,' she observed.

'Was that Peter Goodfellow I saw talking to David?'

Harriet nodded. 'Yes, I expect so.'

It was almost four o'clock. They had left the Swanbridges' and Cecil had suggested they walk the short distance northwards to Athelstan Gardens instead of hailing a cab.

'I understood he was tipped for a Cabinet post, but nothing happened in the reshuffle.'

'No.' Harriet slowed her pace as she was already a step ahead of Cecil. Why had he insisted on walking? Hadn't he said he was going to the office?

Kings Road was quiet and sultry in a summer Sunday afternoon way. Few cars drove past and the only people out walking were nannies with small children and a scattering of elderly Eastern European migrants dragging reluctant pugs.

Perhaps Cecil was no longer thinking of going to the office? Perhaps he had decided the Rocastle thing was not an urgent matter? So far he had said nothing about the policemen who had come to the house the day before. After dinner the previous evening he had retired to his study and had not emerged until after she had gone to bed. This morning over breakfast the talk had chiefly been of the televising of the Coronation—Julius had overheard something yesterday at Leo's. Cecil had had plenty to say on the matter and a rather tense exchange had followed, resulting in them all finishing their breakfasts in silence. Cecil had retired once more to his study. Did he think she had simply forgotten? Did he think she would accept no explanation? It was a man's prerogative, he would have said, had she questioned him, to keep his business to himself.

Well, it was a wife's prerogative to assess and, if need be, repair the damage one's husband had got them into.

'Cecil, I was thinking we ought to invite Jeremy Rocastle and that lovely wife of his—Jenny, is it?—over to lunch one weekend. They seem like such a nice couple.'

Beside her, Cecil had fallen silent. He walked stiffly, upright, no creases spoiling the line of his Sunday blazer, but she didn't need to look at his face to picture the furrow between his brows that her words had invoked. One did not argue in marriage; one never created a scene. One merely forced the issue in a calm and polite fashion.

'I don't believe that will be possible,' he replied and he might have been discussing the possibility of a day out at Ascot rather than an ex-employee who had absconded in the dead of night with the entire contents of the firm's safe.

'Really? Why not?'

Cecil paused. And no wonder—he could hardly say: because I was wrong about Rocastle. He turned out bad. We have been taken for a ride, ripped off, duped. Swindled.

'Rocastle no longer works at Empire and Colonial.'

'I see. And where has he gone?'

'I am not at liberty to say.'

'Why not? Have the police told you not to?'

They continued to walk in silence, turning left into Portchester Crescent. Many of the houses along this street were now owned by embassies—East European, Middle Eastern—and the faces that one occasionally saw at the windows were dark and bearded, sometimes in white suits or sporting strangely shaped black hats and the occasional turban. Cecil paused beside the first house and adjusted his cufflinks. They were silver, a present from her on his fortieth birthday.

'Harriet.'

She waited.

'I met the new nanny this morning. A Miss Corbett. She appeared to be taking Anne to church.'

Harriet neither confirmed nor denied this statement.

'I never question your decisions,' he continued, 'where matters of the house or the children's well-being are concerned.'

Ah, now she could see where this was going.

'And by the same token I don't expect to involve you in matters of business.'

She said nothing. It was as close to an argument as Cecil would allow himself to get, this putting his foot down, this principled stand. If he found out about the telephone call she had received on Thursday she knew he would make a fuss about that too. Well, she would not give him the opportunity.

'All I ask, Cecil, is that you tell me if it will be in the newspapers.'

He paused. A wood-pigeon cooed loudly overhead and, further away, a small terrier yapped excitedly then fell silent.

'I can't say … It's possible,' he conceded at last. 'But it's poor Mrs Rocastle who will bear the brunt of it, I'm afraid. Thank God they have no children.'

They resumed walking.

'This man, Rocastle. He reported directly to you, didn't he?'

Cecil took a deep breath.

'Yes, that's so, but—'

'So it's inevitable that questions will be asked. That your name will be linked with this scandal. That the police will return and make enquiries—'

Cecil turned to her indignantly.

'What are you suggesting, Harriet? This man broke into the safe and absconded with a large amount of company money—do you think I had any idea of what was he was planning? That I was aware—?'

He paused as a door opened in the basement of one of the houses and a young man in a dark suit came up the steps to the street, glancing at them as he passed.

No, she did not think he had had any idea. That was not Cecil's way. If he had suspected he would have acted at once. He wouldn't have been able to stop himself.

'I shall speak to Sir Maurice this afternoon,' Cecil said when the man had gone.

And, in his eyes, that was the matter closed. Yet the police would make enquiries; they were bound to.

'Mother, I've been blessed,' Anne announced, pausing dramatically on the stairs.

Harriet stood in the hall and regarded her younger child. She was wearing her school hat, a hideous wide-brimmed straw thing with a red ribbon that went under the chin.

'Have you, dear?'

'Yes, the man put his hand on my head and said "Bless you, my child" and I hadn't even sneezed. It was terrifically funny!'

Behind Anne the new nanny appeared, tall and gaunt and her face like thunder and Harriet thought, oh they've been to church. And Anne had behaved—well, like Anne, by the sound of it. Harriet experienced a flash of annoyance that the new nanny—a mere girl of twenty—was standing there scowling at her daughter as though Anne had used the wrong knife at dinner.

'Perhaps he thought you were about to sneeze,' she suggested. 'Was it very dusty in the church?'

Anne gave this question some thought. 'It was a bit, I suppose. And I went out without my handkerchief, too.'

She came clattering down the remaining stairs, the nanny following two steps behind her at a more sedate pace, her face stony, but rearranging her features as she reached the bottom stair so that her face became that of an East End girl once more.

'We're off to the garden, Mrs Wallis,' she announced, and it seemed like a challenge thrown down. 'As you suggested,' she added, as though this gave her immunity to criticism.

'Don't go to the garden over the road,' Harriet instructed. 'Take the children to Kensington Gardens, it's better exercise for them. Take Julius with you.'

Harriet went into the drawing room and picked up yesterday's *Times* and skimmed the headlines: *La Bohème* was playing tonight at Sadler's Wells, there was talk of tea being de-rationed, the War Office had provided its daily list of casualties in Korea. Her eyes skipped over the page and refused to settle long enough to take in more than the headlines.

There were footsteps in the hallway and the front door opened.

'I can walk down the steps backwards with my eyes shut!' called Anne from outside.

'She likes to throw stones at the squirrels, you know,' were Julius's parting words and a moment later the front door shut.

Downstairs in the kitchen Mrs Thompson could be heard slamming baking trays around. Cecil was at the office. He had gone straight there in a cab after their return from the Swanbridges', though what exactly he hoped to achieve there was unclear. Harriet imagined him at his desk surrounded by his ships and an empty safe, the outer office silent and deserted, everyone at home for the weekend and his secretary, Miss James, tending her elderly mother in Rickmansworth or Norwood or wherever such people lived.

It was almost half past four. Harriet stood at the window. Athelstan Gardens was still and silent. She stood up, reaching for a scarf to cover her hair and a pair of sunglasses and, after a moment's hesitation, her handbag. She wasn't sure if she would need it, if she might need some money or not.

Outside the sky was clear and a pale blue; the sun was still high and she felt it slowly warm her arms. The house was cold; even on the hottest summer day its high ceilings and narrow windows were an effective defence against sunlight.

She paused on the doorstep, listening. The tinny strains of light music from Mrs Thompson's wireless drifted up from the kitchen. Harriet pulled the front door closed behind her and went down the steps, her pumps making no sound on the stonework. Resisting the urge to pause again at the gate she lifted the latch and crossed the street. She wanted a cigarette, but one didn't smoke in the street so she walked, head up—this was, after all, her own street. No traffic came by, no front doors opened or closed. No one appeared at their windows. It was almost eerie. She walked on the opposite side of the street along the length of the garden, the black railings and the privet hedge on her right until she reached the padlocked gate. As she eased the key into the padlock she looked over the gate into the garden beyond. An elderly couple, the Pashkints, émigrés from some extinct Eastern European state, were seated at the bench nearest the gate, both muffled up for a Moscow winter, she with a dusty fur stole, he with a long gabardine coat, sitting side by side, silent and staring straight ahead.

Harriet entered the garden, wondering whether to wish them a good afternoon, but it was simpler not to. She walked soundlessly past them and neither looked up, only the eyes of the dead animal around Mrs Pashkint's neck followed Harriet's progress, an animal that had probably been killed in another century.

There were four benches in the garden, one on each side of the square of lawn. Two of the benches were empty, aside from a lone pigeon strutting importantly back and forth. The bench on the far side of the lawn was occupied by a young man in a linen suit and hat. Even from a distance one could see how tall he was. He leaned back, an arm resting along the back of the bench in a posture that seemed to want you to believe he was relaxed and unconcerned, but the arm in its pressed linen sleeve was stiff and awkward, the fingers of the hand beat a rapid tattoo on the spotted wood of the bench.

Her footsteps made a sound on the path and he looked up at once and met her eyes. His was a handsome face, clean-shaven, dark hair cut short, dark eyes and a light tan—a face she had never expected to see again, and for a moment her footsteps faltered. But only for a moment. She smiled. Moisture stood out on his forehead and upper lip and, as though aware of her gaze, he reached for a handkerchief and dabbed at his face. He looked like someone who had been sitting here a while.

'Well, finally!' he said by way of greeting, uncrossing his legs and standing up. 'Do you know how long I've been sitting here?'

They were not the words she had anticipated and Harriet felt her smile dissolve into a frown but she embraced him anyway, clinging to him, her fingers digging into his arm, then abruptly releasing him.

'I've no idea, Freddie. I didn't tell you to come at a certain time. In fact, as I recall, I didn't tell you to come at all.'

'One o'clock I got here, one o'-bloody-clock!' he complained, as though she hadn't spoken. '*And* I was here all yesterday afternoon too. I've had to suffer the gaze of every child and old biddy in the district, not to mention the faecal matter of every pigeon in this part of London. It's a wonder I haven't been moved on or arrested. One charming young lady took her children away, obviously under the impression I was just waiting for the opportunity to expose some part of my anatomy to her young charges. Really, I'm quite fed up.'

'Things came up expectedly yesterday. And you did just ring up out of the blue! I warned you it would be difficult—'

She could hear her voicing rising and she made herself stop. She would not cry; she had told herself she would not cry. Freddie didn't need tears. What did he need? She couldn't imagine. She took a deep breath.

'—and today we went out to lunch and, really, what do you expect me to do? Invite you along?'

She sat down beside him and as Freddie made no reply to this they sat in silence and stared at the pigeons. She laughed suddenly. 'Do you know, you sound just like Julius. That same petulant schoolboy manner.'

Freddie stirred and she regretted at once saying that.

'Well, I wouldn't know, would I? Haven't seen the little blighter since he was five.'

They fell silent again.

It's no good blaming me, Harriet thought bitterly. Wasn't she taking enough of a risk just being seen out with him? She allowed herself a quick glance to left and right, but cautiously, not wanting Freddie to notice. At the far end of the garden the Pashkints hadn't stirred. Just then Mr Pashkint lifted a mournful head and said something, holding his right hand out before him, palm upwards in a gesture that said, What can you do?

What *could* you do? Freddie was back. He had rung up out of the blue on Thursday. They had spoken briefly on the telephone, but nothing had been resolved. They had spoken about the past. And what *could* be resolved? Freddie couldn't stay here.

'You didn't tell Cecil?' he said suddenly and Harriet shook her head irritably.

'No, of course not. Why on earth do you think I would tell him? Besides, there's something going on with him. A police matter—'

Beside her Freddie stiffened.

'No, it's something at work. One of Cecil's employees stole from the company and disappeared. That's all he's concerned about at the moment.'

Freddie settled back down again. 'But will you tell him?'

'I don't see what can be gained from it.'

Freddie almost seemed to want Cecil to know he was back, as though he wanted to force things. But he didn't know Cecil, he didn't know what Cecil might do. Harriet did. And because of that she wasn't going to let Freddie coerce her into anything.

'Why *did* you come back, Freddie?' she demanded and even though she could see the sudden hurt in his eyes she couldn't hold back. After all, it was his fault, all this, not hers. He had brought it on himself. 'It's not that I don't want to see you, Lord knows, but for God's sake why didn't you stay in Canada? You had a life there. You said you had a new life.'

Freddie said nothing. He didn't have to. He reached over and took her hand and held it and they sat like that for a long time until Mr Pashkint had stood up and offered his wife his arm and tottered back with her through the gate and away.

Chapter Six
OCTOBER 1952

Anne was proving to a be something of a handful.

It was Monday morning. The smell of bacon wafted up from below and Mr Wallis could be heard, distantly and petulantly, complaining that there was no newspaper. *The Times* came some mornings but not others—for no adequately explained reason. Julius was up, Jean could hear him rummaging about in his room, flinging open doors and banging them shut again. But from Anne's room there was silence.

'Good morning, Anne. Oh, you still in bed? Come on, then, let's get your things together for school.'

Jean came into the room, pulled Anne's school uniform out of the wardrobe and handed it to her. Anne reached out to take it then withdrew her hand at the last minute so that the tunic fell to the floor.

'I don't want you going through my wardrobe, Nanny,' she announced getting out of bed and flouncing over to the window.

Jean looked down at the uniform where it lay on the floor.

'Oh. So how am I to get you ready for school then, Anne?'

'I can get my self ready.'

'Suit yourself. I'll go and see if breakfast's ready. Don't forget your hat,' and Jean indicated the St Lydwina's straw hat hanging on its hook on the door. It was the third such hat Anne had had this month. The previous two were now at the bottom of the school pond and Anne was on double report with her teacher.

'I did it on purpose,' Anne had declared after the first incident. 'My friend Patricia Pritchard said I was stupid because I'd done it while everyone was watching. She said they can't get you if you do it when no one's looking. But what's the point of doing it when no one's looking? *She's* the one who's stupid.'

What *was* the point of doing anything if no one was looking? That appeared to be Anne's motto.

Downstairs *The Times* had made a miraculous, if tardy, appearance and Mr Wallis could now be heard exclaiming indignantly from the breakfast room. As Jean passed the door, Mrs Wallis looked up from her cup of coffee and saw her.

'Nanny, where's Anne got to? Her father will be leaving for the office soon and she must come and say goodbye.'

'She's coming down directly,' replied Jean, though Anne had indicated no intention to do any such thing. It was strange, this insistence on saying goodbye to their father each morning, the three of them—Anne, Julius and Mrs Wallis—lined up at the front door as though Mr Wallis were going off to war rather than simply catching the Piccadilly Line to Holborn.

'Oh. Goodfellow's resigned,' she heard Mr Wallis remark. 'Harriet, your old school chum Daphne's husband has resigned from the Ministry, '… in order', it says here, 'to concentrate on his electorate'. Wonder what that means?'

'Anne, come and say goodbye to your father,' Jean called up the stairs and, getting no response, went back up to the girl's room.

'I said goodbye to him last night,' replied Anne and she got out of bed and wandered over to the window. 'Father prefers it that way.'

There was silence while Jean attempted to make sense of this. She decided Anne was just being difficult.

Downstairs the front door slammed shut and a moment later they could hear the smart click of Mr Wallis's shoes on the front steps.

'Anyway, it's too late, Daddy's already left,' Anne pointed out, gazing down at the street below where Mr Wallis's rapidly retreating figure could be seen.

'Well. It's high time we got ready for school,' Jean countered, feeling that she had somehow been out-played by the child.

'We? Oh, are you coming too, Nanny?' Before Jean could reply to this Anne returned to her bed and sat down heavily, placing a weak hand to her forehead. 'Anyway, I shan't be able to go to school today, I'm afraid, as I don't feel well.'

Jean was about to reply that Anne was clearly well enough to get up out of bed and go and stand by the window, but stopped herself. What would a nanny do in such a situation?

'Oh poor lamb,' she said. 'Yes, you do look a little poorly. Let me get you into bed,' and Anne submitted to having her forehead felt and a thermometer placed beneath her tongue, lying perfectly still until Jean had removed the thermometer and studied it for a while with narrowed eyes, holding it up to the light and twisting it this way and that.

'Oh. Can't you read a thermometer, Nanny?' asked Anne, sounding less wan than she had a few moments ago.

In the end, Jean went to fetch Mrs Wallis.

Mrs Wallis, it appeared, was about to go out. She was standing in the hallway pulling on her gloves and she looked blankly at Jean as Jean related the news of her daughter's illness to her. Mrs Wallis picked up a spotted black and white silk head scarf and paused before the hallway mirror.

'And in your opinion, Nanny, is it real or is she faking?' she enquired.

Jean was a little nonplussed.

'I took her temperature,' she replied carefully. 'But these things, well, you never can tell—'

'Yes, quite.' Mrs Wallis replaced the scarf on the hall table and followed her. Upstairs, Anne lay curled up on her bed.

'Anne, dear, what is it?'

'Don't feel well,' Anne replied feebly.

'Well, is it your head? Your throat? Your stomach?'

'My … head,' Anne replied after a moment's consideration and she delicately touched that afflicted part of her anatomy.

Mrs Wallis nodded as though she had expected this.

'I suppose you had better stay home from school.' The patient nodded meekly at this suggestion. 'Nanny, please telephone the school and notify them that Anne will not be in today.' And with that she turned and left the room.

Jean followed her out and back down the stairs.

'Are you going out, then, Mrs Wallis?'

'Yes. I have an appointment,' she replied, clearly surprised at the question.

'Dr Rolley's number is in the address book downstairs on the telephone table should Anne's medical condition … deteriorate.' Mrs Wallis had now reached the hall mirror. Jean watched from her position on the stairs as she tied the scarf over her head and reached for a coat. 'And of course Mr Wallis's number at the office is in there too, should there be any kind of emergency,' and she put on the coat, picked up her handbag and left.

Jean went back upstairs and found Anne standing by the window, absorbed by something down below. She spun around as Jean came in, her eyes flew wide open and she raced back over to her bed.

'I think it's rude to come into a person's room without knocking first,' she declared from the safety of her bed.

'Do you? And I think it's rude to lie about being ill,' and Jean marched over to the window.

'I'm *not* lying! I *am* ill!' Anne insisted, curling into a ball on her bed.

Outside, Mrs Wallis could be seen walking purposefully along the opposite pavement. She wore gloves and a long raincoat and her face was almost hidden behind a pair of enormous sunglasses. She walked with her head down and her arms folded tightly over her chest. She stopped at the locked gate to the garden, pulled a key from her pocket and let herself in, locking the gate behind her and for a moment she was obscured by the tall privet hedges.

Jean's eyes swept ahead and from her viewpoint, two storeys up, the garden was spread out before her. An elderly lady sat on a bench on the far side, staring gloomily at a small white dog that sniffed at one of the rose beds. A young man in a hat and a dark grey raincoat sat on another bench opposite them. Mrs Wallis came into view and made straight for the young man who stood up and went to her. They embraced briefly and sat down side by side on the bench. They too sat staring gloomily at the same white dog that a moment earlier had preoccupied the elderly lady.

Jean turned away and stared at Anne, who returned her gaze wordlessly.

'Anne, get back into bed now,' Jean said.

Anne huffed moodily but did as she was told.

Downstairs in the garden the young man turned towards Mrs Wallis and took her hand.

A moment later Jean left the bedroom and went quickly down two flights of stairs to the hallway. She opened the address book and picked up the telephone, but it was not Doctor Rolley's number that she dialled.

Chapter Seven

OCTOBER 1952

At the newly relocated offices of Empire and Colonial Shipping Lines off Chancery Lane, Jeremy Rocastle's office was still cordoned off. Yellow incident tape, of the variety one had got used to during the war, marked off an area around the doorway of his now vacant office. One expected such a thing around a bombsite filled with rubble and debris but here in the office, amid the soft olive-green carpet and the red leather armchairs and the forbidding portraits of former directors, it was incongruous. It was indecent.

Cecil averted his eyes from the sealed office door and its distasteful yellow tape.

In the first week following Rocastle's disappearance Scotland Yard had gone through the building like a bout of influenza and statements had been taken from everyone from Sir Maurice himself down to the fluctuating team of Jamaican women who nightly cleaned the offices.

Cecil himself had been among the first to make his statement: Rocastle had worked in his department. He had known the man for a little over a year. He had trusted Rocastle, naturally. The man had dined at his house. He had met Rocastle's wife. On the evening in question Cecil had noticed nothing unusual. He had left the office at around 6 pm and had not seen Rocastle since.

It was a simple and truthful statement of fact. No one had asked: did Rocastle ever behave suspiciously? Did he ever do anything to make you question his honesty? Had you ever resolved to report his actions to a fellow director and then failed to do so?

Cecil had signed the statement and it had been taken away in a cardboard box along with all the others.

The investigation had continued, photographs had been taken, descriptions had been circulated, doorknobs, desks and the company safe had been coated in powder and dusted for fingerprints. Why? What was the point? They all knew who had perpetrated the crime.

The share price had dropped, of course. It was only to be expected. Foolish to suppose a story like this would remain out of the press for long, and the newspapers had had a field day. And they hadn't spared Rocastle: old Etonian, Cambridge man, a trusted position in a highly respected firm, a respectable wife. ('Respectable'! That was the word the newspapers used when someone's family origins were rather obscure. Poor Mrs Rocastle.) Any whiff of scandal was eagerly pounced upon. At least there was no question anyone else was involved; that anyone else in the firm had even the slightest idea what was going on.

Cecil had stayed in his office each evening late into the night. If one worked extra hard, if one could prove one's loyalty to the firm, to one's colleagues, by excelling, by working through the night if need be—Lord knows, he had done it often enough during the war—if one could just do that, night after night—

But he didn't work. He simply sat and went over it all in his head, and in the end he got no work done at all. Night after night. And in the mornings Miss James looked at him oddly and gave timid smiles and said nothing.

And then it had suddenly stopped. The police had packed up and gone. Now, two weeks later, all that remained was the yellow incident tape. Had the police simply forgotten to remove it? He must remember to get Miss James to telephone them.

Rocastle's name had been removed from his office door. There were four small holes where his name plate had been unscrewed. Cecil had passed this very door that Monday morning in August on his way to a hastily arranged meeting with Standforth. But one could not simply destroy another man's career without at least warning him; without at least giving the fellow a chance to explain himself, to prepare some sort of defence. He had gone back and knocked on Rocastle's door—

'Morning, Wallis.'

Cecil started as McAnley Stanforth, the senior director and Sir Maurice's right-hand man, passed him in the corridor.

'Morning, Standforth.'

'Still trying to come to terms with our black sheep, are you?' Standforth said, nodding towards the cordoned office.

Cecil forced a smile.

'Yes. Something like that.

'Well, I shouldn't worry too much about it, old man. Someone like that, a rotten apple if you like, well, they're bad through and through. Chaps like you and I can't imagine it. Makes it hard for us to spot them.'

'Yes, no doubt you're right,' Cecil agreed, but as he watched Standforth stride down the corridor and disappear into his office, he thought: but I *did* spot it. And I knocked on this door and I confronted the man.

Rocastle had been sitting at his desk when Cecil had entered, sipping a cup of tea and reading the *Daily Mail*. Well, that ought to have sounded warning bells straight away. The *Daily Mail*! At Empire and Colonial! Rocastle had looked up calmly enough, almost cheerfully, and there had been nothing in his face to indicate guilt. Nothing to even suggest he recalled the conversation he and Cecil had had the previous Friday about the erroneous entries in the wages ledger.

Cecil had felt a moment of disquiet. Had he made a mistake? Was he about to make an even bigger mistake and, in the process, jeopardise this young man's career?

But there had been a principle at stake.

'Rocastle, I have given the incident we discussed on Friday a great deal of thought,' he had announced, 'and I feel it incumbent upon me to advise you that I have resolved to report it to Standforth.'

He had seen the slightest flicker of something—fear? surprise?— pass across Rocastle's face, but otherwise the fellow had remained remarkably cool. Cecil had pressed on.

'An error has been made—whether purposely or by accident—and it needs to be reported. And as Standforth is director of finance, he needs to be advised. It is, I am sure you understand, nothing more than a precaution. There can be no question of fraud. Everything must be out in the open.'

As he had outlined this course of action Cecil had had every intention of carrying it out. And yet he had not done so.

'Oh, Mr Wallis. Mr Sayid telephoned while you were out. I took down his number. He's staying at the Ritz and asks that you telephone him there this afternoon.'

Cecil looked up to see Miss James rising from her station, a modest teak desk outside his own office, her shorthand pad and her pencil stub poised to record his reply.

And here was the antidote, he realised; here was the cure to the yellow incident tape and the unsteady share price and the unwelcome boots of Scotland Yard in the corridors and the rotten apples like Rocastle: Miss James. Steady, reliable, faithful secretary of more than fifteen years standing, still manning her station with that same effortless determination, that stalwart and flawless professionalism, that utter dependability. Why didn't the blasted newspapers ever report that?

'Thank you, Miss James,' he replied. And then because he could think of nothing to add he smiled.

Miss James blushed a deep red and sat down still flourishing her pad and pencil as though she didn't quite know what to do with them.

Cecil stepped into his office and closed the door, pausing to draw breath. The sense of calm order that his office provided had been a steady comfort over the years but in the past two weeks it had become almost a craving. The office door was shut and Miss James was a formidable barrier against the world and the worst that it could throw at him.

He crossed the office and settled himself in the large leather chair at his desk. It was a rosewood partner's desk, Victorian, though not as old as the desk in his study. This was a functional desk, a daily desk. The rich rust-brown rosewood shone pleasantly in the late October sunlight. The telephone, an ink-well, the in- and out-trays and a large leather writing pad were precisely positioned. That morning's *Times* was the only thing that spoilt the order. Nothing about the Rocastle affair in it, thank God. (How had it got to the point where he viewed his morning paper with a sinking feeling that did not abate until he had passed the editorial and letters pages?) Today all there had been was a story on Peter Goodfellow resigning from the Ministry, which was surprising—well, it seemed to have surprised Harriet, at any rate, who had rushed off to telephone Valerie for the gossip—but it was not a story that was going to affect the firm's share price. He picked up the *Times* and deposited it in the bin.

Photographs of the fleet lined his office: the *Tostig* which had made the run to New York in five days in 1910; the *Harold* which had shipped troops to Cape Town during the Boer War; the *Ethulwulf*, which had done the Peninsular mail run at the turn of the century and was now in dry dock at Plymouth awaiting break up; and the *Alfred* and the *Eadred*, which had been sunk by enemy action in the North Atlantic in '41 and '43. Above his head was the *Swane*, flagship of the Empire and Colonial fleet, taken by a *New York Times* photographer at the climax of that final record-breaking crossing in '38. Four days, one hour and eight minutes! It had been thrilling—even Harriet had been caught up in the excitement of the moment.

Then the following month the *Queen Mary* had done it in three days and twenty hours.

He frowned. It seemed odd now to imagine Harriet excited. Perhaps his own excitement had carried them both along. And now, looking back, even his own excitement seemed to belong to another person.

It had not been Harriet's first Atlantic crossing, of course. More than a year before the *Swane*'s triumph she had visited New York to stay with an aunt and uncle, a voyage that had ended with the King's abdication and Harriet's arrival at his office one cold morning in December '36, where she had sat before this very desk in a cherry-red coat and hat.

It had been Miss James's predecessor, the elderly Miss Clough, who had knocked on his office door—the old office, then, over at Moorgate—and he had started up from this desk feeling guilty because he had been staring at the wall for the last half hour trying to take in the news from the Palace.

'There's a Miss Paget to see you,' Miss Clough had calmly announced, standing in the doorway, so that for a brief second or two one could believe that all was right with the world and one's

King had not just abdicated. But two red patches stood out on Miss Clough's cheeks.

Miss Paget? Oh dear Lord, yes.

'Thank you, Miss Clough. Please show her in.'

Duty called and one must put the abdication to one side, for this particular interview was going to be tricky.

This Miss Paget, even now waiting outside his office, had just returned from New York aboard the *Swane*, which had docked the previous evening. According to Miss Clough, she had been travelling with her elderly father and unfortunately the father had died about two days out from Southampton. Heart failure, a natural death, but any death on board was a diplomatic and bureaucratic nightmare. Empire and Colonial Lines definitely frowned upon it. But sometimes it could not be avoided. And today was just such a day—and what a day to be dealing with such matters!

The young lady who came into Cecil's office and who had just lost her father in such distressing circumstances was not dressed in mourning. Mourning clothes were already going out of fashion by then, particularly so amongst the young, so perhaps the cherry-red winter coat was not so very remarkable, and yet he remembered so well the impression the young lady made as she strode into his suddenly rather stuffy and shabby office. She had been wearing a fur tippet, he recalled—though every lady wore furs in those days—and a small hat, cherry red to match the coat. And long black gloves. It was 1936, of course—December, so Harriet had been 24.

He came quickly out from behind his desk holding out both hands in a way that was both greeting and discreet sympathy.

'Miss Paget. How do you do? I am Mr Wallis. Cecil Wallis. Thank you for making this journey to our office at such a difficult time.'

Miss Paget shook his hand with a tight smile as though she was uncertain whether he was referring to her father's sudden demise or to the abdication of the King. Cecil realised he wasn't sure himself. He hovered for a moment, hands clasped before him.

'Please do sit down.' He indicated the padded Edwardian chair before his desk. 'May I start by offering my sympathy to you at this distressing time?'

Miss Paget shrugged. 'Oh, well. These things happen. No use crying over spilt milk. Do you mind if I smoke?'

Cecil blinked, a little flustered by her off-hand response. 'No, indeed. Please do.'

Actually, he loathed the habit, but had trained himself to prepare for every social eventuality. He opened a desk drawer and produced a silver ashtray. It was a little too chilly to think of opening the window. Besides, that would have been rude.

She really was a striking-looking young lady. Strong features, dark eyes—what colour? One couldn't really see, but dark, and her face had colour to it as though she had returned, not from New York where it was currently 20 degrees, but from South Africa or the West Indies. She was very self-assured, didn't look at him at all as she concentrated on lighting her cigarette. Perhaps she was keeping a tight rein over her feelings; persons in a state of shock often did.

Miss Paget's father was not Cecil's first trans-Atlantic death.

'May we offer you a cup of tea, Miss Paget? I find tea often helps in these circumstances.' He smiled in a way that offered both friendship and comfort.

Miss Paget raised a curious eyebrow.

'Does it?' she asked, frowning. 'Do you get a lot of this on your ships, Mr ...?'

'Wallis. Not a lot, no. But I'm afraid it is probably a lot more common than the average passenger would expect. We don't advertise the fact, naturally. That would alarm our passengers. Nevertheless, we are prepared for all circumstances and I trust that we may offer a swift and, where possible, painless resolution to ease your distress.'

The eyebrow raised a second time.

'Well. You amaze me, Mr Wallis.' She drew on her cigarette. 'Shall we get on with it? I have an engagement at the Café Royal in one hour.'

She certainly was a cool customer. But no doubt the young lady had not been close to her father, one often read of such things ... Indeed he recalled when his own father had passed away ...

Cecil shook his head to clear it.

'Certainly. Though I should warn you, Miss Paget, the paperwork is rather lengthy in these situations. Any shipboard incident when one is, shall we say, in *terra nullius*, always results in a great deal of bureaucratic and diplomatic to-ing and fro-ing. I'm sure you understand? But we shall endeavour to make it as speedy as possible.'

He opened another drawer and began to assemble the various forms that Miss Paget would be required to complete.

'*Diplomatic?*' exclaimed Miss Paget, rather indignantly. 'Surely you are joking, Mr Wallis? I hardly see what there is of a diplomatic nature about this.'

Cecil smiled sympathetically. Most young ladies, in his experience, had little understanding of the machinations of State and Commonwealth, of the intricate nature of bureaucracy—indeed, they rarely needed to know. It was a pity she did not have a husband to accompany her in this unpleasant task. Then he sat up. She had not brought a husband. Had not, in fact, mentioned a husband—was in fact, a *Miss*. Somehow this seemed ... miraculous.

He realised he was leaning forward and smiling in a way that was neither friendly nor comforting, but eager, bordering on fervent.

'Please do not distress yourself, Miss Paget. I am entirely at your disposal and we shall navigate the treacherous waters of international diplomacy together!'

This was intended to sound heroic. Instead it sounded a little gushy. He hoped he wasn't going to blush.

Miss Paget held her cigarette a little distance from her lips and regarded him silently; regarded him—it had to be said—a little warily.

'It's really just the insurance I'm concerned about, Mr Wallis,' she said.

She really was a cool one! Had the father been a tyrant? Somehow one couldn't imagine anyone tyrannising Miss Paget ...

'Of course, all such matters must be attended to—I commend your practicality, Miss Paget. Let us start with the general release form. I would be honoured to complete it on your behalf,' he announced, brandishing his engraved fountain pen in what he hoped was an official manner. 'Shall we begin?'

She nodded her assent.

'Now, then. When and where exactly did the … unfortunate incident occur? You see, if we can establish that, it may save a great deal of paperwork further down the line.'

Again she paused with the cigarette poised before her lips. She really was quite striking.

'Well, it was evening. Our last evening at sea. Must have been around ten o'clock, as we had all finished dinner. I had been in my cabin but it was dreadfully stuffy, there was no breeze at all, so I went up on deck. I suppose I wandered about a bit on the pool deck. A pair of young men were trying to play quoits but it was far too dark and really they were quite drunk so it was just a bit of silliness, really. They asked me to join them but I didn't feel like it, so I stood a little further away, near the rail, and watched the stars and … whatnot.'

She paused and drew on her cigarette and it was almost as though she was a little embarrassed at having to admit to such a thing. But where was the father during all this? In his cabin having a fatal heart attack, one presumed. Poor girl, no doubt she was experiencing a little guilt—people generally did, in Cecil's experience.

'What happened then, Miss Paget?' he prompted gently.

She shrugged. 'It's rather hard to explain really. I wasn't wearing my gloves, you see—well, it was an unseasonably mild evening—and one doesn't follow all the usual rules on board ship, does one? You must have noticed.'

'Of course.'

'And all I can say is, I was twisting my ring round and round on my finger—it's just a habit one has. And—well, the next moment it had gone. Fallen over the side.'

There was a silence.

'I … see. How unfortunate.' Cecil nodded to give himself time to phrase his next question. 'And your father …?'

Miss Paget blinked at him. 'I beg your pardon?'

'Your father. Where was he during this time?'

She gave him the oddest look. 'At his home in Belgravia, one would imagine. Why on earth would you need to know that?'

This time the silence lasted a great deal longer. Cecil reached discreetly into a different drawer and pulled out another form.

'You said it was an insurance claim?'

'Yes, of course. My engagement ring. It was diamond. It was fully insured, naturally, but the insurance company are demanding I obtain a form from you before I proceed with the claim.'

There was a discreet knock and the elderly Miss Clough appeared around the door.

'Sorry to disturb you, Mr Wallis, but a Miss Hatchett has arrived— it's about her father.'

'A Miss *Hatchett*?'

'Yes, Mr Wallis.' Miss Clough returned his gaze expressionlessly.

'Ask her to wait outside. I shall be with her directly.'

Cecil sat back in his chair. Miss Paget had lost an engagement ring. Not her father, just a ring. An engagement ring. She was engaged.

'I'll take this with me, shall I?' she said, indicating the form, and he nodded, summoning a weak smile. Then he watched silently as Miss Paget opened her handbag, folded the form and placed it inside. She took a final pull on her cigarette, stubbed it out in the ashtray and stood up. 'Goodbye, then, Mr Wallis. And thank you for your assistance. I shall certainly know where to come the next time I mislay an engagement ring.'

And she had gone. Off, no doubt, to get married to some fabulously rich New York businessman.

But the odd thing was that Harriet hadn't married some fabulously rich New York businessman—she had married him.

And they had honeymooned on board the *Swane*. He smiled, remembering.

He was disturbed by a soft tap on his office door. A moment later the door opened and Miss James appeared.

Cecil felt a slightly uncomfortably constriction in his chest. What on earth was it now? Ever since the Rocastle affair one felt like one could count on nothing; there were no certainties any longer.

'Just your morning tea, Mr Wallis,' she said, pushing the door open with her foot and sliding soundlessly into the office with the silver tea tray.

Tea. Of course. Everything settled once more into calm order. The silver Victorian tea tray and the elegant Royal Worcester tea set, more than fifty years old now, salvaged from Father's house, its red and gold rim decoration as fresh now as the day it left the factory. Miss James placed the tray on his desk and departed, returning a moment later with a tea plate containing two biscuits— one digestive, one garibaldi—resting serenely on its cool china surface.

'Mr Wallis, a Miss Corbett just telephoned. She seemed most anxious to talk with you. I didn't put her through because I knew you were very busy.'

'Miss Corbett? The nanny?'

'So I am led to believe.' Miss James never took anything at face value. She placed the teacup on Cecil's desk. 'Should be nicely brewed now,' she observed, as she always did.

'What did she want?'

Miss James paused to consider. 'She didn't indicate, other than to request that you telephone the house as soon as it is convenient.'

'Thank you, Miss James,' and as she retired to the outer office, he reached for the digestive and broke the biscuit in two with a satisfying snap. But it wasn't satisfying. The biscuit may as well have been stale for all the enjoyment he was going to get from it. He lay both halves down on the plate. The nanny had rung. Something, clearly, was amiss and one couldn't simply ignore it.

He picked up the telephone receiver and dialled the number. The telephone rang once and was picked up.

'Kensington 8578,' came Miss Corbett's oddly formal voice.

'Ah, Miss Corbett. It's Mr Wallis. Miss James said you had telephoned me. Is everything all right?'

'I'm afraid I'm not sure, Mr Wallis. I thought it best to telephone. Anne is unwell, you see, and Mrs Wallis has gone out, and Dr Rolley is out on call and cannot be contacted.'

He was baffled, then remembered that Anne had not come downstairs this morning to see him off.

'I'm not entirely certain I follow you. Is Anne at home from school?'

'Yes. She is unwell. A headache—of course, it could well be nothing, children get all sorts of aches and pains all the time, but I remember a girl in our street before the war who had a headache, and in three days she was down with the scarlet fever.'

'Well. But I'm sure you are over-reacting, Miss Corbett. And you say Dr Rolley is unavailable?'

'I'm afraid so. Of course, I would have consulted Mrs Wallis, but she went out early. To an appointment.'

What appointment? Harriet had mentioned nothing over breakfast. No doubt it was her hairdresser or something. Well, then, obviously Harriet did not deem it to be too serious.

'I feel sure if Mrs Wallis thinks it is all right—'

'I'm afraid Mrs Wallis left before.'

'Before? Left before what?'

'Before things took a turn for the worse. I believe it would be best if you were to come home, Mr Wallis.'

Cecil was nonplussed. Yet the girl's calm insistence was unnerving.

'Exactly how sick is she, Miss Corbett?'

'It's hard to say. You can never tell, can you, with children?'

'I can't very well simply drop everything and come home. Now, listen, I want you to telephone Dr Rolley's surgery again and find out when he will be available. Mrs Wallis is likely to return home soon, in any case. I shall telephone you again in an hour to ascertain further developments.'

Afterwards he sat at his desk while the tea grew cold and a skin formed over its surface. Scarlet fever? The woman was hysterical. He picked up the pile of papers in his in-tray and began to sort through them. After ten minutes he pushed himself up from his chair, grabbed his coat, hat and umbrella and left the office.

'I shan't be going to my club for lunch, Miss James; I shall be going home. I shall return sometime around two o'clock,' and Miss James signalled her total astonishment at this unprecedented turn of events with a brief nod of her head and returned to her typing.

The traffic along Piccadilly was like a funeral procession and the cab crawled along at barely five miles an hour before coming to a complete halt at Hyde Park Corner. Cecil peered out of the window to take his mind off his growing frustration.

The day had begun unpromisingly when a low and menacing bank of apparently unending grey clouds had settled over London. Now, seemingly against all odds, the sky had brightened and, as the cab slunk through Knightsbridge, a shaft of sunlight shone down in a way that made one suddenly appreciate being alive, and made Cecil glad he had abandoned habit and decided to come home for lunch.

'Just drop me here, driver,' he called, leaning forward to tap on the glass. An impulse (the second impulse in an hour!) urged him to quit the cab and walk the remaining distance in the sunshine. It would probably be quicker, in any case. 'Thank you, my good man,' and he threw in a small tip.

He rarely walked along Old Brompton Road and certainly never found himself in Old Brompton Road at lunchtime on a Monday.

The road was busy with late morning shoppers, mothers with smart prams and smartly turned out babies, neatly attired shopgirls on their lunch breaks, bank clerks carrying packets of sandwiches in search of benches to sit on. It was perfect. London functioning exactly as London had for two millennia: mothers and babies, commerce, life. It made him proud to be a functioning part of a functioning city.

He turned left into Palmerston Terrace, then into Athelstan Gardens with a pleasant sense of homecoming just as the sun slid beneath a large bank of dirty brown cloud and a few spots of rain began to fall. But he would make it home before the shower took hold. The private garden was deserted, as though everyone had anticipated the turn in the weather. Not even the wretched elderly couple, who seemed as permanent a fixture as the pigeons, were there.

I ought to have telephoned ahead, Cecil realised, the awkwardness of arriving home unannounced and unexpected in the middle of the day striking him keenly. His pace slowed. Harriet would think it very strange. But Harriet was out. And damn it, it's my house, he reasoned.

He picked up his pace again and began to cross the road, seeing for the first time a couple standing just inside the padlocked gate. So the garden had not been empty; the privet hedge had simply obscured them, and indeed one of the two people in the garden appeared to be Harriet.

And the other person was Freddie.

Cecil paused, forgetting for one dizzying moment how to walk. He willed his legs to move onwards and they jerked forwards stiffly. It could not be Freddie. Freddie had gone abroad.

The man said something indistinctly and repositioned his hat. It was Freddie. No question about it.

Keep moving. Don't let them see you.

Cecil continued walking yet it was impossible not to look back. They hadn't moved. Harriet was saying something with a frown, looking off behind her—not this way, thank God. Something final had been said and now they were embracing, briefly, almost bitterly.

Keep walking, eyes straight ahead. Don't look back.

When he turned again Harriet had come through the gate and was walking briskly across the road towards the house without a backward glance, apparently not having noticed him. Freddie, too, had crossed the road but was walking in the other direction, back towards Old Brompton Road, his head down, thoughts somewhere else.

Cecil kept on walking, past the house and round the corner into Fulham Road. He ought to have telephoned first.

Chapter Eight

OCTOBER 1952

Jean watched from the window of her room as three storeys below, on the far side of the street in the enclosed confines of that unwelcoming and closed-off garden, Mrs Wallis embraced the young man. Then she strode from him with her head held high as though she had no conscience at all. And the man stood and watched her go, then he too left.

Mrs Wallis wore a spotted black and white head scarf, the sort of head scarf the new Queen wore at Sandringham, and a large pair of sunglasses and a long raincoat that covered her from neck to mid-calf. She was dressed like someone who did not wish to be recognised. But someone *had* recognised her. Two people, in fact. Herself and another—and it looked very much like Mr Wallis.

She had watched him as he drew almost level with the two lovers

108

and began to cross the road. His step faltered, then he continued on his way, though now his head was bowed.

Was it Mr Wallis? All the men in this street wore identical raincoats and hats and brandished the same rolled umbrella. But something about the way he walked, the angle of his head, the curve of that slightly beaked nose, told her it was him. She recognised him even from three storeys up. And she had summoned him.

Just as God had summoned her here.

She had gone to the Festival of Britain—and so had a great many other people that day.

It had been a hot and dry Saturday in early August, last year, and she had gone with the O'Riordans—Eddie and his brother, Liam— and Liam's girl, Maureen. The O'Riordans were Mrs McIlwraith's sister's boys and Jean had had misgivings right from the start.

They were Catholics, of course, and Dad did not approve of Catholics. One of the O'Riordan sisters was an unmarried mother and the older boy was on remand at Brixton. But what had it mattered by then, by that hot Saturday in August when Dad had been gone six years already?

Liam's girl, Maureen, had said, 'Come with us, Jean. Us girls, we got to stick to together'. What Maureen had meant by this was hard to say, but Jean had agreed, because it was the Festival and she was a little excited, though she made it clear it was with Maureen that she was going.

And so it had turned out … as far as the bus stop on Commercial Road. As soon as the number 11 turned up Maureen and Liam had hopped down the back and made it pretty clear they didn't need any company.

'Back seat for us then, Jean?' Eddie had asked her with a wink and she had glared at him and taken a seat directly behind the driver.

'You can forget any of that funny business, Eddie O'Riordan. I'm not interested. I'm just here to see the Festival.'

And so, it turned out, was everyone else. The Festival site was heaving that Saturday; they seemed to have chosen the most popular day of the year for their visit.

'Right then, where's the beer tent?' said Liam, standing on the riverbank and staring all about him as though he expected to see a large sign that read: *Welcome to the Festival of Britain—beer tent this way*.

There hadn't been a beer tent. Instead there had been striped umbrellas and open-air cafés. There had been a funny little railway and a Mississippi Showboat and a spindly metal spiral staircase that went up and up but didn't go anywhere. And a vast silvery pointy thing hanging in the air, pointy-end downwards, so that you wondered how it stayed up. Everyone ate ice-cream and strode about in 3-D Polaroid spectacles, wandering in and out of the pavilions. One pavilion showed you what the world would be like in the future. It had a car from the future which made Eddie whistle appreciatively and Liam said, 'It ain't no good, Eddie, me old son—ain't got no back seat', and he and Maureen had giggled.

'Ships and Sea Pavilion,' read Eddie as they stood outside the next hall. 'Sounds boring.' He paused to light a cigarette.

They had eaten their ice-creams and worn their 3-D Polaroid spectacles until the cardboard had rubbed a sore spot on the bridges of their noses. They had drunk four pints of Bass at the Festival Bar (well, Eddie and Liam had—Maureen had had a gin and orange, thank you very much, and Jean had had a cup of tea), they had ridden on the paddle steamer and Liam and Eddie had taken turns seeing who could spit the furthest over the side, and now Eddie was getting restless.

'Where them other two got to, then?' he had muttered, irritably thrusting his 3-D spectacles further up his nose, then pulling them off and tossing them into the river. Liam and Maureen had had a row outside the Dome of Discovery. Something to do with a girl in a red hat and a man whom Liam had thought was the girl's father and who had turned out to be her fella.

'There's Maureen,' said Jean pointing. Maureen could just be seen clipping angrily through the crowd on her very high heels some distance ahead of them.

'Leave 'er, moody cow... Blimey, what's this?' said Eddie, pointing through the entrance-way of the Ships and Sea Pavilion with his cigarette. It was the front of a huge ship, the pointed bit. MV *Titania* it said in black lettering on the side. It was so big you had to crane your neck to see the top and it must have scraped the roof of the pavilion near enough, even though the pavilion was so big.

'Where's the rest of it, then?' called Eddie as they walked around to the side of the giant hull, and Jean could see that it was really just the front bit of the ship and the rest of the ship wasn't there at all, which was a bit of a swiz. Jean followed Eddie into a small room that was made up to look like the ship's engine-room and there were noises and sudden bursts of steam that made a small girl burst into tears. Her mother led her out and Eddie made a grab for one of the levers.

'Hey, look at me! Full steam ahead!'

'Careful! Don't break it, Eddie!'

'I ain't breakin' it, am I! It's fake, innit? It ain't goin' nowhere. 'Ere, you know what? Me old man worked in one of these. Hundred degree heat in midwinter, he used to say, while the toffs is bein' served gin and wotsits upstairs.'

'You said your old Dad worked the Woolwich ferry.'

'Same difference. Here, Jean, how's about it?' and he grabbed her and pulled her close and tried to kiss her.

'Give over, Eddie. I told you I weren't interested.' She could feel one of the levers pressing painfully into her back and she pushed him away. An elderly couple appeared in the doorway and stared at them both with a frown. 'Well, *really!*' said the man.

'What you lookin' at, Grandad?' demanded Eddie menacingly.

Alarmed, the couple backed rapidly out.

Jean pushed furiously past Eddie. She was tired and hungry and a little sick from all the ice-cream and the 3-D Polaroid spectacles had given her a headache. Why had Eddie even come here? Just so that he could act the fool with Liam and get drunk and make fun of everyone and embarrass her in front of all these people and spoil it for them all? She threw her spectacles in a rubbish bin and marched off.

There was Maureen, standing in the distance near the entrance to the pavilion smoking an angry cigarette, tapping her foot furiously. Of Liam there was no sign. He'd be for it when he did eventually turn up, that was certain. Jean veered towards her. At least she and Maureen could leave together—that was a bit more dignified than flouncing off home on your own. But a large group of nuns appeared out of nowhere and in the swirling black confusion of habits and wimples Jean lost her bearings, and when she looked again Maureen had gone. She waited and walked up and down for a bit, but there was no sign of her.

So be it. If they had chosen to desert her, she would go home on her own.

The nuns reappeared out of nowhere, surrounding her in an excitable cluster like pigeons at Trafalgar Square, and suddenly it felt as though everyone had chosen that exact moment to visit the Ships and Sea Pavilion.

Jean fought her way through the swirling black mass, using her elbows for leverage, until finally she was back at the huge hull of the *Titania*. Then she saw where the nuns had just been and why they had so suddenly emerged and were twittering so excitedly: beside the hull was a small room made up to look like the first-class cabin of a luxury liner, complete with two neat little compartments cut into the cabin wall containing beds, and a porthole overlooking a picture of the sea. There were little red curtains across both berths and if you pulled one aside what you saw wasn't just a neat little berth, you saw Eddie. And Maureen. Lying on the bed, having it away.

'Excuse me, I need to get past,' she said, pushing past a young couple who were rooted, wide-eyed, to the spot right behind her.

She couldn't seem to find her way out of this wretched pavilion; instead she found her face practically pressed up against a large glass display case. What was inside the glass case she could not make out; there was only the image of Maureen and Eddie, obliterating all else.

The words 'The History of Ocean Travel' gradually came into focus. Behind it were photographs of big-masted sailing ships and passengers, dressed from before the first war, climbing up long gangways carrying boxes and trunks, and other people waving goodbye from the railings on the ships, all with big smiles on their faces as if sailing off into the unknown was a good thing. And there were the big modern ocean liners, the sort that went to New York and Australia, and beside each one was the name of the shipping company—Union-Castle, P&O, Cunard, Empire and Colonial— and in important curly print beneath were the names of the men who ran each line. They were all 'Sir' this and 'Lord' that and 'The Hon' someone else and they all had lots of meaningless letters after their names: *Sir Maurice Debden, Mr St. John MacIntosh DSO.* They didn't seem like real people at all. *Mr McAuley Standforth CBE, Mr Cecil Wallis.*

She stepped backwards, not caring that she had trodden on a small child's foot. The Festival, Eddie and Maureen having it away in the first-class cabin, the swirling mass of nuns, even the small child whose foot she had trodden on, had all been for this. They had guided her here, to this one spot. To Mr Cecil Wallis.

The window in her bedroom rattled. It rattled a lot as the days moved deeper into autumn. This morning a sharp chill had whistled around the upstairs rooms, then the sun had briefly come out; but now the wind was getting up again and it had started to rain. A door slammed somewhere downstairs—Mrs Thompson, perhaps, returning from the shops. Putting the shopping away, sitting down, taking the weight off. Putting the kettle on.

Outside, Mrs Wallis and the man had parted, he walking rapidly away towards Old Brompton Road. He was a youngish man, quite handsome and well dressed, though perhaps a little shabby. A poor bank clerk, perhaps; an aspiring writer; an out-of-work musician. Did they carry on right there in the garden, within sight of Mrs Wallis's own house?

There were voices downstairs. Mrs Wallis was back already, and was even now giving orders to Mrs Thompson about the weekly menus and the housekeeping budget as if nothing had happened, and with not the slightest notion that Mr Wallis had practically caught them in the act. It was just as she had pictured it and there could be no avoiding a scene now, there could be no denial—

And yet his step had faltered. He had pulled his hat down as though he didn't wish to see them. What kind of man did that?

Mr Cecil Wallis. A name in a glass cabinet at the Festival of Britain.

But the festival was long over, the pavilions dismantled, the glass cabinets removed and in storage, or perhaps broken up and destroyed, and Mr Cecil Wallis had walked right past his wife and her lover; had walked right past his own house and continued round the corner into Fulham Road.

Chapter Nine

OCTOBER 1952

A Piccadilly Line train came in, bound for Kings Cross and Finsbury Park. The doors opened, a number of lunchtime office workers and West End shoppers got in and the doors closed again. The train rattled noisily out of the station with a screech of metal and a shower of sparks. And Cecil found that he had failed to board and was still standing on the platform.

Freddie was back. And Harriet had lied to him.

A mother with a little girl in tow pushed past and stood in front of him, the mother peering at the mirror of a powder compact with one hand and firmly holding onto the little girl with the other. The girl looked over her shoulder and regarded Cecil wordlessly.

He remembered the last time he had seen Freddie—in the tea rooms at Harrods in March '44—and the last time Harriet had lied to him. Or perhaps it was not the last time she had lied to him? Perhaps Freddie had been back for some time?

The child's unwavering gaze was unnerving. Cecil glared at her but she only stared more intently.

He had been surprised to see Freddie that bleak and drizzling March afternoon in Harrods. He had presumed Freddie was somewhere in North Africa. That was what he had been told, though during the war one never knew for certain where anyone was and even if one did, one was not meant to say. It was a question of national security. But Harriet had said, Freddie is in North Africa and he had seen no reason to question it.

He had arranged to meet Harriet and the children in Harrods tea room. In those days, particularly towards the end of the war, when the Blitz had ended but the V1s and V2s had yet to start up, he had got into the habit of meeting Harriet and the children every couple of weeks for afternoon tea and scones. There was no jam and no one could remember the last time they'd seen double cream, but at Harrods one could, at least, still get scones. And tea. Harrods had always managed to put on a magnificent array of teas, even during the darkest hours of rationing.

A convoy of ships had just made it across the Atlantic, and Cecil, who had been seconded by the Admiralty to oversee merchant ship repairs and refits at the docks, had not been home in a week. Security around the docked ships had been stepped up and a black-marketeer had been shot by guards the previous evening. Cecil had not slept for three nights, other than hastily snatched catnaps on the chair in his office. But one did not complain; it was much worse for the troops. It was much worse for Freddie, who was in North Africa.

Or not in North Africa, for there he had been, bold as brass, sitting at the table, sipping his tea and jiggling one-year-old Anne on his lap. And beside him Julius was fairly jumping up and down with excitement, pleading to try Freddie's officer's hat on. Opposite him Harriet had been sitting with her gloved hands folded over each other on the table and a teacup untouched before her. And once Cecil had got over his surprise at seeing Freddie it was this that struck him the most—the expression on her face, which he at first mistook for a sort of serenity but was, instead (as he saw, drawing closer), a kind of studied tension, her teeth clenched so tightly he could see the muscles in her jaw and the tendons standing out in her neck.

'Dada!'

Anne had seen him and pointed a chubby arm at him over Freddie's shoulder. The effect this single word had had on the little gathering had been remarkable. Freddie had reacted first, springing up and almost knocking Anne to the floor. Seeming belatedly to remember her presence, he had scooped her up and handed her to her mother. Harriet's face had assumed a greyish tinge but aside from turning her head towards Cecil and taking the squirming child she had not moved.

'Daddy! Uncle Freddie's back!' Julius had announced, somewhat unnecessarily, and he had tried once more to reach Freddie's hat. But as Freddie had now placed the hat on his head and appeared to be making ready to leave, he was again thwarted.

'What's this?' Cecil had said, walking towards them, a bemused smile on his face. 'Didn't realise we were expecting you, Freddie. When did you get back?'

Freddie had not replied. He had instead turned to Harriet.

'It's just a flying visit,' Harriet had explained, and her voice had been strained. 'We only heard from him today.'

Freddie had appeared to find his voice. 'Yes, short notice. Sorry, can't stay,' and he had dismissed Cecil and turned, rather helplessly it had seemed, towards Harriet. She had got up and hugged him, though she had not looked at his face, and had quickly resumed her seat. 'Be seeing you, Julius,' Freddie had said, and he had picked up

117

first one child and then the other and hugged them rather fiercely. Anne had squirmed and wriggled to be free. And the next moment Freddie was gone.

Cecil had watched him go and sat down at the space Freddie had just vacated. His wife, he had realised with a shock, was silently crying.

Another Piccadilly Line train was approaching, and this distracted the little girl from whose merciless scrutiny Cecil was at last spared. The doors opened and he stepped on board and located a seat, and found that the little girl and her mother were now sitting directly opposite. The girl resumed her gaze and began to pick her nose.

Eight years. And now Freddie was back.

I ought to have confronted them, Cecil realised. Why had he just slunk away as though *he* were the guilty one?

The train pulled away and gathered speed as it entered the tunnel.

Eight years. He remembered his shock at seeing Harriet crying like that, sitting there perfectly still with the tears steaming down her face, in the middle of Harrods tea room. Had he avoided a confrontation today because he had known—just as he had known eight years before—that Harriet would choose Freddie over him?

Chapter Ten

According to the society page of *The Times* the Swanbridges had last night attended a charity ball also attended by Princess Margaret. That would have pleased Valerie, Harriet thought with a brief smile. She would be dining out on that for a month.

There was nothing in *The Times* about Empire and Colonial, or about the man who had stolen from Cecil's firm. Instead there had been another piece about Daphne's husband, Peter Goodfellow, only this time the story was less about Peter himself and more about revelations that Mr Goodfellow's nephew, a junior naval officer in the war, had been convicted on a charge of dereliction of duty in June of '43 and had duly been court-martialled. It had been suggested in some quarters that the Honourable Mr Goodfellow's recent resignation from the Ministry and his earlier failure to win a Cabinet posting in the recent reshuffle—a post he had been widely tipped to win—were connected to this revelation. *The Times* concluded by noting that, while it was not the British way to lay the guilt for one man's action at the doorstep of another, would the Honourable Mr Goodfellow feel himself able, in light of the above-mentioned revelations about his family, to continue to serve his constituents?

It was a horrid, vindictive story. Harriet folded the paper over and pushed it to the far side of the table. Dereliction of duty. The war had been over seven years, but people did not forget. Poor Daphne.

The newspaper was a complimentary copy provided for the enjoyment of members and their guests at Simon's club, so naturally it was *The Times*. It was revolutionary enough that his club now had a sitting room where members could entertain ladies. But to read a newspaper other than *The Times* would have been inconceivable.

The Planters Club was a minor establishment as far as gentlemen's clubs went, which explained why it had recently opened its doors (albeit its back doors) to ladies. It was located near to, but not actually in, St James, and catered largely for returned administrators and overseers from the remnants of Britain's empire. Harriet's father, a long-time District Officer in the Indian Civil Service, had become a member following his return from India in 1930 and had thoughtfully bequeathed his membership to Simon. Harriet was reasonably certain that, left to his own devices, Simon would never have bothered with such a place. But having had membership thrust upon him, and especially since the war, he had taken to spending a large amount of time in its reading room. Reading, he was quick to stress, not in conversation with the other members, the majority of whom sat in gloomy silence, sunk within ancient winged armchairs, each turned at an angle away from its neighbour. No one spoke other than to order a port, a newspaper or a cab and the only movement came from the ancient, white-gloved staff who padded about carrying silver trays—trays on which important missives ought to have arrived from Whitehall and Westminster but on which, instead, were balanced crystal tumblers of not-quite-vintage port and dusty-looking sherry. Hanging over it all was a fug of pipe and cigar smoke thick enough to make your eyes water.

Harriet was seated in the Guests' Room, which was an antechamber off the Reading Room and was reached by an uncarpeted back corridor and a side entrance that led off, via an alleyway, to the rear entrance of the nearby tube station. One was left in no doubt as to one's status as a lady in a gentlemen's club. On the wall above the door to the Reading Room was a crest. Whose crest it was impossible to tell, even if one cared to know—and Harriet did not—because it was half obscured by a large creamy-white topi that someone had hung up there.

This seemed an unusually rakish thing for a member of the Planters Club to have done.

A topi. She hadn't seen one for—well, it must be all of thirty years. Bombay bowlers, that was what they were colloquially called, and everyone in India wore them back then, simply everyone. If you didn't, you were regarded with disdain. All the Europeans, that is. The Indians, of course, never wore them.

She stood up abruptly. God, the place was insufferably hot. She went to the window and attempted to open it. But windows in this sort of place were purely ornamental. In the street below, leaves swirled and a young couple, both in raincoats, hurried past with their collars turned up and heads down, side-stepping to avoid a puddle. She watched the scene for a moment. There was a time when England in November had seemed monstrous, when the mildest late-summer breeze had cut through her tropically thinned blood like ice and the sight of endless grey buildings, of dull grey streets and duller grey people, had filled her with horror. Despair.

But that was long ago. Another lifetime. A time when she had expected to return to India. When India had been her home. When she had expected to see her mother again.

She turned and faced the room. A Bombay bowler! Funny how one could remember exactly what it felt like, the shape of it beneath one's hands. The weight of it on one's head.

Their father's district had been in Jhelum, in the Rawalpindi division of the Punjab, an area half the size of Wales with a population of over half a million. It had taken 15 days march to cross it—and consequently half of Father's time each month was spent touring the district. Did Simon ever think about that time? He had left India even longer ago than she had, in 1918. It had been right after the Armistice was declared in Europe. And Simon had been only eight, which was late. Many European children were packed off to England for schooling when they were six. She had stayed in India another six years. A girl's schooling wasn't so important. One could get by with a governess, at least till one was twelve.

Funny how they never spoke about India, she and Simon.

Her eyes were drawn again to that crest above the door and the hat that hung incongruously from it. Mother had been wearing a topi the last time she had seen her. She had been lying on a bed on the veranda of the bungalow in Jhelum, one of the punkah-wallahs cooling her half-heartedly. It had been early summer, perhaps May or June, and already crushingly hot. Usually Father would have removed the entire household to Murree by then. All the Europeans fled to the hill stations to escape the oppressive lowland summer. But this summer Mother had become ill and the journey to Murree—made on horseback and elephant—had been considered too risky. So Mother had lain on a bed on the veranda and Father had ordered ice to be sent up by train from Delhi, when usually the cost would have been prohibitive.

Ice must have been the only luxury that *was* prohibitive. The bungalow they had lived in was enormous, rooms for all the family plus any number of servants. And yet sparsely furnished, as though they all knew it was only temporary. And most postings in India were temporary—though they had lived in that bungalow five or six years already by that summer. So many servants. It seemed ludicrous now. And in England one had practically no servants. And one got used to that, too, after a while.

With Father away so much, Mother had spent a great deal of her time organising the servants and attempting to train various ayahs in the finer details of child rearing, about which she had had very precise and strongly held views. This had all changed dramatically when the Great War had ended and Simon had been packed off to school in England. It was as though Mother had put all her time, all her effort, into this one child and now that he had gone she simply gave up. Instead she had spent her time at the tennis club and at the Surrey Club, a large wooden hut in a clearing about five miles away with a makeshift bar and an ice box, where all the local Europeans congregated.

Mother had become ill quite suddenly that May of '24. She had appeared at breakfast one morning pale, feverish and listless and had retired to bed mid-morning. It was one of those lingering fevers that one got from time to time and that weakened the whole body almost overnight. Father had been at home that day, had been preparing the household for the move to Murree, but instead he had ordered the bed to be placed on the veranda and for someone to send for the doctor. There was a European doctor in the district, though he was half a day's ride away. The doctor had come, had examined her, had spoken to Father and had ridden off. Father had looked concerned. The move to Murree would have to be delayed.

But there was more at stake than the planned relocation. There was Freddie.

Freddie had just turned eight. He needed to go to school. And Harriet herself, at twelve, needed to go to an English school sooner or later. Passages from Bombay to Liverpool had been booked weeks earlier and Mother was to accompany them on the month-long voyage in June.

It must have been late May, then, that she had watched Mother lying on the bed on the veranda with the punkah-wallah sporadically fanning her and the bearer proffering tea on a silver tray from time to time. In the hallway, trunks and bags were stacked, awaiting loading onto the bullock cart, handwritten labels identifying a ship's name and a school outside Chatham in Kent and another in Sussex. Freddie, she remembered, had been excited about the voyage, but eight-year-old boys got excited about anything. Harriet had watched her mother from the garden and wondered for about the hundredth time if they were going to postpone the voyage; if they could just stay here. Perhaps forever.

Father had said not. Father had announced the previous evening that a man called Stephens, a junior subdivisional officer recently arrived from England, and whom they had met only once, would accompany them to Bombay and ensure they reached their ship in good time. They would be met by their grandparents at the other end.

At the time it had seemed surreal. A dream. A two-day train journey, a ship, a voyage. A different country. A school. Harriet's mind had simply baulked at it all. Refused to take it all in. It had simply shut down and concentrated on the matter in hand: Mother on her bed on the veranda.

She had looked beautiful. But then didn't every mother look beautiful on the last day that one saw them? Especially if one was a child. Mother was such a solid presence—more solid than Father, because she was always there. Built for colonial life, Father called it, and Mother would frown crossly because it implied she was stockier than she actually was. But that day she had been—what? Wispy. Insubstantial. Or was it merely with the wisdom of hindsight that one thought that? Certainly they were not accustomed to seeing Mother lying prostrate on a bed on the veranda in her thin white cotton dressing gown. Her wrists had been so thin, and the skin over her face pulled taut and shiny, not with the red glow of the summer heat but with a paleness than was unnerving.

'Dearest, do get me a drink,' Mother had said that final day, her eyes half-closed, and Harriet had passed her the glass of water the bearer had left by her side. But Mother hadn't taken it. She had waved it aside at the last minute as though she had lost interest in it, the same way she had lost interest in motherhood.

Moments had passed. Harriet had thought, we are leaving soon. If Mother gets up now she could accompany us. There's still time.

'Are you off soon?' Mother had said, suddenly opening her eyes, and the way she had said 'Are *you* off?' meant she had not been intending to come.

'Soon, yes. The trunks are in the hallway. The men are loading them into the cart. Father says Stephens is to accompany us to Bombay.'

'Good, dear. I'm sure Father knows best. I hear Stephens is a very good man … There were some Stephenses at Minehead. Mr Stephens was in tin, as I recall. I wonder if they are related.' After this she had lain back again and closed her eyes. 'This wretched heat,' she had murmured, waving a hand over her face, and it had seemed as though she might not rouse herself even to say goodbye.

The trunks had been secured and checked and Freddie had been marched past and placed in the cart and finally Harriet had stood beside the bed to say goodbye. She had put out a hand, instinctively, tentatively, to touch her mother's face, but before she could do so Mother had opened her eyes very wide.

'You'll look after Freddie, dear, won't you?' she had said. 'He is in your care.'

Harriet had withdrawn her hand and looked over at Freddie, already in the cart, sucking on a stick of sugar-cane. She had taken him to church on her own once or twice, had held tightly on to his hand in the market, had read to him when he had been sick with a fever last year. But now he was in her care. All the way to England.

What if she were to refuse?

But one didn't refuse. She had nodded, though Mother, by then, had already fallen asleep.

So Harriet and Freddie and the man called Stephens had made the journey to Bombay on their own.

'Would you care for some refreshments, madam?'

Harriet looked up and half expected to see a bearer in his turban and white tunic standing there, offering her a planter's punch. But it was the ancient waiter from the club in his black tailcoat and white gloves and with an unpleasantly swollen red nose and burst purple veins in his cheeks.

'Yes, all right. Get me a vodka martini.'

It was early to be drinking but, Lord knew, one needed some defence against this oppressive mausoleum.

'Harriet.'

Simon strode through the door of the Reading Room, dressed in his usual fashion—a tweed jacket, good quality, of course, but God, it made him made him look years older than 42, and those endless dreary brown trousers and a nondescript tie of indeterminate colour and design. It was almost as though he was at pains to disguise the fact he was a decorated Battle of Britain hero. He was still lean, his chin scrupulously clean-shaven, his hair recently cut and neatly parted. Once upon a time, in the years leading up to the war, he had been something of a catch. Cut quite a dash, one might say. And in those days he was simply a lowly clerk in a law firm. Now he had every reason to throw himself about and yet he kept himself tucked away. Perhaps it was the approach of middle age. Perhaps it was the war. Perhaps it was a hasty and unwise marriage and an even hastier divorce—the war again. Lord knew, it had enough to answer for. Still, there was no need to let oneself go.

'How are you, old girl?' he enquired mildly, stooping to kiss her. The kiss was somewhat stiff and awkward. Their relationship had never quite recovered from Simon being sent away to school at age eight. By the time she and Freddie had arrived in England Simon was fourteen and had had very little time for two younger siblings whom he barely knew.

'I'm well. You?'

'Oh, you know. Sorry I'm a bit late. There was a flap on at the Palace.' He laughed suddenly and sat down. 'Sorry. That's the sort of nonsense we tell the press when a silver teaspoon has been mislaid before some dreadfully important State dinner. Actually, I lost track of the time, then it took an absolute age to fight one's way through the hordes of tourists in The Mall.'

Harriet smiled vaguely. He was going to give an update on preparations for the Coronation if she didn't cut him off at once. But he didn't give an update on the preparations for the Coronation. Instead he said, 'There's a great deal about Emp and Col in the press. Is Cecil at all concerned?'

Harriet sighed crossly. Of course Cecil was concerned. This blasted business with the stolen money and the absconding employee didn't seem to want to go away. The police had returned, twice, to the house to talk to him. A 'talk', apparently, was not an interview; it was less serious than an interview. It suggested they were asking for Cecil's advice, picking his brains, rather than accusing him of anything. At least his name had been kept out of the newspapers.

'He's not concerned, no,' she replied. 'That silly affair with the ex-employee has all but blown over.'

'I thought they'd uncovered all sorts of fraud? And the chap's still at large, isn't he?'

'I've really no idea.'

'Is anyone else implicated?'

Harriet reached for a cigarette. Everyone asked about it, of course, everywhere one went. It was rather as though Cecil had been caught out in some lurid affair that had been splashed across the tabloids—everyone falling over themselves to feign sympathy with the poor wife but privately agog with curiosity. And the wife, naturally, held her head high and smiled and never, *never* betrayed her husband.

'I shouldn't think so.'

Simon frowned. 'But that's why you wanted to meet, isn't it? Because of Cecil?'

Well. Here it was. She took a deep breath.

'No. It's nothing to do with Cecil.' She opened her cigarette case and took out a cigarette. 'Freddie's back. He's been back a couple of months. I thought you ought to know.'

She closed the cigarette case and it was only when the cigarette was in her mouth and alight that she allowed herself to notice Simon's reaction.

He was observing her silently and his face was expressionless. Quite expressionless, but she could see now that his hands, resting on the arms of the ancient leather armchair, were rigid, his entire body tense.

'I see. When did he arrive?' he asked finally. 'And who knows he's here?'

Yes, that was Simon. She could almost see the questions, the implications, flitting across his brain, one after another. Harriet drew on her cigarette. The smoke from its tip drifted in a single column towards the once ornate ceiling.

'August. And no one knows.'

'August!' The fingers clenched tightly together for a moment then carefully stretched out again on the armrests. 'Why in God's name didn't you tell me earlier?'

'He asked me not to. Thought you might feel ... compromised.'

'Compromised! Too damned right! Good Lord.' Simon fell silent, mulling this over. Finally he took a deep breath. 'All right. But why now? What does he hope to accomplish?'

'For God's sake, he wanted to come home. Is that so hard to understand?'

'Yes, damn it!' and now Simon got to his feet, walked over to the window. Walked back again. Sat down. 'He's forfeited any right to come home. It's not his decision to make. He can never come home.'

'Well, he has.'

The silence that followed was lengthy.

Finally Simon spoke.

'Have you assisted him?'

His eyes locked onto hers and Harriet wordlessly returned the look. Would Simon know if she were lying? He would think he would, but Harriet rather doubted it.

128

'You sound like a barrister, Simon. No. I did not assist him. He didn't ask me to. He telephoned me one morning in September after Cecil had gone to work and the children were at school.'

'You mean he's been to the *house*?'

'No, I do not.' She spoke slowly and calmly. 'I'm hardly going to risk letting him come to the house, am I?' She crushed her cigarette in the ashtray and searched for another. 'I met him in the garden.'

'But good God, Harri, anyone could have seen him—could have seen the two of you!'

'It's a private garden, only residents have a key. You know that. And it's secluded. Besides, what the hell would it matter if someone did see him? He's perfectly anonymous. He looks just like every other young man in London, Simon. Or did you think he'd have a mark on his forehead?'

'For God's sake!'

'Madam?' The ancient waiter appeared with a martini glass on a silver tray. He bowed stiffly and placed the glass on the table beside Harriet. 'Good morning, Group Captain Paget. Your usual, sir?'

Simon nodded curtly. When the waiter had gone he turned again to Harriet.

'I still fail to understand what Freddie hopes to achieve by coming back. And what on earth is he living on?'

'The money Father left him? What he saved working overseas? Lord, I don't know.' Harriet shrugged impatiently. Why did Simon always get so caught up in the unnecessary details? Perhaps it was working at the Palace that did it. No doubt every minute of every day was timetabled, every item of one's wardrobe was worked out in advance, every meal, every occasion, planned down to the finest detail.

Simon looked aghast.

'You mean he's just walked into his bank and made a withdrawal?'

'How the devil should I know?'

'Well, didn't you ask him?'

'Obviously not.'

From the Reading Room came the sound of a particularly unpleasant fit of coughing. While it lasted Harriet took the opportunity to knock back her Martini. She grimaced. It was hideous—drowning in vermouth. A small and wrinkled olive rolled about at the bottom of the glass, looking as though it dated from before the war.

'Your scotch and soda, sir.'

Simon took the drink and nodded at the ancient waiter without looking at him, a frown creasing his brow and a vein twitching on his left temple. Harriet watched him through the haze of cigarette smoke, aware a similar frown had appeared on her own face.

'May I?'

Simon reached over and took a cigarette from her case and lit it silently.

I shouldn't have come, Harriet realised. It had been a mistake. She had come here for Simon's sake because surely he had the right to know; would want to know? But now she realised the opposite was true: Simon would rather not know.

She looked around for the waiter, but he had vanished and perhaps that was just as well: she felt bloody-minded enough to inform him just how undrinkable his martini was. She placed her glass on the table and sank back into the uncomfortable leather upholstery of the chair. She had come here, she realised, not for Simon's sake at all, but because she needed his help. Help that Simon did not have, and had never had, any intention of giving.

'And not even Cecil knows?' said Simon, leaning forward and speaking in a low tone.

'*No.* I haven't said anything.'

'Well *don't*, for God's sake. The fewer people who know—'

'No one knows! God, you can be so bloody conventional sometimes, Simon.'

He glared at her and they smoked in silence.

'All right, then, where has he been? Where was he living all this time?'

'Canada, I understand. I think he was in the States for a while, too, but mostly Canada. Toronto, Alberta, Vancouver. He appears to have moved around.'

'Doing what?'

'All kinds of things. Clerical. I think he said he was a clerk for a railway company out west. And for a shipping company in Hudson Bay.'

Simon nodded, then he sighed.

'But what does he intend to do here? Nothing's changed.'

'He thinks it has.'

'Then he's mistaken.'

'No, he believes there'll be an amnesty. Soon.'

Simon picked up the scotch and soda again and swirled it around in the tumbler. His eye was caught by the folded copy of *The Times* that Harriet had discarded. The headline about Peter Goodfellow lay between them in bold, 18-point serif typeface.

'Perhaps there will be,' Simon replied at last. 'But it changes nothing. Don't you see that, Harriet? He's a deserter. That can't be changed, amnesty or no amnesty. '

Chapter Eleven

He would wait for Harriet to tell him herself about Freddie's return.

Cecil reached for his cufflinks and fixed them to his shirt cuffs. He had made this resolution two weeks ago, when he had come home from the office during his lunch-hour and seen Freddie in the garden, and, so far, Harriet had not said a word. Instead, she continued to make polite conversation over breakfast and dinner and was always ready with his scotch and water each evening. She appeared to be attending the usual number of committees, charity events, lunches, dinners, appointments with her dressmaker, gallery openings and first nights. Indeed, here they were off to Sadler's Wells to see *Don Giovanni* just like any other married couple. Just as though Freddie had not come back.

'Don't fiddle with that, please, Anne.'

She was next-door in her dressing room now, arranging her hair. He could tell by the way she spoke that she had a hairclip stuck in the corner of her mouth. And by the sound of it, Anne was assisting her.

'Which ones will you wear tonight, Mummy?' Anne could be heard inquiring in her mock-adult voice.

'Hmm? Oh, just the pearls.'

'Shall I help you put them on?'

'No, dear. The catch is very easy. And I'd rather not have your sticky fingers all over them.'

'I don't think my fingers *are* sticky.'

Perhaps the spell was broken? Perhaps whatever hold Freddie appeared to have over her was no longer there, she had cast it off? But if that were true, why had she failed to tell him that Freddie had returned?

'This is from India, isn't it?' said Anne, and he knew she was opening her mother's jewellery box.

'Yes, I believe so, originally.'

'Did grandfather bring it back from India with him?'

'No, dear. Your father picked it up in a shop on the Fulham Road.'

Cecil paused in his attempt to fix the cufflink and looked at his reflection in the dressing-table mirror. He *had* picked it up in the Fulham Road, years ago, one balmy July evening on his way home from the office. He had seen it in the window of the old antique shop that used to be on the corner—long gone now—and on the spur of the moment had walked in and purchased it. It had come from India, originally, and perhaps that was what had made him buy it for her.

The catch on the cufflink refused to snap back into place no matter how hard he tried to force it and eventually it broke in two, and he stared down at it in disbelief. They had been his father's cufflinks, a present from his mother to his father, and now they were broken.

At a sound on the landing he looked up and saw Anne in the mirror, standing in his bedroom doorway, silently watching him. He turned around and smiled at her, though he could think of nothing to say.

'What are you going to see, Daddy?' she asked, though he knew she already knew.

'*Don Giovanni*.'

'What is *Don Giovanni*, Daddy?'

'Not what, who. He was a Spanish nobleman who treated women badly and came to a very sticky end. Or that's the myth anyway. And then he was made into an opera by Mozart.'

She nodded thoughtfully, and encouraged by this, Cecil added:

'We'll take you, in a few years. You and Julius. Would you like that?'

'I don't think I shall like opera,' she replied, and drifted off.

Cecil turned back to the mirror and after a moment he undid the first cufflink and laid it and the two halves of the broken one side by side on his dressing-table.

Less than a week after he had seen her in the tea room at Harrods, the meaning of his wife's tears had become horribly apparent.

The police had come to the house in March of '44 and at first Cecil had assumed they had come to report that Freddie had been killed in action.

They had all been sitting down to Sunday lunch, a rare enough event in those days, and exactly what this wartime Sunday lunch had consisted of it was hard now to imagine, though sometime around 1943 Mrs Thompson had begun producing pigeon pie, and by March '44 it had felt as though they had been subsisting on pigeon and boiled turnips for some months, though it had probably only been a few weeks. The windows, he remembered, had had tape stuck diagonally across each pane in case of shrapnel, and during the week the black-out curtains were simply left in place and half rooms not used. But that day, it being a Sunday and Cecil being at home for once, Mrs Thompson had pulled back the curtains and lit a fire in the grate.

The two men had rung the doorbell. Somehow one did not expect bad news when people rang the doorbell. It would be a sharp rap on the front door, not this dignified chime that ought to have heralded guests for lunch but instead brought two officers of the military police.

Julius had jumped down from his chair, his spoon in his hand, and had run down the stairs shrieking excitedly. Harriet had got up, calling sharply after him, and Cecil had remained in his chair, wondering where Julius had picked up such atrocious table manners.

'Soldiers!' cried Julius, and he could be heard now pelting back up the stairs. 'Mummy, it's soldiers!' and Cecil and Harriet had exchanged a look.

What look, then, had they exchanged? Cecil had thought, well, that's it, it's Freddie, wounded or worse … Harriet's look, he remembered clearly, was one of sheer panic.

Mrs Thompson had appeared in the doorway, wheezing and holding onto the doorframe.

'Two young men for you,' she had announced and it seemed now, in hindsight, that her words had been spoken portentously. But perhaps she had merely been trying to catch her breath.

'What young men, Mrs Thompson?' Cecil had enquired calmly.

'Military police! Or so they claim.'

And that was the point at which he had assumed Freddie had been killed in action. A gasp from Harriet had seemed to confirm that this was what she, too, believed.

'What do they want?' Harriet had demanded, and he had looked at her in time to see the blood draining from her face.

'Buggered if I know,' Mrs Thompson had replied, and it had been a measure of everyone's growing alarm that no one had chastised her.

135

'We had better go and find out,' Cecil had said and, grimly, he and Harriet had gone downstairs.

The two MPs had been standing in the hallway, men in their late thirties, both over six foot in winter great-coats and holding their hats at their sides. They had looked somehow indecent in the hallway beside the tubular steel Le Corbusier telephone table and the Ivon Hitchens abstract on the wall that Harriet had picked up in a small gallery in Mayfair before the war. Julius had been standing on the stairs, half hiding behind the banisters and staring wide-eyed at the two men, who had studiously ignored him.

'Julius, go back to your lunch,' Cecil had ordered. 'And kindly do not leave the table again until I give you permission to do so, do you understand?'

Julius had glared mutinously and turned and stomped back up the stairs, and Cecil had experienced a moment of irritation. But there were two military policemen standing in the hallway.

'How do you do? I am Mr Cecil Wallis. This is my wife, Harriet. How may we assist you?' he had said, because it was important to remain calm and in control. And because Harriet had been holding onto the banister with fingers that looked as though they were going to cut right through the wood.

'Captains Milton and Peters. May we find somewhere private to talk?'

No one had said, sorry to trouble you on a Sunday, sir. Please excuse this intrusion. Cecil had felt a little sick.

'Of course,' and he had led them into the ground floor reception room. They had all sat down, the two officers on the settee, himself and Harriet in the armchairs. It had been noticeable that no one had leaned back in their chair; they had all placed themselves right on the very edges. One of the officers had been carrying a small leather attaché case, which he had placed on his lap. Cecil had hitched up his trousers at the knee and stared at the small case.

'Are you the sister of Second-Lieutenant Frederick Paget of the 1st Royal Tank Regiment, Mrs Wallis?' the officer who had spoken earlier—Peters or Milton?—had said to Harriet, and Cecil, convinced now that they would all be attending Freddie's memorial service before the week was up, had reached across and touched her hand. She had pulled her hand away at once and laid it on her lap, flat, pressing down hard the same way she had on the table at Harrods a few days earlier.

'Yes,' she had replied.

'And have you seen or heard from Lieutenant Paget in the last few weeks?'

'No.'

No. She had answered, no. It was an unequivocal 'no' and Cecil had looked sharply at her and remembered the tears in the tea room five days ago. He had felt a rising sense of panic. What was going on here? And what was he going to do if the officer now turned to him and asked the same question?

But he hadn't. Instead the man had opened his case and pulled out a sheet of typed paper.

'Lieutenant Paget failed to report for duty on the twenty-ninth of last month. His division is presently stationed in Southern Italy—we are not at liberty to say exactly where. We have reason to believe that he is now back in this country. There is a warrant out for his arrest on a charge of desertion. May I remind you that harbouring or assisting a deserter during wartime is a very serious offence?'

It was difficult to remember with any certainty how they had both reacted. Cecil had somehow found himself standing by the window gazing out over the street. A young nurse had walked past, pushing a bicycle in the direction of the Brompton Hospital. He could remember her clearly, remember the click her shoes made on the pavement below the window.

Harriet, he had presumed, was still seated. He had not been able to turn around to look at her. It was impossible. Those tears in the tea room at Harrods.

Who had spoken next? He couldn't remember. There had been no further details forthcoming from the two officers. They had 'not been at liberty' to say more. So he himself must have said something, mumbled some reply, expressed his shock—though that must have been patently evident—had probably thanked them for coming! At any rate, they had gone and he and Harriet had waited in the room as the men's footsteps had receded down the front steps and the little gate had creaked open and snapped shut and two car doors had opened and closed, and a moment later an engine had started up. He had been standing by the window and yet he could not recall seeing them depart. Had no recollection of seeing their vehicle, some military staff car, presumably.

And after they had gone—

Yes, there was a period of time, a long, long time, it had seemed, when neither of them had spoken. He had left the window, finally, with a sense of dread at the words that must be spoken, had to, simply could not be avoided.

'You knew, of course,' he had said and it had seemed as though these words must break something, something that might never be repaired.

'Yes.'

Still he not been able to look at her.

'You knew last week when you saw Freddie. He told you then. He came to you to tell you. Didn't he?'

'Yes.'

He had nodded and had felt himself beginning to lose control, had felt his breath coming faster and faster while not quite catching enough of it to be able to breathe.

'And you lied to the military police.'

'Of course.'

'Of course.' He had nodded a second time. 'And you mentioned nothing to me—'

She had abruptly got up and they had stood facing each other.

'How could I "mention" it to you? That would have implicated you.'

'You lied! To the MPs. Do you have any idea—'

'I did *not* assist him. I am *not* harbouring him.'

'*But they asked if you had seen him*! My *God*, what if they had asked me?' He had gaped at her as the implications of this had washed over him. 'Do you suppose I would have lied *too*? Is that what you expected me to do? And if I had told the truth, what then? They would have known you had lied. You could have been *arrested*! Dear *God*, you still could be. We *both* could be!'

He had reached blindly behind him for the chair and sunk down into it, feeling nauseous. In a second he had got up again, finding it impossible to remain still, and had begun to pace the room.

'Are you expecting me to *help* you? To help *him*? Because I won't! *I will not*—do you understand? How *dare* you put me in this position? How dare Freddie put *you* in this position!'

Harriet had gone back to her chair and slowly and calmly sat down.

'All that matters is Freddie's safety,' she said in a low tone. 'He has made plans to leave the country; indeed, he may already have done so. You do not need to concern yourself with him or this matter any longer.'

Cecil had stared at her in disbelief.

'How can you be so *naïve*? This isn't simply going to go away. What you have done is *reprehensible*! You have put yourself, me, our children, at risk!'

She had appeared to be listening, though there had been no expression on her face, and it had been this that made him stop. She had turned and looked him, the same way she might have looked at him were she offering him a second cup of tea.

'Cecil, if you think I am concerned about you or about me then you are mistaken. I am not.'

Cecil lifted his gaze from the broken cufflink that lay on the dressing-table before him and looked at his own face in the mirror.

He had never been back to the tea room at Harrods, he realised. That had been the end of that particular ritual. And he had somehow avoided setting foot in Harrods for the last eight years.

So, Freddie had returned. But what difference did it make, really? Freddie, he realised, had been with them all along.

Chapter Twelve

On the stage the unscrupulous Don Giovanni attempted to woo the recently betrothed Zerlina away from her fiancé and in the second row of the circle Harriet thought: maybe it will all be all right. Freddie had come home, there would be an amnesty and maybe everything would be fine.

She leaned back in her seat. Her shoulders felt stiff and she realised they had been hunched up beneath her ears since the opera had begun—and perhaps for much longer.

Zerlina, now offstage, let out a terrified scream as Don Giovannni's seduction turned violent.

Was it possible? Could things simply slip back to how they had once been, before the war? Freddie living his rakish bachelor existence in Maida Vale, a string of vapid girls following him about and Simon coming over every so often and shaking his head and making those irritating tutting noises, as though all that mattered was that Freddie hadn't got married yet and settled down?

On the stage a grand ball was in full swing at Don Giovanni's castle but, unfortunately for the host, his guests had turned on him and he was obliged to fight his way through a crowd and flee. There was much clashing of swords and flashing of lights and rolling of drums.

Harriet narrowed her eyes and lifted a discreet hand to shield her eyes from the worst of it. Beside her Cecil sat perfectly still and in the darkness she could sense rather than see his utter absorption in the production. How would he react if he knew Freddie was back?

She resolved to tell him. And once Cecil had got over his initial outrage, and there had been an amnesty, everything would be all right.

Around them the audience burst into applause and the lights came up to indicate the end of the first act. Cecil started slightly and began belatedly to applaud and it occurred to Harriet that he had not been absorbed in the production at all; indeed, he appeared to have seen as little of it as she had. They got to their feet and in the confusion of retrieving gloves and bags and programs Harriet found it easy enough to avoid catching his eye. As they filed out, Cecil was waylaid by a merchant banker and his wife and Harriet slipped out alone, anxious suddenly to be outside in the light and air.

In the auditorium David and Valerie Swanbridge were at the bar already, collecting their interval champagne. Valerie waved and she and David fought their way through the crowd towards her.

'Darling, how are you?' said Valerie, kissing her. 'It's been ages. You look wan. She looks wan, doesn't she, David? Cecil, what have you been doing to her?'

Cecil, who had just that moment appeared at her elbow, met this accusation with a look of consternation and Harriet turned quickly away.

'You're looking well, Cecil. All going well in the shipping industry?' asked David, who didn't give two hoots about the shipping industry. Of course, Cecil couldn't see it. As far as he was concerned the whole world was as much in thrall to big ships as he was.

'Oh well, it has its ups and downs. We—'

'Excellent. Harriet, you're looking ravishing as ever. Have some champagne.'

'I think she's looking wan.' Valerie had stepped back from kissing Harriet and now passed an eye over her dress. 'Dior?'

Harriet nodded and took a sip of the champagne as Valerie cast a critical eye over her shoes.

'Jordan?' and Harriet nodded again.

'Good God!' exclaimed David, 'You ladies talk in some form of secret code half the time.'

'It's merely to hide the fact that our entire existence is taken up with the latest fashion, being seen at the right places and our husbands' careers,' replied Harriet and, as no one seemed willing to offer a reply to this observation, she took another sip of her champagne.

'Are you enjoying the production, Valerie?' enquired Cecil, after a moment of silence.

'Oh, I don't think anyone ever *enjoys* opera,' replied Valerie, surprised. 'Enjoy it ending, quite probably. Surely we are all here simply to get dressed up? To go out? For the occasion of it? Seeing people. Being somewhere—isn't that right, Harri?'

Valerie placed her lips on a just-lit Gauloises and removed them with a sound like a kiss. A perfect red imprint of her lips stained the cigarette.

'I married my wife for her shallowness, you know,' said David, leaning over and kissing her cheek.

'And he's rarely disappointed, are you, my love?' replied his wife.

'Practically never. Cecil, what do you make of this Eisenhower fellow?'

Cecil took a mouthful of champagne and seemed to give David's question a great deal of consideration.

'We-ell. He was a formidable general, no question that he's proved himself capable in war. But peacetime politics is a whole other kettle of fish.'

'Certainly a very convincing victory,' David mused. 'Perhaps it means this war in Korea might end soon and everyone might stop testing these ghastly atomic bombs.'

'Oh, I doubt that very much,' said Valerie in a bored voice. 'What would all you boys do if you weren't playing at war games?' and she whipped out her powder compact and flipped open the lid with a single, practised move. 'Harriet,' she said a moment later in an aside, and Harriet moved closer, sensing gossip. 'You saw Peter Goodfellow resigned his seat?'

Harriet moved away again and looked off towards the far side of the auditorium. No, she had not seen that. She had stopped reading the paper and if Cecil had read it he had not mentioned it.

'No, I've not seen the paper,' she murmured with a shrug, hoping Valerie would take the hint. But Valerie was not one for hints.

'It was in this morning's *Times*. He's stood down. All this stuff about the blasted nephew. It'll be a divorce now for sure. Daphne won't stand for it. Poor Peter. I always rather liked him.'

'You did not! You always described him as "widely disliked"!'

'Quite possibly. But now that this has happened one can't help but feel dreadfully sorry for him. I mean, it's not his fault his blasted nephew did a bolt in the war, is it?'

Harriet looked helplessly at the queue of people standing at the bar and could summon no reply. Valerie knew nothing about Freddie's desertion; no one did aside from herself, Simon and Cecil. As far as anyone knew, Freddie had emigrated. Indeed, it was quite possible most of her old friends had forgotten she had ever had a younger brother.

Except that her younger brother was, at this minute, standing in the crush at the bar ordering a glass of champagne.

'What is it, darling? Champagne not agreeing with you?' said Valerie, at once sensing her disquiet. 'It's a Montaudon '38, I saw the man pour it from the bottle myself.'

'No, it's divine. But I think I need a glass of water.'

'David will get you one—'

'Don't bother, I can get it myself. Oh, Cecil, you heard David and Valerie sat next to Princess Margaret at the van den Berg's charity lunch a couple of weeks ago?'

And with Valerie thus distracted Harriet slipped away and forced her way into the crowd at the bar.

'Harriet! Thought it was you. Marilyn, look who it is!'

A hand had reached out and fingers had closed around her forearm. Harriet turned around to see a haze of faces leering at her. The hand and the voice belonged to Montgomery Pine and standing beside him was Marilyn, his wife. Montgomery, an octogenarian whose grip on her arm belied his frail and wasted body, had been a contemporary of Father's, serving with him in the Indian Civil Service. Beside him were Eustace and Phyllis Bing—he had been a member of Simon's squadron during the war and she had debuted the same year as Harriet. They all knew Freddie, of course, every single one of them, and they encircled her now, pressing in on her from all sides with their greetings and their enquiries and their entreaties. Harriet grinned at them wildly, kissing and simpering and trusting that what felt like panic might somehow manifest as unbridled enthusiasm.

'Marilyn, Monty. How *lovely*. Yes, I'm well. Phyllis, you're looking *marvellous*. Eustace, how *are* you? I'm sorry, you must excuse me.'

They would think she had an assignation but there was nothing to be done about it. Unbridled enthusiasm had been a mistake. Now they would know for certain something was up. Blast Freddie!

She plunged once more into the crowd at the bar but now she could no longer see him and perhaps, after all, she had been mistaken? What could Freddie possibly be doing—

145

But there he was, off to the right, trying to get the barman's attention, dressed in an evening suit, his hair brushed a little differently, but Freddie, nonetheless, right there at the bar, at Sadler's Wells on opening night just as though it was still 1938 and the last fourteen years had never happened.

Harriet seized his arm so that he swung around in alarm. When he saw her, his alarm diminished only slightly.

'What the *devil* are you playing at?' she hissed. 'Are you *mad*?'

'Steady on, Harri!' he protested as she bundled him out of the queue and they finished up in a far corner behind a vast rubber plant, away from curious eyes. 'Oh well, that was subtle! If no one had noticed me before they jolly well have now!'

'But what are you *doing*? This is *madness*!'

'It's *Don Giovanni*. I always rather liked *Don Giovanni*.'

'Oh well, that's all right, then, isn't it? Why don't you put an advertisement in *The Times*? "Freddie Paget, back from Canada, still on the run, still officially wanted for desertion. All enquiries care of Her Majesty's Prison, Brixton".' She regretted it as soon as she had said it. 'I'm sorry, that was cruel.'

'No matter,' said Freddie and gave a slight shrug.

'But what are you *doing* here? You're taking a dreadful risk.'

'Simon's not here, is he?'

'No, but just about everybody else is. How did you even get a ticket?'

'Oh, through the job,' he replied with a shrug. 'I've found some casual work doing the books for an actor's agency in Kilburn. It's rather squalid, but it has some perks. And frankly, I'm tired of all this skulking about.'

Harriet gripped his arm even more tightly and before her the crowd of jostling faces swam in and out of focus.

'But. *You. Don't. Have. A. Choice*. Do you *want* people to know you're back? Freddie, you don't seem to realise there's still a great deal of anger and resentment, even after seven years.'

'Look, I'm not the only chap who did a bunk. And I'm not the only one in my platoon, for that matter—'

'I don't care about them. You could still be arrested.'

'Stop being so absurdly melodramatic, Harri. Don't I deserve some fun?'

She could see a gleam of excitement in his eye. Could he have *forgotten*? Did he no longer remember that day in the tea room at Harrods? Eight years on the run? Was it all so quickly dismissed? She looked at him helplessly.

'I don't know. I just—'

'Harri, do you remember that production of *Tosca*?' He took her arm, laughing.

Harriet did remember and despite herself she smiled. 'Tosca ran up the castle steps to chuck herself off the ramparts and tripped over her dress—'

'And fell flat on her face! And some chap in the front row jumped up on stage to help her up and she had to shake him off so she could hurl herself to her death. Priceless!'

'And Cecil had dozed off and missed the whole thing.'

'That's right, I'd forgotten that. Woke up to find the entire house in hoots of laughter and he with not the foggiest idea what was going on.'

They both shook with laughter but at that moment Harriet saw Montgomery Pine looking in their direction. Montgomery put his head on one side, frowned and took a step towards them and Harriet gripped Freddie's arm again.

'Freddie, you can't stay. There are too many people who still know you.'

'Oh relax. I'm not to going to run into some chap from my platoon here, am I?'

'How do you *know* you're not? I would have thought this was precisely the sort of place you would run into someone.'

She thought at first he hadn't heard her, for he made no reply. But when she looked at him the gleam had gone, replaced by a look she couldn't read, and her stomach dropped.

'Because most of them were killed, Harri, that's how I know,' he said.

The bell sounded to indicate the second act was about to commence. They stood silently and watched as the crush at the bar became a crush at the doorways leading back to the stalls and circle.

'Cecil will be looking for me,' said Harriet, without moving.

She saw him a moment later, standing some distance off, tapping his rolled-up program impatiently against his thigh. Freddie spotted him too, and his head went back defiantly.

'You know what,' he said, 'I've seen *Don Giovanni*. I know what happens in the second act. I suddenly find I have no desire to see it again. Give my love to old Ceec, won't you?' and with that he squeezed her arm and went quickly down the stairs and was gone.

Chapter Thirteen

DECEMBER 1952

Somewhere in the distance a single bell was tolling. It was the bell from the church off Queen's Gate on the other side of Old Brompton Road and it was heralding in Christmas Day.

Cecil opened his eyes. It was still dark, just a hint of greyish-yellow light through the curtains. And that was probably as light as it was going to get. The pea-souper that had descended on the city in early December looked set to continue until spring.

Christmas morning. He lay perfectly still, listening to the bell and to the distant traffic on Fulham Road.

And then he thought: has it snowed? *Could* it snow with all this smog?

He felt a thrill of excitement: Christmas morning and the promise of snow. Extraordinary that he could still feel it in middle age; that he could be rendered instantly a small boy excitedly opening his stocking.

In those days, during and just after the First War, the stocking would have been one of Father's old military socks and it would have contained an orange, some nuts ... What else? Some coins, yes, a few pennies or whatever was appropriate. It would have been presented somewhat formally over breakfast, rather like a diploma at a graduation. Father hadn't gone in for hanging the things at the end of one's bed and there was never any suggestion of a chap on a reindeer delivering said stockings. Nowadays it was all Father Christmas this and Father Christmas that so that the real value of Christmas seemed muddied. Father had done the presentation, of course, and Mother—or would it have been Nanny?—had said, 'What do you say, Cecil?' And what he had said was, 'Thank you, Father'. And then Father had presented Mother with something—one never really knew what—and Mother would dutifully open it and say, 'Thank you, dear', and then the whole thing was reversed as she gave her present to Father. And that was the main part of Christmas over and done with.

One Christmas morning Mother had not appeared until late in the afternoon and Father had said she was ill. When she had finally appeared, flushed and sleepy, she had lain as though exhausted on the chaise longue near the hearth and Father had sat rigidly in his armchair, his hands gripping the arms and his knuckles white. When Nanny had said it was time Cecil return to the nursery Mother had called him over and held his chin. She had called him her little man and kissed him on the lips and her breath had smelt of brandy. Nanny had said what a shame it was that Mrs Wallis was unwell, and on Christmas Day, too.

And where was Felicity during all this? Perhaps she had not yet been born. The Great War had come and Father had been away with his regiment until the first Christmas after the Armistice. By then Mother had been dead nearly a year. Felicity must have been two, three years old by then and Nanny would wheel her out every now and then, like a thoroughbred at a show.

Nowadays no one wanted oranges and nuts in their stockings. They wanted train sets and bicycles and dolls and guns and cowboy hats and complicated board games and Lord knew what else. The children told you what they wanted and where was the spirit of Christmas in all this? Where was the innocence? Anne hadn't believed in Father Christmas since she was three. Julius had at least pretended to believe until he was about nine.

What would Christmas morning be like when the children had gone? Himself and Harriet in the house alone. Presumably they would still go to church. Leo and Felicity would still come over for an afternoon drink. What would they all have to talk about, after so many years? What would he and Harriet have to talk about?

He stirred uneasily. His feet felt like blocks of ice and the hot-water bottle at the bottom of the bed was an unwelcome cold, rubbery presence. The grey light at the window had become brighter and the traffic heavier. The bell still tolled, urgent and mournful.

It hadn't always been like this. That first Christmas together, the Christmas of '38, they had been married less than a year. They had walked to the top of Primrose Hill and watched Christmas morning from the summit, and the city had been theirs and no one else's, and it would always be like this.

His father had died—quite suddenly in the end—soon after his and Harriet's wedding in the late spring of '38. A stroke. The housekeeper had found him face down on the lawn in the early morning as though he had taken an early morning stroll and simply given up all of a sudden.

They had been in New York at the time, he and Harriet, almost at the end of the honeymoon, and the news had meant they had cut short their trip and brought forward their homeward passage. It had been a nuisance, he recalled, and he felt guilty even now for feeling so. One ought to have been sad, but the only things one had felt sad about were the closing of a part of one's life, the end of the old house, the selling of furniture he had grown up with. The servants were barely a skeleton staff by that stage, whose names he had hardly known, and Nanny had long since passed away. Mother was buried in a graveyard beside the village church and he had not visited it once in twenty years. He wondered if Felicity had ever visited. He could not imagine ever asking her.

Father's house had been sold by an agent to an American couple from Wisconsin and by Christmas he and Harriet had purchased the house in Athelstan Gardens and stuffed it full of father's old furniture. The better pieces, of course. And it had looked ghastly! Rococo armoires, oak bureaux, rosewood piano stools, a Thomas Brooks centre table that completely blocked the entrance hall. They had stood it for a fortnight then they had passed most of it over to Sotheby's and lived in a virtually empty house for, oh, months it had seemed. And it had been glorious! Liberating! Hilarious! To have such a place, all to themselves, to roam about sleeping in one room one night, another the next, sometimes on the bed, sometimes simply on a mattress, sometimes on the landing just because one could. And none of it had mattered! No one had bothered them for weeks on end. They had needed no one else.

By that Christmas of '38 Harriet must have been carrying Julius, though they hadn't realised it—or he hadn't—until late into January, February. That time, then, the time they had had together before the children came, had been short, so very, very short.

That Christmas morning in '38 they had still been free. Father was dead. For the first time ever there was no need to go down to the family house in Sussex. They had the day to themselves. Had they bought each other presents? He had an idea Harriet's present had been something silly—yet with more meaning than any present he had received before or since. A paper hat, that was it—just a silly paper hat, handmade out of bright wrapping paper, that Harriet had plonked on his head, laughing when it had fallen down over his ears. And he had presented her with a Christmas cracker that he had laboriously opened the night before and resealed so that, when she pulled it, out fell a heart. A red, paper heart.

Incredible.

They had taken a cab to Regent's Park and walked through the frosty grass hand in hand. They had crossed the canal and climbed up Primrose Hill and sat on the bench at the top watching the city glisten in the frosty morning.

Christmas Day and they had had the city to themselves.

Had there been snow? He couldn't remember. When one looked back at any Christmas, it was always snowing. On this Christmas Day the snow must have been thick and fresh and bright on the ground. Their footsteps must have squeaked and crunched and left a trail. How could it have been otherwise?

They had gone to her father's flat in Belgravia.

It was hard to recall the flat as it had been then when the old man was still alive; they had only visited a handful of times. Cecil had had an impression of tiger-skin rugs, romanticised Victorian landscapes crowded on the walls showing Indian scenes of men pigsticking or troops of red-coated soldiers defending some mountain pass. There had been a hideous elephant's foot umbrella stand. And the whole flat heated to such an unbearable temperature that he had felt he was suffocating. Old Mr Paget had been well into his seventies by then, brown as a walnut from all those years in India, but frail and querulous, bitter with the way his life had ended. He'd been dead within the year.

They had gone to the flat at lunchtime on Christmas Day; no way out of it, really. His own father was gone, but hers was still alive. And the visit would not cut into their day too much: just a light lunch prepared by the woman who did for him, nothing too rich, nothing too strenuous, a sherry or two and then they would be off. The rest of the afternoon, the evening, was still theirs.

Freddie had been there.

Always Freddie. Even then. Had they known he was going to be there? But why wouldn't he be—it was Christmas Day, after all— though Cecil was fairly certain Simon hadn't been there. And there had been a suggestion, even before this, that Freddie and the old man didn't get on. Freddie would have been twenty-two or thereabouts, and recently come down from University College. Lord, Mr Paget must have been into his fifties when he fathered the boy. No wonder they didn't see eye to eye, they were separated by two generations. And University College—not Cambridge like his father and elder brother. Not even Oxford, but University College, London.

Freddie had been a good-looking fellow, perhaps a little cocksure, not as bad as some, but worse than others. And there was something—what? How did one characterise it?

But no, that was absurd. People didn't have signs on their foreheads marking them out as deserters. And Freddie wasn't a deserter, not then. It was the war that had made him a deserter.

There had been barbed comments, he recalled, over the sherries. Why had the boy gone to *that* university? Why had he studied modern subjects, literature, the arts? Why had he come down *six months ago* and yet failed to secure a place in a firm? In a law office? In a Ministry? In the armed forces?

Harriet had become increasingly restless and Cecil had thought, perhaps we will leave soon? She had snapped at the old man, at her own father, and Cecil had been surprised. Freddie had been unconcerned, both by the old man's jibes and by Harriet's increasing annoyance. And Cecil had thought, perhaps this was how such things played themselves out in this household. He only had his own household to compare it to and there no one had said anything of consequence, good or bad.

'*India*, my boy!' the old man had said, practically shouting the words and it had seemed as though he had been leading up to this point throughout the whole unpleasant visit.

Harriet had got up and walked away.

'It's still the best option, boy! It's still the jewel in our diminishing crown! It will be the making of you. It's been the making of better men than you.'

Meaning himself, presumably, Cecil had thought, a little uncharitably. Really, the old boy was quite insufferable.

'If there's going to be a war, one hardly wants to be shuffling paper in Calcutta, does one?' Freddie had replied laconically, which had only infuriated the old man further.

'There isn't going to *be* a war!'

Mr Paget had spoken and Herr Hitler had jolly well better listen.

'You can still get into the Civil Service, despite having a second-rate degree,' he had insisted. 'I still have some influence, you know. These old hands can still pull a few strings.'

The old hands he was referring to were curled, claw-like, around the top of a knobbly cane planted on the ground between his knees. They were wizened things, the fingers narrow and dried up, the knuckles swollen, the nails an unpleasant yellow. Like dragon's claws from some childhood fairytale.

'No, thanks,' Freddie had replied, unwinding his long legs and reaching for the sherry decanter. 'Refill, anyone?'

'Thirty-five years of my life I gave to India!' the old man had shouted, thumping the floor with his cane, and Cecil had shifted uneasily.

'And Mother gave her life,' Harriet had said, reappearing at his elbow. Cecil remembered flinching at that. But the old man had not heard, or had chosen not to hear.

'And it was a wild place back then. By God, you've no idea. The natives were little more than savages in some places. Head-hunters, cannibals, uprisings, mutinies. Butchered, we were, whole families, whole *settlements*. And we had come to *save* them!'

'There's ingratitude for you!' Freddie had remarked, refilling his glass and putting the stopper back in the decanter.

Increasingly agitated, the old man had lifted his cane and pointed it angrily, almost violently, at his young son.

'I was glad to serve my country, my Queen. And some of the men who went out there never came back. They never returned!'

This was clearly Freddie's fault.

'I remember one young man, about your age. Fresh out from Chatham. Bright future ahead of him. Only been out a few weeks. *Just a few weeks. Butchered.* In broad daylight. Not in the jungle, in a park in the middle of a city. Struck down in broad daylight.'

Harriet, quite suddenly, had become almost hysterical.

'*He's not going to India!* He's *not*! Don't you under*stand*? There's nothing there for us, *nothing*! It's dead. *Gone!*'

Her words had rebounded off the walls of the small, over-furnished flat and echoed around them like a cannon shot. They had all sat there in horrid silence, Freddie staring wordlessly at the floor, his jaws clenched tightly; the old man, his face purple, his mouth opening and closing like a great, stupid carp in a pond; and Cecil, clutching the arms of his chair and hearing his heart beating too loudly.

'Come, Cecil. It's time we were off,' Harriet had announced, and even though they had not even eaten lunch and he had been horribly, horribly embarrassed at the thought of simply getting up and leaving, he'd been relieved and had jumped up, too quickly, to join her.

Afterwards—what? They must have returned home. Had they walked or taken a cab? Did they talk about it? He couldn't remember.

By the following Christmas they had had Julius, and a nanny of course, and that dreadful woman, Mrs Flowers, Mrs Thompson's predecessor, who had cooked and kept house for them. By the following Christmas the spell had been broken. He had made one of the rooms his study, another was the day nursery, another the night nursery. No one roamed from room to room anymore. And by the end of the war Harriet had her own bedroom.

Inside the house all was silent.

Mrs Thompson did not stir before dawn for anyone, Christmas or no Christmas, and Julius and Anne had never been the sort of children to rise before dawn on Christmas Day, even when they were very small. Would Harriet be up? What time did she awaken usually? She had been a late riser in the early years of their marriage, had resented the dawn. But now? Did she lie in bed for a time, reading, smoking, thinking? Did she stand at the window and look out at the world? He realised he didn't know.

He sat up, wondered whether to venture as far as the window, decided it was too early yet. His toes pushed against the cold hot-water bottle and it slid out of the bottom of the bed and fell with a sloppy thud onto the floor. A draft of cold air shot in through the gap in the sheets and he pulled them more closely about his legs. In the old house in the days before the Great War they had required a housemaid to start a fire in each of the bedrooms and to pour hot water into a large enamel washing bowl on the dressing table before they would even think of getting up, and still the cold had chilled the bones. He shivered. The past was always colder than the present.

And yet still one wanted to return there.

The tolling of the church bell had given way to a peal. He got out of bed, thrusting his feet into slippers and reaching quickly for his dressing gown. It really was bitterly cold; even the carpet seemed icy. It got colder still as he crossed to the window and drew the curtains aside. Had it snowed?

It hadn't. The dawn was hidden in the greyish-yellow smog. Frost laced the windows and glistened wetly on the lawn below.

From down the hallway a door opened. A muffled voice could be heard—Julius? Then a reply, in a higher voice—Anne, presumably. A thump followed, then silence. The children were up, discovering their stockings. He sighed. He had carefully wrapped the presents the night before, sometime after midnight, and had silently entered their rooms and placed one bulging stocking at the end of each bed. The task ought to have brought pleasure but it had saddened him.

The bells ceased suddenly and silence fell. It was Christmas morning—it hadn't snowed and once again Father Christmas had not come.

Chapter Fourteen

DECEMBER 1952

She could have sat in the same pew as the family but Jean chose the pew behind, from where she stared at the back of Mr Wallis's head for the duration of the Christmas morning service. No one had asked her to move. No one had said, 'Nanny, why are you sitting there? Why don't you sit with us?' Instead, Anne had said, 'But Mummy, I don't *want* to keep my gloves on, it's too *hot!*' And Julius had said, 'Oh, look what some wag's drawn on the front of this hymn book!' Mr Wallis had pretended not to hear and Mrs Wallis had sat down looking cross and announced in an aside, 'Really, the hypocrisy of it all makes me sick.'

And that appeared to sum up Christmas for the Wallises.

Jean closed her eyes. She did not hold out much hope that the Church of England Christmas morning service, nor the fresh-faced and eager-looking rector who was going to deliver it, would provide the sort of nourishment her soul craved on such an important day.

The pews had cushions on them: red lipstick-coloured cushions of a velvety material tied to the wooden pews with lengths of gold cord. In her own Chapel in Stepney the pews were pews: long wooden benches, and Dad used to say if you sat on them for an hour you remembered God's grace and that Christ had died for you on the Cross. Here, you thought about Christmas dinner and the presents in your stocking and how much your neighbour earned and what hat his wife was wearing.

Sometimes it was hard to love your neighbour.

In the pew in front of her, Mr Wallis sat very straight, his hymn book resting in his lap, an attentive look on his face as the rector spoke of the three wise men. The bringing of gifts, of course, appealed to this congregation. The gold, the frankincense, the myrrh—the children sat up on their cushions imagining the wonders that such words implied; imagining the presents that were awaiting them in their homes. How the service dragged on when there was a splendid dinner to consume and splendid presents in brightly coloured paper to unwrap!

A child dropped her hymn book with a loud thud and everyone turned to look—a congregation so easily distracted from the word of God. Mr Wallis did not turn, he continued to stare at the eager-faced rector, but the rector's words surely did not penetrate; it seemed his attentiveness was on his own thoughts, with no room left for God's word.

She could have gone to her own Chapel for the Christmas service; Mrs Wallis had said as much, had seemed surprised that Jean had not wanted to take the day off. But why would she, when she had no family to go home to? She had gone to Chapel last Christmas eager for the word of God to fill her as it had always done on this holy day. But instead the ghosts of Mum and Dad and Gladys and Nerys and Edward and little Bertie had surrounded her and she had left before the final prayer. She had craved their presence, sought their spirits every day for seven years, and yet when she had found them—when *they* had found *her*—she had fled.

And now another year had passed; it was eight years since that final Christmas and sometimes she found she could not remember a face, could no longer hear their voices in her head.

'Oh *what* an occasion it must have *been*!' sang out the rector, clapping his hands enthusiastically as he related the story of Christ's birth to his once-a-year captive audience. 'A saviour is born! A *king* is born! And Jesus had no coronation, remember. No golden carriage with horses and footmen to transport him to his throne; no crown studded with jewels awaiting him; no adoring crowds cheering him on.'

The Coronation. It was less than six months away. Was this the only way the rector could get his message through to his congregation, by comparing Christ's birth to the Coronation, so that, in their closed and addled minds, they confused the crowning of a new queen with the birth of God's only son?

'Mummy, if we buy a television set we will be able to watch the Coronation!' said Anne in a loud voice, and a number of people laughed.

Jean closed her eyes.

On that final Christmas in '44, Dad had read from the New Testament—Matthew's account of Christ's birth, as he did each year—and they had sat silently around the table in the parlour, breathlessly it seemed now, listening in awe and wonder. Afterwards Dad had closed the Bible and laid it on the table and looked around at each of their silent faces, his own face shiny with the glory of God, and that glory was reflected in the face of each of them, even Bertie, who was only just five. Even he had sat still and quiet.

'Well, now,' Dad had said, 'what a glorious day it was. And we thank the good Lord that we are all here together on this special day to celebrate the birth of His only son.'

'Amen!' said Mum, squeezing Dad's hand.

'Amen!' replied Gladys and Nerys and Edward and little Bertie.

And in Jean's memory, Nerys was wearing the buttercup-yellow ribbon in her hair and Edward his dark green cardigan that Mum had knitted the previous winter, two buttons already missing. Mum was wearing her best, sturdy navy-blue shoes and behind them on the mantelpiece was the little china horse Gladys had won at the fair two summers earlier.

'The tin! The tin!' cried Edward, and Bertie joined in, thumping the table excitedly.

And Dad reached behind him for the tobacco tin with the dented yellow lid that showed a sailor in a jersey and a peaked cap. He laid the tin carefully on the table with almost as much reverence as he had shown the Bible.

'My turn! My turn!' said Bertie, his eyes sparkling with excitement.

'It was Bertie on Sunday,' said Nerys primly, looking to Jean and Gladys for confirmation.

'That's 'cause it was his birthday,' pointed out Edward, becoming all serious. Edward believed strongly in fairness and justice.

'It must be Dad's turn again!' said Gladys, who was good at sums and had worked out that if Bertie had done it last, then Dad, as the eldest, was next in turn.

'Oh, I don't mind missing out,' said Dad, with a smile. 'What about it, girl?' and he smiled at Jean.

Taking the tin Dad held out to her, she lifted the dented lid and closed her eyes—she always closed her eyes—and her fingers dipped into the tiny strips of paper nestled within. She didn't fish about the way Gladys did, trying first one and then another, or dive in with her whole fist like Edward did. No, she allowed her fingers to hover for a moment then reached out, and the first piece of paper they touched, that was the one. She opened her eyes. Unfolding the tiny strip she read aloud:

'You shall not be afraid of the terror by night, nor of the arrow that flies by day: Psalm 91, verse 5.'

She looked up and saw them all watching her. No one questioned what it meant. They had survived the Blitz when many thousands of others had perished. And now the Germans were sending flying rockets that came in the daytime and destroyed whole streets and whole families.

'Well, by God's grace, we 'ave made it safely to another Christmas, intact and in one piece,' Mum declared, saying out loud what they were all thinking. 'And now it is time to eat!'

The Bible and the tin had been put away and from the kitchen Mum had brought in the Christmas dinner. There had been a rabbit and five potatoes—one for each of the children—a sliced carrot, parsnips and a turnip, all from the vegetable patch in the back yard, and bread too, and Mum had made a custard from two month's ration of dried egg and a jug of milk courtesy of Mrs McGuiness down the street who had a daughter who worked on the land. Gladys, Nerys and Jean had saved their sweet ration for a month and with their coupons they got two chocolate bars and some gobstoppers which they all ate noisily and happily that evening and for once no one had worried about how little there was in the pantry for tomorrow.

Dad had worked extra night shifts at the docks that Christmas to provide the rabbit on Christmas day. Other men turned to the black market to get hold of an egg, some bananas, a whole chicken sometimes. But not Dad. His conscience wouldn't allow it—not when others were starving. He had saved his money and gone up west where there were shops that still had food. He hadn't said how much he had paid and they had known better than to ask.

'Go in peace to love and serve the Lord!' said the rector triumphantly and the congregation rose to its feet, relieved and released, their duty done for another year.

'Mrs Shehan-Knowles wore that same hat last Christmas,' said Mrs Wallis.

'Pops, I thought I'd stroll over to Alistair Kellett's house this afternoon after lunch, just to wish them a merry Christmas,' said Julius.

'You most certainly will not, Julius,' said Mr Wallis, turning to his son in some astonishment. 'On Christmas *Day*?'

'What better day to wish a chap Merry Christmas?' Julius replied.

'I've lost my glove!' said Anne plaintively.

And so the service ended.

The walk back to Athelstan Gardens was made, for the most part, in silence. Anne walked with one hand stuffed into the pocket of her thick winter coat—despite an intensive search the missing glove had remained missing. Everyone had handkerchiefs tied over their faces against the pea-souper, hats pulled low. Ahead of them the houses halfway down the street vanished into a murky fog. Of those houses they could make out, each had a large holly wreath on its front door, glistening with shiny red berries and tied with a scarlet ribbon. A man had come around a week earlier, knocking on each door and selling wreaths from a large barrow, but as most of the residents had already ordered their wreaths from Harrods and Peter Jones and Barkers of Kensington and had them hand-delivered and attached to the front door by a boy, he failed to sell very many at all.

In Stepney a wreath meant someone had died. Jean had seen them—home-made from daisies, willowherb and roses—in the early part of the Blitz, laid on the remains of someone's house or hanging from a makeshift cross someone had fashioned from two pieces of timber. By Christmas '44 you didn't see them so much—too many houses destroyed, too many families wiped out.

'What do I do if Alistair comes here to wish me a Merry Christmas then, Pops?' said Julius, opening the gate to the Wallises' front steps.

Cecil frowned. 'Then you would return the greeting and invite him in for a hot drink and a mince pie.'

'Even though it's Christmas?'

They all trooped up the front steps and waited while Cecil unlocked the front door. A smell of pine needles and roast turkey spilled out.

'Exactly, Julius. We cannot hold ourselves responsible for the ill manners of others in coming to visit us. In that circumstance we show our own good manners by returning the season's greetings and offering hospitality. By not alluding to another's bad manners one shows oneself a true gentleman.'

'I see.' Julius nodded thoughtfully as he followed his father into the hallway. 'And yet you pointed out my bad manners to me, Pops, didn't you?'

'Anne, please remove your shoes—you are shedding pine needles all over the floor,' Cecil said, seeming not to hear Julius's last remark.

There were indeed pine needles all over the floor, though they had been there for over a week, ever since Mr Addison, the man who did the garden, had arrived with the five-foot Christmas tree and had dragged it by its trunk the length of the hallway and up the stairs to the drawing room, installing it beside the baby grand. Mrs Thompson had stomped up the stairs after him with a dustpan and brush and a number of colourful phrases, and had succeeded only in embedding them more firmly into the carpet. It therefore seemed a little unfair to blame Anne for this. But Anne seemed unconcerned.

'Presents! It's time to open the presents!' she announced, stripping off her shoes, coat, scarf, hat and remaining glove and diving up the stairs.

Jean stooped to retrieve the various articles.

'Anne! We do not remove our shoes without first untying the laces,' said Mrs Wallis crossly. 'And pick these things up at once! You are not a savage. Please act in a civilised fashion.'

Pouting, Anne turned around and came back down the stairs, though by now Jean had collected most of the discarded clothing. She handed the items silently to the child, who glared at her as though it had been Jean who had shouted at her and ordered her back. And perhaps it ought to have been? Jean wondered. It was undoubtedly part of the nanny's job to teach good manners, but she couldn't very well shout at the child in front of her mother. And now Anne was angry and Mrs Wallis was looking at Jean silently, condemningly.

Or perhaps she was simply attempting to light her cigarette, you just couldn't tell with Mrs Wallis.

Mrs Thompson emerged from the kitchen, red-faced and sweating, wiping her hands on her apron.

'Oh! You've made it home, then!' she announced, as though they had returned from some dangerous and lengthy overseas expedition rather than the Christmas Day service at church.

'Yes, here we all are!' replied Julius brightly, getting into the spirit of the day. 'How's things in the galley, Mrs T?' he enquired. 'Shipshape and Bristol fashion?'

'Never you mind, Master Julius,' said Mrs Thompson darkly and Anne smirked.

'You are doing a sterling job, Mrs Thompson,' said Cecil firmly, as though he were settling an argument.

'Nanny, did you hear what happened last year—' Anne began.

'Anne, go and brush your hair,' her father interrupted. 'We shall open presents in ten minutes when everyone has tidied themselves up.' And Cecil went upstairs to his study and closed the door.

But Anne was determined to relate her story. 'Last year Mrs Thompson forgot to light the oven so the turkey wasn't cooked until *Boxing* Day!' she explained, her eyes bright with the memory of it all. 'We had to have *lamb cutlets* for Christmas dinner!'

'Utter rot,' said Julius in his usual mild way as he brushed past her to go up the stairs. 'We had Christmas dinner at teatime instead. So really we had two Christmas dinners that Christmas.' He paused halfway up the stairs. 'Which means technically we've had more Christmas dinners than we've had Christmases, so this year we should probably have Christmas with no Christmas dinner, then things would be in sync again.'

'Fine. I'll let Mrs T know not to serve you any then,' remarked Mrs Wallis dryly as she passed him on the stairs. Anne laughed and skipped up the stairs after her mother.

Jean stood alone in the hallway, Anne's scarf still in her hand.

Upstairs doors opened and slammed shut and feet ran excitedly across the landing.

'Nanny, help me with my hair-band! I can't get it right!'

'I told you the tree was lop-sided, Pops. Look at it!'

'Anne, we do not slam doors in this house. Nor do we shout.'

Where was the love, God's love, on this holiest of holy days? There was only spite, bickering, a desire to outdo each other. They were spending the day together because they had to. And she was spending it with them.

'Nanny! Help me!'

So she assisted Anne with her hair-band and she coordinated the reluctant retrieval of various items of footwear and clothing from the bedroom floor then she retired to her own room to tidy herself up. The ceremony of the present opening was set to occur in the drawing room and it was unclear to Jean whether she was expected to participate in these festivities or not. Probably it did not matter either way. In which case she might as well go down and join in.

She thought of the presents she had purchased yesterday in a panic-stricken last-minute rush. She had gone to Barkers, the department store, because that was where Mrs Wallis shopped and surely if she bought something from Barkers it would be suitable, classy. But what ought she to get? In the end she had made a furtive dash into Mrs Wallis's bathroom and noted what soap she used (an expensive-looking one with a French name) and hurried off to Kensington High Street an hour before the shops closed. The rest of the family were getting sweets—a tasteful selection in a gold box for Mr Wallis, some peppermint crèmes for Julius and some garish liquorice allsorts for Anne. She had saved up her sweet ration, but even so the quantities were pathetically small. Mrs Wallis's soap had proved elusive—and was probably too expensive anyway—so she had found a substitute in a similar wrapper and hoped Mrs Wallis wasn't too fussy. Eightpence it had cost, twice what she'd usually pay for soap.

The presents sat in a sad little pile on Jean's bed, all neatly wrapped in the same rather cheap-looking wrapping paper covered in angels and trumpets. It hadn't looked so cheap in the shop.

She closed her eyes very tightly and held on to the edge of the bed.

On that final Christmas, the last one before the bomb, Mum had presented Gladys and Nerys each with a pair of gloves. Mum had painstakingly knitted them through the autumn from wool she had unpicked from an old jumper of Dad's. The jumper had made two pairs of gloves and one scarf for Bertie, and Mum had sat up night after night knitting by candlelight, or sometimes in the tube station if there was a raid on, waiting for the all-clear, her fingers turning blue with cold. It was wicked, Mum had said, to see the girls go off to school with frozen hands, and now they each had gloves, dark blue they were, and made with love from Dad's old jumper. Gladys and Nerys had put them on right then and there and kept them on all Christmas Day because the paraffin heater was small and the windows had ice on them so that you could hardly see out.

A shout of laughter from downstairs suggested the present opening had begun. Evidently the nanny's attendance was not required. Jean looked at the small pile of presents on the bed and wondered if she could stomach the chocolates herself. Probably. Not the liquorice, though. Edward had loved liquorice, she remembered. Or was that

Bertie? She couldn't remember anymore. It couldn't have been Bertie, though; he was too young—there had been no liquorice around then. Probably he had never even tasted it.

She sat down on the narrow little bed and wondered if she had the energy for Christmas. For any Christmas ever again.

'Nanny! Nanny come and look at my presents!'

She must go down; she couldn't hide up here all day. But to take the presents or not? No, leave them. She could always come back up for them if necessary. She ventured cautiously downstairs. The drawing room door was open and a chaos of gaudy wrapping paper, tangled ribbons, gift tags and cards littered the floor. As she approached, a chorus of laughter erupted from the room.

'Look, Nanny! Look what Great-Aunt Hermione sent!' said Anne, gleefully holding up a pair of large and obviously home-knitted socks in a delicate shade of lavender. 'What do you think they are?'

'Looks like an elephant's nightcap!' observed Julius, not waiting for Jean's reply.

'But they're mauve!'

'Are you meant to wear them?'

'I think they're bed socks.'

'But for whom? The Jolly Green Giant?'

Jean stood in the doorway. 'Aren't you going to show me your presents, Anne?' she said, cutting into the laughter.

Anne didn't need to be asked twice. She led the way over to a gleaming red and chrome bicycle that stood proudly against the wall.

'See?' she said. 'It has adjustable handles, brakes here and here, and a bell!' and she rang the bell as proof that it was indeed as she claimed. There was also a dolls' house in the style of a large Victorian country house with a miniature family to inhabit it, two *Girl's Own* annuals, a new pair of soft pink ballet shoes and a book on ballet, a brightly coloured woollen jersey with a teddy bear on the front, which Anne held up rather dubiously, and a tiny gold-coloured evening dress with matching shoes that apparently was for one of the row of dolls that sat silently on Anne's top shelf. Anne displayed the dress with some reluctance also and Jean tried to remember the last time—any time—she had seen Anne play with her dolls.

'How wonderful!' Jean exclaimed, as this seemed to be expected.

'Not really,' said Julius cheerfully. 'She wanted that dress last Christmas. I expect dolly has grown too big for it now.'

Anne slowly folded the little gold dress up and put it away in the corner.

'I had thought there would be something from Uncle Simon,' she said aggrievedly.

'The books were from Uncle Simon,' said Mrs Wallis a little crossly as she bent to pick up some of the rolls of wrapping paper.

'Oh yes,' said Anne and she sighed.

'Not a bad haul, all things considered,' remarked Julius, surveying his own presents critically. A collection of cricket pads and bats and assorted other sporting paraphernalia was stacked in a neat pile on the floor.

'What about Nanny's Christmas present?' cried Anne suddenly and Jean felt a moment of horror. 'Mummy, we didn't get Nanny a Christmas present!' Jean felt the smile stiffen on her face and she busied herself with stooping down to retrieve the discarded wrapping paper.

'We don't usually get Nanny a Christmas present,' said Julius. 'Do we, Mummy? We didn't last year for Nanny Peters.'

'She never got *us* presents,' said Anne, thoughtfully. 'Nanny, did you buy us Christmas presents?'

Jean froze, picturing the mean little pile of cheap presents on her bed upstairs. The mass of wrapping paper scrunched noisily in her arms.

'Well—'

'Anne, dear, we always get Nanny a little something,' interrupted Mrs Wallis. 'There is Nanny's card, over on the mantelpiece,' and she nodded to where an envelope leaned against the clock. Anne went over and retrieved it, reading the single word—'Nanny'—that was neatly written across it. She turned it over, a faintly disappointed look on her face that clearly said adults gave each other the dullest presents.

'Here you are, Nanny. Merry Christmas.'

Jean took the envelope with a hesitant smile. 'Thank you.'

'Aren't you going to open it?' Anne demanded.

Jean's fingers fumbled with the envelope. Why were they all watching her? In desperation she tore at the corner of the envelope and ripped it open. Inside was a Christmas card. She pulled it out. On the front was a picture of a merry Father Christmas with a snowy beard, red robes and round, rosy cheeks, a bulging sack beside him. There was a silence. Were they waiting for her to open the card? She did so, and a ten-shilling note fluttered out.

Ten shillings. It was quite a good sum. More than the cost of the presents upstairs.

'Thank you—' she began, but Anne was already on her hands and knees rearranging her dolls' house kitchen, Mr Wallis was reading a card he had just opened, Mrs Wallis was studying a list on her knee and Julius seemed to have left the room. Jean folded the note back inside the card and slid the card back inside the envelope.

'Mummy, is there time before lunch for me to ride my bike?' said Anne, tiring of the miniature kitchen.

'You may get Nanny to take you out in the back garden. Mind you don't get your best clothes dirty. And wrap up. You're not to go out unless you're wearing gloves, hat and scarf.'

'But I've *lost* my other glove!' protested Anne indignantly as though the request were unreasonable and the missing glove had deliberately got itself lost.

'I'm sure Julius will let you borrow one of his,' Jean replied.

Mrs Wallis ignored this suggestion. 'Well, you have plenty of other pairs, don't you? Just wear one of those.'

Anne grumbled something about *that* pair being absolutely her most *favourite* pair and hating all her other pairs but she allowed Jean to lead her upstairs to a bedroom drawer stuffed with various pairs of gloves, and eventually they retrieved a pair that met with Anne's satisfaction.

'And I must get my own gloves, Anne,' Jean said. She had no winter gloves, but it was imperative she go up to her room, just for a moment, to catch her breath.

She went quickly, hoping Mrs Thompson was downstairs in the kitchen. She entered her room and closed the door and saw again the pathetic little pile of presents. All that chocolate ... Her stomach closed up with nausea.

'Nanny, are you coming?'

She looked up and saw her own face staring back at her from the little silver-backed bedside mirror that Mrs McIlwraith had given her. A parting present. The face in the mirror was thin and pale with a small patch of red on either cheek, as though she had pinched them to give herself colour. Her nose was too narrow, her hair too dull and brown, her lips too thin. The girl that stared back at her wasn't a girl at all; she was a person who had lived beyond childhood and now could hardly remember what it had felt like.

And now the mirror was in tiny pieces on the hard wooden floor and Jean looked down in silent astonishment at the fragments of glass that were scattered in all directions. One fragment was lodged in her left hand and, as she stared at it, bright-red blood seeped out around the fragment and began to gather in a pool in the palm of her hand.

For a moment the house was silent and Jean stood perfectly still. Little pin-points of light flickered before her eyes. A moment later footsteps thudded up the stairs and a hand knocked quickly on the door.

'Miss Corbett? Is everything all right? Are you all right in there?'

It was Mr Wallis. A drop of blood splashed onto the floorboards.

'Yes, fine, thank you,' and her voice sounded quite normal; a little strained perhaps, but quite normal. 'A minor accident, that's all. Everything's all right.'

'Well. That's good. Thought you'd hurt yourself.' There was a pause. 'Shall I ask Mrs Thompson to pop up and help?'

'No need. There's no mess, really.'

Why didn't he just go away?

'All right. Very good,' and at last she heard him pick his ponderous way back down the stairs again.

She found she was holding her breath. She exhaled and her chest ached. She stepped backwards and glass crunched beneath her feet. It was everywhere: on the floor, under the wardrobe, beneath the bed. And her blood had made a small, glistening pool in the centre of the room. She sat down on the bed.

'*Nanny!* Where are you?'

Chapter Fifteen
DECEMBER 1952

'The King-Pattersons have given us another of those ghastly faux Ming vases,' said Harriet, regarding a tall, brightly patterned porcelain receptacle that stood on the baby grand surrounded by a mound of white tissue paper. Downstairs she heard a thud as Anne negotiated her new bicycle down the back step and out into the garden. The nanny, one presumed, was keeping an eye on her.

'Nigel imports them from India, I told you that last year,' replied Cecil.

Harriet returned to the neatly handwritten list on her lap. The list showed this year's Christmas presents divided into two headings and two subheadings: Presents: Received and Sent; Card Only: Received and Sent. Attached to this was last year's list, against which this year's had been meticulously cross-referenced.

Cecil was curiously studying a small gold object. 'What the *devil* is this?'

'Snuff box,' Harriet replied without looking up.

'But why on *earth*—'

'Never mind that. It's from the Carsons. We didn't send anything to the Carsons this year.'

'Didn't we?' Cecil regarded her with some surprise. 'Why on earth not?'

'They're in Egypt. Besides, we sent them something last year—toiletries I think—and they didn't send us anything.'

'I see. So next year we send them something because they sent us something this year, but they don't send us anything as we didn't send them anything?'

'Yes.' Harriet studied the list with a frown. 'Would you believe the Park-Crichtons only sent us a card? A rather cheap one at that.'

'His shares have hit rock bottom,' replied Cecil, replacing the snuff box. 'The Americans are churning out cars at half the cost and about a thousand times the volume. Old Jonathon Park-Crichton will be lucky to afford Christmas dinner this year.'

'Poor Eleanor,' Harriet mused, pausing for a moment to gaze into the middle distance. She had seen Eleanor Park-Crichton at the Hatfields' dinner party only last month. Eleanor had worn a rather super silver gauze Hardy Amies gown and spoken of her acquaintance with one of the minor royals. One would never have guessed …

She returned to the list and drew a neat line through the Park-Crichtons, removing them from the 'Present' list and adding them to the 'Card Only' list.

Harriet laid down her pencil and removed her reading glasses.

Were she and Cecil really going to spend another Christmas morning opening and cataloguing a collection of dreadful Egyptian glassware, tasteless Spanish vases, gaudy Chinese silk scarves and various inedible luxury food items imported at great expense and sold in the month before Christmas for outrageous sums in the food halls of London's department stores?

'Peruvian dates,' said Cecil curiously, holding up a small tin. 'Do they grow dates in Peru? I suppose they must.' He turned the tin over. 'Oh. It says packed in Staines, Middlesex ... The card says, "All the compliments of the season, with love from Sue and Robert". Who the devil are Sue and Robert?'

Yes, it did indeed look as if that was how she and Cecil were going to spend Christmas morning. And yet, if they weren't cataloguing unwanted presents from people they saw once a year, what *would* they be doing on Christmas morning? Not so many years ago they had helped the children play with their new toys. But increasingly one left that sort of thing to the nanny.

Cecil was kneeling in the middle of the room surrounded by the many and varied oddities that fifteen years' worth of relatives, friends, colleagues, associates, clients and vague acquaintances had sent them both. A pile of unopened gifts lay beside him and at his elbow was a pile of gift tags and cards, upon which he was transcribing a brief description of each item. He looked thoroughly absorbed, a child contemplating a tricky jigsaw puzzle or the construction of a particularly complicated model aircraft.

He had looked like that, she remembered, the first time she had met him at his office all those years ago, jumping up eagerly from his desk when she had come in to report the loss of her engagement ring. Eager and desperate to please, and yet so very grave—just as though someone had died. And so touchingly dismayed when she had mentioned that the ring was an engagement ring.

What would life have been like had she remained engaged to John; if she had gone ahead with the marriage?

'It's a watercolour,' announced Cecil, unwrapping a flat rectangular parcel and holding up a small and modestly framed painting. 'Looks like the veldt or the Serengeti or some such ... Lord, you don't think old Godfrey Canbourne painted it himself, do you?'

John had been a captain in the 1st Royal Dragoons when she

had met him in the late autumn of '36 and he had looked very fine in his blue and red tunic and his shiny helmet—which was exactly the point, of course—and what girl in her early twenties wouldn't have fallen for him? And it had turned out that a large number of girls in their early twenties—and some a great deal older and one or two somewhat younger—had indeed fallen for him. Naturally, he had neglected to mention any of this on that romantic evening in New York, the culmination of a whirlwind fortnight of carriage rides muffled up against the cold in Central Park; of Broadway shows and vodka martinis at the Algonquin Hotel. By the time the *Swane* had sailed triumphantly out of New York harbour amid a storm of ticker-tape and streamers, they had been engaged. By the time Southampton was almost in sight, John had made the acquaintance of a young actress from California, on her way over to London to 'shoot a movie', and the engagement was off.

By rights the ring—removed in a furious fit of pique one day out from port—ought to have ended up in the North Atlantic, lost forever. But some part of Harriet (the cautious, practical part ... or perhaps simply the part with a bad aim) had dropped it on the deck of the ship instead, where it had rolled immediately out of sight and could not be found. Naturally John had been left in no doubt that she had thrown the ring overboard, as to admit one had merely dropped it on the deck and lost it sounded rather feeble.

So when the young man from Empire and Colonial Lines had pulled up in a cab outside her father's flat in Belgravia, a week after she had reported the loss of the ring, to announce with appropriate ceremony that the ring, thought lost at sea, had turned up—and had not only turned up, but had been handed in and was now being miraculously returned to its owner!—it could have proved a trifle awkward. But the eager Mr Wallis from the shipping firm had appeared so genuinely excited by the reappearance of the ring that no explanation had been necessary. And when she had admitted to Mr Wallis that her engagement had, sadly, reached an end, his sympathy, his eagerness, knew no bounds. They had arranged to have lunch in Piccadilly the following day.

The eager Mr Wallis. She had joked about him with Freddie that evening. And yet she had gone to the lunch. She had gone to a number of lunches, and a lunchtime recital at St Martin's-in-the-Fields, a concert at the Royal Albert Hall, and it had all been very pleasant, very safe, very predictable. Not at all like John. When one had got one's engagement wrong the first time, one did not make the same mistake twice.

'More quails eggs from the Hendley-Joneses,' announced Cecil, solemnly studying a cellophane-wrapped package. 'Does Tom have shares in a quail farm?'

Cecil had asked this very same question last year.

'Or perhaps he's of the mistaken belief that we *like* quails eggs? Have we ever given that impression, do you think? I feel fairly certain I've never told a living soul I like quail eggs.'

'Certainly you've never told *me* you liked quail eggs,' Harriet replied.

'And that's because I don't.'

Perhaps they had had this entire conversation last year?

At the end of their third month of lunchtime recitals and Saturday evening concerts, Cecil had proposed. And she had said yes. Freddie had been amazed.

'But Harri, he's so dreadfully *dull*!' he had protested tactlessly on hearing the announcement. 'What about John, old thing? He was much more fun, surely?'

'Darling, take John, if you want him. But I can assure you he's no more marriage material than you are.'

'I say. That's a bit strong!'

'No, darling, it's not. Girls adore you, you know that. But they aren't going to marry you. You aren't the marriage type. Cecil *is* the marriage type, and I know that. It's a question of suitability, you see. Dependability and suitability. This is probably the most important decision I'll ever have to make.'

Freddie had looked startled and not a little dismayed.

'Well, I'm sure you're right, old thing.'

And she had been right. On both counts.

Thank God Freddie had not married.

'Surely this is the exact same paperweight we sent to the Marsh-Hamptons last Christmas?' Cecil held up an oversized and rather ugly glass paperweight that was shot through with vivid lilac and scarlet in a way that drew the eyes and repelled them at the same time.

I should tell him about Freddie, she thought.

It was going to come out eventually and better he hear it from her first. He had taken it personally, Freddie's desertion, the visit from the police. Had forbade mention of Freddie's name. Had struck Freddie's very existence from their lives; had lived in fear of someone finding out their shame. *His* shame.

But she had refused to submit to Cecil's shame.

After the war a postcard had arrived showing a quiet street in a French-speaking part of Canada. There were only three lines, no return address, not even a signature—just an apology in Freddie's handwriting. She hadn't shown it to Cecil and it had cost her a lot to destroy the card the day it arrived. The military police had not returned. She and Cecil hadn't spoken of Freddie since.

But that was eight years ago and there was talk of an amnesty. She would tell him. He was going to find out anyway and better she tell him than he found out from someone else.

She set aside the two lists and sat back on her heels.

'Cecil—'

She was interrupted by a loud thud from outside in the back garden, followed a moment later by a cry of pain.

At once she was on her feet at the window. Down below, half sticking out of the rose bed, Anne's new bicycle lay on its side, one wheel spinning. Of Anne there was no sign. Harriet wrenched open the drawing room window and leaned out. And now she could see her youngest child almost directly beneath the window, sitting on her bottom rubbing her knee and gulping back a sob. The nanny appeared and knelt down beside her, producing a white handkerchief with which she dabbed the knee. Just a graze then. No harm done. Yet Harriet found her heart was racing as though she had run up three flights of stairs. She closed the window and turned away.

She found Cecil had got up too and was standing beside her.

'Do you remember when she fell over that step in the garden when she was two?' he said. 'So much blood, we'd thought she'd cracked her skull open, poor little mite.'

Yes, Harriet did remember.

'We had no petrol for the car because of the war,' she replied, 'so you carried her all the way to the hospital and we had to sit on the floor in the corridor till midnight before someone could see us, because there had been a bomb blast.'

She had wrapped Anne up in a blanket, cradling her in her arms and watching her little face grow paler and paler, convincing herself Anne was going to die. In the end it had been a mild concussion and the hospital had kept her in the next day as a precaution. Anne still had a tiny scar on the left side of her forehead. The accident, Harriet remembered, had happened because she had gone out into the back garden to smoke a cigarette, despite it being a frosty Sunday afternoon in March, and Anne had seen her and had come running headlong out of the dining room door towards her.

Cecil had turned away and now picked up a small jade pig that someone with whom he had once worked had seen fit to send them. As she watched him, Harriet suddenly remembered that she had gone out into the garden that day, despite it being a frosty Sunday afternoon in March, not just to smoke a cigarette. She had gone out to catch her breath, to calm herself, to try to work out what to do, because that morning two military policemen had come to the house looking for Freddie.

Was Cecil remembering that day too?

She left the window, picked up her pen and the two lists and resumed her cataloguing of the presents.

Christmas lunch was a success, as much as Christmas lunch could ever be. The turkey was dry and tended to stick to the roof of one's mouth and in the back of one's throat but that was how turkey was and that was how Mrs Thompson liked to serve it, and no amount of hints about basting and sauces and gravy appeared to have any effect. Crackers were pulled and the nanny jumped as though she had never pulled a cracker before in her life and laughed at the feeble jokes inside as though she found them genuinely amusing. The children regarded her with mild concern. Cecil made a point of placing the pink paper hat on his head, as he did each year. The vast steaming Christmas pudding was brought up from the kitchen and Cecil set fire to it. The nanny shrieked when the brandy caught fire and the blue flame shot upwards, burned brightly for a moment then flickered away into nothing and Anne said, 'Don't you have brandy sauce on your Christmas puddings, Nanny?'

Mrs Thompson departed for the remainder of the day to visit her elderly mother and the family retired to the drawing room to sit quietly and digest and listen to the radio, at which point a fight broke out over a toy whose ownership was in dispute. Anne ran from the room in tears and Julius was sent to his room to consider the true meaning of Christmas.

It was four o'clock and dark outside. It hadn't really got light all day, had merely achieved a sort of sinister yellowish glow. Now, with fires being lit and coal beginning to burn in every hearth, the pea-souper outside was thickening by the minute.

Harriet watched silently as Cecil drew the curtains, turned on the lights and shovelled some more coal into the grate. He had just sat down when the doorbell rang.

'That'll be Leo and Felicity,' he announced and paused to smooth down his trousers and adjust his shirt collar before going out to answer the door.

Leo and Felicity usually popped around for sherry and mince pies sometime on Christmas afternoon. Leo would be drunk. Felicity would be disapproving. Harriet closed her eyes for a moment, not moving. Downstairs the front door opened and a blast of cold air shot up the stairs and into the drawing room causing the curtains to rustle and the fire to flicker.

Well, there was no getting out of it.

'Anne! Julius! Make yourselves presentable, please. Uncle Leo and Aunt Felicity are here. Nanny! Oh, there you are. Mr and Mrs Mumford are here. Would you mind bringing up the plate of mince pies Mrs Thompson left in the pantry? And see if you can rustle up some sherry glasses.'

Would the nanny know what a sherry glass looked like? Unlikely. Well, what of it? It was only Leo and Felicity.

'Cecil! How the devil are you, old man?' came Leo's voice loudly up the stairs. Presumably Felicity had driven the car. Felicity never drank.

Harriet smoothed down her hair and cast a glance around the drawing room, adjusted one or two Christmas cards on the mantelpiece and went out into the hallway. Anne and Julius were ahead of her, standing reluctantly and rather resentfully at the bottom of the stairs, and the nanny emerged from the kitchen bearing the plate of mince pies in one hand and a tray of whisky tumblers in the other. Oh dear. Leo appeared at the bottom of the stairs at the same time and almost knocked the nanny clean off her feet.

'Hello there and a merry Christmas to one and all! Whoops! Sorry, m'dear. '

He careered into the banister in an effort to avoid knocking

Nanny, the mince pies and the tumblers to the ground, staggered slightly, and came to a stop leaning at an angle on the wall.

Felicity stepped forward with a tight smile. 'Harriet. How are you? Happy Christmas,' and she placed an arm beneath Leo's elbow and pushed him up the stairs.

When they had all made it to the safety of the upstairs landing, Harriet kissed her sister-in-law and allowed Leo to come at her with a sherry-tinged embrace.

'Hello, Uncle Leo. Awfully chilly, isn't it?' said Julius, solemnly shaking Leo's hand.

'The roads were ghastly,' declared Felicity. 'Visibility down to about ten feet.'

'Did you bring us any presents?' said Anne.

'We damn near hit a policeman in Mayfair!' said Leo, with a laugh.

'Who's for a mince pie?' said Harriet.

'That's when we switched drivers,' explained Felicity, with another of her tight smiles.

'Sherry for me, old girl,' announced Leo with a wink.

'Did you bring us any presents?' said Anne again.

They moved into the drawing room and Leo dropped down onto the armchair. Nanny served the sherry and filled the glasses too full so that the sherry spilled into a little pool on the tray and dripped down the side of the glasses. Harriet slid a coaster beneath Leo's glass just in time to prevent a drop of sherry splashing onto the René Drouet coffee table. Leo had removed his overcoat to reveal flannels, an extraordinary mustard-yellow jersey and an open-necked shirt, a look that might have passed muster on the golf course but seemed a little gay for Christmas Day. Felicity, in stark contrast, was dressed in her matron's outfit: a dull olive-green skirt and white blouse, flesh-coloured nylons and horrid sturdy black shoes. She too had removed her coat, but carried it over one arm as though she were expecting to leave straight away.

'Please, do sit down, Felicity,' Harriet suggested, indicating an empty chair. For heaven's sake, she thought irritably, why did one always feel so damned formal with her? They had been sisters-in-law for fifteen years. Lord knew, she didn't wish to have an intimate chat with the woman, but for heaven's sake, a bit of warmth, a sign of friendship wouldn't go amiss.

'Thank you, Harriet. But I'd prefer to stand,' was the reply.

'And how's your Christmas day been, kids?' said Leo, who always seemed to need to over-compensate for his wife's formality. 'Lots of lovely goodies from Father C?'

'Not a bad haul, thanks, Uncle Leo,' replied Julius. 'And you?'

One never knew if Julius was being facetious or not. It was probably safe to assume he was.

'Felicity, a mince pie?'

'Thank you, but I can't abide them. It's the orange peel ...'

Felicity did not go on to explain what it was about the orange peel that particularly offended her.

'Show us what you've got there, Anne,' said Cecil in his indulgent-parent voice.

Anne was busily unwrapping a large present that Leo had just handed her. She placed it now on the armchair and knelt down on the carpet, all her attention focused on the gaudy red and green wrapping paper and the gold ribbon tied around it. She unpeeled the sticking tape at one end carefully, so as not to tear the paper. It tore at one corner and she winced. But now the paper was unwrapped and Anne reached inside—

'Oh ...' The word was little more than a breath, but the disappointment it contained was evident—to her mother at least. The present was a doll-sized gold ball gown, a vague copy of a Dior dress that had been fashionable a couple of seasons ago. It was exactly the same dress she and Cecil had purchased and given to her earlier in the day.

There was a silence as Anne held up the dress and looked at it. Someone needed to say something.

'How beautiful!' Cecil observed, as though ball gowns—and

miniature Dior ball gowns in particular—were of particular interest to him. 'What do you say, Anne?'

'Thank you,' said Anne dutifully, the dress already laid down on its wrapping paper.

'But Pops, she's already—' began Julius.

'Nanny, do be a sweetie and top up the glasses.'

'Saw it in Hamleys,' said Leo, obviously pleased with himself. 'Remembered last year you were talking about it, Annie.'

'Yes,' said Anne quietly.

'The bottle's empty, Mrs Wallis,' said the nanny in a loud whisper, leaning over and catching Harriet's eye in some dismay.

'Not to worry, Harriet, old girl—there's more where that came from!' and Leo produced a bottle-shaped present wrapped in the same gaudy paper. 'Didn't think we'd forget, did you?'

No, Harriet hadn't thought for one moment that Leo would forget to bring his customary bottle of Christmas sherry. He had brought one every Christmas for the past ten years. Neither she nor Cecil had ever mentioned that they did not, in fact, drink sherry, and the only time a bottle was opened was when Leo and Felicity came around. Some they had managed to pass on as gifts, but in the main the bottles collected dust on a shelf in the pantry.

'Thank you, Leo. How kind,' and she took the bottle and passed it to the nanny.

The girl took the bottle and held it gingerly as though it were a stick of dynamite.

'There's a corkscrew in the kitchen, Nanny.'

The girl gave her a panic-stricken look and Harriet, exasperated, thought, good Lord, hasn't the girl ever opened a bottle of sherry before? She smiled pleasantly.

'Give it to me, I'll do it. Do excuse me a moment,' and she took the bottle outside.

'Harriet, I—do you mind if I join you?'

Harriet turned in surprise as Felicity came out behind her and gave a rather wild smile.

'Of course not,' she said and led the way downstairs to the kitchen.

Well! What did this mean? Had something happened? Was Leo— had Leo done something? Were Felicity and Leo having problems? Dear God, surely not a divorce!

Harriet turned on the kitchen light and began sorting through the drawers to see where Mrs Thompson kept the corkscrew. Felicity had paused in the kitchen doorway and appeared to be waiting for something.

'Ah, here it is. Now, let's see if we can get this out.' Harriet unpeeled the foil and stabbed the point of the corkscrew into the cork. The silence drew out uncomfortably as Harriet twisted the corkscrew then slowly began to ease the cork out. It came out with a satisfying pop and a warm, sickly-sweet aroma seeped out.

'Fresh glasses, I think,' she said, not really knowing what she was saying but wanting to fill the silence. She rummaged in a cupboard and retrieved two more glasses—genuine sherry glasses this time— gave them a quick polish and poured two small amounts, one into each glass, and held one out to Felicity. It reminded her suddenly of her youth, those endless cocktail parties at little flats in Bloomsbury and in large country houses where one inevitably found oneself in the kitchen at two in the morning half sloshed with some girlfriend or other, discussing some man or what some other girl had done with some man. One did not associate Felicity with such scenes. And Felicity didn't drink.

Felicity took the glass and took a quick sip. She grimaced.

'Harriet, I must talk to you about something. It's—rather delicate.'

Oh Lord.

'Of course, anything I can do, naturally …?'

'The thing is—' Felicity paused. 'It's the silliest thing, you'll laugh …'

Upstairs Leo did laugh, loudly, and Felicity winced.

'I don't quite know how it can have happened ...'

'For heaven's sake, just tell me!' What the devil had she done? Been caught shop lifting?

'I'm pregnant.'

'*Pregnant?!*' Felicity was dead right—she did want to laugh.

'Yes. I can't think how it can have happened ...' she repeated.

'Can't you?' Harriet shook her head in some confusion. Pregnant! Felicity!

'Well, obviously one understands *how* it happened. What I meant was, well—' She paused (and one's mind baulked at the thought of Felicity discussing birth control). By the look of it, Felicity's mind had similarly baulked as she was unable to complete the sentence.

'Are you sure?' said Harriet, getting down to business—after all, this wasn't the first such conversation she had had with a girlfriend in a kitchen. Although it had been some years since the last time. And she did not exactly put Felicity in that category.

'Yes, quite. It's been two months. And I went to a doctor. Not our doctor, naturally, but he confirmed it.'

'Why not your doctor?'

Felicity stared at her. 'Because I can't keep it! Obviously.'

Now it was Harriet's turn to stare.

'Why on earth not?' she replied, but even as she said it the reasons seemed clear enough. Felicity was not mother material; had not the slightest interest in babies; was approaching her forties. And she had her career.

'But I can't! I simply *cannot* have a baby. It would destroy everything. *Everything*! Don't you see?' Felicity's voice rose a little hysterically. 'I would have to give up my job!'

'Now, darling, take a deep breath. It's quite all right, it's all going to be fine,' said Harriet automatically though she didn't, at this moment, see how. She waited as Felicity took a deep breath and another sip of the sherry. 'Good. That's better. Now, let's just think clearly and rationally about this. Leo—does he know?'

'No, of course not. I couldn't tell him; he'd want it.'

'But, my dear, doesn't he have a right to know?'

'Yes, I'm sure he does, and I'm sure he has a right to be a father, but he doesn't have to give up everything to do it, does he? No, I'm sorry, Harriet, but I've made up my mind. He isn't going to find out.'

'But, then, why are you telling me, if you've already made up your mind?'

Felicity closed her eyes for a moment.

'I need help, Harriet. I don't know … how to go about it. How to get rid of it,' and for the first time her eyes became pleading, desperate. Frightened.

Harriet leant back against the kitchen cupboard and took a sip of the sherry. It tasted sweet and sickly and she put the glass down on the kitchen table. She reached around for a cigarette, but they were upstairs; there was only a packet of Mrs Thompson's wretched Craven A's by the sink.

There had been other occasions, of course, before the war, when girls had got themselves into trouble and she had heard a name mentioned, seen an address passed furtively from hand to hand—a doctor with a foreign-sounding name, a woman with a kind heart in the East End. But so many years ago now, she had nothing she could pass on as useful advice. And there were the horror stories, too, of coat-hangers and blood poisoning and lice-infested rooms and girls who could no longer have babies. Of girls who had died.

Besides, it was illegal.

'Darling, I don't really see what I can do.'

'But surely you must know someone—someone who can help?'

'I'm afraid I can't think of anyone. It's not the sort of thing one—'

'You *must* know something!' There was a note of something close to panic in Felicity's voice.

Harriet turned away and replaced the corkscrew in the draw. She slowly slid the draw back into the dresser. Cecil had said, in this very house eight years ago:

'Are you expecting me to help you? To help him? Because I won't! I will not—do you understand? How dare you put me in this position? How dare Freddie put you in this position!'

And she *had* expected him to help, or at least to understand. But he hadn't. He had not helped her. He had refused.

She turned to face Felicity, holding out both her hands.

'I'm so sorry, Felicity.'

Felicity stared at her. For a moment she said nothing and it seemed as though she had pinned all her hopes, had gathered all her strength, had sacrificed all her dignity, for this one conversation, this single plea for help—and it had come to nothing.

Her eyes hardened and she nodded slowly.

'Well. No matter, I'm sure I can sort it out myself,' she said briskly.

There was a silence during which Harriet could have said, 'Look, I don't know who to go to but I can ask around, I can see if anyone knows something ...' But she remained silent, and in another moment Felicity turned and went back upstairs.

'There you are!' exclaimed Leo loudly, as though they had been gone for some hours. 'Thought you'd got lost,' he added brilliantly, but not even Anne laughed. Felicity stood stiffly at the back of the room and smiled, but it was a rather grim smile that made Harriet look away and wish they would leave.

They did leave eventually, but only after Leo had downed two more sherries and Cecil had reminisced about some childhood Christmas that he obviously felt surprisingly sentimental about, but which Felicity refused to get drawn into. Anne had got bored and gone off to her room and Julius had stood surreptitiously beside the sherry decanter and then edged out of the room and fled upstairs so that one assumed he had taken a furtive swig. Let Cecil deal with it. And finally Felicity had announced that it really was time they were off and there was relief in the flurry of coats and hats and farewells.

'Goodbye, Harriet,' said Felicity, leaning forward and brushing against her cheek. Her hands were cold and stiff and her eyes turned away before Harriet could reply. The door closed behind them and Harriet stood in the hallway for a long moment.

It was too bad. One couldn't help everyone. Sometimes one was unable to help even those one cared the most deeply for. There was nothing to be done about it.

Chapter Sixteen

JANUARY 1953

The Bentley boy was to be executed at Wandsworth Prison that morning at nine o'clock for the murder of a police constable. The papers were full of it. A crowd had gathered at dawn outside the prison, petitions had been submitted. A last-minute appeal for clemency had been rejected and the Home Secretary had not intervened.

Cecil glanced at his watch. It was almost twelve-thirty and by now the boy was dead. To be hanged by the neck until you were dead, to wait in a cell and count down each day until you were scheduled to be put to death by your own government, your own countrymen. It was unthinkable, barbaric.

The boy's face stared at him from every newspaper in the carriage.

The Central Line train rattled into Tottenham Court Road station and screeched to a halt. It was lunchtime and the platform was crowded with office workers and shoppers making the most of the last days of the post-Christmas sales. The doors opened and a sea of people swept out and a sea of other people surged in, shopping bags knocking against each other, briefcases, hats, umbrellas, small children, all jumbled together. Jostling each other, talking, rustling newspapers, stepping on toes. Just as though it were a normal Wednesday in January; as though a nineteen-year-old boy had not been executed at Wandsworth Prison barely three-and-a-half hours ago.

It was twelve thirty-five. He was going to be late. Felicity got cross with people when they were late. The doors closed and the train rattled onward on its journey westbound.

It was a nuisance, this lunchtime appointment with Felicity. Things were busy at the office; it was awkward making excuses to take such a long lunch break. It didn't set a good example to the junior staff. But it was the old girl's birthday and, after all, he was her only brother. And this was her fortieth. Lunch was preferable to an evening appointment, anyway—one couldn't go anywhere after dark in these dreadful pea-soupers. It was bad enough in the middle of the day, when some ghost of daylight seeped through the yellowish smog, but after dark it was quite impossible.

The train pulled into Oxford Circus, the doors opened and somehow more people squeezed on. One of them was a young woman in a long beige overcoat, a scarf tied around her head and under her chin.

It was Jenny Rocastle!

Cecil half stood up before realising that it was not Jenny Rocastle at all, just a girl who looked a bit like her; who didn't look very much like her at all, now he could see her properly. And much younger than Mrs Rocastle. The girl pushed her way into the carriage and found a seat opposite Cecil. She sat staring vacantly at the advertisements above his head. The doors closed and the train moved off again.

He hadn't seen Mrs Rocastle since the week before Christmas.

He stirred uneasily, crossing and uncrossing his legs. His umbrella rolled onto the floor and a large man in a Homburg stepped on it. Cecil reached quickly for the umbrella. There was a large muddy footprint marking the black silk and he experienced a moment of revulsion, but resisted the urge to pull out his handkerchief and wipe it off.

He had gone to visit Mrs Rocastle soon after her husband's disappearance. It seemed the decent thing to do, one didn't condemn someone simply because their husband had gone bad. He had made a point of making a return visit a fortnight later and again before Christmas, just to show his support. And Mrs Rocastle had appeared grateful, pleased even, at his visits.

Yet he had said nothing of his visits to Harriet.

The whole Rocastle incident was an office matter and as such had no bearing on Harriet. Nevertheless he continued to feel uneasy, leaving work on a pretext, travelling in a taxi at lunchtime to a West London residence like a man visiting his mistress, head tucked into his collar as he climbed the stairs to her flat—it seemed to Cecil that mistresses always lived in upstairs flats—and half expecting her to come to the door in a dressing gown. She never had. She was always dressed very soberly, very properly. Each time she had sat on the edge of an armchair, pressing tea and biscuits on him and listening, gravely, as he told her of the lack of news of her husband, of the extent of the damage to the firm. She had never asked questions, only sat there nodding silently in agreement as though it was all to be expected.

And soon he had ceased to talk to her of her husband and the investigation at all and had instead talked to her about the office: about Sir Maurice, a take-over scare, the ships scheduled for breaking up, the flu epidemic that had felled the typing pool, things he never told Harriet, and Mrs Rocastle—Jenny—listened and made comments and was interested. Or was that just politeness?

And still he had said nothing of his visits to Harriet.

'Wot chew starin' at then? Bloody pervert!'

Cecil froze in horror as the young girl opposite spat out these words and every head in the carriage turned and stared at him.

That the girl could utter such vulgar words with such a pretty mouth was shocking. That she could make such an accusation so loudly and in front of a carriage full of people, appalling.

Cecil started to his feet even before the train had rolled into Bond Street station and stumbled towards the door feeling twenty, thirty pairs of eyes watching him. He stood facing the doorway as the train rumbled to a halt and waited an eternity for the doors to open. Finally they did and he stepped quickly through and away down the platform as fast as decorum permitted. A man in a tweed suit passed him on the escalators and gave Cecil a long frowning look.

Had he been staring at the girl? If she *had* been Mrs Rocastle, would he have stared at her? All the times he had sat in her armchair sipping her tea and nibbling her biscuits and she had sat perched on the opposite chair, nodding and saying very little—had he been staring at her?

Cecil passed through the ticket barrier waving his ticket at the West Indian ticket collector and braced himself for the street.

Outside it was like the war again, only instead of gas masks everyone wore handkerchiefs over their mouths and noses, and instead of bomb smoke there was the smog. Almost two months of it now and still no sign of it letting up.

Was this the world we fought for? Cecil wondered, as he fumbled for his handkerchief. This half-life lived in a half-light?

He retrieved his handkerchief and held it to his mouth as he stepped out onto the street. It was a quarter to one but it may as well have been five o'clock in the evening for all the daylight there was. All around people appeared out of the gloom, only their eyes visible above scarves, collars and white handkerchiefs, then they were swallowed up again by the fog. Cecil thought again of the boy who had been executed. Was it so terrible, after all, to be taken from the world, to be delivered from a future such as this?

He turned northwards—was it northwards?—and made for Wigmore Street, and if he hadn't done this walk a dozen times before, hadn't met Felicity at this café many times in the past, he would have lost his way instantly. As it was he felt a moment of panicked disorientation as he crossed Manchester Place. But there was the pub on the corner, and beside it the old bookshop, and beside that the cafe. Relieved, he almost took a deep breath, thought better of it and dived inside.

Inside a bell tinkled somewhere at the back of the shop and echoed around the all-but-empty room. Tables and chairs were placed too close together and if the place had been full it would have been impossible to negotiate a way between them. But the café was deserted save for two elderly ladies who huddled in a corner clutching vast handbags, and Felicity, who sat at her usual table by the window reading a book.

'Hello,' he called and waved apologetically. 'Train didn't turn up. Transport's completely up the creek with this fog.' He pulled out a chair, remembering to kiss her before sitting down.

This fog! It was all anyone said these days. One could blame it for practically anything. A few years ago everyone blamed the unions for everything that was wrong with Britain. Or delinquents, or spivs, or Americans. Now one blamed the fog.

Felicity inserted a bookmark at her page and placed the book on the table. It was Dostoevsky. She smiled at him a little wanly.

'Oh, many happy returns of the day,' he said cheerfully.

Her smile became a little more wan.

'Thank you.'

There was a pause while he waited for her to add something, but she didn't.

'Well, I'd better order lunch then, hadn't I?' he said brightly. Why am I pretending to be cheerful, he wondered as he stared at the cardboard menu on the table. And why am I studying the menu? I only ever have the roast beef and Yorkshire pud.

He was doing it because Felicity was being so oddly quiet. And wan; yes, she looked distinctly wan. Ought he to mention it?

'What'll it be, old girl?' he asked and cringed at his own cheerfulness.

'I'll have my usual,' she said.

'Right you are.' The waitress hovered—a slatternly girl in a black dress and a white apron with a purple stain on it and her hair piled high on her head in a stiff bouffant. Cecil beamed at her. 'We'll have one toad in the hole and I'll have'—he felt reckless—'I'll have the fish of the day.'

'Fish is off.'

'Oh. Well. The roast beef and Yorkshire pudding, then, please.' He smiled at the girl then he remembered the girl on the tube train and turned abruptly away. The waitress flounced away and they were left in silence.

'Leo at work?' Cecil inquired.

'Yes.'

He nodded. Of course Leo was at work, where else would he be? Felicity had mornings free as her television program didn't go out until five o'clock in the afternoon.

'His Spitfire drama begins broadcasting this week,' she said.

'Oh, right. Very good. Must look out for it. What's it called?'

'*Spitfire*.'

'Oh.' He nodded, and they both knew the Wallises did not own a television set and would never watch a program called *Spitfire* even if they did.

'Simon Paget still acting as advisor, is he?'

'No. He left before Christmas. He was unhappy with the dialogue and the actors. And the plot. And most of the technical details.'

'Really? Well, old Simon always was a fusspot. Can't imagine why he got himself involved in such a vulgar scheme in the first place.'

Felicity frowned and Cecil realised belatedly that the vulgar scheme had been principally Leo's idea.

'And how's the hippo? Still got lots of friends, I trust?'

'We've been told we have to include a West Indian hippo. There's a concern we won't appeal to the children of immigrants.'

Cecil stared at her as the roast beef and Yorkshire pudding was slammed down onto the table in front of him. He waited until the waitress had thrust the toad-in-the-hole at Felicity. It was served with a handful of green peas which rolled in a cluster around the plate like a school of tiny green fish.

'Do many West Indian families have television sets?' replied Cecil in some surprise.

'I really have no idea,' said Felicity, unfolding a paper napkin and laying it on her lap.

'And of course one has to question whether hippos do in fact come from the West Indies,' added Cecil, attempting to lighten the tone.

'I doubt it,' replied Felicity, taking the question at face value. 'No more than they come from the home counties.'

She had a point. The hippo in *Hippo and Friends* had a distinct home counties plum in his mouth. No doubt the BBC was not too concerned about zoological accuracy. It was, evidently, concerned about audience numbers.

'Oh, I almost forgot,' and Cecil reached inside his coat pocket and placed her present on the table. 'Happy birthday, old girl.'

There was a moment of awkwardness as they decided whether it was appropriate to kiss, decided not to risk it and instead smiled at each other.

Cecil was rather pleased with the present. After all, it wasn't every day one turned forty, was it? It called for something a bit special. Felicity took the present and unwrapped it carefully. It was a box and she looked up at him curiously. He smiled back and suddenly felt a moment of shyness. She opened the lid and looked at the ring nestling inside.

'It's mother's,' he explained quickly. 'Don't you remember—no, of course, you were too young. It was her engagement ring. After she died, father kept all her rings in his desk drawer. I found them after he died. I mentioned it to you at the time. Anyway, I completely forgot about them until I found them in my own desk a few months ago. I got it altered to your size—Leo lent me one of your rings.'

He stopped, feeling pleased with this story, with his efforts.

Felicity looked at the ring again and her eyes filled with tears. Cecil was appalled. Somehow he had not imagined this. He attacked his roast beef with vigour.

'What a lovely idea,' said Felicity after a moment or two. There was a silence and Cecil continued to eat, concentrating on his Yorkshire pudding which was thankfully a little leathery and therefore took all his attention to saw through. 'Thank you, Cecil,' she said finally.

'Don't mention it, old girl. Hmm, the Yorkshire's very good. How's yours?'

'Super,' she replied though she hadn't taken a mouthful.

Her hand was shaking. He noticed it out of the corner of his eye as he lifted a forkful of roast beef to his mouth. He looked away with a frown, alarmed. Was it the ring? Lord, one wanted her to be pleased. Hadn't occurred to him she might be upset by it.

'Oh. Forgot to ask: how were Margery and the kids?'

He had rung her three nights ago to confirm the lunch and Leo had answered the telephone, reporting that Felicity was away overnight, staying with an old school-chum in Maidenhead.

She looked up at him, her fork poised mid-air.

'Leo mentioned it when I rang. Didn't he say I'd called?'

She looked almost unwell.

'No. No, he didn't.'

'Well, and how *was* Margery?'

'Fine. I mean, she's been a little down since John died, you know. Did you know John had died? It was a while ago, of course, but I think she still misses him a great deal.' She smiled, but the smile did not touch her eyes.

'No, I didn't know. Poor Margery.' Cecil ate for a moment in silence. Then he looked up. 'Felicity, are you all right? You look … quite unwell.'

He couldn't recall ever saying such a thing to her before. Ever *noticing* such a thing before.

She blinked at him.

'Of course I'm all right. Quite all right. Why do you ask?' She laughed uncertainly.

'Sorry, old girl. Don't mean to appear rude. Just a little concerned, that's all.'

'I was feeling a little queasy,' she admitted, then she appeared to regret this admission and turned back to her toad-in-the-hole.

Cecil looked at her and a sudden, an astonishing thought came to him.

'Good Lord, you're not expecting a baby, are you?'

He regretted it as soon as the words left his mouth. She looked at him aghast and he realised his mistake.

'Of course not, Cecil. What a thing to suggest.' She smiled that same unnerving smile again. 'Leo and I have never wanted children, you know that.'

'Of course.' He hadn't known that—how would he? Though it came as no surprise. And better not to want children than to have childlessness forced upon you.

'Anyway, I've been meaning to tell you, I have had some ideas for a new television program,' said Felicity, leaning forward and placing her fork and knife on the plate though she had eaten almost nothing. 'It has puppets—I mean puppets with strings rather than a glove puppet like Hippo, and that allows for much great movement around the set, you see.'

Cecil nodded. 'Yes, I see,' and he listened silently while outside the fog closed in.

Chapter Seventeen

FEBRUARY 1953

The news hoarding outside Knightsbridge tube station announced in dramatic black letters that the Government had offered a general amnesty for deserters. It was to be a special measure during Coronation year.

From the top deck of the number 14 bus Jean looked down at the paper-boy, muffled up in a long scarf, who shouted these words as he tossed papers at passers-by and neatly caught their coins. A lady in a wide-brimmed hat side-stepped the noisy paper-boy and climbed into the back of a black cab.

During the war men had died and other men had survived, some had fought and some had not. Now, eight years on, what mattered to the people of Knightsbridge late on a chilly Tuesday afternoon was hailing a cab ahead of someone else further up the street, avoiding the frozen puddles on Old Brompton Road and getting home before dark.

The bus pulled away from the kerb and a young couple, giggling and clutching a wet packet of chips, emerged onto the top deck and took a seat at the front of the bus. Behind the couple came a man, a little older, in a long overcoat and hat and carrying a hastily folded newspaper. The bus swerved and he swung into the seat in front of Jean, grabbing the handrail to steady himself.

Tuesdays were Jean's afternoon off. Often she took the bus to Kensington High Street and had a slice of cake and a cup of tea at the Lyons tea shop and watched the people going by, then took a walk in Kensington Gardens. If there was something good showing, she went to the pictures, then she bought fish and chips and ate them on the bus coming home. But this Tuesday she had left the house as soon as the clock in the hallway had struck twelve, and taken the bus east to the City. She had got off and walked along the river past the Tower and the crowds of tourists. She had avoided the docks, turning north into Cable Street towards Shadwell, and then into Stepney.

It had been a shock to see all those empty, bombed-out streets, the few remaining rows of ugly, overcrowded tenements, the lines of grey washing criss-crossing the lanes and alleyways; to see so many filthy children playing in the dirt, inadequately dressed against the cold February day. And it was a shock to realise that she was shocked, when she ought not to have been, when she had grown up right here.

The bombsites were in every street. Dreadful gaping wounds in the roadside, remnants of a wall here, a doorway there, and everywhere rosebay willowherb choking and consuming everything in its path. And so few cars. The streets were as full of craters as they had been when the war ended. What was the Government doing? And where was everyone living? On top of each other, seemed to be the answer—all that washing outside one grimy window, all those children playing outside a single doorstep.

As she passed them, the children paused in their games to stare at her.

One little boy stooped and picked up a stone and hurled it at her, not with any obvious anger, it seemed, but out of boredom, or habit. The stone sailed past Jean's ear and landed with a thud on the pavement, bouncing and rolling into the gutter.

Jean quickened her pace. It had only been six months and yet she hurried with her head down like a stranger.

Turning into Malacca Row she paused. Half the street was gone, of course, from number twelve right the way down to number twenty—an open sore of scorched bricks and piles of rubble that had lain undisturbed for eight years. The willowherb crept over every surface, strangling, reclaiming, gradually turning city back into country. Into wasteland.

And behind the hole that had once been the north side of Malacca Row was the gasworks, looming five storeys high and making her stand and stare because for the first twelve years of her life the gasworks had been hidden. Now, even after eight years, it was still a shock to see it, so vast and exposed, like a bone when the flesh had been blasted off. If the rocket had fallen one street to the north, everyone had said—if the rocket had landed on the gasworks and not on the north side of Malacca Row—the whole area would have been blown sky high. But it had fallen on Malacca Row and numbers twelve to twenty had been reduced to rubble and five families had been wiped out. It could have been more—*would* have been more, but the rocket had fallen on a Sunday, and in the daytime when folk were outside hanging out their washing and waiting for the pub to open. The Corbetts hadn't been hanging out their washing, as Sunday was Chapel day. But that Sunday—for the first Sunday in living memory—the Corbetts had not gone to Chapel.

The McIlwraiths lived at number ten. When the bomb had hit, their house had lost all its windows and most of its tiles and a couple of outside walls, but it was, generally speaking, still standing. Mr McIlwraith was long gone by then, but in the years since the rocket

Eddie or Liam or one of Mrs McIlwraith's other nephews had shored up a wall here, a roofing joist there, a doorway somewhere else, using bricks and bits of timber salvaged from the debris of the other houses. Jean had long ago trained herself not to wonder if the particular piece of timber shoring up the doorframe or replacing the banisters had once been part of her own house. Life went on. And Mrs McIlwraith had been good to her.

She crossed the road and the front door of number 10 opened just as though she was expected, and there was Mrs McIlwraith standing in the doorway, a scarf tied around her head, a fag in the corner of her mouth as always, the rug—it looked like the rug from the hallway—in her hands, and she began to beat it vigorously against the doorpost. She looked up and paused in her beating, seeing Jean.

'Well, if it in't little Jeanie Corbett,' she announced as though addressing a third person. And Jean almost skipped over to her, ten years old and with her socks fallen down to her ankles.

'You ain't 'ere to see Eddie, I 'ope?' Mrs McIlwraith added, placing a hand on her hip and blocking the doorway.

Jean stopped.

'Hello, Mrs McIlwraith. No, I—'

'Because he's upped and gone off with that Brenda Sykes from the Dog and Rabbit. Her that was goin' with young Ted Henshaw before he got himself banged up for them fake ration books.'

There was a pause. Mrs McIlwraith gave the rug a brisk shake to indicate what she thought of Ted Henshaw, and perhaps what she thought of Brenda Sykes too.

'No, I was just poppin' round. Say hello, that's all,' said Jean feeling, a little awkward.

'Yeah, well.'

Mrs McIlwraith appeared not to think much of someone 'poppin' round'. She scowled.

'They feedin' you all right, are they?' she inquired suspiciously, as though Jean were at a girls' reformatory school.

'Yeah, course,' Jean replied, a little defensively. She stood and watched the rug beating and found she hadn't much else to say.

Mrs McIlwraith rolled the cigarette from one corner of her mouth to the other and regarded Jean for a moment.

'I daresay you're too posh for the likes of us now,' she observed.

Jean made no reply to this.

'Well, I can't be standin' round here all day yackin', can I? There's work to be done,' and with that Mrs McIlwrath gave the rug a final thump and turned and closed the door behind her.

Jean left Malacca Row and turned south towards Wapping and the docks.

Soon the oily, salty, vaguely fishy smell of the river filled her head. The boom of a large ship sounded once, twice, then faded, a haze of smoke filled the horizon and the blood quickened in her veins. Up west the river was a quaint waterway of pleasure craft bobbing up and down and going nowhere. Not a real river at all. Here it was a working river, a proper river, and her heart leapt to think of it. But she was not here to see the river.

Ahead of her was a narrow laneway into which she turned. At the end of the laneway in between two warehouses, one mostly intact, one reduced to rubble, was the Chapel. It was a squat brick building, not fancy like the Catholic or the Church of England churches with all their stained glass and their stone carvings and what have you. No, this was a plain sort of building—ugly, really—yet her heart swelled with joy when she saw its four tiny windows, its green-painted door and two tatty posters flapping in the breeze, one proclaiming God's love, the other—handwritten in bold blue ink—listing the service times. Hitler's bombs had fallen to right and left but the Chapel, by God's mercy, had been kept safe. Even Hitler's rockets had proved no match for His protection.

Jean marched boldly up to the peeling green front door and pushed it open. Inside a familiar warm and musty smell greeted her, of wood and disinfectant and dust and damp. Of paper and candles burning. Some things hadn't changed. And there were the eight rows of hard wooden pews—room for only 30 worshippers and not a cushion in sight. At the far end of the hall was the altar, a simple wooden affair constructed years ago by one of the brethren, and on it the cross and the candles in their candleholders—they were wooden too. Gold, Pastor Bellamy had always said, was too much of a temptation to the weak-minded and He didn't mind if you used gold or wood to worship Him.

There was no pulpit. Pastor Bellamy, or whichever of the elders was preaching that day, stood behind a crude wooden lectern. Dad had stood there himself on many a Sunday, not that he ever required a lectern to hold his sermon notes for it was all inside him. Fire in the belly was how he described it, and he could summon that fire at will, it had seemed, to the awe and delight of the little congregation. Sometimes it had been frightening. How many times as a small child, and then when she was a little older, with Gladys and Nerys squeezed in tightly beside her on the pew, had she sat quaking with fear as Dad's eyes had blazed and those terrible words had poured forth, evoking the damnation and torment that awaited the sinner.

There had been one Sunday during the war when a member of the congregation, a young girl, had made some transgression—the exact nature of this transgression was never mentioned, though it seemed obvious now that the girl had got herself in the family way— and Dad had railed against her furiously, urging the congregation to expel the sinner, and his wrath and indignation when Pastor Bellamy had suggested they show the girl mercy and allow her to remain in the church had been terrifying to behold. Dad had leapt up and stood right here, addressing the other elders and their wives and families, demanding they act decisively. 'Temptation leads only to damnation!' he had roared, thumping the lectern, and eventually they had come round to his way of thinking and the girl had been expelled.

What had become of her? Perhaps she had joined the Catholics. Perhaps she had turned from God completely.

The chapel was silent. The echo of Dad's words was just that: an echo, and only Jean could hear it.

'Hello? Is anyone in? Pastor Bellamy?'

She went to the door that led to the tiny room at the back of the hall that served as both office and Pastor Bellamy's vestry, then stepped back in surprise when another man entirely came out of the room.

'Hello. Can I help you?' said the man, pausing and peering curiously at her. He was a young man, only a few years older than herself, with a narrow frame and a narrow face, thinning hair, dark eyes that studied her closely. He wore a collar and seemed vaguely familiar. He stood in the doorway of the office as if he had business to be there. Jean stepped back and felt a moment of alarm, confusion.

'Yes ... I was looking for Pastor Bellamy.'

'Well, I'm Pastor Lennard,' he replied, as though that somehow answered her question. 'Bob Lennard—I was an elder over at Hackney. And what's your name?'

Yes, she remembered him, he had helped out one Christmas when the Pastor had been unwell and had visited on other occasions.

'I'm Jean. Jean Corbett. You'll know of my Dad, Owen? Owen Corbett—he was an elder here for twenty years. And my Mum. We all came here, the Corbetts ...'

He smiled politely, but there was no recognition in his eyes.

'Please, where is Pastor Bellamy?'

'I'm afraid he passed away some months ago.'

He delivered this news, then—perhaps out of respect—he paused, though if it was respect, the pause was hardly long enough.

'November it was. There was a break-in.' He began to close the door to the office, pulling out a large key and inserting it in a new-looking lock. 'Poor Pastor Bellamy was here on his own and they struck him down. The Lord alone knows what they were after, but desperate times ...' He shrugged a little sadly. 'Mrs Angel found him next morning. Still alive, but insensible. They took him to the

London Hospital at Whitechapel, but he only lived a few days. May he rest in eternal peace,' he finished with a helpful smile.

Jean stared at him as another part of her old life crumbled into dust and vanished.

'No one told me,' she said at last.

'No, I'm sure,' he replied, nodding. 'You've left the district, then?'

Jean heard him but her head began to hurt at her temples, a pounding that pressed against her eyes.

'Yes, I ... Yes. I had to get work ...'

'Of course. God helps those that help themselves.'

He nodded again. Why did he keep nodding? And smiling? What was there to smile about?

'And what is it that you do in your work?'

Jean sat down heavily on the nearest pew. They had sat just here, Dad and Mum and Gladys and Nerys and Edward and little Bertie and her, all of them, Sunday after Sunday and sometimes in the evening too, Dad with the Bible open before him following the pastor's words. Year after year. Even that winter in the war when Mum had been laid up bad with her feet and Dad had barely been able to stand up because his back was so bad, still they had made the journey to Chapel to thank God for their lives. The Corbetts had worshipped here for forty years, but now they were gone and no one remembered them. It was as though they had never been here at all.

'Nanny. I'm a nanny. For a family. Up west.'

'A nanny, is it?' he repeated with a raised eyebrow, as though this were a calling located somewhere between a whore and a Catholic. 'And is it a wealthy family, this family up west, Jean?'

She nodded. What other sort of family could afford a nanny?

Mr Lennard—she couldn't think of him as Pastor—nodded slowly.

'Well. I'm sure their need is great,' he observed. 'And will you be returning to us, Jean? Our need is great too, as I'm certain you are aware. Very great. The war has brought such suffering to many and the peacetime has not provided as it should. Not here, at any rate. There is a great deal of work to be done.'

He looked down at her, coldly, it seemed. Condemningly. She looked away, lowering her eyes.

'Fares, please,' said the West Indian clippie, scanning the faces of the people on the top deck of the bus. The young man in the hat who had joined at Knightsbridge held out some coins and the conductor cranked up his machine so that a strip of ticket was disgorged and torn off and presented to the passenger. The man took it without looking up. He sat low in his seat watching the street below from beneath the brim of his hat.

Would she go back?

Mr Lennard had said a lot of people had suffered. As though it were her fault. As though she were to blame for the suffering of others. But what about her? Hadn't *she* suffered? Hadn't she suffered more than most?

Today was the 24th of February. The newspapers screamed it from every hoarding but not a single one noted that it was eight years ago today that a rocket had landed on Malacca Row and five families had been wiped out.

Mr Lennard could keep his suffering and his guilt. There were other important jobs to do. And sometimes God showed you what job had to be done and if that job took you away from the only home you had ever known, well, so be it.

'Sout' Kensin'ton! Sout' Kensin'ton!' sang out the clippie urgently, looking around at the passengers on the top deck as though to warn them that this was their final chance to alight before being sucked forever into Hammersmith and Chiswick.

Jean started up, caught up in the urgency of the moment, grabbing her bag and diving towards the steps. The young man in the hat stood up too and they became momentarily entangled in the aisle. Jean extricated herself and the man stood aside, murmuring an apology, though it sounded half-hearted, as though his thoughts were elsewhere.

It was dark as Jean stepped off the bus, crossed Cromwell Place and headed along Old Brompton Road, but at least the pea-souper had mostly gone and she could see the streetlights and know, with reasonable certainty, where she was. Thousands had died, they said, old folk and the sick and babies, of the smog! It was only just now coming out—folk right across the city choking to death! It was hard to imagine. At least with a bomb you could see it, hear it. But this—it was a sort of creeping death.

Jean shivered and pulled her scarf up over her mouth and took shallow breaths.

Old Brompton Road was almost deserted. The smog had lifted but, even so, folk were afraid: it might return at any time without warning.

A man's footsteps crunched loudly only a few feet behind her and Jean pulled her coat closer around her shoulders and walked a little more quickly. It was safer here than in Wapping, of course, but still, you couldn't be too careful.

The footsteps grew louder and closer.

She saw a young courting couple standing in a doorway ahead and felt a moment of relief. She was safe if other people were around. As she approached the couple they began kissing. The man put his hands on the girl's shoulders then around her waist and she put her hands beneath his hat, dislodging it, so that it slipped back. Jean could see their mouths, open, their jaws working as though they were eating each other. She reached them and passed them and so did the footsteps behind her. She continued on a few feet until she came to a dress shop, where she paused to look in the window at the expensive French dresses displayed on the mannequins. The footsteps stopped. She looked up then and saw it was the man from the bus. He had paused too, and was now busily lighting a cigarette. A stiff breeze was making it difficult and he had to cup his hand and light match after match to get his cigarette alight.

Had he really wanted a cigarette, or was he waiting for her to go on?

She set off again, more quickly this time, waiting for the corner of Palmerston Terrace to come into view. Palmerston Terrace was a short, quiet street, tree-lined, with its own private residents' garden. You had no business to go down there unless you lived there or in Athelstan Gardens, which led off it. Jean turned down Palmerston Terrace and a moment later the footsteps behind her turned too.

She felt a moment of panic. Should she run? She was already walking fast; he would know by now that she was on to him. There had been a knife attack on a young girl in Sloane Square only two weeks ago—a man, or two men, had followed the girl home from the bus one evening and accosted her with a knife, threatened her, dragged her into an laneway and attacked her. The girl had survived. The men hadn't been caught yet.

There was a policeman standing on the corner of Athelstan Gardens.

Jean swerved towards him, her heart thudding painfully in her chest. The policeman stood in a circle of light cast by the streetlight and watched impassively as she careered towards him out of the darkness. At the last moment he raised a curious eyebrow and took a step towards her.

'Evening, madam. Ev'thing all right?'

Jean stopped before him and paused to catch her breath. He was a young constable, just a boy really, his face fresh and clean-shaven, his frame tall but lanky. The huge black dome on his head looked outsized and almost alien. But he was a policeman.

'I don't know,' she gasped, looking over her shoulder. 'I think that man's followin' me.'

They both looked as the young man crossed over Palmerston Terrace and headed off down Athelstan Gardens. He looked up briefly and appeared to take in both policeman and Jean in one expressionless glance. His step didn't falter and he was soon lost in the darkness.

'D'you know 'im, then? This fella?' said the policeman.

'No. Never seen 'im before. Except he was on my bus. Got on at Knightsbridge, he did. Sat in front of me, then got off at the same stop. He's been about three foot behind me all the way from the station.'

The policeman nodded, though whether this was because he fully understood her predicament and sympathised or because he thought she was a hysterical young girl who had read too many cheap thrillers she couldn't tell.

'Well, looks like he's gone now. Want me to go and see where he's gone?'

Jean nodded and she waited as the constable loped off down Athelstan Gardens after the young man in the hat. She shivered. She was alone again and it was silent and deserted here on the corner. And standing here beneath the streetlight anyone could see her. Suppose the man had doubled back?

He didn't look the sort to carry a knife. But what did the sort to carry a knife look like? The sorts of kids she had just seen hanging around in Wapping, most probably, but they would stick out round here like a dustman at a Buckingham Palace garden party.

She could always run into someone's yard if it came to it—though all the houses looked cold and solidly barred against just such an event. And how much would someone in one of these houses want to help her?

'All safe,' called the young policeman, emerging from the gloom with a cheery smile. 'Followed 'im all the way and he went into one of them houses at the end of the street.' He looked back over his shoulder thoughtfully. 'Pretty sure we was called to that same house, once. Few months back. Think it was that one, anyway. They all look alike to me.'

Jean took a deep breath and suddenly felt angry because she'd been so frightened and just because one man had turned out not to be a knife-wielding madman didn't mean the next one would.

'Well, that's all right then. Thank you,' she said to the policeman, as he seemed to be expecting it.

'Not from round 'ere, are ya?' he said, peering at her in the half light.

Jean hitched her handbag up over her shoulder and admitted that no, she was not from round here.

'I live 'ere, though,' she added, just in case he was implying she didn't belong here.

'Want me to escort you 'ome?' he suggested, and at once she wondered if he'd suggested this because he didn't believe her story, or because he thought she might break in to one of the rich houses and steal something?

'No, thank you, I can find me own way.'

'Suit yourself. But I'm often here. This is my beat. PC Clarkson.'

Jean nodded and hurried off.

It was freezing. Spring surely wasn't that far off and yet the tips of the branches on the cherry trees were lined with frost. Her face, despite the cold, was damp with perspiration and she could feel the moisture quickly turning to ice.

Escort her home, indeed! Fine impression she'd make turning up at the Wallises' house after her afternoon off with a policeman at her elbow!

She fumbled for her key and pushed it with shivering fingers into the front door lock. A blast of heat hit her as she stumbled inside. It was wicked how hot they kept the house—rooms that weren't even used were heated so that it was almost like summer!

She removed her coat and hat and scarf and hung them up in the cupboard. There were voices upstairs.

'And how does it change *anything*?'

It sounded like Mr Wallis.

Jean paused, halfway up the stairs, but there came no reply, so she continued upwards. The drawing room door was ajar and beyond it she could see Mr Wallis standing over by the fireplace, tall and erect, his hands clenched behind his back, his face slightly flushed. She paused. If she moved he would notice her. She had never seen him angry before, never seen him anything but affable, occasionally friendly, often distracted.

Now she saw there was a second man in the drawing room, and it was him! The young man from the bus, sitting there as bold as brass, in the Wallises' drawing room! He was still wearing his beige overcoat, but he had removed his hat, which he held tightly in his hands, and for the first time she could see his face.

It was the face of the man who had embraced Mrs Wallis in the garden.

Yes, of course it was. Stupid not to have realised before. Mrs Wallis's lover! Come to confront her husband—or be confronted by him.

The rasp of a cigarette lighter and the abrupt and unmistakable waft of a du Maurier indicated the two men were not alone.

'For God's sake, Cecil. Everything *has* changed. That is the point.' It was Mrs Wallis, her presence obscured till now by the door.

'The law may have changed, but people's opinions have not,' replied Mr Wallis, to which Mrs Wallis responded with an angry noise.

'The law reflects public opinion. The law is made *by* the people,' she explained patiently.

Jean considered this. That the law could be a thing made by the people was a strange idea. A rich person's idea.

'Look here, Wallis. I'm not naïve enough to think all people's opinions have changed overnight,' said the young man, speaking for the first time, and he had a BBC voice, the same voice as Mr and Mrs Wallis.

'The fact remains,' the young man continued, 'I shall no longer need to remain … incognito.'

'You mean to announce your return in *The Times*, then?' said Mr Wallis.

'No, of course he doesn't,' said Mrs Wallis impatiently. 'He simply means he no longer has to risk imprisonment. He can apply for this certificate of protection.'

A certificate of protection? Could an adulterer get such a thing?

'Well, I am sorry, but I am unable to offer you any assistance,' said Cecil with finality.

They had come to the cuckolded husband for help? Jean almost felt sorry for him.

'You are perfectly able to assist, Cecil,' retorted Mrs Wallis. 'You are simply choosing not to.'

There was a silence. The clock on the mantelpiece ticked loudly.

'And what sort of firm do you think will want to take him on, eh?' said Mr Wallis at last. 'What kind of employer, when there are good men out there who have served their country?'

Inside the drawing room there was a thud as though something had fallen over, footsteps muffled by the thick carpet, the rasp of a match being struck.

'I'm sorry, Freddie, but surely you must see how it is?' he continued.

'I see exactly how it is,' replied the lover—Freddie—in a strange voice, almost bored. 'Must have been tough for you during the war, old man, going off to the office each day while every other fellow was on foreign soil fighting for his damned life.'

'That's enough!' replied Cecil sharply. 'I refuse to discuss this further. You will kindly leave my house immediately.'

Jean moved through the open door of the breakfast room and closed it behind her just as the drawing room door opened. She stood perfectly still as angry footsteps passed her, then hurried down the stairs. A moment later other, lighter, footsteps followed.

'*Freddie*! Freddie, *wait*!' It was Mrs Wallis. 'For God's sake, don't be such an idiot!'

'I'm sorry, Harri,' the young man replied from some way down the stairs. 'I refuse to be insulted by—by *him*. This was a mistake—a stupid, blasted mistake. Lord knows how I let you talk me into it.'

'Please,' said Mrs Wallis, 'just—just telephone me tomorrow when you are little calmer.' Jean couldn't hear the man's reply, but a moment later she heard Mrs Wallis return to the drawing room.

Jean opened the breakfast room door and peered out. The coast was clear. She ventured out.

'Well, are you satisfied?' demanded Mrs Wallis indistinctly. She had closed the drawing room door after her this time. Jean found herself glued to the same spot on the carpet.

'I *cannot* believe you put me in such a—a *compromising* position!' said Mr Wallis.

'You feel compromised, do you? This is Freddie's life we are discussing, not some awkward social faux pas.'

'For God's sake, how can you be so damned naïve, Harriet? I know he's your brother, but you can't let that blind you to the facts.'

Her brother.

'I understand the facts of this situation perfectly, Cecil. Do not patronise me.'

'All I am saying, Harriet, is that public opinion has not changed. It was the same after the last war, no matter what you may think, no matter what law the government may have passed—and, for God's sake, if it wasn't Coronation year do you think there would ever have *been* an amnesty?'

The amnesty. The young man—Mrs Wallis's brother—was a deserter. Jean stepped back from the room. She had no desire to hear any more.

'It would be so easy for you to help him,' said Mrs Wallis indistinctly. 'All he needs is a job in some dull little insurance firm, some boring city bank. All he needs is a reference, a word from you. Is that so much to ask?'

There was a silence—thick and heavy. It was broken by a slow intake of breath.

'What kind of a man *are* you?'

'The kind of man who has standards, Harriet. Moral standards. And I will not compromise those standards. I simply *will not*.'

'For God's *sake!*'

The door opened and had Mrs Wallis turned right rather than gone down the stairs she would have seen the nanny disappearing into the breakfast room at some speed. In another moment the front door opened and closed with a slam.

Jean waited behind the door. Mrs Wallis's brother was a deserter. Well, and so were hundreds, thousands of other men. Everyone knew someone whose son or friend or cousin had done a bunk. The streets round home were crawling with them: men who only emerged at night and who scuttled about with their collars turned up and one eye always behind them. But those men were just kids, boys from poor families, from the slums. Not Freddie. He was one of Them. You never heard of one of Them deserting.

But why should *he* get an amnesty? Did any of those dead young men get another chance? Did the families killed in the Blitz get a second go?

The drawing room door opened and Mr Wallis went into his study and closed the door behind him, and from the shadows Jean stood and watched.

And what had Mr Wallis done while other folk risked their lives? He had worked in an office. Sent others to their deaths and gone home for his tea.

Chapter Eighteen

MARCH 1953

A black cab drew up outside Cecil's office just off Chancery Lane and Harriet paid the driver and got out, closing the door behind her and smoothing down her dress. It was a pleasant spring morning. One almost didn't need a coat. A scattering of early blossoms was visible on the trees in the little park opposite. A young couple sat on the bench in the park laughing and tearing off pieces of bread and tossing them to the pigeons.

Harriet pulled out her cigarette case, took out a cigarette and lit it carefully.

She had found Freddie a position. It hadn't been easy. Three weeks of masterfully arranged dinner parties with some of the dullest men in England and their dreadfully dreary wives, of opportune conversations during intervals at the theatre, of sitting through the most ghastly charity lunches and writing fat cheques for everyone's pet charity from Yugoslavian orphans to elderly pit ponies. And the phone calls! There had been too many to count. But it had finally paid off. She had, to put it somewhat vulgarly, 'hit the jackpot'.

Now all she needed was to find a way to convince Cecil that he should help.

In the three weeks since Freddie had come to the house and left in such a fury she had seen him only once and that an unsatisfactory meeting at a café in Baker Street. Freddie had been sullen, taciturn. Angry at her, it seemed, for the world's condemnation, for Cecil's belligerence, for her own belief in him. He had been restless, had talked of leaving, of returning to Canada. It was certainly what Cecil wanted. But why must they all do what Cecil wanted? It was Freddie's life, after all. She had come away angry herself, at Cecil, at the world, at Freddie.

But last night, and from an unlikely source, something had come up. They had dined at White Gables, the Richmond home of Nobby Caruthers. Nobby and Cecil were both VPS Old Boys, though Nobby was some years Cecil's senior. Now for the most part retired, Caruthers sat on the board of Home Counties Equity and Insurance in the City. The dinner—an annual affair made up of retired bankers and stockbrokers and their wives—was, generally speaking, as dull as ditchwater, but with the men finishing their port and cigars in the other room, Harriet had found herself seated next to Trixie Caruthers, Nobby's wife.

'My brother, Freddie, has recently returned from overseas,' she had remarked. 'He was in Canada, you know? Did rather well. But now he's returned and is looking for a suitable position. His area is finance. Accounting, administration—well, one is never entirely clear about these things, but it's all money, isn't it?'

It had been a desperate gambit, not to mention an appalling lie to her host, who would surely see right through it. What kind of person, after all, returned from overseas having done 'rather well' and yet had no position to go to?

Yet Trixie had responded with a smile and a pat of her hand. 'My dear, I'm sure if your brother is as good as you say he is, Nobby would be delighted to help him out. Why don't I ask him if he is agreeable to a meeting?'

And there it was. So very simple in the end. Trixie had been true to her word, had telephoned that morning to report that Nobby was more than happy to meet Harriet's brother and that the brother in question should telephone Nobby's office to arrange a meeting. Harriet had telephoned Freddie at once.

'Caruthers?' Freddie had said suspiciously down the telephone. 'There was a Caruthers made a big splash in New York before the war. That him?'

'I think so. He's semi-retired now, but he still holds a fair bit of influence. Well, the way Cecil and all the others kow-tow to him one would think he was the chairman of the Bank of England.'

'And you went to him cap in hand, did you, begging for a job for the wayward younger brother?'

'For God's sake, it wasn't like that, Freddie. Trixie, his wife, mentioned Caruthers had just given a job to Phyllis Bing's ghastly eldest boy and how he was always scratching around trying to find good men. It just seemed the perfect opportunity. And once you're in, in a place like that, well, that's it. You're set for life. No one gives a damn where you were before.'

'You mean no one gives a damn what I did in the war? It's the first thing they look at—a chap's blasted war record. It's no good, Harri. People like that—places like that—simply can't see beyond it.'

'Cecil and Caruthers were at the same school. A word from Cecil, a character reference, call it whatever you like—and you're in.'

There had been a silence.

'You can't seriously believe Cecil would give it?'

'He'll have to.'

On the corner of Chancery Lane Harriet drew heavily on her cigarette, thinking hard.

She hadn't rung to let Cecil know she was coming.

But no matter. She cast the cigarette into the gutter and walked up to the front entrance of Empire and Colonial's head office.

The building was a large, modern tower block, all glass and concrete. Utterly bleak, of course. Cecil's old office in Moorgate had been a marvellous old place, originally a Masonic hall, all coats of arms and gargoyles and intricate little cornices. Over two hundred years old. But an incendiary in the building next door in early '41 had rendered it unsafe and the place had been abandoned. Empire and Colonial had operated out of temporary offices near Liverpool Street for some years, finally moving into these new premises off Chancery Lane in late '49. Functional, that was about the only word one could use to describe this building. It was as though the war had made everyone too wary of wasting time and money putting up something rather grand or beautiful that a rocket could destroy in a matter of seconds.

She went briskly up the front steps and pushed her way through the ghastly revolving doorway. (Really! Such doors appeared to have been designed purely to repel visitors. And Lord knew, Empire and Colonial could ill afford to repel anyone.)

'May I help you, madam?' said the receptionist, a pert young girl in a steel grey blouse and horn-rimmed glasses. Her manner was slightly confronting, slightly hostile, utterly efficient. Harriet took an immediate dislike to her.

'Yes, you may.' She paused to put a cigarette in her mouth. 'Do you have a light?'

The receptionist raised one eyebrow a fraction of an inch then reached beneath her desk. She pulled out a lighter and silently lit Harriet's cigarette.

'Good. Thank you. Now, I should like to see Mr Cecil Wallis, please.'

'Certainly.' The girl was at once all smiling efficiency. 'Do you have an appointment?'

'No.'

The smiling efficiency disappeared, replaced by cool impenetrability. 'Then I shall need to consult with Miss James, Mr Wallis's secretary,' she said, as though she had little expectation of such a course of action actually achieving anything.

'You do that,' Harriet blew a stream of smoke from her nostrils upwards into the atrium.

The receptionist picked up the receiver of her telephone with some importance. 'And what name shall I give?'

'Your own, I would imagine. Then you may inform Miss James that Mrs Cecil Wallis is here.'

The receptionist reddened and asked no further questions.

It had been two or more years since she had last visited Cecil at his office. She had visited the old Moorgate office many times during those first years of marriage, when the children were very young. They had gone to Cecil's club for lunch or taken sandwiches into the park. But it had been years since they had eaten sandwiches in the park together.

She took the lift to the tenth floor where the carpet was a bilious pea-green and the walls lined with self-important portraits of stuffy elderly Victorians sporting absurd whiskers. There were four secretaries stationed here, four versions of the one model: fifty-ish, grey hair pulled into a severe bun, glasses hanging from cords around their necks, stiff white blouses and pastel woollen cardigans.

'Miss James. How lovely. Are you well?'

'I am Miss Stuart,' came the rather frosty reply. 'Miss James is over there.'

'I do beg your pardon. Miss James. How lovely. Are you well?'

'Quite well, Mrs Wallis, thank you for inquiring.'

Miss James was perhaps a little older than her three colleagues, her bun perhaps a little more severe, the pencils in her jar arranged just a little more precisely—graded, no doubt, by height and colour.

'Mr Wallis has an Indian gentleman with him just at the moment,' Miss James explained, 'a rather important meeting, though I'm sure it won't go on too much longer. Would you care to take a seat?'

From this Mrs Wallis was to infer that she ranked somewhere beneath unknown Indian gentlemen in the office pecking order.

'Yes, very well.' Harriet sat down on the over-stuffed red leather chair indicated by Miss James and slowly crossed her legs. She drew on her cigarette and exhaled noiselessly. Miss James smothered a slight cough.

Minutes passed. Miss James completed a page of typing and pulled the page from the typewriter with a rip, then placed it on top of a pile of similar pages. She knocked them together into one neat pile and placed them in a tray marked 'Out' with a satisfied look. Having completed this task she pushed her chair back and stood up.

'I'm just taking this in to Mr Wallis now,' she explained, indicating the documents. 'I shall inform him you are here.'

She emerged a moment or two later, closing the door behind her, made her way back to her desk, sat down, rearranged her skirt and finally turned towards Harriet.

'I have informed Mr Wallis of your presence, Mrs Wallis—'

'I'm most grateful.'

Miss James produced a tight smile. 'And he apologises for keeping you waiting and asks that you wait another ten minutes while he concludes his meeting and makes an important telephone call.'

Before Harriet could make a suitable reply, the office door opened and the Indian gentleman came out. He was a distinguished-looking man, very tall and very dark, white tunic and trousers, a snow-white turban with a delicate wispy feather at the crown. And patent leather shoes—Italian, by the look of them—a rolled black umbrella and a smart little briefcase. He paused at Miss James's desk and bowed deeply.

'Thanking you, dear lady, for your most generous hospitality,' he said in a deep musical voice.

Miss James flushed and simpered.

'Oh, my pleasure, Mr Gupta. Any time, I'm sure.'

Mr Gupta inclined his head, then nodded briefly at the other secretaries, noticed Harriet and nodded at her too, for good measure, then strode from the room.

Perhaps Mr Gupta was employed at the Bombay office. His dark colouring suggested he came from the south of India, Madras or Mysore or Bangalore perhaps, and Harriet was reminded of the maharaja who had ruled a state neighbouring Father's district. He had the same bearing, the same extreme politeness. But this man was darker, much darker, more like the coolies you saw piled three deep on the roof of the trains that travelled from Delhi to Bombay. She had travelled on that train herself once.

Harriet abruptly stood up and Miss James looked at her.

'I have decided to wait outside. Please tell my husband I shall wait in the park opposite.'

'Of course,' said Miss James and she looked as though she would have liked to add something further but Harriet had picked up her handbag and left the office.

The park was busier now. The young couple had gone, replaced by groups of tourists studying guides and maps. The pigeons were still there and the only vacant bench was spotted with their droppings. Harriet found a clean patch on the bench and sat down. Her cigarette had expired and she tossed it on the ground and reached for another. She could see Mr Gupta standing on the pavement waving his umbrella at a passing cab. The cab pulled up and the Indian stood and waited as though expecting the door to be opened for him. After an exchange with the driver Mr Gupta opened the door himself and climbed in. The cab drove off.

Freddie. And now this Indian man, this Mr Gupta.

It was important not to think about that train journey.

Two small children ran into the park, a girl and a boy, perhaps nine and five, the girl older, leading her little brother importantly by the hand, the boy following demurely, trusting her to lead him safely through the park.

She remembered the train journey.

The locals had ridden on the roof of the train all the way from Jhelum to Bombay and eight-year-old Freddie had been amazed.

'But they won't fall off, will they, Mr Stephens?' he had asked over and over, and Mr Stephens, who had been in India a month, had shaken his head and said, 'No, Freddie, of course they won't. These chaps are used to it.'

The train journey to Bombay went via Delhi and took two days, so Father had reserved sleeping compartments for them all. He had been unable to accompany them to the train station and Mother was too unwell to move from the veranda. So they had all stood outside the house and made a rather sombre and restrained farewell. Mother had said, You'll look after Freddie, dear, won't you? He is in your care.

Mohammed had driven them in a bullock cart to the station, found them their compartment, stowed the luggage and then waited patiently for the train to depart.

'Goodbye, Mohammed,' Freddie had called excitedly again and again from the window and as the train had pulled away from the station Mohammed had finally raised a hand in farewell and stood there, unmoving, a slowly disappearing figure, still as a statue on the platform. Harriet had raised her hand once and let it fall onto her lap. Someone one had known forever, who had always been there, was now disappearing into the distance.

They had never seen him again.

The luggage had become lost almost immediately and Mr Stephens had remonstrated with the train guard and the porters, and finally the luggage had been returned to them, some hours into their journey.

'Absolutely *bloody* outrageous,' he had exclaimed, and Harriet had stared at him in shock.

'Not in front of Freddie,' she had told him and he had blushed.

'Well, but *really*. These chaps are nothing but nasty little thieves. Pretending to help a fellow, wearing a uniform to try and fool one they're all above board and tickety-boo, then one hands over some local currency and hey presto! One's luggage miraculously reappears. It's a damned scam ... Oh, I'm sorry ...'

They were leaving India, going Home to England, though neither she nor Freddie had ever been to England before. They were supposed to be travelling with Mother, but with Mother too ill to travel Mr Stephens would be escorting them to Bombay instead, and putting them on the ship to England. And Mr Stephens, who had been in India for a month, had been angry about the luggage.

Harriet hadn't minded about the luggage. Things went missing all the time. One expected it. This was India, after all, as everyone always said—as though India was a magical land where solid objects simply vanished into thin air, never to be seen again. Mr Stephens seemed not to be aware of this.

She and Freddie had sat in the open doorway of the train carriage, their legs dangling and the wind blowing in their faces, and Mr Stephens had said, 'Come away from there, it's not safe.' But of *course* it was safe, everyone did it, and the trains travelled so slowly one could practically jump out and run alongside it. And some people did just that. It was terrifically hot and the carriage was unbearable, so really they were forced to sit by the door. Mr Stephens had softened a bit after that and had come and joined them in the doorway, and he had told Freddie about the voyage out. He had come out from Liverpool, he explained, then Marseilles, then Port Said, then through the Suez Canal. It had taken four weeks. Freddie had been very interested because of course they were about to make the same voyage themselves, only in reverse, and he had asked Mr Stephens all sorts of questions about the ship, the cabins, what the crew wore, what food was served, and he'd got very excited when Mr Stephens had said there was a swimming pool on the deck.

'And what will England be like?' Freddie had asked, and Mr Stephens had got all peculiar and seemed not to hear the question so that Freddie had had to ask it again. Eventually he had answered, 'Well, Freddie. It's green fields and beautiful villages and lovely old trees and wonderful old cities. It's quite the most marvellous place in the world, my boy,' and Freddie had said, 'But there are trees and fields and villages and cities *here*,' and Mr Stephens had replied that that was hardly the same thing. Freddie had asked why was it not the same thing? and Mr Stephens had looked annoyed and had stood up and said he would see about tiffin.

Mohammed had packed them all off with tiffin trays for the journey and Mr Stephens now broke these open. They had eaten in companionable silence and when the train had pulled into some tiny halt in the middle of nowhere, small children had crowded around the doorway begging for food. Mr Stephens had shooed them away and, encouraged by this, they had run enthusiastically alongside the train as it pulled out of the station.

At last night had come and the mosquitoes had swarmed around them. Freddie had fallen asleep against Mr Stephens's shoulder and Mr Stephens had stood up saying, Up we go, lifting Freddie up in his arms and carrying him to the sleeping compartment. There were nets over the bunks, but the mosquitoes were relentless, and Mr Stephens could be heard in the next compartment swatting and cursing and twisting around and opening and closing the window.

In the morning the train had stopped for hours at an important junction and they had got out and stretched their legs, walking up and down the platform as railway staff swarmed around and all over the engine, refuelling and decoupling cars and coupling other cars.

They had eaten their breakfast tiffin sitting on the platform, and suddenly the whistle had blown and they had had only seconds to scramble back on board before the train left.

Freddie and Mr Stephens were the best of friends by this stage and at one point when Freddie had needed to visit the lavatory Mr Stephens had offered to take him. Freddie had returned red faced and silent and Mr Stephens had explained in an aside that he had had a little accident. That was typical of Freddie, who tended to get over-excited; Mother was always saying it.

They had stopped at another big station and as it was lunchtime they had disembarked and had a rather splendid luncheon at the station restaurant before the train moved off again.

'Really!' Mr Stephens had exclaimed as the train had eventually set off once more, 'It's a wonder these trains ever reach their destination.' But as their ship wasn't scheduled to sail until the ten o'clock tide that evening Harriet couldn't see that it mattered if they spent an hour at lunch. And anyway, it meant they could stretch their legs some more.

Freddie had said little since his accident and had picked at his food and Mr Stephens had jollied him along and played the fool a bit to help him over his embarrassment.

The train had trundled on and on across endless plains, jerking to a halt every now and again to let people on and off, stopping sometimes when there wasn't even a station, and eventually she and Freddie had slept. Mr Stephens had said he would stay awake 'to keep watch'. When Harriet had jerked awake an hour later she saw that he had dozed off too. As the afternoon had rushed towards the tropical night and the sun had plunged into the western horizon ahead of them, they had approached Bombay.

Mr Stephens had woken and they had had tea.

'Not far now,' he had observed.

Bombay, it turned out, was an island, connected to the mainland on its northernmost tip by a causeway. Mr Stephens, who had spent a day here a month before, was an expert on Bombay.

'You know, Freddie, if they knocked down the causeway, Bombay would float off into the Arabian Sea,' he had explained solemnly as the train rattled across the narrow strip of land.

'No, it wouldn't,' replied Freddie, who was old enough to understand the nature of some things but not yet old enough to appreciate Mr Stephens's feeble attempt at humour.

The city was at the far end of the island and the train had ground its way painfully southwards, the island gradually narrowing to a point until they were able to see the sea from both sides of the train. On the east, Mr Stephens had explained, was Bombay Harbour, and on the west, Back Bay, and beyond that the Arabian Sea. The train had finally trundled into the grandly named Victoria Railway Terminus at a little after five o'clock in the afternoon.

'Come along, then,' Mr Stephens had said, shepherding them off the train and flagging down a porter to take the luggage.

How she and Freddie had gazed about them in amazement at the railway station in which they now found themselves! It had been a fantastical place of domes and fascinating turrets and coloured glass windows that made one think more of a church than a station. Outside the station were ornate gardens and wide avenues and prettily dressed ladies and gentlemen wandered back and forth beneath white parasols. The harbour was directly ahead but the P&O landing place, explained Mr Stephens, was further south. Harriet had grabbed Freddie's hand and they had climbed into a taxi and let themselves be taken to the docks.

The journey to the dock had been a slow stop-and-start affair and the ornate gardens and wide avenues outside the station had rapidly turned into a chaos of people teeming in every direction in every sort of dress, selling every sort of wares, riding every mode of transport and speaking in every language. The taxi had negotiated an overturned cart, then a fresh bullock carcass spurting blood in a wide crimson arc and finally a man with a bald head and red eyes who had leapt in front of the taxi shouting and waving his arms at them, his arms had ended in two shiney stumps.

'All right, it's quite all right,' Mr Stephens had assured them, shielding Freddie's eyes. 'We're quite safe in here,' and indeed the taxi driver had steered a path through the chaos without batting an eye. Eventually the hull of a vast ocean liner had come into view at the end of a street—the *Tiberius*!—and they had been able to smell the sea, to taste it on their lips. Seagulls had dipped and swooped and shrieked and coolies had run this way and that carrying vast trunks and boxes of luggage.

'Here we are,' Mr Stephens had announced with some satisfaction, rapping the driver on the shoulder with his umbrella as they pulled up alongside the ship.

That umbrella. It had been a large black affair and someone in England must have told Mr Stephens about the monsoons as he never let it leave his side. He used it now to direct the unloading of luggage at the dockside and its stowage in their cabin. They had climbed excitedly up the steep gangway, a sailor in a white uniform had saluted them and Mr Stephens had shown him their tickets. They had inspected the cabin, the lavatory and the beds and opened all sorts of cleverly hidden little cupboards and drawers and found everything to their satisfaction.

'Now,' Mr Stephens had said, with the air of a job well done, 'you don't sail until ten o'clock this evening, so what do you say to tea and cakes at the yacht club? My treat.'

Freddie had sulked and said 'No' and Harriet had reprimanded him for his rudeness, pointing out that Mr Stephens had been extremely kind to them, and she had accepted the invitation on both their behalves. They had disembarked once more and walked along the harbour wall in the quickly thickening darkness.

His mission now complete, Mr Stephens had been in an enthusiastic and expansive mood, pointing out first the Gateway of India ('Built in 1911 to commemorate the King's visit') and then the magnificent Taj Mahal Hotel.

'Isn't it magnificent?' he said, indicating the vast building on their left, and they had nodded in agreement.

Housed beside the hotel was the splendid Royal Bombay Yacht Club in a building almost as grand. They had sat at a table on the lawn overlooking the water and the crowd of gently bobbing yachts. A white-coated Indian with a wide cummerbund had served them tea and Battenburg cake from silver trays. Mr Stephens himself had poured the tea.

Harriet had found it hard to concentrate or to eat. There had been so much to see, to take in—all the sounds, the sights, the smells. And she had had butterflies in her tummy at the impending departure. It was past six o'clock, which was very late for tea, almost Freddie's bedtime, but everything, it had appeared, was now upside-down.

Mr Stephens had done most of the talking and had spent some time explaining to Freddie how he had gone to Oxford—he had made a point of mentioning which college—and how, because he had studied exceptionally hard, he had been one of only a few accepted into the Indian Civil Service. This had entailed a gruelling year of extensive training in Chatham before he had received his posting. Freddie had listened in polite silence before announcing that he intended to join the Indian Army and fight on the northwest frontier. Mr Stephens had replied—a little crossly it had seemed to Harriet—that of course we all had our different skills and destinies and that the Indian Army was always keen to recruit new officers.

A silence had fallen.

'Well, time we were off,' Mr Stephens had announced at last.

The dense tropical night had long fallen when she and Freddie had made their way back to their cabin and Mr Stephens was gone. Freddie had slept almost at once and Harriet had sat by herself listening as the mooring ropes were untied and the ship's funnel boomed over and over. Most of the passengers had crowded the ship's side to wave goodbye to friends and family, but Harriet had preferred to stay in the cabin with Freddie.

She had pulled out a sheet of paper from the little desk and begun her first letter.

Dearest Mother and Father,

I hope you are both well and that Mother is feeling much better. I am writing from the cabin of the Tiberius as it disembarks. A lot of people are up on deck waving and cheering and dear Mr Stephens is standing at the dockside waving to us. He was so kind to bring us here and he looked after both Freddie and I most attentively ...

The letter she had received in reply from Father, two months later, had reached her during her first term at Maldeville. The letter had been to announce Mother's death some weeks earlier.

She had never returned to India. Father had retired five years later and installed himself in the flat in Belgravia, and neither she nor Freddie nor Simon had ever visited Mother's grave. India was full of European graves. Or perhaps, now, it wasn't. Perhaps many had been destroyed during Independence and the Partition. Either way, everything had changed. There was no reason to go back, nothing to go back to.

And here was Cecil coming towards her across the small park, side-stepping a stubborn pigeon.

'Harriet,' he said as he approached and she was acutely aware they had hardly exchanged two words since she had brought Freddie to the house three weeks ago. Cecil paused at the bench upon which she was sitting, surveyed it dubiously, pulled out a handkerchief and gave the bench a cursory flick, then sat down, lifting his trousers at the knee at the last moment. He produced the bright smile he gave when he wanted to appear relaxed and wasn't.

'What brings you here?' he said.

He knew of, course, hence the smile. In the car on the drive home from White Gables she had mentioned the conversation with Trixie, and he had said nothing. He said nothing now.

Harriet smiled suddenly. 'Cecil, do you remember that little park outside the old Moorgate office? Where we went for sandwiches sometimes in your lunch hour, and that little man was often there feeding that bird. What was it? Some kind of parrot?'

She glanced sideways and saw him smile, despite himself.

'A cockatoo. White with a sort of yellow quiff on its head.'

'That was it. How it used to squawk!'

They sat for a moment in silence, remembering—not the squawking cockatoo but the young couple sharing their packet of sandwiches side by side on a bench so many years ago.

'I used to bring you lemon curd in your sandwiches, do you remember? And it must have been months before you could bring yourself to tell me you didn't like lemon curd.'

Cecil smiled. 'Still ate them though, didn't I?'

They watched the two children playing, the girl and her little brother.

'Cecil, Freddie has a good chance of a position with Home Counties.' Well, there was no use delaying it. 'Nobby Caruthers has agreed to a meeting. This is Freddie's chance to—'

She paused. She had lived with Freddie's desertion for so long it seemed odd to imagine it finally being all over.

'His chance to start again. To fix everything.'

Cecil remained silent. A pigeon walked over, its head bobbing in step with its feet. It was a dirty, scruffy-looking specimen, but so were most of its fellows. Cecil joggled his foot at the pigeon and it swayed away and set off in another direction.

'By which you mean,' he said at last, 'that this is *our* chance to fix everything.'

'Yes, if you like.' Harriet narrowed her eyes as she drew on her cigarette. He was going to make this as hard for her as he could. But if that meant he would do it, so be it.

'And never mind that, by lying to Caruthers in this way, we— by which I mean, *I*—would be compromising my own moral standards.'

Harriet closed her eyes for a moment. Then she turned to him.

'Cecil, I am asking you, politely, as your wife—the mother of your children—to put in a good word for my brother. Is that so onerous?'

She had spoken more sharply than she intended, but his suggestion that what she was asking was somehow immoral, was beyond the pale.

A silence settled over them and lengthened uncomfortably.

'What you are asking me to do is unfair.' Cecil sat very upright on the bench, looking straight ahead at the buses turning into Holborn and Fleet Street. His voice was as calm and level as always. Harriet sat up straight beside him, her eyes fixed firmly on the traffic.

'Unfair?' she repeated quite pleasantly. 'Cecil, Freddie is my brother.'

'Of course. And I am your husband. The father of your children.'

A well-dressed nanny turned into the little park pushing a large black pram and leading a small child by the hand. They stopped at the statue in the centre of the park and the small child began chasing the pigeons. The nanny lit a cigarette and rocked the pram with her foot.

'Does Felicity ever come to you when she's in trouble?' said Harriet after a moment.

'What does Felicity have to do with this?'

'Does she ever come to you for help?'

She could feel Cecil stir uneasily beside her.

'Naturally, were she ever in trouble, I should like to believe that she felt she could always turn to me for assistance, yes. However, as she never—'

'You're wrong, Cecil. She came to me. She was in trouble. She's pregnant. She didn't know what to do so she came to me.'

The small child slid over and began to howl, and the nanny hastily put out her cigarette and knelt down beside him, asking soothing questions and rubbing the afflicted limb.

Beside her Cecil was silent and Harriet knew she should feel bad; after all, she had betrayed a confidence, and on top of that she had implied that she had, in fact, come to Felicity's aid when she had not. But she didn't feel bad. She felt angry.

'Naturally, Felicity would know there was nothing I could do to help,' Cecil replied at last, his voice quiet. 'Not in that kind of situation. What could I do? I know nothing of such things. That's a woman's world.'

'And this is a man's world, Cecil. Will you help?'

After a long moment he nodded.

Chapter Nineteen

MARCH 1953

'It's Nanny Peters!' shrieked Anne, pointing an astonished finger at a woman on the far side of the playground.

Anne was standing at the top of the slide where she had lately taken to presiding, perhaps because it provided such an excellent vantage point over the rest of the playground in the park they occasionally visited after school. If other, smaller, children attempted to use the slide she could usually frighten them off with a look, but she was not averse to using physical persuasion if required.

Jean, watching from a nearby bench, usually found it best to let nature take its course. But at these words, she got at once to her feet and looked to where Anne was pointing. A young woman in a long raincoat, with a green silk headscarf tied around her head and a cigarette in the corner of her mouth, was standing beside a small child on a red tricycle. She looked up as Anne waved and called to her, but she not did wave back.

'Anne, come down from there. It's time we went back home,' Jean ordered, beckoning to her, but Anne was already scrambling backwards down the slide, thrusting another child bodily out of the way. Jean swooped to rescue the child—a little girl in pigtails who was too stunned to burst into tears—and placed her on the ground.

'Look, it's Nanny Peters,' said Anne again and set off towards the woman in the raincoat.

'*Anne!*'

Jean started after her, then hesitated. Ought she to follow or remain where she was? She couldn't think. She would wait here behind the slide, almost, in fact, hidden by it, and eventually Anne would return, would come looking for her and they could leave.

'Nanny! Nanny Peters!' Anne called again, and this time, Anne having skidded to a halt in front of her, the woman acknowledged her.

'Oh, it's you, is it?' the woman remarked with a single jerk of her head and without removing her cigarette from her mouth.

'What are you doing here?' Anne demanded. 'We were told you had gone to Leicester.' Her tone was accusing, as though 'gone to Leicester' was a euphemism for prison or a home for wayward girls.

'Aye, I did go to Leicester, but I come back, didn't I?' was all the reply Nanny Peters seemed prepared to give.

'Oh.' Anne was clearly a little perturbed by this. 'But why didn't you come back to *us*, then?'

Nanny Peters raised her eyebrows at this suggestion, which seemed to strike her as amusing. Then she looked away, over Anne's head, and at once saw Jean, despite Jean being largely obscured by the slide.

'Oh, I remember you,' she called over. 'So you followed my suggestion then? Bet you regretted it soon enough.'

Jean gave a non-committal smile.

'Anne, come on, it's time we went home,' she called again.

Nanny Peters had recognised her.

They had met once before, months earlier, on a warm autumnal day last September. On that day a woman with a small child had emerged from one of the large houses at the far end of Athelstan Gardens and, after a moment of hesitation, Jean had followed them.

The woman had not looked at all how Jean had pictured someone from such a house would look. She had sported a fuzz of peroxided hair in a very tight perm, a figure-hugging blouse of some cheap, clinging material, and lipstick so vivid you could see it from the other side of the street. And she had been young, perhaps a year or two older than Jean herself. The child that had accompanied her was around eight or nine, a girl with very straight brown hair in two demure pigtails and wearing a tunic—the sort of tunic children who went to exclusive private schools might wear.

They had walked up Palmerston Terrace, crossed Old Brompton Road and come here, to the park, and Jean had followed them.

At the park the child had immediately disengaged herself from the woman and marched over to the swings where she had sat sullenly kicking the dirt before picking a fight with another, much smaller child who had run off in tears. The woman with the tight perm had parked herself on a bench and lit a cigarette.

Jean had walked over and sat down. And after a moment she had spoken.

'Fun at that age, in't they?' she had said to the woman, because this was what she imagined people—mothers—might say to one another.

The woman had shrugged.

'I don't know, love. Some of 'em in't fun at any age,' she had replied.

Jean had searched for a suitable reply to this observation, but found none. After a moment she had said 'Do you just 'ave the one, then?' and nodded at the sullen child.

At this the young woman had raised both eyebrows and her nostrils had flared.

'Oh, she in't mine, pet. I'm the nanny.'

'Oh.'

Yes, the young woman would be the nanny, of course.

'I've been a nanny too,' Jean had replied. 'For a family back east.'

'What—China?'

'No. Stepney.'

'Oh.' The woman had nodded without appearing much interested. 'Well, I'm out of it soon,' she had added unexpectedly. 'Next week, in fact. Back 'ome to Leicester. And not a day too soon.'

'Oh. What will they do?'

'Who?' The nanny had looked mystified.

'The family you work for.'

'Oh, them.' She had shrugged again. 'Don't know. Not my problem, is it?' and she had paused to draw heavily on her cigarette. Then she had turned and looked at Jean, a long, appraising look that took in the dull brown hair in a dull, plain style, the pale face unadorned with make up, the plain white blouse and unstylishly narrow skirt, and the heavy navy shoes, unfashionably low. 'You *are* a nanny, in't yer!' she had added in summary and Jean had had a sense she was being judged. 'Well, if you're looking for a job, love, they're always desperate these days. My lot got me through the agency in the High Street. Simpson's is the name. I'll give you the address if you like.'

And she had pulled out an old bus ticket and scribbled down the address of an employment agency in Kensington High Street and handed it to Jean.

'I'm Nellie. Nellie Peters,' she had added, standing up and smoothing down her skirts. She hadn't held out her hand or even met Jean's eye as she said this as she was too busy adjusting her petticoat, the cigarette wedged firmly in the side of her mouth.

'Thanks. I'm Jean. Jean Corbett,' but the nanny had been scowling over at her charge and seemed not to be listening. The child, it appeared, had pushed another child off the swing and an anxious and overdressed young woman had run frantically over. A scene had appeared inevitable.

'Bloody little bitch,' the nanny had muttered and marched over.

Jean hadn't stayed to watch. A few days later she had sat in the offices of Simpson's in Kensington High Street across from a Miss Anderson and, yes, it had appeared that everyone wanted a nanny and, despite Jean's shaky references, she had been given the name and address of eleven potential clients. In the end she had agreed to visit only one, the Wallises in Athelstan Gardens.

'*Anne!*' Jean called. 'Come on, your mother will be wondering where we've got to and it's your piano lesson at five.'

As Nanny Peters had begun to herd her small charge away and appeared in no hurry to prolong the interview, Anne capitulated and came moodily away.

'I wonder why Nanny Peters came back and didn't tell us,' she mused as they began the walk home.

'Perhaps she was too busy with her new family.'

Anne considered this. 'Nanny, what did she mean about you following her suggestion?'

'I have no idea, Anne. I think she was mistaking me for someone else.'

Chapter Twenty

MARCH 1953

The telephone was ringing as Harriet arrived back home from visiting Cecil at his office.

She dropped her front-door key so that by the time she had let herself in Mrs Thompson had already got to the telephone and was standing in the hallway in her apron, the usual cigarette clenched in her mouth. Harriet reached for the glass ashtray that lived on the hallway table and whipped it beneath Mrs Thompson's cigarette moments before a dusting of ash toppled from the end and tumbled towards the carpet.

'Mr Paget,' announced Mrs Thompson, unimpressed by Harriet's quick thinking with the ashtray.

'Thank you, Mrs Thompson.' Harriet took the telephone receiver and, even though Freddie had been back seven months, it was a moment before she realised it was him on the other end of the telephone and not Simon.

'Listen, sis, you won't believe it but Caruthers has offered me the job.'

Harriet heard herself gasp and she put her hand to her mouth.

'I can't believe it! I only just spoke to Cecil a couple of hours ago.'

'Oh, I already had it in the bag by then. Looks like I didn't need Old Ceec's help after all. Apparently just being the brother-in-law did the trick. What do you think? Accounts clerk in some finance department near Liverpool Street, starting tomorrow.' He paused to laugh. 'Not quite the glittering career in high finance Father had planned for me.'

'Father didn't plan for the war.'

'No.'

'Oh, Freddie, it's marvellous. Look, why don't you come over? Come and meet the children, I know they'd be thrilled. Come for afternoon tea. Cecil won't be back for ages yet.'

It was going to be all right. And Freddie was coming to tea to meet the children.

'Mrs Thompson! Mr Paget will be coming for afternoon tea at a quarter past five. Please set up the tea in the drawing room rather than in the kitchen.'

Harriet did not wait to observe Mrs Thompson's reaction to this request, which was both unprecedented and spontaneous. Instead, she went upstairs and almost ran into the nanny.

'Miss Corbett. Are the children back from school yet?'

'Yes, Mrs Wallis,' the girl replied. 'We've just this moment returned from the park and Anne is getting ready to go to her piano lesson and Julius is in his room doing homework.'

She delivered these statement, then waited on the stairs.

Harriet smiled and that seemed to unbalance the girl, who didn't know where to look. Nanny had gone for the austere look today: a dull, white blouse over a navy skirt, offset with flesh-coloured tights and her ugly navy shoes. To supplement this she had dug up a dun-coloured cardigan. Come to think of it, every day was austere day for

Nanny. And it was a pity too, for the girl was quite pretty. She had good bone structure and a good figure, if a little … well, austere. All she needed was a hair-do, a decent outfit and some good lipstick. Surely there must be one or two unused tubes upstairs. She would give them to Nanny. And perhaps it was time the girl got a pay-rise; after all, she had been with them now for six or seven months.

'Well, let's be very naughty and skip piano lesson for today,' Harriet declared. 'Would you telephone Miss Dalrymple and let her know? We have a visitor coming for afternoon tea: Mr Paget, the children's uncle will be joining us.

'Mr Paget? The children's uncle Simon?'

'No … their Uncle Freddie. They haven't seen him in a long while.'

'Oh. Has Mr Paget been away, then?'

'Yes, obviously, or they would have seen him, wouldn't they?'

The girl made no reply to this.

'Well. Would you let the children know? No, wait—I'll tell them myself.'

Really, the girl was beyond sullen! It quite spoilt her features when she pulled such a face. Perhaps the lipstick wouldn't suit her after all.

Harriet went quickly up the stairs and found Anne in her room rummaging around in her wardrobe.

'Anne, I—oh!'

Harriet had trodden on Anne's school hat which lay in a dishevelled state in the middle of the room. It squelched as her foot made contact with the crown and water seeped out onto the carpet.

'It's my hat,' Anne explained, emerging from the cupboard. 'It ended up in the pond. I really can't say how.'

'Oh. Well, never mind. Anne, what do you think? Your Uncle Freddie has returned to England and he's coming to tea this afternoon to see you.'

Anne digested this information thoughtfully.

'I don't have an Uncle Freddie,' she declared at last.

241

'Yes, you do,' Harriet explained patiently. 'He is my and Uncle Simon's younger brother. You met him at Harrods once during the war, though you probably won't remember it as you were only a year old. Julius would remember it.'

Anne appeared less than impressed.

'*What* would I remember?' said Julius behind her.

'Uncle Freddie. He's coming to tea. You met him at Harrods once. In the tea room. During the war.'

'Oh yes, I do remember that … We had scones. They served them on a sort of multi-layered plate thing. One of them had peel or something in it—so I don't think that can have been a scone after all. More likely it was a kind of bun—'

'Yes, but don't you remember Uncle Freddie being there?'

Julius frowned in concentration, but it was clear the scones had made a bigger impression on his five-year-old brain than his uncle had.

'Well, anyway he's coming to tea and he's very much looking forward to seeing you both again. In fact—I have a super idea! Why don't we go and meet him at the tube station?'

Anne and Julius regarded their mother in astonished silence.

'You want us to go to the tube station to meet him?' Julius repeated. 'All of us?'

'Yes!' God, children could be so maddeningly slow sometimes!

And so, after some minutes spent assembling the appropriate outdoor clothing they were ready to set off, and when it became apparent that they were going out sans nanny and with just their mother, Anne grabbed Harriet's hand and skipped down the front steps, almost falling head-first in her excitement. Julius followed at a more sedate pace, preferring to walk a little apart with his hands in his trouser pockets and clearly still dubious as to the nature of the expedition.

'What will Uncle Freddie look like?' Anne asked, swinging Harriet's arm madly as she walked. 'Will he look like Uncle Simon?'

Harriet laughed. 'No, he's much younger than Uncle Simon.

And they don't look a bit alike. Uncle Freddie has darker hair and he's a bit taller and thinner. And he doesn't smoke a pipe.'

'That's good.'

'And Mother, where has Uncle Freddie been?'

'Canada. He's been in Canada. And America. Working.'

'Doing what?' asked Julius.

'Oh, lots of things. Important work for a railway company and a shipping firm and—oh, lots of things.'

'A shipping firm? You mean like Daddy?' said Anne, looking up at her mother with a frown as though she could not quite understand anyone, aside from her own father, choosing to work in such a place.

'Yes, that's right. Or rather, not quite the same, because this was a company that has commercial ships rather than passenger liners and it was around Hudson Bay and not across the ocean. And Uncle Freddie worked in their accounts department, I believe.'

'And why has he come back?' Julius asked.

'Because he misses us all and he was homesick.'

'So why didn't he come back before? If he missed us, I mean?'

'Well, I'm not sure. You'll have to ask him.'

Freddie would not exactly relish such a question, but he was just going to have to deal with the children himself.

'I don't think Uncle Freddie missed us at all,' Anne mused. 'In fact, I don't think he remembered us at all, because he never sent birthday presents or Christmas presents, did he? Or birthday cards or Christmas cards. Not once.'

'Yes, that's true,' Julius grudgingly agreed. 'One has to concede the old girl has a point,' and he looked to his mother for an explanation.

They had reached the busy junction outside the station so that Harriet stopped at the pedestrian crossing and it proved quite impossible to continue the conversation.

It was approaching five o'clock as they arrived at South Kensington tube station and already early rush-hour workers were streaming out of the entrance. Harriet, Julius and Anne took up a position just outside the ticket barrier from where they could observe people who had arrived on either the Circle or the Piccadilly Line.

'If Uncle Freddie left sometime after the war ended, that's at least eight years.' Julius was standing slightly off to the right of his mother and sister as though to minimise the possibility that people should assume he was with them. He surveyed the passing crowd thoughtfully. 'So that's sixteen Christmases and birthdays combined. Or thirty-two, if you count all my Christmases and birthdays and all Anne's. That's a frightful lot of presents we didn't get,' he concluded.

Anne stared at him, clearly shocked by these figures.

'I'm certain that, now that he is back, he will put things right,' Harriet replied.

She felt fairly sure Freddie was in no position to provide the thirty-two missing presents—and had not, in all probability, given them any thought at all—but she had no doubt that, with a little persuasion and the loan of a cheque-book, he could be coerced into a trip to Hamleys.

'And when did Uncle Freddie get back?' asked Julius.

Harriet opened her mouth to reply, then found that there was simply no correct answer to this question, or rather, none that would satisfy the children's curiosity while at the same time alluding, at least partially, to the truth.

'Anne, please stop twisting about and stand still—oh, I can see him!'

Freddie had somehow come through the ticket barrier without them spotting him and was standing on the other side of the concourse. Harriet started up and was about to wave before she realised that he was pressed against the tiled wall of the station, beside a chocolate vending machine and a litter bin. As she watched, her hand poised mid-wave, he raised both hands to his face and began to rub his temples violently, then he ran both hands through his hair. He looked wildly from side to side and at last seemed to see them. His face registered dismay.

Harriet let go of Anne's hand.

'Children, I want you both to wait here for me. Don't leave this spot; I shall be back in a just a moment,' she said, not looking at them, and she pushed her way through the crowd until she had reached him.

'Freddie, what is it? What's happened?'

He looked at her with a face so pale she felt her stomach lurch.

'Would you believe, I just ran smack into my old C.O.?' he said and he laughed humourlessly. 'Straight into him. Doors opened, me on the Circle Line train, him on the platform just about to board the train. Face to face. Not sure which one of us was the most surprised.' He paused, then shook his head and Harriet saw that his hands were shaking. 'And do you know what I did? I ran. Pushed past him and got out of there just as fast as I could. Suppose that's what I do best, isn't it—running.'

They stood in silence as all around them the station filled up and on the far side of the concourse the children waved at them excitedly.

Chapter Twenty-one

APRIL 1953

There was going to come a point, Cecil realised uneasily, when his behaviour could no longer be construed as courteous and would, instead, be regarded as improper. Had he reached that point? Perhaps it could already be regarded as improper and he was simply deluding himself about his real motives?

He paused for a moment, frowning.

'Oy, watch your step, deary. Them stairs is slippery as a bar of soap once they bin washed down. I should know—damn near broke me neck on 'em just last week.'

Cecil started and almost lost his footing. He grabbed at the banister of the stairwell and steadied himself.

A charwoman in a grubby headscarf, a cigarette dangling from her lip, leered down at him from the first floor landing, at her feet a mop and bucket and a slosh of water in a puddle that was dripping in steadily growing rivers down the stairs towards him. Cecil side-stepped a trickle that was inches from his shoe.

'Thank you. I shall take care to mind my step,' he replied with a curt nod of his head as he advanced up the stairs towards her.

The charwoman grunted but didn't move, observing him silently and seemingly in no hurry to step out of his way.

'You'll be after that Miss Squires, top floor,' she said shifting her position so that she was leaning on the other hip.

Cecil paused, his face reddening and the thoughts of a moment ago rushing back into his head.

'I beg your pardon! I am not acquainted with a Miss Squires.'

'Anyways you're outta luck,' continued the woman, as though he hadn't spoken. 'She's gorn off into the country for the weekend. Over'eard her tellin' Mr Barnes, the caretaker. Won't be back till Monday mornin'.' The woman removed her cigarette and knocked ash onto the nearby window-sill. 'All right for some,' she added, as though Miss Squires had done her a personal injury by going away for the weekend.

Cecil did not dignify her comment, nor her insinuation, with a reply and stepped firmly past her, taking some satisfaction in leaving a large and rather muddy footprint on her newly washed floor. He could still hear her grumbling as he reached the third floor of the block of flats.

Leinster Mansions was a four-storey block of apartments built for gentlemen bachelors in the late twenties and a little shabby now, the carpets worn and faded, the paint peeling in places, a number of light-fittings minus their bulbs. The building, situated on a main thoroughfare in the heart of Hammersmith, was a little too close to the tube station to be entirely desirable, but nevertheless it retained a certain faded elegance, a pre-war charm that Cecil still felt drawn to in these austere times of concrete and prefabs. The Rocastles lived here; or rather, Jenny Rocastle lived here alone, at flat number 9 on the third floor.

Cecil looked up the stairwell towards the top floor and for a fleeting moment wondered which was the flat of the absent Miss

Squires. He hadn't seen a lady of the type Miss Squires appeared to be during his previous three visits. Indeed, he had encountered no one at all during his previous visits, excepting Mrs Rocastle herself. And that, perhaps, was a good thing.

But good Lord, he was doing nothing improper! He could just as easily have brought Harriet with him.

And yet he had not. He had in fact (while not uttering an out-and-out lie) certainly given the impression that he was going into the office on this Saturday morning to transact some rather urgent shipping business. But instead he had taken the Piccadilly Line westbound five stops and was even now standing outside the flat of a young lady in Hammersmith.

It did not look good.

He hesitated at the door of number 9. Ought one to have telephoned beforehand to announce one's intentions? Under normal circumstances he would have done just that, but he had information to relay that had come to light very late the previous afternoon, after the time that a gentleman could respectably telephone a young lady at home. Cecil paused and slowly adjusted his tie. He had not, he now realised, wished to convey the information to Mrs Rocastle yesterday afternoon over the telephone; he had wanted to deliver it himself and in person to her flat.

He raised his hand and pressed his finger on the front doorbell. A tinny buzz sounded distantly on the other side of the door. He waited, but could hear nothing. He ought to have telephoned after all, because it appeared that, like Miss Squires, Mrs Rocastle was not at home.

Blast!

He felt a little annoyed. And a little foolish. He would pass the unpleasant charwoman again on his way down. And she would think he had called on Miss Squires.

Blast!

A sound from behind the front door startled him and a moment later the door opened. Jenny Rocastle stood in the doorway and regarded him with some surprise.

'Oh. Mr Wallis.'

She was dressed in a pale-blue sweater and a matching blue skirt, her face showed the traces of make-up, but she wore no jewellery. Her hair, freshly permed, shone in a darkly golden way. Harriet would have called it rather cheap, but Mrs Rocastle was ten years Harriet's junior and the hairstyle she sported suited her. Well, in Cecil's view it did.

'Mrs Rocastle. I do apologise for just turning up at your door unannounced like this, but I was in the vicinity and I had some information I wished to relay to you. I do hope it's not an inconvenient moment?'

'Well, I do have someone here—'

'Oh, I do apologise, of course I'll leave at once.'

'No, it's quite all right. It's only Peter—Jeremy's brother. Do come in.'

Cecil smiled, but felt a moment's hesitation. He had not reckoned on another guest. Somehow his own presence now felt a little … questionable.

And Rocastle had a brother?

'Peter, this is Mr Cecil Wallis—Jeremy's old boss from Empire and Colonial. Mr Wallis, this is Peter Rocastle, my husband's brother.'

Peter Rocastle was in the little drawing room positioned at one end of the cramped two-seater settee. He rose as they came in and held out a hand to Cecil. He was a tall man, taller by some inches than Jeremy. There was a slight family resemblance, the same round face and ruddy complexion, but Peter's hair was fairer and longer than his brother's and his clothes were somewhat more casual— loose-fitting flannel, brown brogues and a yellow sweater.

'Hello. Good to meet you, sir. Jenny—you didn't mention you were expecting visitors?'

Cecil smiled again and began to repeat his words of a moment earlier, but Mrs Rocastle spoke first.

'Oh, Mr Wallis was in the vicinity,' she explained, as though 'the vicinity' was a vintage motor car of questionable mechanical reliability.

'Really?' said Mr Rocastle readily. 'Splendid.'

'Yes. I must say, I really had no idea Jeremy had a brother,' said Cecil politely.

'Neither did I,' replied Jenny confidingly.

'And *I* had no idea Jeremy had a wife,' said Peter Rocastle cheerfully as he resumed his place on the settee, then on seeing Cecil's startled face he leant forward and added: 'Turns out old Jezzer was something of a dark horse.'

'If not a complete black sheep,' added Jenny.

'In fact, he was a veritable monochrome menagerie,' said Rocastle and Cecil stood in the centre of the room with a polite smile on his face. Neither Jenny nor Mr Rocastle seemed particularly perturbed by this state of affairs, so that Cecil wondered if this was all some sort of bizarre joke.

'Really?' he said simply, nodding to cover his confusion.

'Mr Wallis says he has some information,' said Jenny, seating herself on the settee and tucking both legs beneath her. She held out a hand and Peter passed her a cigarette then tossed her a box of matches which she caught neatly one-handed. Cecil watched as she lit the cigarette, shook the match to make it go out, then looked up at him expectantly.

It was strange, almost disconcerting. She had not looked like this the previous times he had come to visit. On those occasions she had been ... what? Vulnerable, shocked, upset? She had needed help, protection. Now, sitting on the sofa with her cigarette and her expectant look she appeared quite at ease, almost, one might say ... confrontational. Mocking.

Cecil sat down on the edge of an armchair and realised they were both watching him. The information. Of course.

'Yes, indeed. I thought you ought to know, Mrs Rocastle. I came straight round. Or rather, I made the discovery in the office late last evening and came round first thing this morning—'

'And because you happened to be in the vicinity?' added Peter Rocastle, helpfully.

'Quite.' Cecil hitched up his trousers at the knee. 'As you know, Mrs Rocastle, the police have been conducting an ongoing investigation into your husband's disappearance and the theft that occurred at the firm and that was—we must presume—perpetrated by him.' He paused. Of course she knew that—why was he telling her? 'And so, naturally, a great deal of time has been spent going through the firm's records over the period that your husband held his position. A great deal of time has been spent by myself going through those records. Purely to ascertain the extent of the theft, as I am sure you can appreciate.'

Mrs Rocastle smoked silently and gave no indication of whether she appreciated this or not.

'Anyway, it was as I was perusing records from a year ago that I made the discovery,' he leaned forward, 'that your husband made a number of long-distance telephone calls and sent a significant number of telegrams to an establishment in Johannesburg, South Africa. A *financial* establishment.' He paused, but no one said anything. 'This may not, in itself, appear to you to be anything out of the ordinary—Empire and Colonial is, of course, a firm with world-wide holdings and interests. But the point is, *we have no dealings with any establishments of this nature in Johannesburg.*' He paused. 'It is my firm belief, Mrs Rocastle, that your husband had been planning this crime for some time and is even now at large in South Africa!'

He sat back.

'Well, I wouldn't be at all surprised,' said Peter Rocastle, pausing to smoke. 'He grew up there—we both did. First place I'd look for him. Told Scotland Yard so about six months ago.'

There was a long pause during which Cecil nodded again and re-hitched his trousers.

'I see. Well, nevertheless, I think it prudent that I pass on this information to Scotland Yard so that they may continue their investigations anew.'

Peter nodded. 'Good idea, old boy. Very good idea.'

Jenny Rocastle had finished her cigarette and she now crushed it out on the ashtray on the coffee table. She didn't reach for another, but instead sat and regarded Cecil in a way that seemed to imply the interview had ended. And it was at this point that it occurred to Cecil that Mrs Rocastle was not wearing any nylons, nor indeed, a brassiere and that Mr Rocastle was wearing no socks beneath his shoes. That his shoe-laces were untied. That they both, in fact, appeared to have dressed in something of a hurry.

He stood up.

'Good. Well, I ought to leave; must get back to the office. It's a busy time of year, of course.'

They both stood up.

'Yes. I remember Jeremy saying how April was a busy time of year,' said Mrs Rocastle. 'Thank you so much for taking the trouble to come over in person, Mr Wallis.'

'Oh, it's no trouble, let me assure you.'

'Goodbye, then. Lovely to meet you,' said Peter Rocastle from the settee with a cheery wave of the hand.

'Thank you again, Mr Wallis, you've been so kind,' said Mrs Rocastle holding the front door open.

'Oh, it's no trouble,' Cecil repeated, stepping out onto the third floor landing. Jenny Rocastle smiled vaguely and closed the door.

Cecil stood for a moment in some confusion. You've *been* so kind. It was what you said to someone when you did not expect to meet them again.

He turned away and a moment later heard smothered guffaws of laughter from the other side of the front door. He walked quickly towards the stairs and went rapidly down them.

'Told you she weren't there,' said the charwoman, who was now on the second floor landing. Cecil passed her in cold silence. 'Gorn away for the weekend, she 'as!' she called after him.

Outside a light spring shower had just begun. Cecil stood beneath the porch of Leinster Mansions, trying to decide whether it was worth opening his umbrella or not. A young man in a dirty beige macintosh, his head sunk low in his shoulders, his collar turned up and a cigarette dangling from his lower lip turned into the porchway. He gave Cecil a sideways but otherwise expressionless look and disappeared inside. Cecil regarded him warily. He looked a decidedly shady sort of character. Indeed, this whole building was shady; he had always thought so; indeed, he had often wondered why Mrs Rocastle lived here.

Now, however, it seemed entirely appropriate that she lived here.

He stepped out into the street and made a dash for the tube station. He would go to the office. No point in going home; they weren't expecting him. He had said he would go to the office, and to the office he would go. There was work to be done, important work. One could get a great deal done on a Saturday morning, no interruptions, the place quiet for once. He would go to the office and get a great deal done.

The office was indeed quiet. Pickering the caretaker was nominally on duty at the door and he tipped his hat and offered a surprised 'Morning, Mr Wallis, sir,' as Cecil entered the building and signed in. Upstairs, each of the typewriters was covered and silent, all the pens and pencils arranged neatly in jars, papers sorted into discrete piles, teacups washed and stowed away.

He unlocked his office door and went in. There was a great deal on at the moment. The West Indies route was under review. It had been losing money for years and there was talk of pulling out altogether. (How, when there were clearly West Indians pouring into England on every tide, could the route be losing money?) India was proving difficult, too—there were intense negotiations underway with the Bombay authorities to extend docking privileges in the face of increasing competition from other lines. And plans to commence building of the *Canute*—the line's biggest, fastest, most up-to-date and modern liner, a liner to put all others to shame, to smash the London to New York record once and for all—had been shelved, indefinitely. There was no money for it, apparently. The unions were up in arms, of course: hundreds of men likely to lose their positions. And the prestige to the firm that such a flagship would bring—lost. Just like that. And no indication as to when the ship would be built—or indeed if it ever would. Passenger numbers were dropping. Plummeting, Sir Maurice had said. One simply couldn't compete with the new aeroplanes.

It was nonsense! Could an aircraft offer the sort of luxury, the sheer *thrill* of crossing an ocean in a vast ocean-going liner?

With a sigh Cecil picked up the first unanswered letter in his in-tray and began to compose a reply.

An hour passed and then a another. It was nearing lunchtime, and five letters, two memoranda and three telegrams had been composed and left on Miss James's desk. Three other letters, already typed, had been signed and were in the 'To Post' tray. Cecil sat at his desk and did nothing for a while. Eventually he stood up, left his office, closed and locked his door behind him and went down to the ground floor. Mr Pickering looked up from his racing guide and said 'Afternoon, Mr Wallis, sir,' and tipped his hat and Cecil went out into the street.

The day had become overcast again, though the rain was holding off for the time being. Cecil stood on the corner and thought about going home. He could go home now. He had gone to the office. It had been quiet. He had not been interrupted. He had got a great deal done.

Instead he turned southwards down Chancery Lane, then attempted to cross Fleet Street, scowling at the driver of a black cab that bore down on him. The cab driver tooted loudly and Cecil jumped back on to the kerb.

He had got a great deal done and Miss James would no doubt comment on this fact on Monday morning. Perhaps she would do so when Sir Maurice was passing, or Mr Standforth, though not

Mr McIntosh who was in the Kingston office attempting to patch up things in the West Indies. But it certainly wouldn't hurt if Sir Maurice or Mr Standforth learnt he had been here over the weekend. He had not, in truth, achieved all that he ought this week. Too much time spent tracking down Rocastle—all in the firm's best interests, naturally, but not perhaps as pressing as other matters.

He made a second attempt to cross Fleet Street, this time without mishap.

Yesterday he had rung Felicity. He had suggested, quite matter-of-factly, that they meet up, hinted that perhaps she might wish to discuss certain matters, and she had coldly informed him she had a production meeting all day and it would have to wait. Really, one attempted to do a good turn and it was simply thrown back in one's face. And this morning he had gone to the trouble of visiting Mrs Rocastle at her flat in Hammersmith to pass on helpful information, to ascertain her situation—and he had been treated indifferently, almost to the point of impertinence. To top it all, he had agreed to assist Freddie—purely for Harriet's sake and against his better judgement. He had agreed to talk to Nobby, and what happened? Next thing he knew, Harriet was telling him that Caruthers had gone and offered Freddie a position anyway, with or without Cecil's recommendation.

'It would seem that we didn't need your assistance after all,' Harriet had announced over dinner a few nights earlier. 'So now there's no question of you having to compromise your moral standards, is there?'

She had spoken these words pleasantly enough, yet when he had glanced up there had been a look on her face that had rooted him to his seat, unable to move, his spoon hovering somewhere above his soup bowl. She had left the room then, and he had silently resumed eating.

There was a public house on the corner of Mitre Court, the Printer's Apprentice, a dimly lit and ramshackle den, all uneven floorboards and low-hanging beams, into which about half a dozen customers could comfortably squeeze. Cecil went in and breathed in the fug of stale ale and cigarettes that hung in the air.

'A half pint of your own brew, my good man,' he requested of the young barman. The barman, sporting slippery Brylcreemed hair and an open-necked shirt, sighed patiently.

'Ain't got our own brew, 'ave we? We 'ave what the brewery gives us, see?'

'I see. In that case I shall have some of that.' Cecil pointed randomly to a tap and turned away to fish out some coins from his pocket, and so that he wouldn't have to engage the barman in further fruitless discussion.

'Wallis? My dear chap, how are you?'

And there was Nobby Caruthers coming at him out of the fug and brandishing a small glass just as though it was all pre-arranged. Cecil experienced that moment of disorientation one always felt when one ran into someone one had just been thinking about.

'Didn't know you drank here,' Nobby added with a beaming smile.

Cecil smiled back and shook Nobby's hand. He was glad to see the old boy, naturally, though he felt a trifle uncomfortable at Nobby's assumption that he drank regularly—here or anywhere.

'I don't as a rule,' he assured him. 'Just popped in on my way home. Been putting in a few extra hours at the office.'

'Good God, Wallis, you don't want to be doing that sort of thing. Not at your age. Let the young 'uns waste their Saturdays trying to impress the bosses, eh? Men like you and I have already climbed the greasy pole. We can afford to settle back and make up our own hours. Here, have a cigarette. Moroccan Turkish blend. Curzons of Jermyn Street make them up for me.'

'Fourpence, mate,' said the barman.

'Oh, let me, Wallis,' said Nobby reaching over and paying the man. 'What are you drinking this rot for? You know it's made in some ghastly factory in Essex or somewhere, don't you?'

Cecil took his beer and declined the cigarette.

'I haven't the faintest idea where it's made. But thank you. Your good health.'

'Bottoms up! Never touch the stuff myself. A good malt whisky is the only tipple passes these lips. That and a damn fine vintage port. Let's sit down—I've a table over there.'

They made their way around the corner of the bar and into a dimly lit alcove. A copy of *The Sporting Life* lay open on the table. Nobby was fond of horses. Owned a couple, too, rumour had it.

'Oh, reminds me: your brother-in-law started working for me this week. Did you know?'

Cecil placed his glass on the table and removed his raincoat and neatly folded it. He squeezed into a long wooden bench, hitched up his trousers and placed his folded raincoat on his lap.

'Oh. Yes. Yes, indeed, I had heard something to that effect.'

Nobby seemed to regard him closely. 'Seems like a good fellow. Been overseas, I understand. Canada.'

'Yes, so I believe.' Cecil took a sip of the beer. It was watery and chilled. He suppressed a shudder.

'Used to work at Moderate Assurance and Equity in the City before the war. Knew a chap worked there, before they crashed. Fine war record, too, by all accounts.'

Cecil took another sip. Was Nobby referring to Freddie or the chap he knew before the war?

'North Africa. Royal Tank Regiment.' Nobby took a large gulp of his whisky. 'Pretty tough they had it, those desert rats. Pretty damned tough.'

'Yes,' said Cecil not looking up. How did Nobby know about Freddie's war record? If he knew about it from some official source, then surely he would know the truth? Freddie must have told him— or told him this part of it. Dear God, he was shameless.

He took a second gulp of the beer and closed his eyes for a moment.

Harriet had said: 'So now there's no question of you having to compromise your moral standards, is there?'

But he *had* compromised his moral standards. Last August he had confronted Rocastle in his office. He had said: 'Rocastle, I have given this incident a great deal of thought, and I feel it incumbent upon me to advise you that I have resolved to report it to Standforth ... There can be no question of fraud. Everything must be out in the open.'

And Rocastle ought to have been dismayed, or perhaps angry, at the very least concerned. But instead he had smiled.

'Wallis, I think you're making a bit of a mountain out of what is clearly a rather insignificant molehill,' he had replied. 'Do you seriously want to jeopardise my career on a whim? Mud like this, well—it sticks, doesn't it? You must know that, better than anyone?'

What the devil had the fellow meant by that? But Rocastle had explained without further encouragement:

'I mean, your wife moves in the best circles, doesn't she? Opening nights, charity balls—that sort of thing? And your brother-in-law works at the Palace. Imagine the repercussions if there was gossip— oh not malicious, necessarily, just gossip, you know how people are—about some wayward family member? Oh, meant to tell you, I ran into an old chum the other day. Turns out this chum was in the same regiment as your wife's younger brother. North Africa. Royal Tank, wasn't it? What's he up to these days, anyway, your brother-in-law?'

When Cecil opened his eyes Nobby was peering at him.

'What's up, Wallis? You got something against the boy?'

'Of course not.'

'I mean, you'd tell me if there was any reason I shouldn't hire him?'

But he had known something about Rocastle and he had said nothing. He had compromised his moral standards—for what? To protect Harriet and Simon; to protect Freddie. And where had it got him? He had practically given Rocastle free rein to help himself to the proceeds of the company safe; Freddie was strutting about like a bloated peacock boasting about his new job ... And Harriet despised him.

To hell with them. To hell with Freddie.

'Look here, Nobby. I'm sorry, I really am,' he said, suddenly facing the old man at last. 'I do wish I had had time to speak to you as we had arranged. My wife—Mr Paget is her younger brother; it's only natural she wishes to assist him. I really ought to have spoken to you ...'

Nobby frowned at him and leaned forward. 'Well, out with it, Wallis! Is the fellow a crook of some kind?'

'Good Lord, no. Nothing of the sort. It's simply that—' Cecil paused and took another sip of the dreadful beer. 'I'm afraid I'm not sure how best to put this. The fact is, Freddie is a decent enough young man; he's certainly not dishonest. It's simply that his war record is not ... It's not quite as you may have been led to believe.'

'He wasn't in North Africa after all?'

'Oh, he was, for a number of years. No question of it. Fact is, though, he came home on leave—early '44 or thereabouts—and never went back.'

Nobby sat back in his chair and regarded him silently for a moment.

'You're telling me he was a deserter?'

Spoken out loud like that, the word was appalling. Bald, uncompromising. Cecil looked down at the wooden table. A cluster of circular stains made by the glasses of numerous patrons pock-marked the wood. The beer was undrinkable. He felt a little queasy.

''Fraid so. Of course, there's a general amnesty now. Water under the bridge and all that. And as I said, young Freddie served creditably for some years before that, and he's a decent enough sort.'

Nobby made no comment.

'Apologies, Nobby, for not speaking up earlier. Truth is, I didn't get the chance. Didn't realise things were so … advanced. Trust this won't put you in a difficult position?'

'I rather think it will, Wallis; I rather think it will.' Nobby's frown deepened. Cecil swallowed the remainder of the beer.

'Shall I get us both another round?'

'I think not.' Nobby looked up sharply. 'Now, look here, Wallis. You're absolutely certain about this? I mean, there's no possibility you might be mistaken?'

Cecil tried to think. He had done the right thing—of course he had, no one could question that—and yet, was it right to jeopardise a man's career? But damn it all—to whom ought one's loyalty be? Should he give the impression there was an element of doubt? But no, that was dishonest—and this was, after all, about honesty.

''Fraid not. Wouldn't have brought the wretched thing up had I had the slightest doubt. Truth is, the MPs actually fronted up at the house searching for him. Dashed awkward.'

He had not intended to say that. No, he really would have preferred not to have said that.

'I see,' said Nobby gravely. 'Well, that rather puts the thing beyond any doubt.'

Caruthers stood up, gathering up his newspaper.

'I'd better be off. Meeting my good lady at Covent Garden in half an hour. She's making me sit through *Giselle* again. Daren't be late.' He paused. 'Thanks for the chat, old man. Sorry we couldn't have had it earlier but … no matter.'

When he had gone, Cecil remained where he was for some time. He could buy another beer, but the effort seemed immense. And the end result hardly justified it. He could go home now, there was nothing stopping him. He had achieved a great deal this morning. A great deal.

It was a shame about Freddie. A real shame. But they ought to have allowed him time to talk to Nobby first. It need not have got this far. He had done the right thing, no one could question that he had. It was best for all concerned.

He got up, put on his coat and left the pub.

Chapter Twenty-two

APRIL 1953

And for four days, nothing happened.

On Sunday he and Harriet attended a charity luncheon in Knightsbridge, then set about discussing the arrangements for a Coronation Day party. On Monday Cecil went in to the office and sat through a tedious and lengthy meeting with two representatives of the Cairo office, and on Tuesday he made the important decision to scale back operations on the Argentinean route. By Wednesday he had almost pushed the meeting with Caruthers out of his head: perhaps Caruthers had not, in fact, taken the thing too seriously and there would not be any repercussions after all.

Well, so be it. A large part of him was relieved. A small part thought Freddie damn well deserved what he got!

On Wednesday evening he arrived home at the same time as

Julius, who, judging by his muddy appearance, was returning from pre-season cricket-net practice.

'Double maths tomorrow,' announced Julius grimly as he pulled off his coat. 'Followed by Latin vocab, and it's rumoured Mr Alexander'll be handing out the results of last week's mid-term paper.'

'Oh, I feel quite certain you'll have acquitted yourself adequately,' Cecil replied, pleased the boy had volunteered this information when increasingly he appeared not to wish to divulge anything of any significance to either of his parents. (Oh, for the days when mid-term papers were one's only concern!)

Cecil had by now hung up his coat and arranged his shoes precisely side by side on the shoe rack. He paused in the hallway, listening. There were voices overhead. Curious, he started up the stairs.

'Don't see how you can possibly know that,' Julius retorted. 'Sometimes one thinks one's done quite badly in a test, then one's pleasantly surprised … Other times you just know you've done really badly and nothing can save you.'

Cecil paused at the bend in the staircase in time to see Julius furtively nudge his father's shoes with his toe until they were no longer precisely side by. Then he took off his own shoes and placed them neatly on the rack.

Cecil was about to comment on this when he heard voices again, coming from the drawing room. He looked up. One of the voices was Harriet's, but it was difficult to make out the other as a car chose that exact moment to idle loudly in the street outside.

'And really, what rot it all is!' continued Julius, following his father up the stairs. 'As if one needed to know Latin verbs in order to pilot a plane!'

Cecil began to reply that, actually, Julius, you'll find that a basic grounding in the classics is pretty damned useful, not to say essential to one's—

But outside the car finally revved up and drove away and the street fell silent.

'Do you know what that old bastard *did*—'

'It's Uncle Freddie!'

Julius thrust past him on the stairs, crossed the landing and flung open the drawing room door.

'Hello, Uncle Freddie!'

Cecil hesitated, then, with a growing sense of foreboding, followed. Freddie was standing at one end of the mantelpiece, but he spun around at Julius's entrance. Harriet stood in the centre of the room, her face pale, a loose strand of hair falling over her eyes and a vivid spot of red visible one on either cheek. She looked over Julius's head and for a moment her eyes met Cecil's. He looked away.

'Julius. Wait outside, please!' he ordered.

'I don't see why—'

'I said wait outside!'

'Oh, all right then. I've got things to be getting on with, anyhow,' and Julius sauntered off.

Cecil went into the drawing room and closed the door behind him, going immediately over to the fireplace, where he stood with his back to the empty grate. They both regarded him silently.

'You haven't told the children my dirty little secret, then, Wallis?' demanded Freddie.

'Freddie. How are you? No, I have certainly not told the children!'

'All too shameful, is it?'

'Freddie!' said Harriet, and she took a step towards him, her arms outstretched almost as though she would embrace him, then she hesitated and her arms fell to her sides. Freddie seemed not to notice, or to care.

'Well, I'm terribly sorry to turn up like this and embarrass you, but I wonder has it occurred to you what it's been like for me? What I've been through—'

'No!' retorted Cecil, cutting him off. 'And frankly I do not wish to—'

'Nine years I've been moving from place to place, using a different name, trying to avoid running into someone who might know me—'

'It was your choice, Freddie—'

'Hiding every time I saw a policeman, a soldier, an Englishman. Moving to a new town simply because I thought I'd seen someone from my old regiment. Terrified I'd trip myself up on my own lies, that I'd give myself away with some slip—'

'It was your choice!'

Perhaps that was too much, perhaps he had gone too far, for Harriet's face registered dismay.

'Cecil!' she gasped.

'We have done everything in our power to help you—'

'*Help*? Exactly *how*—'

'We could have contacted the authorities nine years ago, but we did not. Against my better judgement, I can tell you. And not for your sake, for Harriet's.'

'Freddie, just tell me what's happened, for heaven's sake!' said Harriet.

Cecil turned away and faced the window. In the street below two nurses in capes hurried past in the direction of the hospital to start their shift.

'That old bastard Caruthers, that's what!'

Cecil closed his eyes and was glad he was facing the window.

'Your old pal, Cecil, took me into his office—all nice and friendly, just a fireside chat, doncha know? Then he lays it out to me: sorry, old boy, don't know how to tell you this, but I've found out your dirty little secret, and frankly it's simply not on. Can't have chaps like you working in a distinguished firm like this. Bad luck and all that, but pack your bag and leave the premises. Oh and here's a letter terminating your employment just to make it all official and above board.'

'Oh Freddie ...'

It would have been better to have worked late at the office; to let this little scene play itself out without him.

'Hardly had time to settle into my new desk before I was out! The old bastard all but had me frog-marched out of the building and thrown onto the street.'

'But the amnesty! He has no right—'

And how *dare* Harriet sound so close to tears? Was this the only thing that mattered, her blasted brother!

'He's got every bloody *right*, Harri. Men like him are born with the right, didn't you know? They play with people's lives the way they played with tin soldiers when they were little boys in the nursery.'

A floorboard creaked loudly on the other side of the door and Cecil looked up sharply, catching Harriet's eye. Freddie appeared not to have heard it.

'I actually thought, it's all over,' he said, pacing the room. 'I thought; this is it, I've done my time. I've paid for my mistakes, and now, finally, I can live a normal life.'

'Cecil, you must call Nobby, you must talk to him—'

He could not turn and face her. There was nothing he could say. Outside, a small green sports car driven by two young men pulled up alongside the nurses.

'I don't know how he found out, Harri. I don't know how the *hell* the old bastard found out!'

'Cecil, you *must* call him! I can't believe Nobby would do this if—'

After a brief exchange, the two nurses climbed into the car and were driven away. Perhaps, after all, their shifts were not due to start soon. Perhaps it did not matter to them if they arrived on time or not. Perhaps it no longer mattered what anyone did.

'For *God's* sake, Harriet, it's got nothing to *do* with me. Don't you understand? I want *nothing* to do with this!'

He left the fireplace, crossed the room and flung open the door, finding himself face to face with Julius. The boy returned his gaze wordlessly.

'Go upstairs, Julius,' Cecil ordered, coming out and closing the door behind him. Julius turned and fled upstairs to his room.

Cecil walked towards his study and, despite the drawing room door being closed, he could still hear Harriet. She spoke in a curiously quiet voice: 'We must do something … Cecil will come round.'

'No, he won't. I don't know why you can't see it, Harri. He has no intention of helping. He'd prefer it if I left for good and never showed my face again.'

'*No*! Freddie, that's nonsense … Where are you going?'

The door opened again and Freddie came out. He paused in the doorway, staring at Cecil, and for a second their eyes met before Freddie dived down the stairs. Cecil stepped back into the doorway of his study and a moment later Harriet emerged, breathless, and ran down the stairs.

'*Freddie! Freddie, come back!*'

Downstairs the front door opened, then shut with a slam. Cecil closed his study door and realised that, in fifteen years of married life, he had never seen Harriet run before.

Chapter Twenty-three

APRIL 1953

Mrs Wallis's brother was leaving. He had only just got here, and now he was leaving. And by the look of it, Mrs Wallis was going with him.

Jean watched from her top-floor window and a moment later a door slammed on the floor below. That was the third door slammed in as many minutes. She came out of her room and stood at the top of the stairs. The door sounded like one of the children's.

She was the nanny, she ought to go and investigate. But this evening was her night off, she had asked Mrs Wallis especially. But she had plenty of time. And the children hadn't had their tea yet.

Jean had ventured halfway down the stairs when she heard a loud thump from Anne's room. It sounded as though Anne had fallen off her bed or dropped something. A moment later Julius burst from his room and banged angrily on his sister's door.

'What's going on in there?' he demanded, opening her door and going in.

From her vantage point on the stairs, Jean could see past him to where Anne was kneeling on her bed, leaning down as though searching for something on the floor. She jumped up as Julius came in, her face pink, and glared at him furiously.

'Don't come into my room without asking—it's very rude!'

'What the *devil* are you playing at in here?' Julius demanded a second time. 'Sounds like a herd of blasted elephants.'

'None of your business, Nosy Parker!'

'Fine. Suit yourself. I shall find out, anyway.'

Julius leaned against the wall, taking his time when Anne clearly wanted him out and wasn't being very subtle about it.

Jean was about to intervene when Julius added, 'I don't suppose you have the slightest idea what's going on downstairs, do you?'

'What do you mean? Nothing's going on!'

'Oh really? Shows how much *you* know.'

Behind him, Jean came silently the rest of the way down the stairs. Here she paused. Something told her that if Julius saw her, if he realised she could overhear him, he would clam up. And she very much wanted to hear what he had to say.

'While you were thumping about in here with your stupid little-girl secrets, Uncle Freddie was downstairs, except that Father has just kicked him out.' Julius paused dramatically. 'I just saw the whole thing. Father threw him out. I doubt he'll ever come back, and we'll never see him again,' he added.

'You're *lying*!' screamed Anne. 'I don't believe you!'

'Doesn't actually matter a damn if you believe it or not, old girl. It happens to be true.'

'Go *away*! Get out of my room!'

'And that's not all. I know *why* Father threw him out, too, *and* why Uncle Freddie's been away all this time. And you'd better listen, because people are going to find out and when they do, it'll be the worse for us.'

'*What* is? What are you *talking* about?'

'Uncle Freddie. Turns out he wasn't doing important work on the railways in Canada. Or for a shipping firm or for anyone at all, really. He was on the run. He's a deserter, so there!'

'He is not! You're lying! That's a *rotten* thing to say!'

'Fine. I shan't tell you then,' and Julius shrugged and turned to leave.

'What do you mean? Tell me! I *demand* you tell me! It's not *fair*!'

'Oh? I thought you didn't believe me. I thought you said I was lying.'

'*Tell me!*'

'All right, old girl, keep your hair on. If you really want to know, I just overheard them all talking. In the drawing room. Mother and Father and Uncle Freddie. And Uncle Freddie said he'd been sacked from a job and it was because the firm had found out he's a deserter.'

Anne walked right up to him, her cheeks puffed out and her fists clenched as though she would make him shut up if she could.

'And then Mother said, Well, Father must help Freddie get his job back. And Father got very angry and said it wasn't any of his business, anyway, and he stormed out. And Uncle Freddie said it wasn't fair, and then he stormed out too and Mother went running out after him.'

'Mummy doesn't run,' Anne countered, evidently latching onto that image as though it undermined the veracity of Julius's story.

'Well, she does now, I just heard it. Mother was absolutely *furious* with Father. I expect they'll be getting a divorce now.'

'*That's not true!* And anyway, Uncle Freddie's not a deserter, I know he's not.'

'How do you know it? You don't know anything. And you know what? Everyone will find out, all your friends and everyone at school, they'll know that your uncle is a deserter *and they'll never let you forget it, ever!*'

'*Shut up! Shut up! Shut up! They won't! It's not true!*'

Anne stood furiously before him, her fists held tightly by her sides.

'It *is* true and you standing there saying it isn't isn't going to change a bally thing, so you'd better get used to it because nothing will be the same again after this, you'll see.'

'Go away, get out!' and Anne pushed him with both hands, only stopping when she saw Jean. Her hands at once dropped to her sides and her face registered dismay. Julius, seeing this, turned around and stared at Jean too.

'Oh, it's quite all right,' said Jean. 'No one knows but us, do they? I mean about your Uncle Freddie, the deserter,' and she smiled from one child to the other. They gazed back at her expressionlessly. 'Well, now, shall we see if Mrs Thompson has tea ready? I'm starving— aren't you?'

Tea was a somewhat tense affair.

Jean sat on one side of the kitchen table absorbed in the task of pouring the tea, passing around the butter dish and carefully policing the order in which items were consumed, which meant ensuring everyone ate their slice of bread before starting in on the cakes. Anne sat opposite her glaring at her plate and moodily heaping dollops of raspberry jam onto her bread. Julius sat at the end of the table and appeared to take some satisfaction in spreading lemon curd to each corner of his bread as thinly as possible. This involved, turning the plate on its axis ninety degrees then spreading the lemon curd again from a difference angle until Jean remarked, 'Julius, I would prefer it if you would just spread it and eat it,' at which Julius threw his knife down and stuffed an angry mouthful of bread into his mouth.

'I don't want any more bread and jam,' announced Anne, even though she had barely nibbled the slice on her plate. 'I shall have a piece of fruit instead. Mother likes us to have fruit. What do you think, an orange or a banana?'

She contemplated the large bowl of fruit on the dresser. It was piled high with tangerines and mandarins, a grapefruit, some red apples and two large bunches of bananas. Anne picked up the bananas and surveyed them with a critical eye. They were overripe and turning a little brown. In the end she discarded them and went with a mandarin.

'Do you want one, Nanny?' she said, deliberately not offering one to her brother. 'I should avoid the bananas. They look a little off.'

Jean shook her head.

So much fruit. It swam before her eyes. The smell of it nauseated her. She knew the cost of an orange, of a banana, during the war, and it was more than mere money. It had cost everything in the world.

Eventually the torturous meal was over and Anne made a point of leaving the table without saying 'Please may I leave the table?' and Julius made a point of pointing this out to Jean. Jean surprised him by replying that today was her birthday.

'Oh. Well, many happy returns of the day,' he replied grudgingly. 'Are you going out this evening to celebrate?'

'I am going out this evening, yes,' she replied and Julius stared at her, clearly not expecting this.

'Oh. Who with? Your young man?'

'Never you mind, Julius. That's my business, not yours. Now, let me get on with the clearing up.'

She got up and went over to the sink, but not before she had seen the blood rush to his face.

Julius turned and left the kitchen without another word and Jean sat down and finished her tea alone.

It's my birthday, thought Jean.

Once it had snowed on her birthday. She must have been ten, eleven perhaps. It had been during the war and the snow had fallen a couple of nights before so that by the morning of her birthday it was a brown slush on the streets, though small piles still lay undisturbed on the bombsites. It had mostly melted away by the end of the day, but not before all the kids in Malacca Row had worked together to fashion a crude snowman. Someone had stuck a twig beneath the snowman's pebble nose and a funny peaked cap on its head so that it resembled Herr Hitler—in a lopsided, lumpy kind of way—then they had all thrown hard little snowballs at it, and when the snow had run out they had thrown stones at it, then bricks, then they had all rushed up and kicked it to bits and stamped on it until there was nothing left but a pile of slush, and someone's mum had come out and told them all off. It hadn't snowed on her birthday since.

The wind had got up and was blowing newspaper and dust down the street. Jean pulled her coat closer around her shoulders. She had told Julius she was going out and if he had supposed from this that she was going out with her young man, well, that was his mistake. But it was her birthday, after all. You had to go out on your birthday.

As she approached the old hospital an ambulance trundled past and turned in through the gates and she paused, watching for a moment as the driver and a nurse climbed out, opened the doors and wheeled a patient out. All she could see of the patient was a shape outlined by a blanket. The person could have been dead. Or not.

It reminded her of the war.

She turned away and walked the short distance up Athelstan Gardens until she reached the little wrought-iron gate into the private garden. She had, once or twice, used her key herself to go into the garden without the children and on each occasion she had been peered at frostily by the dried-up old biddies who sat, all day, on its moss-covered benches. But by evening the gardens were deserted.

She reached inside her bag, pulled out the key and inserted it into the padlock. The gate creaked in a harsh, rusted way that you never noticed in the daylight, and banged shut behind her. She paused, listening, then stepped silently into the shadows, picking her way carefully. The privet hedge that bordered the garden and kept it safe from prying eyes meant that at night the garden was all but pitch dark. The sky was overcast, but a break in the clouds allowed a single shaft of moonlight to illuminate the neat square of lawn. The benches were deserted now—even the pigeons had vacated—and she walked over to the furthest one, the one Mrs Wallis's brother used to sit on.

It was her birthday.

Always, on your birthday, Dad would pull out the old tobacco tin and, as well as your presents, you got to dip into the tin and select a quote from the Bible, the same as the family did on Christmas Day. Last year Jean had gone through the Bible making her own tin of quotes. She had found an old pair of scissors and, though it felt wrong, an old and battered copy of the New Testament which she had cut up, mostly concentrating on the Psalms. Very soon she had amassed a collection of quotes and her tobacco tin was full. On the morning of her birthday she had opened the tin, closed her eyes and thrust her fingers inside. She had pulled out Matthew 5, verse 41, 'And whoever compels you to go one mile, go with him two', which hadn't been very good as no one was compelling her to go a mile with them, or indeed, to go anywhere at all. So she had pulled out another quote but that hadn't been much better, nor the next one, nor the next. And very soon it had become apparent that, if there was no one to stop you from pulling out all of the quotes, then you might as well pull them all out. And it had become apparent, too, that not one of the quotes was exactly right. And how could that be when she had selected them so carefully? When they were always so exactly right in the old days, when you pulled them out of this same tin and the whole family was watching you?

This birthday she had not bothered with the quotes. Instead she had come out to be by herself. She had come to the private garden.

The bench was cold. The coldness seeped up through her coat and through her dress and over her entire body. Beneath her feet the grass smelt damp and earthy. There had been a frost every morning this week, despite it being April, and it looked like there'd be another tomorrow. She shivered and wondered what time it was; whether it was too early to return to the house. They would notice if she got back too soon.

Except that she knew that no one would notice what time the nanny got back from her night off.

She got up off the bench and crossed the lawn, finding her way back to the gate and lifting the heavy latch silently as though someone in one of the houses might hear her.

'Oy! What's your game, then?'

Jean jumped as a tall figure loomed out of the shadows.

'Oh, it's you,' added the figure, a man, and Jean realised it was the young constable she'd run into weeks back.

'What do you mean by jumping out at me like that?' she replied indignantly. 'Almost give me a turn.'

'I though you was a burglar or something, didn't I?' He eyed her suspiciously. 'What you doin' in them gardens, anyway, this time of night?'

'Praying,' Jean replied.

'Oh.' He seemed uncertain how to reply to this. 'This your street, then?' he said instead and Jean nodded. 'Looks pretty quiet, don't it?' he added.

Jean gazed down the length of Athelstan Gardens and could see no one. She shivered slightly and hoped he didn't notice.

'It's usually pretty quiet, I s'pose.'

'Ha! You wouldn't believe what goes on behind them curtains. Believe me, I seen it every night—husbands walkin' out on their wives, kids runnin' away from home, husbands comin' home and findin' their wives in bed with the fella next-door, housewives knockin' back a bottle of sherry during the day then laying into the kids—or their husbands. You wouldn't believe it.'

Jean took a second look at the rows of discreetly painted front doors and elegant wrought iron railings and tried to imagine the chaos behind each door that he had just described.

'Well, that's as may be, but it ain't like that in the household I live in, I tell can you that.'

'Oh, I ain't saying they're all like it. Just some, that's all.'

Jean nodded noncommittally. What he had just described—well, it sounded more like Stepney than South Ken. He was just showing off. Trying to impress her.

'What's it like, then, livin' with these posh people?' and he jerked his head at the silent row of houses opposite.

'Oh, they're very well-to-do. Mr Wallis is in business. Very important, he is. A big shipping firm. Empire and Colonial.'

'Oh.' The policeman nodded without much interest.

'Mrs Wallis goes to lunch and the hairdresser most days, and the theatre and all these cocktail evenings and big charity dos and what-have-you. She's ever so elegant. And her brother works at the Palace.'

She paused. Now it was she who was showing off.

'How they treat you, then?' he said. 'Being a servant.'

'I ain't a servant. I'm the nanny. It's hardly the same thing. And anyway, they treat me like one of the family.'

She studied his profile in the moonlight. He had a boy's face, the features still soft, a rash of acne on his cheek, his chin inexpertly shaved. His Adam's apple bobbed as he swallowed.

'Do you have a gun, then?' she said, and he turned and stared at her.

'A gun? Course I don't have a gun!'

'But they teach you how to use one?'

'We're coppers, not squaddies. What do we need with a gun? This ain't Chicago, is it?'

She said nothing in reply to this. Then, 'Well, I gotta get back. They worry if I'm out late. Like I said, they treat me like one of the family.'

He walked with her a short way up the street, then he paused, bathed in a circle of light from the streetlamp.

'That your house, then?' He peered up at it. 'We did a call to that house a while back. Sure it was that one. I never forget a house we get called out to. Likely as not you end up back there, sooner or later.'

'Oh, I don't think so,' said Jean. 'Not this house.'

Chapter Twenty-four

MAY 1953

On the last Tuesday in May a van drew up outside the house at a little after eleven o'clock in the morning and two men got out. It was the half-term holiday and the children were both at home, so Jean joined Anne at her bedroom window and watched. The two men stood in the street and stretched and scratched themselves as though they had driven some considerable distance. As the address on their van indicated they had come from Fulham their stretching seemed excessive.

One of the two men, the younger, reached for a cigarette and lit it then offered the packet to the second man. Only once both cigarettes had been lit and half smoked did either of the men survey the street in which they found themselves. A discussion broke out, a delivery chit on a clipboard was retrieved from the van's cab and studied. Fingers were pointed and at last the two men appeared to reach a decision. They dropped their cigarettes on the pavement, crushed them underfoot and went up to the Wallises' front gate.

'Nanny, what do you think it is?' demanded Anne.

Downstairs the front door bell rang and Anne unfastened her bedroom window and, after a brief struggle, opened it.

'They're delivering something,' Jean replied, and Anne groaned and rolled her eyes.

'*Obviously* they're delivering something—but what?'

She leaned precariously out of the window, the way she had done on that very first day in the drawing room last September, only now she was two storeys up and if she fell from this height she probably would not survive. Through the open window they could hear the two men deep in discussion with Mrs Thompson.

'I don't care what you're delivering. You're not comin' in 'ere with your muddy shoes. You'll take 'em off before you come in or you ain't comin' in at all.'

'Suits me, missus,' said the younger of the two men with a shrug. 'We'll be only too happy to leave it 'ere on the doorstep, won't we, Ted? Fifteen of these we gotta deliver today.'

Anne leaned out even further, but by the time she had done so the discussion about footwear appeared to have been concluded and a compromise reached as both men had returned to their van and were even now opening up the doors at the back. But at this point, agonisingly, they paused for another cigarette break and Anne kicked impatiently at the wall beneath the window-sill with the toes of her shoes as she waited. After an excruciating delay they resumed their unloading, one disappearing inside the back of the van, the other waiting on the street outside.

And what they unloaded was a box. A large cardboard box, square or perhaps oblong in shape and large enough that it took both of them to heave it out and ease it onto a little two-wheeled trolley. The box was obviously very heavy indeed as the two men puffed and panted as they pulled it through the gate and hitched it up over the first step.

'Careful!' said the elder man as the younger man pushed a little too vigorously.

Clearly Anne could not be expected to stand by and watch, so she left the window and ran out of her room. Jean followed at a more sedate pace in time to see Anne run smack into Julius who was emerging from his own bedroom.

'Did you see? Something's being delivered,' she gasped breathlessly.

Julius regarded them both wearily and appeared less than impressed.

'Oh that, yes,' he replied, off-handedly. 'I'm well aware of that.'

'No, you're not. You're just saying that.'

'Am I? All right then, I shan't tell you,' and he turned and went with a shrug back into his bedroom.

Anne stood in an apparent agony of indecision, then turned and noticed Jean standing in her bedroom doorway. Anne scowled at her as though Jean had no right to be watching her and Jean smiled back.

'All right,' Anne declared, marching into Julius's room. 'What is it, then?'

Jean followed, two steps behind.

Julius was sitting at his desk, apparently studying. He sighed at her question and laboriously closed his book.

'*Ob*viously,' he began, drawing out the moment, 'it's a television set. They're getting it in time for the Coronation. Surely you knew?'

A television! thought Jean. Of course: the Coronation Day party. A few weeks ago Mr and Mrs Wallis had begun making arrangements for a party on the day of the Coronation—a list of attendees, the merits of various caterers, a possible menu of food items, had all been discussed at length. Mr Wallis, she remembered, had been curiously excited by the idea of a party. But then Mr Paget had come around and words had been spoken and Mrs Wallis had stormed out. There had been no mention of the party since.

Anne actually gasped. Then she scowled.

'Anyway, I already knew that,' she said. 'We both knew, didn't we, Nanny?'

'No, you didn't,' sighed Julius. 'Anyway, I don't know why you're wetting your knickers. It's just television. It's hardly something to get excited about. In fact,' and now he turned around and solemnly laid down his pen, 'it's actually a very bad thing. Television heralds the end of all cultural and intellectual endeavour, Anne, my girl. It's the thin end of the wedge for civilisation as we know it,' and he fixed her with a disapproving look.

'But now we shall be able to watch Aunt Felicity!' Anne replied as all the manifold implications of Television began to formulate in her mind.

Julius raised a shocked eyebrow. 'And why on earth should we want to do that?'

But Anne, it was apparent, was in heaven. Television had arrived at number 83 Athelstan Gardens, and in time for the Coronation! Nothing would ever be the same again.

The television set was positioned, not without much straining and cursing on the part of the two delivery men, in the drawing room on the first floor.

Television came in a large mahogany case with its own little doors that locked with a small gold key so that it was a separate piece of furniture like the cocktail cabinet. Television came with a lead and a plug which you had to wire up with a screwdriver by following a complicated diagram, and by this stage the delivery men were halfway back to Fulham, so that you had to do such things on your own. Mr Wallis was at work, so Julius wired the plug. Mrs Wallis, recently returned from a hair appointment, smoked and watched through narrowed eyes.

'Careful it doesn't blow up,' she observed. Jean, standing in the doorway, jumped back in alarm and Julius scoffed.

Television had to be plugged into the wall, which meant unplugging the lamp standard and this meant moving the lamp to another corner of the room, where it fell over each time you opened the drawing room door. The lamp was banished to the breakfast room. Television had a silver knob on the front which you pulled out to turn it on. Then it hissed and crackled and onto the screen came a strange grey and white grid with a circle in the middle and the letters 'BBC' in black at the bottom.

'That's the test card,' explained Julius, who, for one so contemptuous of it, appeared to know a great deal about Television.

'What does it do?' asked Anne.

'Nothing, obviously,' was the reply.

'Well, what's it for then?' she demanded.

'It's a piece of card that appears on one's screen when there are no programmes scheduled. If one can see the test card, then one's television is working properly, you see. Test. Card.'

'Well, I think it's a stupid idea.'

'Don't tease your sister, Julius,' said Mrs Wallis.

'Well, now. I wonder when the programs start?' said Julius, sitting back on his haunches and studying the test card as though a schedule for that evening's programmes could be seen there.

'I haven't the faintest idea,' said Mrs Wallis. 'Nanny, the children needn't think they are going to be allowed to sit here all day staring at this thing.'

'No, that would never do ...' said Jean, wondering how you *did* know when the programmes started ...?

'Their father purchased the television strictly so that we could all watch the Coronation in some comfort, and not have to wait for endless hours behind a barrier in Park Lane—or worse, go to some other person's house to watch it on their set. Please turn it off now, Julius, and close the doors.'

Julius did as his mother bid, closing the doors with some ceremony as though it were the final curtain coming down at the end of a successful West End production. Then they all stood in silence and stared at this new addition to the family.

It was the half-term school holiday and a trip to the park had been organised. At the last moment Julius had announced he had homework to do and would not, therefore, be accompanying them. So Jean and Anne had set out alone. The trip was not a success. At the park Anne had fallen off the slide and grazed her knee and Jean had stepped in some dog dirt. On the way home the rain had started and by the time they reached Athelstan Gardens it was falling in large, fat drops that ran down the backs of their necks.

When they got home Mrs Wallis was out and Julius was watching the television.

Jean stopped and stood in the doorway of the drawing room staring in silent fascination at the screen. Anne danced around in the hallway in her socks, obviously waiting, with barely suppressed glee, for Nanny to enquire why Julius was not doing the aforementioned homework, but instead Jean simply said 'Wash your hands before tea', and continued to stare at the screen. It was hypnotic.

Anne sat down in Mr Wallis's upright armchair and sulked.

On the television a man was sitting in a black leather chair with his legs crossed talking to another man who also had his legs crossed. The first man wore a grey suit—well, one presumed it was grey—and the second man wore a tweed jacket and had a pipe in the corner of his mouth.

'That does sound truly fascinating. And can you tell the children, Professor Robbins, how you stayed warm on your Antarctic adventure?' said the man in the suit. 'Yes. I wore warm clothes,' replied the second man and the man in the suit nodded vigorously.

'Mummy said we weren't to watch it,' Anne observed petulantly.

'I think you'll find, old girl, that what she actually said was, don't watch it *all day*. And I have no intention of watching it all day. I have more important things to do, even if you don't.'

'Anyway, what is it?' said Anne sulkily.

'It's a man talking to another man about visiting the Antarctic.'

'I suppose what we are all dying to know, Professor Robbins, is how many polar bears you saw?' said the man in the suit. 'None,' replied the Professor wearily. 'There aren't any polar bears in the Antarctic. You're probably thinking of the Arctic.'

'You haven't been studying at all!' declared Anne accusingly.

'Ssh, Anne, I'm trying to watch,' said Jean.

Anne fell into a furious silence.

The two men in the studio had gone and Jean heard the words of a song:

Hip, hip, hip hooray
It's hip, hip, Hippo day!
We've all come to play
It's hip, hip, Hippo day!

'It's Aunt Felicity!' screamed Anne, her fury at her brother seemingly forgotten.

'Good grief!' groaned Julius.

The words of the song were written on the screen and as a woman's voice sang each word a finger pointed to it. Then the words vanished and Jean stepped backwards in surprise as, suddenly, there was Mrs Mumford gazing expressionlessly at her. Only she was black and white, of course, her blonde hair grey, her vivid red lipstick grey, her dress a bland, lighter shade of grey, but her gloves were still white. She smiled and her eyebrows raised as though she was surprised to see them all.

'Hello, children,' she said. 'Isn't it a beautiful day today?'

It had rained on and off throughout most of the day.

'We're in the garden.'

She wasn't in a garden at all. She was standing at a counter in what was quite obviously the television studio. On the counter were some flowers in a row, tall-stemmed flowers with large grey petals and happy smiling faces.

'Let's see what Hippo's up to, shall we?' suggested Aunt Felicity, and she indicated with her arm to the end of the row of flowers. 'There he is!' she said, without taking her eyes off the camera.

Hippo was a dull grey colour. Mid-grey fur, a slightly darker shade of grey hat and a darker shade of grey bow tie.

'Hello, Hippo,' said Aunt Felicity. 'What are you up to?'

As Hippo was holding a watering can and was clearly watering the smiling flowers this seemed a pointless question. Hippo paused in his watering and danced around awkwardly for a moment or two.

'Hello, everyone!' he said and his voice was very clipped, like a Wing Commander in a Battle of Britain film. 'I'm watering my flowers,' he explained and as proof he held up his little grey watering can. As his hands were large round grey paws this was no easy task.

'And why are you watering your flowers, Hippo?' asked Aunt Felicity, still smiling at the camera.

'Because it's warm and sunny and my flowers are very thirsty,' replied Hippo.

'Good grief,' observed Julius again. He got up and walked out of the room shaking his head.

Jean, suddenly freed from television's hypnotic spell by Julius's departure, advanced at once on the wooden box.

'What are you *doing*?' shrieked Anne, alarmed.

'I'm turning it off. You oughtn't to be wasting your time watching it.'

Anne leapt up. 'Leave it on, Nanny! I'm watching! I *demand* you leave it on!'

'I'm sorry, Anne, but your mother was quite clear about it. And don't you have piano practice to do?'

Anne gaped at her, her fists clenched in silent fury.

'Is that a new hat, Hippo?' said Aunt Felicity.

But whether or not Hippo was indeed sporting a new hat they were destined never to find out as Jean depressed the silver knob and the screen dissolved into a tiny white dot then disappeared altogether.

'Turn it back on!'

But Jean carefully closed the little wooden doors and turned the little gold key and pocketed it. 'I don't think your mother would be very pleased if she knew you were spending your time watching this kind of thing, Anne. If I recall, she expressly forbade it.'

From upstairs they could faintly make out Julius humming the *Hippo and Friends* song cheerfully to himself.

Furious, Anne stomped after him, then paused in the doorway, breathing heavily.

'It's not fair!' she wailed. 'Why does *he* always get to do what he wants and I never do! Everyone always tells me what to do, or they don't listen when I want to do something, or they only pretend to listen when really they aren't! And everyone always gets to know what's happening first and why did no one tell *me* television was coming? And why is it all right for Julius to watch television, but not me?'

'The sooner you give up expecting life to be fair, Anne, the better off you'll be.'

Angry tears welled up in the girl's eyes and she brushed them furiously away.

'Anyway, *I* know something Julius doesn't know! I know something you and probably even *Mother* doesn't know, so there!'

And she ran out.

Anne did not come down for tea. After a while Jean left Julius to pour the tea and went in search of her. Her room was empty, and as she came back downstairs Jean was surprised to see that the door to Mr Wallis's study was ajar, when he always kept it firmly closed.

She went over and looked in. The study was silent and dark, the curtains half drawn to protect from the sunlight the photographs of ships that lined the walls. There was a different smell in here, different to anywhere else in the house—old, polished wood and dusty bookshelves and ink and ancient creaky leather upholstery—a fatherly sort of smell. The room was dominated by a vast desk and behind it was a tall, glass-fronted wooden cabinet.

But what she could see was Anne squatting down behind the desk, rummaging about in one of the drawers. In a moment she located what she was seeking and turned and fitted a small key into the lock on the cabinet door. The key turned smoothly and the door opened.

The cabinet consisted of four shelves containing a highly polished silver cup with a crest on it, dusty piles of papers and brown cardboard files and various other odds and ends. On the lowest shelf was a small and ornately carved wooden case. It looked like the sort of case that might contain jewellery.

As Jean watched, Anne reached down and lifted the wooden case and lay it on her father's desk. She undid the catch and lifted up the lid and there, nestling on a cream silk lining, was a gun.

It was a large revolver, or perhaps a pistol, a dull, metallic black colour, and beside it was a faded pink cardboard cartridge box. Anne reached in and slowly, reverently, lifted the gun out with both hands, then rested the heavy, stubby barrel of the revolver over her left forearm, then she stared down the barrel, closing one eye and aiming it, just like the cowboys did at the Saturday morning matinee. She carefully got to her feet and took aim at the ships on Father's wall, then pointed the gun at the photograph of herself and Julius on the desk, and finally she turned and stood at the window and took aim at the people down in Athelstan Gardens.

Jean must have moved as a floorboard creaked, making Anne spin around. For a moment that seemed to stretch out into eternity, they stared at each other. The gun was pointing straight at Jean and yet, rather than fear, Jean experienced a surge of power that ran the length of her body. The barrel of the gun swam in and out of focus.

'Anne,' she said calmly, 'what do you think you're doing?'

'You can't do anything, I have the gun,' said Anne, laughing. 'I can make you do whatever I like!'

'What would you like me to do, then?' said Jean.

'And no one else even knows it's here! Or where the key's kept! But I saw it once, when I was standing just there, where you're standing, waiting for Father; I saw him take the key out of the cabinet and put it in the bottom drawer. Then I could open the cabinet whenever I felt like it!' She glanced over at the window and the street below. 'Those stupid, silly people down there have no idea I'm up here with a gun aimed right at them! How surprised they would be, if they found out! How frightened they would be!'

'Or perhaps they would just be angry?' Jean suggested.

'I can see you!' said Anne, peering at Jean through her one open eye, 'and I can make you do anything! Anything at all!'

Jean returned her stare. And Anne pointed the gun and laughed.

Then her laugh ended and she seemed not to know quite what to do next. She scowled at Jean and took aim again, then, because Jean didn't do or say anything and Anne clearly could not think of anything to make Nanny do, she lowered the gun and pretended to shoot the carpet.

'Pow!' she said.

Jean advanced on her and grabbed her by both shoulders.

'You stupid, stupid girl!' she shouted, shaking her violently.

Anne dropped the gun, which fell with a loud thud, and for a second neither of them moved. They both stood staring down at it.

Anne suddenly looked frightened, and Jean shook her again.

'Do you think this is a *toy*? You *stupid* child. *Do you? DO YOU?*'

Anne burst into tears.

'I didn't mean it, I was only pretending. You won't tell Daddy, will you? *Please!*'

'Don't touch it! Move away from it right now!'

Anne leapt backwards in her hurry to move away, leaving Jean to scoop up the gun and lay it back inside its box.

Anne began to sob.

'But I didn't do anything—'

'Don't you *ever*—don't you ever, *EVER* do such a thing again. *Do you hear me?*' And Jean advanced upon her so that Anne shrank back, pressing herself against the door of the cabinet.

'I didn't mean—'

'Do you hear me?'

But Anne pushed past Jean and fled from the room.

Jean remained where she was, in the centre of the room, the gun in its box held before her in both hands.

After a moment, she closed the lid of the box and returned it to its shelf in Mr Wallis's cabinet, turning the key to lock it. Then she hesitated. Of course, she would have to tell Mr Wallis. She slipped the key into her pocket. Yes, Mr Wallis would have to be told. And until then, the key was safe in her keeping.

Chapter Twenty-five

JUNE 1953

The red, white and blue bunting strung from the lampposts in Athelstan Gardens hung limply in the steady drizzle that had begun before dawn and showed no signs of letting up.

Cecil, standing at his bedroom window in the grey dawn, experienced such a crushing disappointment in the pit of his stomach it was almost too much to bear. All everyone wanted was a sunny day for the Coronation, and instead it was raining. In The Mall and in the streets that lined the Coronation route those who had camped out overnight would be waking to a sky that was overcast and a June morning that was as cold and damp as a winter's day. It was like an eagerly awaited Christmas Day at mid-morning, when one's stocking has been opened, the Christmas Day service is over, there is no sign of the promised snow and all the grown-ups are acting as though it were just another day.

But this was a Coronation! And what a Coronation to witness! This was history. An occasion until now only observed by the highest dignitaries in the land would at eleven o'clock on this Tuesday morning in June be witnessed first-hand by millions. Thanks to television and the BBC.

It was important to remember this moment, this day, thought Cecil. And important that the children remember it too, remember it as a special time, a golden time. A time that they might tell their children and their grandchildren about. His own father had witnessed Queen Victoria riding past in a carriage outside Buckingham Palace on her Diamond Jubilee. And earlier still, Grandfather had written a memoir in which he described the celebrations for the young Queen's coronation in 1838.

And now it's my turn, thought Cecil. We must dig out the box brownie. And we should go to The Mall, he thought suddenly. Really, we should go and watch the procession. Why are we staying here in the house? Why are we watching it on the television when we could see it for ourselves?

But he had purchased the television for just this occasion. And there were people coming over—Leo and Felicity, a number of neighbours. Leo's nephew, young Archie and some girl of his, the Swanbridges. The children were looking forward to it. Still, it seemed sad not to be out there amongst the people.

He had purchased Coronation mugs for the children. Such items were everywhere in London: Coronation plates, Coronation spoons, special edition Coronation stamps—indeed, the commercialisation of the Coronation was verging on the vulgar. But a mug was a traditional souvenir item. Most households still had a '37 Coronation mug in a cupboard somewhere. So he had dropped in to Selfridges on his way home and purchased two mugs for the children, cream-coloured and carefully wrapped in white tissue paper. They stood side by side on the dressing table. He would present them this morning—perhaps over breakfast, certainly before all the guests arrived. It would be a private moment, a solemn moment—a family moment.

He walked across to his wardrobe and peered for some moments at its contents. Not a suit, that was too formal. He settled for a pair of new and rather smart beige trousers, a crisp white linen shirt and the green and black striped VPS tie. He topped it off with a navy blazer and added a pair of black loafers.

He heard a sound from the next room—footsteps, the floorboards creaking. Harriet was up.

Well, what of it? The day had begun. He was ready for it.

Last night Harriet had been to see Freddie. He was still residing, it seemed, in the appalling bed-sit off Marylebone Road and Harriet had gone round there three, four times since the incident with Nobby, returning each time angry and irritable, or quiet and concerned.

Last night she had come home to announce that Freddie was returning to Canada.

She had returned late; the children had already gone to bed, and Cecil had been sitting reading the paper in the drawing room, listening to Elgar on the wireless, half waiting for her, half attempting to complete the crossword. There had been one final clue, twelve across: 'A gamble on some sunshine is treacherous', seven letters, ending with 's'.

She had come in, stood for a moment in the doorway, regarding him, it had seemed, and made her announcement.

'Freddie is going to return to Canada.'

And he had been relieved, truth to tell. Who would not have been? His brother-in-law's return to England had been disastrous. It had damaged his marriage, upset the children and jeopardised a friendship with Nobby to boot. And what it had cost Empire and Colonial and his own position there—even before Freddie had turned up—well, that was nothing short of catastrophic. Frankly, Freddie was nothing but trouble.

But he had needed to play it carefully, he had realised that at once.

'I see,' he had replied, folding his paper and placing it on the coffee table.

'You want him to go, don't you?' Harriet had replied immediately, though he had said nothing to indicate this.

'My dear, it makes no difference to me one way or the other. It's his decision.'

'But you're glad, aren't you?'

He had been baffled, irritated by her attack. She had seemed almost hysterical.

'I won't deny it's best all round if he does go. It can't be much fun for him here. And I doubt that things will improve substantially for him in the foreseeable future.'

'You don't know what it's been like for him! He's waited years, *years* to come back; it's been his only glimmer of hope during those dreadful, dreary years in exile.'

'For God's sake! He's not a deposed monarch!'

'Isn't he? He may as well be! It's as though all those years of active service, of fighting for one's country in that dreadful place, in appalling conditions, count for nothing.'

'Harriet, I don't make the rules.'

'No, but you're happy to uphold them when it suits you, when you're safe and secure in your office. No one can touch you there, can they?'

Her words had shocked him. They had been so bitter, so contemptuous. They had rendered him speechless. Was this what she thought of him? Of his work? Of those endless, terrifying nights fire-watching at the docks during the war?

'Do you know what Freddie has been through? Do you have any idea?'

'For God's sake, I am not responsible for what has happened to Freddie!'

Then he had lowered his eyes. The conversation with Nobby at the horrid little pub had come back to him. But Harriet knew nothing of that. No one did, and no one needed to know. And suddenly he had been angry with her for putting him in this position.

'And might I remind you, Harriet, that you are my wife? That your duty, first and foremost, is to me and your family. Not to your younger brother, who, frankly, has been nothing but trouble since he came back—and for a damn sight longer than that too.'

He had had a good mind to let her know exactly what he had done for Freddie, and not just for Freddie but for her and Simon too! He had jeopardised his own career, he had lied to the police, that was what he had done!

He had picked up the newspaper then and shaken it angrily.

'My ... *duty*?' she had repeated, as though the word were foreign to her.

He had thrown the paper down again.

'Yes, your duty. Frankly—and I'm sorry to have to say this—but you appear more concerned about Freddie than you do about your own children, and me, for that matter.'

That had been the deciding blow, it had appeared, as Harriet had turned and walked from the room and a moment later he had heard her bedroom door open and close.

He had gazed at the last clue in the crossword for some considerable time after that, but the answer had continued to elude him.

Cecil surveyed himself in the mirror, adjusted the way the blazer rested on his shoulders and straightened his tie so that the swan and seahorse crest was central, turned to face the window and looked at himself sideways. Good, it would do. The ladies, of course, would take hours to get ready—hair teasing and spraying and make-up, and one dress then another, and first one pair of shoes, then a second, then a third. And which handbag? And how much jewellery? Or just the pearls? And then, of course, this evening, they would spend hours taking it all off. And everyone would go to bed and it would all be over. Tomorrow was another day.

Out of nowhere the pointlessness of it all welled up and threatened to overwhelm him.

He leaned his forehead against the mirror and closed his eyes, remembering the last time—the last Coronation in '37. He and Harriet had just become engaged. He'd been living in lodgings in Bayswater and not yet turned 30—still a young man, filled with a young man's hopes and ambitions. One's whole life ahead of one, the future unknown, a blank canvas. And now here he was in his mid-forties. Life was on a set course, there were no unknowns left. In a few short years the children would leave home, get married, start their own families. And he was left with his job, his wife, his home.

Was it enough?

The Coronation mugs stood on the dressing table. He picked one up and delicately unwrapped the intricately folded tissue paper until the mug was revealed in all its pageantry and splendour, and the face of the new Queen gazed serenely back at him.

He smiled. It was a splendid day—a day to remember.

Cecil was first down to breakfast. He sat alone in the breakfast room and waited for Mrs Thompson to bring in the tea. Upstairs he could hear sounds of movement.

'Mummy, what shoes should I wear? I don't like that black pair, they hurt my feet.'

'I hardly think it's a tie sort of day, Mumsy. After all, it's not as if we were actually attending the service at the Abbey, is it?'

'Could you please just dress yourself, Anne,' came Harriet's irritable reply, audible, though indistinctly, from her dressing room. 'Nanny, would you please see to it.'

Cecil sat and twirled the napkin ring around his napkin silently. The two mugs in their crisp white tissue paper stood on the sideboard.

Eventually his family began to emerge—Anne and Nanny first, the one bursting energetically into the room, the other red-faced and a little flustered, self-consciously bringing up the rear.

'Good morning, Anne. Good morning, Nanny. And a happy Coronation Day to you both,' Cecil remarked.

'Happy Coronation Day!' Anne sang back, plonking herself down at the table and grabbing her napkin.

'Oh. Yes. Same to you, Mr Wallis,' added the Nanny, rather feebly.

'And what are your family doing to mark this momentous occasion, Miss Corbett? Are they attending a street party?'

The question seemed to flummox the girl, then she recovered herself and said, somewhat grimly, 'Oh yes, a street party. They're all going to a lovely party down our street.'

And Anne, who had been fussily rearranging her position on the chair, looked up and said, 'But Father, Nanny doesn't have a family, do you, Nanny? They were all killed.'

No one appeared to know what to reply to this and thankfully Julius strode into the room at that moment with his hands in his pockets.

'Morning, Pops,' he announced blithely, reaching for the discarded *Times* from last night. 'Here we all are then,' he continued. 'The big day finally upon us. A day of pageantry and jollity to thrill the masses, eh?'

Fortunately Mrs Thompson chose that moment to arrive with the tea and coffee pots. She burst into the breakfast room in a gaudy Coronation apron, her hair recently set for the occasion.

'What a mornin'!' she announced breathlessly. 'Thought we was gonna run out of coffee,' she declared, dumping the two pots on the table with a jarring thud and a shake of her tightly permed head. 'But at the last minute I found a spare packet at the back of the shelf.'

'That is a relief, Mrs T,' said Julius. 'Lord knows what we'd have done but for your quick thinking and eagle eyes.'

Mrs Thompson made no reply to this as she was already patting her hair and heading out of the door.

'Oh. Beg your pardon, Mrs Wallis,' she said, and Harriet entered the room looking cross.

'*Why* is that wretched woman always in the way?' said Harriet pulling out her chair and glaring furiously at them all.

There was a surprised silence. As far as anyone knew Mrs Thompson wasn't always in the way. Indeed, she tended to spend the majority of her time downstairs smoking her revolting cigarettes, poring over the *Daily Mail* and listening to *Have a Go* and *Twenty Questions* and *Round Britain Quiz* on the radio. One frequently had to go in search of her.

But Harriet was cross. Had been cross for days. More than cross, truth be told. Downright unpleasant. Cecil poured himself a cup of tea, but he could feel her eyes on him.

'Betrays!' announced Julius and everyone stared at him. 'Twelve across, seven letters. *"A gamble on some sunshine is treacherous"*: bet-rays. *Betrays.*'

The crossword completed, he tossed *The Times* aside and set to work on a piece of toast. Mrs Thompson had prepared kippers for breakfast and she placed the steaming plate on the sideboard with some ceremony.

'I thought kippers for today,' she announced proudly, as though a plate of copper-coloured, steaming kippers was the ultimate tribute to the Coronation. She had also prepared a mountain of toast, which stood stacked two-deep in the silver toast rack in the centre of the table, cooling rapidly.

'Marvellous,' replied Cecil, smiling at her in a way that, he hoped, acknowledged the extra effort she had put in on this auspicious occasion. 'I trust you have prepared enough kippers for yourself too, Mrs Thompson?' he added, on a sudden wave of bonhomie.

'Oh, I can't abide them,' said Mrs Thompson airily. 'Nasty, slippery things they are,' and she sailed out of the room.

'I don't like kippers either,' announced Anne solemnly from the far end of the table. She laid her knife and fork down on either side of her plate and regarded her parents silently as though she had been asked to do something heinous. As she had happily tucked into a kipper the last time they had been served, Cecil felt a flicker of annoyance but Harriet got in before him.

'Don't eat one, then,' she replied crisply and Anne scowled down at her plate.

There was a brief silence.

'Well, I find a kipper is a very satisfying and nourishing way to start the day,' announced Cecil, going over to the silver dish on the sideboard and placing two of the offending items onto his plate. 'And Mrs Thompson is a dab hand at preparing them,' he added.

'And yet she never eats them herself,' observed Julius darkly.

Cecil experienced a second flicker of annoyance—actually, this time it was more a flash than a flicker, and he was glad he had his back to the table. Why were they harping on about kippers on this most special of mornings?

'Mummy, may I go and watch the Coronation with Brigit Myles?' said Anne. 'Her family have a flat with a balcony that overlooks Hyde Park. They are having ever such a grand party and Brigit said she asked her mother and her mother said I could go.'

'As her mother has not seen fit to ask your father or myself whether it is acceptable,' replied Harriet, 'I do not think it appropriate. And we do not announce such invitations at the last moment, Anne. It is impolite.'

Anne's face turned a mottled red and she glared defiantly at her empty plate.

'I want to go! It's not *fair!*'

'Nanny, did you know anything about this?'

Nanny looked up, wide-eyed, from the slice of toast she was nibbling, a rabbit caught in the headlights of a speeding lorry.

'Well, I said Anne ought to ask you ...' she replied slowly, with a glance at Anne.

'Nanny said I could go!' wailed Anne and Nanny looked horrified.

'I most certainly did not! I said it wasn't up to me at all. I said to ask.'

'You said I could go!'

That one of them was lying was apparent to Cecil. And that that person was, in all likelihood, Anne made it no easier to accept. All children lied, of course—it was a natural part of growing up ... Not that he had ever lied to his own father, never. Except about enjoying things. But that was different—it was expected that one would lie about enjoying oneself.

'This is a family day, Anne,' he observed calmly as he returned to the table and seated himself. 'An occasion for spending time with one's family. I'm sure Brigit and her mother will understand.'

Anne fell mutinously silent. He was aware that Harriet was watching him as he reached for a slice of toast and began to spread butter on it. There was so much toast that taking a single slice made no noticeable inroad into the stack. This was not how he had imagined their Coronation breakfast to be. But there were the mugs; he had intended some kind of ceremony, a few words. A presentation.

'Nanny hasn't eaten any breakfast,' said Anne sullenly, as though she was determined to get the girl into trouble. And indeed Nanny's plate was empty. The girl flushed a deep scarlet.

She was an odd one, that girl.

'Anne, we do not make personal comments,' said Harriet coldly.

'That's not a personal comment. I was just saying—'

'I said *no*,' said Harriet, and Anne assumed a look of outraged silence.

'Well,' said Julius, having dispatched a kipper, and placing his napkin on his plate, 'I'm afraid I must dash. Mind if I leave the table?'

'Actually, I'd be obliged if you would stay a moment longer, old man,' said Cecil quickly, and something flashed across the boy's face.

'Of course. Anything you say, old boy.'

'I wanted to say a few words, that's all.' Cecil spoke lightly, cheerily. After all, this was a celebration, wasn't it?

Julius looked down at his plate and something twitched at the side of this mouth. Anne sniffed sulkily and Harriet sat very still. Nanny, who had unfortunately chosen that moment to reach for a second slice of toast, now dropped her hand back onto her lap and stared at her plate in obvious mortification. She, the nanny—alone amongst them all?—understood the gravity, the import of the occasion. He addressed the nanny.

'This is an important day,' he began. No, that wasn't right. 'This may be the most important, the most special, the most historic day of our lives!'

'What about the war ending?' said Anne.

Cecil ignored this interruption.

'Today heralds the start of a new era in the History of Our Nation. A new Elizabethan Age, and we are all privileged to witness it.'

No one said anything. They appeared to be waiting for him to go on—or to finish?

'And I, for one, am delighted to be able to celebrate such a momentous event with my family. And I trust that in later years, when we are all older, when some of us—God forbid—are no longer here, that we may look back on this day with pleasure. With fondness.'

He paused. Was Harriet even listening? Nanny was listening. He wished he had bought the nanny a Coronation mug.

'And to that end, to mark this occasion and this special breakfast at the start of this historic day, I would like to present Julius and Anne with these,' and he went over to the sideboard and picked up the two packages and walked around and handed one to Julius and one to Anne. Then he resumed his seat.

There was a slight pause.

'Oh. Thanks,' said Julius, a trifle awkwardly.

'What is it?' said Anne.

Cecil sat down and poured himself a cup of coffee. Harriet hadn't touched the coffee. He didn't usually drink coffee himself before eleven o'clock, but the pot was there, full and steaming gently, and Mrs Thompson had gone to some trouble to make it.

Both children unwrapped the white tissue paper and simultaneously revealed the creamy Coronation mugs.

'Oh. I've already got one. We got given these at school,' said Anne, putting it down on the table. Julius said nothing.

'Well, now you have two,' said Cecil with a bright smile. 'Perhaps you can present one to your own children in time, as a memento?'

Anne didn't reply to this suggestion.

Julius stifled a yawn.

'Well. This has all been thoroughly entertaining, of course, but I have lots to do, so if no one objects I shall push off.'

'We don't "push off", Julius. We leave the table,' Cecil snapped and Julius froze, half off his chair.

'Then I shall leave the table, if I may?'

'Of course.'

Anne left too. Only the nanny stayed behind to pick up the discarded tissue paper and the two mugs. Cecil watched her over his coffee.

'Why don't you take one, Nanny?' he suggested, wishing for some reason that Nanny had not just witnessed this absurd charade.

Nanny looked up.

'Oh no, they belong to the children,' she said, and left the room.

A car drove past the window below, tooting its horn excitedly. People had begun to celebrate already. There had been talk of a street party in Athelstan Gardens, but most of the households had purchased a television and wanted to watch it at home. Friends, family, neighbours were already beginning to arrive, or to go somewhere else if they had made other arrangements.

'Well, that was a ridiculous little scene,' observed Harriet.

They were alone now, the children, the nanny, Mrs Thompson gone. The coldness of her words, the contempt, froze the blood in his veins. It was the first thing she had said to him since the horrid little scene last night.

Was no one going to eat all this toast?

'Uncle Leo and Aunt Felicity are here!' called Anne excitedly from upstairs. Her bad temper from breakfast was, it seemed, now all but forgotten. Oh, for the simplicity, the short memory of youth, thought Cecil as he straightened his tie for the third time before the mirror. Leo and Felicity were here. The day had begun.

'Hello! Happy Coronation Day, one and all!' called Leo from the hallway.

'Hello, Uncle Leo—have you brought us anything? Hello, Aunt Felicity.'

'Hello, Anne. My, don't you look pretty in your lovely dress!'

'Here you are, kids, Coronation mugs. Keep 'em safe. Could be worth a fortune one day.'

'Smashing. We shall be able to set up a stall in Portobello Road soon,' said Julius.

'Harriet! How the devil are you? Looking a little peaky—or is that just the excitement of the occasion?'

'Hello, Leo. Good of you to come. Felicity.'

And perhaps it was indicative of the mounting excitement that Harriet went straight to Felicity and clasped both her hands and went to kiss her. But Felicity, who never appeared entirely at ease at the best of times, now positively turned to ice and she twisted her head at the last moment so that the kiss ended in mid-air. Then she gave her sister-in-law the most fleeting of smiles, dropped her hands and moved away, and it occurred to Cecil that, in April, Harriet had told him Felicity was pregnant. Yet here she was, two months later, and she and Leo had said nothing, and clearly Felicity was nothing of the sort.

It had been a lie, then, to force him to help Freddie.

'Uncle Leo, is Archie with you?' said Julius, peering past his uncle into the hallway.

'Yes, he's bringing up the rear—got his own car now, you know. And some dolly bird.'

'Don't, Leo,' said Felicity.

'What? I didn't say a thing!'

It was time to go downstairs.

He ran into the nanny as soon as he left his room. Blast.

'Oh, Miss Corbett. I must apologise—'

'Mr and Mrs Mumford are here,' she said, and it seemed to Cecil that the girl had deliberately cut him off.

'Yes, indeed. You'll be joining us, will you? For the broadcast? Might be the last time we're all together.'

There was a silence.

'My wife did explain to you that Anne has been accepted into Wellbeck College—my sister's old school? It's a very good place, and needless to say we're delighted. There was some possibility—her reports from St Lydwina's have not always been ... Well, needless to say, it's a relief. So we won't be requiring your services much longer, then. And as we leave for the south of France at the end of June—'

He paused. Why didn't the girl say something?

'My wife did explain ... ?'

'No, I don't believe Mrs Wallis mentioned it at all.'

'Oh.' Blast Harriet for putting him in this awkward spot. 'Well, I daresay it won't inconvenience you too substantially? Plenty of households crying out for a nanny. Of course, references won't be a problem. Mrs Wallis will take care of all that ...'

'No,' replied the Nanny, 'I don't believe it will inconvenience me.'

'Good. Splendid. And you'll be joining us to watch the broadcast?'

The broadcast was set to commence at a quarter past ten and by ten past the drawing room was filling up. The sliding doors had been opened and the guests now spilled into the breakfast room too. Leo had brought his nephew, Archie Longhurst, who was doing his national service and who had arrived looking dapper in his grey airman's uniform, his ears sticking out and a girl on his arm. The girl was called Mavis or Maeve and had an unfortunate Midlands accent. 'Coventry,' she had corrected, when someone had remarked on this. She clung to Archie's arm and laughed a lot and reached for a new glass each time a tray was brought round.

Valerie and David Swanbridge were here, David all debonair in an open-necked shirt and unseasonable suntan, laughing at everything, Valerie in orange and black, peering at everyone over the rim of her champagne, and as arch as a three-span railway bridge. Mr and Mrs Vincento from number 79 were here, and so too the Paxtons from number 18, neither of whose households had television. Little was known of the Vincentos, who were newly arrived in Athelstan Gardens. Cecil made a special point of introducing them to the Paxtons. Vaughn and Ruth Paxton were long-term Athelstan residents and, as such, key persons to know—at least they thought so. Cecil left Mr Vincento—who, despite his name, heralded from Cirencester—deep in conversation with Vaughn Paxton. The rather portly Mrs Vincento latched onto Archie, leaving Ruth Paxton and Maeve (or Mavis) from Coventry to search desperately for a conversational starting point.

Julius had a couple of his school chums here—Alistair, and a boy called Pemberton whose father was in tinned mackerel, and who was extraordinarily tall and blushed whenever he was addressed.

Anne had none of her friends here. Come to think of it, one was hard put to remember the name of any of Anne's friends. There was this Brigit Myles girl, presumably, though he had never heard mention of her prior to today.

'Mrs Paxton, Valerie—champagne?'

'Thank you, Mr Wallis, but Vaughn and I never take alcohol before lunch.'

'Don't you?' remarked Valerie in some surprise. 'How crushingly dull for you. I'll have hers, Cecil. Cigarette, anyone?'

A catering firm had been hired for the day and a young man of Eastern European appearance was moving expertly between the guests balancing a tray of champagne glasses. Another was distributing Spanish olives on French toast, and smoked salmon, both delivered at an astonishing price from Harrods just after breakfast. There was a crab soufflé, too, cooling on the kitchen table downstairs. Good. All was going well.

'Did you hear, Archie? Hillary has reached the summit of Everest. Swanbridge, did you hear? They announced it earlier over the radio.'

'Good lord, is this smoked salmon, Wallis?'

'It really is a magnificent achievement!'

'It was really just a call to Harrods—'

'They said it could never be done—not humanly possible.'

'David's company supplied them, you know, Mr Longhurst.'

'The smoked salmon?'

'Yes, I just telephoned to Harrods—'

'For God's sake, Cecil, no one cares where you got the blasted salmon.'

'But Daddy, won't all the men on Everest miss the Coronation?'

'Be quiet, Anne.'

'I say, is this real smoked salmon?'

'It's time, it's time for the television!' said Anne in a loud voice and everyone laughed. They began to arrange themselves in chairs around the television and Cecil went over, rather ceremoniously, to turn it on. He paused, wondering whether to mark the occasion with a few words, but the memory of breakfast still smarted, so he pulled the knob and to a loud cheer the screen crackled into life (thank heavens! What if the contraption had failed?) and there was a woman in a long gown smiling at the camera.

'Welcome,' she said, 'to this historic broadcast.'

'Hurrah!' said someone.

'Ssh!' came a chorus of voices.

The picture changed and suddenly they were at the Victoria Memorial, right outside the Palace.

'Is Uncle Simon there? Mummy, is Uncle Simon at the Palace?'

'And here she is!' said the presenter. 'The young Queen Elizabeth, looking serene and radiant, emerging from the Palace, the Duke of Edinburgh beside her in this splendid Gold State Coach drawn by eight magnificent Windsor Greys. It really is an auspicious moment!'

The carriage, of course, was grey on the tiny screen, but it hardly seemed to matter, for this was really happening right now, only a few short miles away.

'In't she bootiful?' said someone with a sigh—presumably the Mavis woman.

'Quite marvellous!'

'Look at the crowds!'

'How many were they expecting, do you know?'

'Is that my champagne?'

'For heaven's sake, Leo, you're sitting on my handbag.'

The carriage made its way along the Embankment and the commentator—a man now—had almost to shout to be heard over the cheers of the crowds who were lined ten, twenty, thirty deep in some places. The route was lined with sailors and marines and Grenadier Guards who snapped to attention as the carriage swung past, liveried footmen walked alongside the carriage and others rode behind in a sea of pageantry that was bewildering. In no time at all the procession had swung into Parliament Square and ahead was the Abbey.

'Apparently something in the region of two million television sets have been sold in the last few weeks. They're expecting a television audience of some eight million! Extraordinary, isn't it?'

'Is that right?'

'So much for the starving masses and their welfare state.'

'Julius!'

'Quite right, old boy. The people no longer want cake, they want television!'

They could see the carriages pull up outside the Abbey, one after another. Princess Margaret and the Queen Mother emerged and went inside, and at last the Queen's Gold State Coach swung around the corner and slowed to a halt.

'Gosh, isn't it exciting?' someone said.

'There are four cameras positioned actually inside the Abbey. The fellows manning the cameras have so little room to move they had to choose only the smallest cameramen to sit there.'

'I really don't think anyone needs to know that, Leo.'

'Uncle Leo said the whole lot's being relayed live to West Germany, Holland and France, didn't you, Uncle Leo?'

'Don't encourage him.'

'Is that right, Mr Mumford?'

'Bang on! And your lot, Archie, the RAF boys, are flying telerecordings to Canada at three points during the day. By this afternoon local time they'll be watching this very same broadcast in North America. Think of it!'

'Canberra jet bombers, Mavis. Takes each one five hours to cross the Atlantic.'

'Fancy!'

'And here she is!' cried the presenter. 'Amid a magnificent hail of bells, the Queen's coach arrives at Westminster Abbey!'

A silence fell as the coachman opened the coach door and the Queen and the Duke of Edinburgh climbed out and, surrounded by a host of white-gowned maids carrying the Royal train, they entered the Abbey. The procession of Royalty, dignitaries and clergy made their slow way down the aisle in stately silence, the Queen flanked by her six ladies-in-waiting.

'What happens now?'

'Ssh!'

'And now the Archbishop of Canterbury speaks,' the presenter continued.

'I here present unto you Queen Elizabeth, your undoubted Queen, wherefore all who are come this day, do you homage and service. Are you willing to do the same?'

The BBC microphones crackled.

'What did she say?'

'Ssh!'

'And now the Queen takes the Coronation Oath,' whispered the presenter.

'Madam, is your Majesty willing to take the oath?' said the Archbishop, and the silence reverberated around the abbey so that it seemed every guest was holding their breath.

'I am willing!' came back the words, strong and vibrant.

More oaths followed before the Queen's maid began to remove her jewels and her robes.

'They're undressing her. Why are they doing that?'

'Because it's a Coronation, you clot.'

'Mummy, Julius just—'

'Ssh!'

'And now the Archbishop of Canterbury anoints her with the holy oil.'

'Why does he do that?'

'Anne! Shut up, there's a dear.'

The Queen was now being solemnly dressed in layers of stiff golden robes before being silently handed the symbols of her monarchy: the sceptre, the orb, the rod of mercy and the royal ring. And finally the Archbishop held the crown aloft and placed it slowly and magnificently on her head.

Again, everyone held their breath.

'God save the Queen!' rang out through the Abbey and beyond, trumpets sounded, guns fired and bells rang in one glorious cacophony across the city.

Cecil watched and felt a moment of perfect peace.

'There's no more champagne. Cecil, old boy—you haven't run out, have you?'

Cecil sat up. 'No, of course not. I'll go and dig some out. Harriet—where's Harriet?'

And Anne, standing by the window, said, 'Daddy, the police are here.'

Chapter Twenty-six

JUNE 1953

Jean stood at the window of her room and saw the people in the street below, laughing and talking excitedly, the children in their Sunday best waving their miniature Union Jacks, the girls with their hair tied in colourful ribbons, the boys in their smartly polished shoes. And the ladies in their pretty dresses, their hair stacked high on their heads or hidden beneath smart hats.

And over it all the grey clouds gathered and a driving rain began to fall.

She bent her head so that her forehead touched the window pane. The glass felt cool against her skin. She raised both hands to shoulder height and pressed them flat against the window, her fingers splayed. Her hands pressed harder against the glass so that the fingers went rigid and her wrists began to ache and the muscles in her forearms twitched. The glass would break, the jagged broken pieces would slice through the delicate flesh and tendons of her wrists and sever the arteries. There would be blood, a great deal of blood. Or perhaps she would fall, would tumble out of the broken window and down, down three storeys to the pavement below. It would kill you, a fall like that. She could already see herself sprawled on the ground far below, her neck broken.

She pushed, but the glass did not break. Her arms fell limply to her sides.

God had deserted her.

Outside the rain suddenly became a downpour and with shrieks and laughter the people picked up their skirts and their children and covered their hair-dos and ran for shelter, splashing through puddles, battling with umbrellas. They returned to their large houses to turn on their televisions and somewhere, not too far away, a queen was being crowned. The lampposts were hung with flapping, soggy bunting.

God had deserted them all.

And Mr Wallis had made a speech.

There had been no speech in this household on Christ's birthday and no marking of the occasion of His death on the cross. But on this day of pomp and ceremony Mr Wallis had made a speech. He, who had never known a single day of discomfort, who had spent his childhood in comfort and security, who had fought the war from behind the safety of a large desk in his important office, was this morning delighted to be celebrating such a momentous event with his family.

The children had received Coronation mugs and, when they had spurned the gifts bestowed on them, Mr Wallis had offered them to her, the nanny. She would rather commit a thousand mortal sins than accept such an offering.

Dad had had a Coronation mug for the old King's Coronation in '37. It had four flags on the side beneath a crown and two oval portraits, one of the King and one of the Queen and the words 'LONG MAY HE REIGN' in fancy writing underneath. It had hung on a hook on the dresser in the kitchen for as long as anyone could remember, and Dad had drunk his cup of tea out of it every morning, regular as clockwork. Even that last Sunday.

Even on that last Sunday, when everything else had changed.

Dad had come home at dawn that February morning, which was odd because his shift usually didn't end till eight o'clock. Had she noticed that at the time? Had she thought, That's odd, Dad's home early? Or was it only afterwards that she had realised that something was amiss?

By that stage of the war, with the shortages so severe, Dad was working every nightshift for the extra money and often, if the shift was undermanned or a big ship was in, he worked the morning shift too. It was looters, mostly, that Dad guarded against. Saboteurs, the government called them, and very anxious they were about it, too, according to Dad, as though the ships that came in for servicing and repairs were top secret when really they were just old tankers and passenger liners refitted as troop ships and supply ships, part of the convoys that sometimes managed to cross the North Atlantic.

When she and Gladys had come down for breakfast Dad had been sitting at the kitchen table, his mug—the old Coronation mug—sitting empty before him, his face pale and blinking from lack of sleep, his eyes red-rimmed like everyone's eyes had been in the Blitz from the smoke and lack of sleep. Mum had looked up at them standing in the doorway, herself and Gladys already in their Sunday best, and she had stood up abruptly, so abruptly she had knocked over her chair.

'Go and play outside, please, children. Your Dad and I have things to discuss,' and she had shut the kitchen door.

No one ever shut the kitchen door. It was always open. She and Gladys had stared at each other in silent confusion.

'Tell the others,' Jean had instructed Gladys. 'Tell them Mum and Dad have something to discuss. Tell them to play outside until it is time to go to Chapel,' and Gladys had nodded wide-eyed and gone upstairs to tell them. For that was what you did, you became Mum and Dad when Mum and Dad weren't there; as the eldest it was expected.

Between them they had shepherded Nerys and Edward and Bertie into the street with the minimum of fuss and set them to a game of 'What's the Time, Mr Wolf?'

'Are you not playing, Jean?' said Gladys, watching her elder sister closely, taking her cue from her.

Jean had shaken her head. 'I'll keep watch,' she had replied. And she had returned to the house and stood outside the kitchen, waiting till it was time to go to Chapel.

But they hadn't gone to Chapel. Half an hour had passed, and at last Mum had emerged from the kitchen, a worried frown on her face, and she had paused when she saw her eldest daughter.

'We're not attending Chapel, Jean. Go and tell the children and get them out of their best clothes. I don't want them spoiling them playing in the street.'

It was a February morning, 1945. The wind, Jean remembered, had been bitingly cold, and, with no coal to burn, the house had been almost as cold as the street outside. And the children out in the wind and in their Sunday clothes. She remembered being worried about their clothes—if they spoiled their best clothes they would be attending Chapel in their week-day clothes, all patched up and hand-me-downs, and Mum would never have allowed that. The clothes were Jean's responsibility; if they were ruined she would be to blame. She would fetch the children in.

But Mum had said, we're not attending Chapel.

Jean had stared at her in astonishment. Not attending Chapel? They always went to Chapel. Even when Dad had done his back in, even when Mum had been bad with a fever. Always, *always* they went.

'But why? Are you not well, Mum? Is it Dad? Do you want me to take the children to Chapel on my own?' Jean had asked anxiously, a sense of something ominous creeping over her.

'No, love, we're quite well, your Dad and me, but something has happened. At your Dad's work—though with God's help, it will be all right.' Mum had paused and frowned. 'And I'll not have you going off to Chapel on your own, it's too far. Now, be a good girl and bring the children in out of the cold. They'll catch their death.'

She had stared in silence, noticing suddenly that Mum was distracted, her hair falling out of her hair net, her fingers twitching restlessly by her sides then reaching up to push her hair out of her face. But saying nothing. Instead Mum had turned and gone back into the kitchen.

Jean had stood and waited. For what, she wasn't sure.

Eventually she had gone outside and brought in the children, hurrying them and ignoring their questions.

'Are we not goin' to Chapel, then, Jean?' said Gladys.

'But it's my turn! It's my turn, Mr Wolf!' cried Bertie, half excited, half annoyed.

'You never wait for your turn,' said Edward. 'And anyway, Mr Wolf would easily 'ave caught you, just you see if he wouldn't!'

'But why are we to go inside and take off our Sunday best, Jean?' said Nerys, standing determinedly in the doorway.

'Just you do what our Mum tells you, Nerys Corbett,' said Jean firmly, counting the last child in through the front door and closing it shut behind them, and behind the cold February morning.

'But what *is* it, Jean?'

'If you know, you 'ave to tell us!'

'I don't know nothin'!'

'She *does* know! Gladys, she does—and she won't tell!'

'Shut up, Nerys, I was with Jean when Mum come out the kitchen and Mum didn't say nothin'!'

'Gladys! Nerys! *Stop* it!'

'I want to go outside and play!'

314

'Well, you can't, it's Sunday.'

'But we went out before and Mum said we could!'

'*Ow!* Edward pulled my 'air!'

'But *why* aren't we goin' to Chapel? Why aren't we?'

'It's 'cause you're an 'orrid little boy, Bertie, and God don't want you in His 'ouse no more!'

'That's not true! That's not true!'

'Oh, put a *sock* in it, Bertie—'

'*SHUT UP!* All of you! Don't you *understand*? Somethin' *bad* 'as 'appened! Somethin' very bad!'

Jean had left them, then, Gladys and Nerys and Edward and Bertie, and those had been her final words to them.

She had gone back downstairs, angry and fearful. She would let Mum know that the children were all inside, that was what she would do. She had done her duty.

The kitchen door had been open. She had seen Dad still sitting at the kitchen table. Dad, who was normally so active, so big, always moving, talking, laughing. Now he was sitting silently, unmoving. He had looked small. When he saw her, he had looked up, given her a look—sad, anxious? No, it had been more than that, a look that she had not been able to understand.

'Dad?'

But Dad had frowned and looked away.

'Come inside, child,' Mum had said. 'And close the door for a moment, there's a good girl.'

Jean had come in and sat down at the table and a great fear had gripped her like a giant pair of hands tightly squeezing her stomach. She was about to be told what had happened, because she was the eldest. For a moment she had longed to be upstairs playing and squabbling with the other children.

'What is it?' she had said, and it had been important to sound normal. Calm. Grown up.

'Well, love. There's been a silly mix up at the dock—'

'Not a silly mix up,' Dad had interrupted gruffly. 'I took somethin'.

Let's not beat around the bush, Gloria. I took somethin' what wasn't mine to take. Thou shalt not steal, says the Lord, and I stole. And I knew it was stealin' and I stole anyway. I have failed you all and there's no two ways about it. I have let you all down, and the Government, and myself. And the Lord.'

Jean had listened silently, wide-eyed, appalled.

'What your Dad's saying is that—'

'What I'm *saying*, girl, is that I got caught and I got the sack. There—I'm not proud of it, it's a shameful thing to admit to, but there you are.'

Jean had put her hand to her mouth while the kitchen, the world, spun uncontrollably around her. She had looked from one to the other to see what it meant, to read in their faces how this would affect them.

'It's unjust!' Mum had burst out suddenly, 'Your Dad took an orange, Jean, for you children. A single, solitary orange from the warehouse—it's downright unjust, Owen. After all the years you've put in at that place, all the extra shifts, all through the Blitz—'

'I broke the law,' Dad had said quietly, his head down. 'Just once, it's true, but I got caught. And I was meant to be watching the place. I was there to keep the looters out. I let them all down. And last night the supervisor from the Ministry was there, otherwise no one would have noticed—except the Lord.' He had bowed his head.

'Will you … go to prison?' Jean had said, the word dry as sandpaper on her tongue.

'Oh, Owen!' Mum had whispered, her voice breaking. 'But you have a family to support! Owen, did you not tell him? What will we live on now? You've worked the docks eighteen years!'

Dad had frowned. 'I'll not be going to prison, child. The supervisor dismissed me, but said he'd not call the police. We ought to be grateful, Gloria.'

But he had glowered at the table in a way that she hadn't seen since Father Bellamy had brought a Catholic to preach at Chapel one Sunday.

'*Grateful*? I'll not be grateful to anyone who dismisses a man for stealing food to feed his family!' Mum had said, pounding the table in sudden fury. 'What do they know, these men in their fine suits sitting in their offices in Whitehall? What do they know of our lives here? They tell *us* to make sacrifices—every day they tell us—but what sacrifices do *they* make? Living in their big houses with their servants! What do they know about what *we* have to put up with?'

Jean had sat frozen to her seat, her stomach twisting in sickening knots. She had never seen Mum angry, never. And Dad so silent, so small. It was frightening.

'I've a good mind to go round there—'

'*Enough!*' Dad had said, thumping the table, and Jean had cowered. 'That is enough, Gloria. What's done is done. There's nothin' more to be said about it.'

And amazingly Mum had defied him.

'*No*. You are wrong, Owen Corbett. You have to fight for your rights in this world, the Good Lord knows I am right. Go back to this supervisor and talk to him. Explain it to him—'

'I said *ENOUGH*!'

This time there was silence.

Upstairs a loud thump followed by a howl of pain made them all look up.

'Jean. You must be a good child,' Mum had said then, barely above a whisper, her face pale. 'We've told you what happened and there'll be changes now, you can be sure of that. Go upstairs and settle the children while we decide what's to be done.'

So Jean had left the kitchen, but instead of joining her brothers and sisters she had gone outside. Out into the space and solitude of the cold February morning. Dad had stolen! It had been inconceivable! It had been too much to take in. It had been a sin against God. And yet—and yet, if you were starving? If your family was starving?

It was wrong because others were starving too. Dad had said he wouldn't go to prison ... But would he go to Hell? Dad was a good man! He was a *good* man!

She had walked quickly away from the house, southward towards the river, going instinctively towards the Chapel because it was a Sunday morning and that was where you went on Sunday morning.

We should go to Chapel, she had thought, pausing on a street corner. They'll notice we're not there, of course they will! And they'll want to know why we're not there. They'll find out, someone will talk. And then what? Everyone would know. Pride was a sin. Forgiveness was heavenly. But Dad had stolen from the warehouse, from Government property—from the war effort. They would all know.

It had been so very cold out and she had been wearing only her thin cardigan. Shivering, she had turned away from the street that led down to the Chapel, not knowing which direction to take. The street had been empty. It had still been early, only church-goers out at that time, and late shift-workers returning home bleary-eyed, clutching empty sandwich boxes. A bird had burst suddenly into raucous song. A dog had barked somewhere in the distance.

The rocket had appeared overhead with no warning. No air-raid siren sounded, people had no time to run onto the street, or to run from the street into a shelter. It had screamed overhead with a whistle, coming from the southeast, from the coast, all the way from Holland. She froze in her tracks, the blood running cold through her veins as it reached her, then passed her, and she sagged with relief. Not here then, not her, not this time.

But then it had stopped. A second, two seconds later and Jean had seen it falling from the sky a little way to the north. And everything had stopped: sound, the wind, time itself.

And a lifetime had passed and then the world had erupted.

She had run. Run back the way she had come, along the deserted streets, tripping over a bottle, the kerb, her thin cardigan flapping, her shoes barely touching the pavement as she flew home.

But there had been no home. There had just been a hole where that section of the street had been. A hole and smoke and flames and rubble. And oddly, at her feet, a shard of white bone china with the King's head and the words *'LONG MAY HE REIGN'* in fancy writing.

They should have been at Chapel. If only they had gone to Chapel. If only.

'You have to fight for your rights in this world, the Good Lord knows I am right,' Mum had said. 'Go back to the supervisor and talk to him. Explain it to him—'

But Dad had shaken his head. Dad had not wanted to fight. 'Wallis won't change his mind. Why should he? You don't know these people.'

No, they did not know these people.

But they knew their names. Jean knew his name: Wallis, the supervisor from the Ministry. Mr Cecil Wallis. And she remembered that name just as she remembered the man who had designed the V2 rocket, though she did not know his name, and the men and the women who had worked in a factory in Holland to build it—slaves, she now knew they had been, and yet still she blamed them—and the soldier, some young man whose mother loved him, stationed in northern Holland who had operated the equipment that sent the rocket up and over the coastline and across the North Sea and over Kent and all the way to Malacca Row, Stepney, so that it could destroy her family and her home. Oh yes, she remembered them all.

But she knew only one name. And she had come across that name again in the most unexpected place—the Festival of Britain. *Mr Cecil Wallis, a director of Empire and Colonial Lines.* Right there in black and white.

She had needed to know, all these years later, if Mum was right: *did* he have fine suits and an office in Whitehall? *Did* he live in a big house with servants? The office, it had turned out, was off Chancery Lane, a big important office in the city, easy enough to track down; and the house—she had followed him home from work—was big, and elegant, with many storeys and many rooms, situated in a tree-lined street in a very smart suburb. And yes, there had been servants, for on a certain day last September she had observed Nanny Peters emerge from the house.

God had led her here as surely as He had led the Israelites out of the desert, yet she still did not know why.

This morning Mr Wallis had asked her what her family were doing to mark the Coronation. Then, barely an hour later, he had dismissed her from his employ, as carelessly, as summarily, as he had dismissed Dad eight years earlier. He had hoped that she would not be too substantially inconvenienced.

Outside the rain continued to fall and a police car drew up in front of the house and two policemen got out. The two policemen came up the steps and knocked on the Wallises' front-door. A moment later they emerged from the house with Mrs Wallis and led her down the steps and into the car, then they drove off.

Jean realised she was missing the Coronation.

Chapter Twenty-seven

JUNE 1924

Harriet and Freddie had travelled home to England from India in the June of 1924.

On the evening of their embarkation their escort, Mr Stephens, had suggested they have tea and cakes at the Royal Bombay Yacht Club. It had been his treat. He had escorted the District Officer's two children on this long and fraught journey from their home in Jhelum to the dockside in Bombay. Now, his mission accomplished, he had poured the tea and handed round the Battenburg cake with an air of satisfaction.

They were due to sail to England on the ten o'clock tide.

'Well, time we were off,' Mr Stephens had said as the sun set in an orange glow in the west, and they made their way back to the ship.

Only they hadn't returned directly to the ship. Instead Mr Stephens had turned away from the quayside and taken them on a path that led into an ornate garden.

Night had fallen, instantly and without warning as it did every night in India, though that never prevented Mother and Father and just about every European who had lived in England remarking upon it in wonder.

'My God, the night falls quickly here,' Mr Stephens had remarked, and yet they had continued into the gardens and a thick foliage of orchids and casuarinas, bamboo and tamarinds reared up on either side of them, making the night darker still. Over their heads mahogany trees towered and on the ground creepers snaked across the path. The cicadas shrilled so that the very air vibrated.

Freddie was moody, hanging back, dragging his heels and not allowing anyone to hold his hand.

Mr Stephens went back and spoke to him then he rejoined Harriet.

'Freddie needs to spend a penny. I'll take him to a discreet spot. Will you be all right here, Harriet?'

Harriet wasn't at all certain that she would be all right there on her own, in a strange garden, in a strange city, in the pitch dark. But she nodded because that was what one did. Then she had watched as Freddie and Mr Stephens stepped off the path and were swallowed up in the undergrowth.

Now what?

She waited. There was no one else in the gardens, so surely they would not have to journey too far to locate a discreet spot for Freddie to spend his penny.

She waited.

The shriek of some animal nearby made her jump and she whirled about trying to locate it. Tiny yellow spots of light flickered in the undergrowth—a mongoose perhaps. The air was thick with tiny flying insects, with animals. But this wasn't the jungle—she had been in the real jungle where a snake, a scorpion, a leopard, a tiger, might jump out at you at any moment. This was just an ornate garden in a big, important city.

The animal shrieked again. It was a monkey, most probably.

Where *were* they? Ages had passed, simply *ages*!

A sudden flurry of wings filled the air and a dark shape flew out of the trees. She jumped and for a moment the only sound was her heart beating. But it was only a bat.

And then she heard another sound, a sound that wasn't an animal at all. It was a thud, like something solid falling onto the ground, then a voice. A man's voice. Distant. She couldn't tell whose voice or what was said, but it came from the same direction that Freddie and Mr Stephens had taken.

Harriet hesitated. Ought she to wait here as instructed? But if they were only a few yards away, why wait here? And what if something had happened?

She waited for the length of another breath then set off down the path and into the undergrowth from where the sound had come. Her heart thudded uncomfortably in her chest as she pushed her way through the overhanging fronds. She would never have run through a real jungle in the dark, never! But this was just a garden in a big city. There were people all around. She only had to call out and someone would come running to help.

She kept on pushing, blindly, her arms before her face to stop the fronds brushing against her. Then, quite suddenly, the trees parted and she was in a clearing. At the same moment the clouds slid apart and a near-full moon cast a pale yellow glow so that she could see quite clearly. And what she saw was a strange figure, a man—she assumed it was a man, it was a man's height and wearing a man's hat—standing in the centre of the clearing. And indeed the figure was wearing Mr Stephens's hat and Mr Stephens's umbrella was lying on the ground beside him. But the figure was misshapen. Horribly misshapen.

She paused and a call, a greeting, froze on her lips. The figure groaned, put its head back—Mr Stephens's head—and groaned.

And then Freddie cried out. And that was the misshapen part of the figure. There was another figure—a much smaller figure, a child's figure—on his knees before Mr Stephens.

Again Harriet nearly called out and again the words froze on her tongue. The child's head was buried in Mr Stephens's lap, in his trousers, and the child was crying, sobbing, but something held him there, the man's hand held him there, held him firmly at the back of his small head, held him firmly in place and the child was gulping for breath, sobbing.

Freddie was sobbing.

And Mr Stephens put his head back and gasped as though he had been hurt, but he didn't let go.

The umbrella, which until a moment ago had lain on a fallen palm frond, arced through the heavy darkness with the force of a hammer, handle first, and connected with Mr Stephens's temple, making a sickening thud. Mr Stephens crumpled and fell sideways.

Behind him stood Harriet, the pointy end of the umbrella still in her hands.

On the ground Mr Stephens lay quite still and his eyes gazed up at her, reflecting the light of the moon. Harriet stepped back in alarm. But the eyes didn't follow her.

She dropped the umbrella and grabbed Freddie's hand, pulling him to his feet, and together they ran blindly through the garden and emerged suddenly onto the well-lit esplanade not far from the big hotel.

Freddie was hysterical, alternately sobbing and trying to sit down on the pavement and refusing to move. But there was no time for this. They *must* get away!

Half dragging, half carrying Freddie, she made for the big black silhouette ahead of them that must be the Gateway. They reached the Gateway at last, somehow, and there beyond it was the *Tiberius*! It was flooded in light. And suddenly there were people, glorious, wonderful busy people all around! They could get lost in all the people and no one would ever find them. Officials from the ship strode about the quayside barking orders. Coolies scurried about loading on the last of the luggage, and last-minute passengers hurried importantly up the gangway.

Harriet had their papers—Mr Stephens had entrusted her with them when they had first boarded the ship. Now she pulled them out and showed them to the official at the top of the gangway. The official looked at them both with a long frown and made an agonising show of inspecting the papers, humming and hah-ing before finally announcing, 'Everything looks to be in order, miss. Welcome aboard.' Then he had frowned again. 'Everything all right? What's wrong with the little chap?'

'We're leaving our parents to go to school in England,' Harriet had replied, the words already rehearsed in her head.

The official had nodded. 'Yes, we get a lot of that. Chin up, young man; don't want your big sister to think you're a sissy, do you?'

Freddie hadn't replied and it was debatable he had even heard the man's words.

There were other passengers waiting to board and Harriet dragged Freddie to their cabin. People were looking at them, she knew, but it didn't matter. She closed and locked the door behind them and finally let Freddie go. For a moment she let him fall as she leant against the door, catching her breath and trying to think. She *must* think.

But Freddie was hysterical.

She picked him up and put him on the bed, stroking his head.

'Freddie, stop! Please stop, it's fine now. We're safe, we're on the ship, in our cabin. There's no one here. We're safe!'

Eventually he began to calm down and then, in a broken, sobbing voice he spoke.

'I didn't w-want to do it, b-but he said Father would be angry with me if I r-refused. He said Father would be angry if I didn't do w-whatever he said!'

Harriet held him tightly and listened and her heart seemed to turn black with hatred.

'He was *lying*, Freddie. Father wouldn't want you to do that. Father would be very, *very* angry with Mr Stephens if he knew. He was a bad, *bad* man. An *evil* man. He *lied* to you.'

'I didn't want to do it!' sobbed Freddie, though more quietly now. 'I thought Father would be angry with me.'

'I know. But it's safe now. Mr Stephens will never hurt you again.' She placed a finger beneath his chin and lifted his head up, looking at him silently for a moment, then she made herself smile. 'And if anyone asks, Mr Stephens took us back to the ship, then left us. That was the last time we saw him, wasn't it?'

Freddie listened, then he nodded silently.

Up on the deck she could hear the shouts from the sailors as the gangway was removed and mooring ropes untied. The ship's funnel boomed loudly and repeatedly. Above them the passengers crowded to the ship's deck to cheer and wave goodbye to friends and family.

Think, she must think. Mr Stephens wouldn't return to Jhelum. Father and Mother would be worried. 'You can always send a telegram,' Father had said, 'in an emergency.'

Well, this was an emergency, though Father would never know about it.

She opened the drawers in the little writing desk and found a telegram form and after a number of false starts wrote: 'SAFELY ABOARD STOP LOVE TO BOTH STOP H AND F STOP.'

Then she pulled out a sheet of writing paper and began her letter.

Dearest Mother and Father,
I hope you are both well and that Mother is feeling much better. I am writing from the cabin of the Tiberius as it disembarks. A lot of people are up on deck waving and cheering and dear Mr Stephens is standing at the dockside waving to us. He was so kind to bring us here and he looked after both Freddie and I most attentively ...

Three or four months after Father's letter announcing their Mother's death she had received a second letter from Father, this time relating the sad death of dear Mr Stephens. He had, it appeared, never made it back to Jhelum, but had been brutally murdered in a park in Bombay by person or persons unknown later that same night—presumably only hours after seeing the children off at the quayside. It was a sad and tragic loss, Father had observed. A young man with such potential, so cruelly struck down in the prime of his life. He would be sadly missed. His replacement, a Mr Downey, had arrived the previous week, and was already showing himself to be a fine worker.

They had never returned to India, she or Freddie.

Chapter Twenty-eight

JUNE 1953

'Is this him?'

A police inspector sporting a seedy little moustache and a rather cheap raincoat asked this question, and he looked at Harriet rather than at the figure lying motionless on the bed.

'Yes,' answered Harriet.

She wanted to add, Yes, this is my brother, but the words stuck fast in her throat.

A small glass pill bottle lay empty on the bed, another larger bottle still with an inch or so of some clear spirit in it was on the floor beside the bed. There were no signs of violence, no blood. Just a man lying on a bed. He could be asleep or drunk.

'There's a note,' said the policeman. He handed her a small unsealed envelope. 'Looks pretty straightforward—well, as far as these things ever are.' He paused to frown as though picking his words carefully. 'There'll be an inquest of course. Standard procedure. Nothing to worry about.'

'Of course.'

The policeman waited. For what, it was hard to tell. Questions, perhaps? For her to leave?

Harriet found that she had the envelope in her hand. She looked down at it. Her name was written on the envelope with a cheap biro in Freddie's flamboyant scribble: *Mrs Harriet Wallis, 83 Athelstan Gardens, SW1*. And so they had found her, really, with no trouble at all. But how had they found *him*? The policeman had said something about a neighbour. Freddie had lain here, it seemed, since last night. Dead some hours. He must have done it soon after she had left him the previous evening.

She swayed and the room lurched unexpectedly. She felt behind her for a wall, a chair.

'Here, let me help you,' said the policeman, springing over with sudden agility to take her elbow. 'There we are,' and he lowered her onto a chair. 'Mullins, where's that tea? Come on!'

He called out to a young WPC who was moving about in the kitchen. Then he turned back to Harriet and produced a kind and unlikely smile.

'Takes people this way sometimes,' he said and patted her hand.

Harriet watched as the police inspector's hand patted hers and she could see that his fingers touched hers and yet she felt nothing. It was as though he were touching some other person's hand.

'I take it the gentleman wasn't married?' he asked after a moment.

The room slowly came back into focus and she looked into the enquiring eyes of the policeman with the seedy moustache.

'No. No, he wasn't married. He never married.'

And now he never would. Oddly, her voice sounded normal. She didn't want it to sound normal.

'And when was it you last saw Mr Paget?'

'Last night. I was here last night.'

'Oh.' The inspector seemed surprised. Had he suspected they weren't close, she and Freddie? That his family had deserted him? Was that what his look implied? Or was he wondering why she had noticed nothing amiss, had done nothing to prevent this happening? And why *had* she noticed nothing amiss? Why *had* she done nothing to prevent this happening?

The WPC emerged bearing a cup and saucer.

'Ah, here we are, then,' observed the inspector approvingly. 'Good and hot and plenty of sugar.'

The WPC handed Harriet the tea with a sympathetic smile. No doubt they were trained in such things. No doubt this was as routine to them as a dinner party was to her. She held out her hand automatically and let the saucer rest on her lap. They seemed to expect her to drink it, so she put the rim of the cup to her lips and let the hot liquid seep over her tongue. It was sweet and milky and her tongue recoiled, but it was easier to drink than to think or to speak.

'Ambulance is here,' called the WPC—Mullins—who had gone to the window and lifted the net curtain. She crossed to the door and opened it and went out.

'We'll let them get on with it in peace, shall we?' said the inspector, and he helped her up and deftly led her through to the tiny kitchenette and pushed the door shut. They sat down on two vinyl-covered stools before a mean-looking table with a cracked yellow Formica surface.

'Lived alone, did he, Mr Paget?'

She tried to think. 'Yes, yes, he lived alone.' She wanted to add, this is not his normal home. This squalid, this horrid little bed-sit is only temporary. But it wasn't true, this was Freddie's home. She put the tea cup to her lips and let the revolting liquid scald her tongue and her throat.

The inspector nodded, then stood up, though he had been seated for less than a minute. 'Well. I'll leave you to it for a little while. Won't be long.'

For a moment it seemed that he would actually pat her knee, but he appeared to think better of it and left the room.

There was the letter in the unsealed envelope. Harriet stared at it and what—*what?*—could a note possibly say to explain this, to excuse this? Her fingers reached into the envelope and pulled out a single small sheet of plain, un-headed note paper, the sort one purchased cheaply at a stationer's and wrote hurried thank-you notes on to the man who had pruned your roses or the lady who had done the flowers at the church.

'Sorry, old girl. It just didn't seem worth the bother anymore.'

And that was the explanation, the excuse. The reason. Just this and nothing more.

She felt a moment of fury so intense the room went red and then black. But it faded as abruptly as it had appeared. Of course that was the reason, and what better reason was there? *It just didn't seem worth the bother anymore.*

There were noises from the other side of the door—men's voices, muted, respectful of her presence. A thump, a door banging open against the wall. Freddie, being manhandled out of his flat by strangers. Taken—where?

Simon. Someone needed to tell Simon. Simon was at the Palace. It was the day of the Coronation.

The door opened and the police inspector came in with a sympathetic smile.

'There now, all done,' he announced as though talking to a child. 'They'll take him to the mortuary. Like I said, there'll have to be an inquest. Just routine. And I'm afraid I'll have to ask you to pop down to the station and do some paperwork.' He glanced discreetly at his watch. 'But not today. It can wait till tomorrow.'

Indeed, since today was the day of the Coronation.

'I'll get Mullins here to drop you back home. Mr Wallis at home, is he?'

Was he? She tried to think. She nodded.

'Might be an idea to take Mr Paget's papers and valuables with you, Mrs Wallis. Once folk see a place is vacant—well, in this area you can't be too careful, in my experience. I'll give you a moment or two to gather his things together.' And he backed discreetly out.

A moment or two? Was that how long it would take to gather Freddie's papers and valuables? To pack up a man's life? And what papers did Freddie have? What valuables did you have when you lived in a bed-sit off the Marylebone Road?

She found them in a drawer in the little desk beside the bed, a tangle of old ration books and void clothing coupons and working permits for other countries; his birth certificate, folded and creased; a passport in the name of some other man entirely. Some coins—Canadian and English. A batch of dog-eared photographs of young men in khaki in the desert, with a gun, a tank, seen casually in the background, the names and dates scribbled on the back and beginning to fade. A single payslip from Home Counties Equity. A typed letter with the Home Counties address at the top and Nobby Caruthers's name at the bottom informing Mr Paget that certain information concerning his past had come to light and that, in view of this, Home Counties regretted they were unable to continue Mr Paget's employment. And in the margin, written in pencil in angry capitals, the single word, heavily underlined: *WALLIS?*

Wallis. Herself? Or Cecil? But the letter of dismissal had come from Nobby. *Certain information had come to light.* How did one check up on a man's military service record anyway? They had not discussed it. She had never asked Freddie how they, his new employer, could know, had found out his secret. Could one simply enquire at the Ministry of Defence? Did the Ministry give out that sort of information? Surely an employer could only find out if someone informed them?

'Mrs Wallis?'

The WPC stood respectfully in the doorway. The girl was in uniform, her heavy A-line skirt cruelly unfashionable, the hat flattening her perm. She looked too young to have left school and yet here she was, waiting to drive Harriet home in a police vehicle.

'We'll lock up, shall we? Just to be on the safe side,' and the girl pulled the front door shut behind them and firmly locked it, testing the door handle to make sure. Then she handed Harriet the key. 'You'd better take charge of this till you decide what to do with it.'

What would she do with it? A squalid bed-sit off the Marylebone Road where Freddie had died. She had no idea who owned the building, who the landlord was. She would give the key to Simon.

Simon. Someone would have to tell Simon.

WALLIS, written in angry pencil and heavily underlined, over and over again.

'All right, Mrs Wallis?'

The girl was peering at her, a hand out to help, but reluctant to make contact.

The journey back was long and convoluted. They appeared to be heading west through Paddington and Bayswater in an attempt to avoid the congestion of crowds around Hyde Park and it was a nightmare of stopping and starting and swerving.

'What a day for it,' observed the WPC, waiting patiently at the lights as hordes of onlookers swarmed across Bayswater Road and headed into the park. Whether she meant what a day for the Coronation or what a day for a suicide was unclear.

'This is you, isn't it?' she said at last, turning into Athelstan Gardens. Harriet nodded.

'Number 83. Towards the end.'

Above them the clouds thinned and a faint streak of sunshine crept across the garden and over the strings of bunting.

'There's someone home, is there, Mrs Wallis? Your husband?'

Her husband? Yes, he was at home; they were all at home.

She got out of the car, thanked the woman and let herself into the house. The WPC in the car waited outside for a time and Harriet stood in the hallway until she could see the car drive away.

Chapter Twenty-nine

'Corbett? Owen Corbett?'

Cecil Wallis appeared to strain every muscle in an effort to remember. Jean could see the tendons stretched taut in his face, the tiny beads of moisture that had burst out on his forehead and upper lip. His eyes never for a moment left the barrel of the revolver—*his* revolver—that was pointing, at this moment, at his chest. He *had* to remember; his very life depended on it.

'The foreman?' he gasped at last. 'Yes, yes, there *was* a man. Corbett. Welsh. Or came from a Welsh family. Worked at the West India Dock, he was the nightwatchman. There had been looting ... We had instructions to step up security.'

He paused, seemingly panic-stricken, staring at the gun, comically cross-eyed.

She could shoot him now, but that wasn't right. That was not how it must be. She must hear him say it: 'I'm sorry'. He must atone.

This then was her mission. This was His plan for her.

'*It was you, wasn't it*? It was *you* who had him sacked.'

The revolver shook wildly in her hands. She gripped it so tightly the butt cut into the flesh of her palms.

Mr Wallis appeared confused. He shook his head as though to clear it, as though to blank her out completely, to make her disappear.

'But I—Are you—is this man in some way *related* to you? Not your father? Yes, of course. I see. My God.' He appeared to stagger, reached behind him blindly for the desktop with which to steady himself. 'But, Miss Corbett.' He licked his lips, blinking rapidly. 'Miss Corbett, you *must* understand. It was *imperative* the docks, the warehouse were kept secure … No one could be trusted in those days. You must realise—the convoys *had to get through*—there were so little food reserves it was an issue of national security—'

'You *destroyed* him! You destroyed *us*!'

Mr Wallis stared at her.

'But I don't—'

'We was *starvin*'! We was all starvin'! Were *you* starvin', Mr Wallis?'

Mr Wallis opened his mouth, but no words came out.

'Dad knew it was wrong! Lord knows, we was brought up to fear the Lord, but what's an orange? A *single orange* to feed his children? And he was so *ashamed*. Do you think he'd have done it if he had thought there was any other way?'

Mr Wallis just stared.

'We didn't go to Chapel that mornin'. You see, don't you, Mr Wallis, what that meant?'

And still Mr Wallis stared.

Downstairs, from a long, long way off, Jean could hear the front door open and slam shut. Mr Wallis's hands gripped the edge of the desk behind him, shaking.

'But Miss Corbett. I don't understand you! I know nothing about an orange. *Nothing*, I *swear* to you! Yes, I remember that night—this incident—quite clearly, of course I do! The man—Corbett, your father—was with a woman, in the office. I found them. A *woman*. Do you understand what I'm saying? She was a prostitute, a young girl—no more than sixteen, seventeen, I don't know—and they were … engaged in a sexual act … Good *God*, if I dismissed the man, it was no more than he deserved. He was in a position of trust and he was carrying on—it was absolutely *untenable*.'

'*STOP!* That's a *lie!* A *lie!* How *dare*—'

'But there were others, not just myself! There were three of us there, myself and two of the docks police. Perkins and—and—oh, I forget the other man's name. We all saw it. Not just me. Ask them!'

The gun was no longer pointing at his chest, but it seemed that now Mr Wallis had begun talking he couldn't stop. She wanted him to stop.

'I'm sorry, so very sorry, Miss Corbett. I don't know what your father has told you about this incident but clearly … clearly …'

He did stop then, finally, as the gun was now lying on its side on his study desk and the nanny had fled from the room.

Chapter Thirty

JUNE 1953

Inside the house the level of noise was unexpected. So many voices. Harriet could hear the boom of the BBC presenter's commentary, the cheers of the crowds. She paused in the hallway and found that she was holding onto the wall, leaning against it. The stairs, the carpet on the floor, the lampshade, the coat cupboard, the telephone on the telephone table spun over and over again before her eyes. Was she going to be sick?

Mullins and her police vehicle had gone. She was alone.

'Cecil, old man? Where the devil are you? We're out of champers again!'

She waited, but when the reply came it was Julius, not Cecil, who made it.

'Nonsense. We've made adequate provision. Even for your extensive appetite, Uncle Leo.' The words seemed to echo around

her head long after they had been spoken. *We've made adequate provision.*
Adequate provision.

'And where the devil is Harriet? She's been gone an absolute
age!'

This wasn't Cecil either. *Had* she been gone an age? It seemed like
only minutes ago that Anne had announced the policemen were at
the door. Harriet had run down to answer it—it had been important
to answer the door before Cecil—and she had left the two police
officers, an inspector and a young WPC, standing in the doorway
as she went back upstairs to explain that the police had come to the
wrong house. No one had thought it odd. No one had noticed her
grab her coat and leave with the police in their car.

And out of nowhere Mrs Thompson loomed, her face red
and shiny and floating like a party balloon just a few inches from
Harriet's eyes.

'Oh, Mrs Wallis!' she announced and it sounded like an accusation.
'That soufflé's ruined. I told them it had to be served at once. *I told*
them!'

The red and shiny face swam before her eyes. Harriet turned
away from it, towards the stairs, but a sense of something urgent,
something horribly wrong, crept over her. The soufflé was ruined.
It was ruined. Had *she* ruined it?

It was an effort to climb the stairs and it was somehow necessary
to hold onto the banisters on both sides and heave oneself up bodily
one step at a time. The landing got further and further away the
higher and the further one climbed.

'I'm sorry, so very sorry!' said a voice, very stark and clear, but not from
the drawing room. From only a few feet away.

Cecil's voice. He was in his study. The door was closed. In a
moment, just as though they had been waiting for her, the door was
flung open and a girl burst out. It was the nanny and her face was
stricken and tearful, her eyes wild. She ran towards the stairs; yes,
one could see that she was running and yet it was as though the girl
moved in slow motion. She saw Mrs Wallis and veered towards the

stairs and away, but her presence, her stricken face, remained long after she had gone.

What did it mean? Why was the girl running? And the soufflé was ruined. Mrs Thompson had said so.

A cheer erupted from the drawing room, but seemed to come from far, far away, down the end of a tunnel.

'I wish we were there! Look at that crowd!'

'When are they going to come onto the balcony? It's taking ages!'

'Because it's official, dunderhead. These things are meant to take ages.'

'Where is Cecil with that champers? He's been a devil of a long time.'

Harriet flattened herself against the wall. The wall would hold her up. It would stop the world from spinning so fast.

We've made adequate provision.

What had the girl been doing in Cecil's study? Where *was* Cecil?

Cecil emerged from the study, but he was not carrying the champagne. He stood in the doorway, his face quite pale, his fingers fiddling nervously with his tie, his eyes going to the drawing room, to the stairs that led up to the nanny's room. He did not look down to where his wife stood, pressed against the wall of the stairs. He took a step and paused outside the door, appearing to think, then he ran his hands over his face, straightened his shoulders and entered the drawing room.

Behind him, the study door stood wide open. The room looked different somehow—the desk chair was on its side. Some papers were scattered across the floor. And on the top of the desk was Cecil's revolver.

Why it was there and who had put it there seemed irrelevant. It was there on the desk top and now it was in Harriet's hand. Was it loaded? Surely Cecil did not keep the thing loaded? It would be irresponsible.

The gun was in her hand. It ought to feel heavy, cold and unnatural in one's hand. And yet it felt like nothing. Was she holding the gun? She stood before the mirror that hung above the bookcase and watched as the gun pointed at the reflection of the woman in the mirror. Yes, she was indeed holding it. Or at least the woman in the mirror was.

The letter had said certain information had come to light. They had made adequate provision, yet the soufflé was ruined.

It was a double-action revolver. That meant one did not have to cock it each time one fired. How did one know such things?

'About time, old man. What the *devil* have you been doing in there? Having it away with the servants?'

'I thought it was all over, Harriet,' Freddie had said not so long ago in this very house. 'I really thought: this is it, I've done my time.'

And Mother had said, 'You'll look after Freddie, dear, won't you? He is in your care.'

The woman in the mirror lowered the gun from her reflection and turned smartly on her heel, crossed the hallway and opened the door to the drawing room.

'And here she is at last! The new Queen, along with the entire Royal Family, stepping onto the balcony at Buckingham Palace.'

There were a dozen people gathered around the television, some standing, some sitting, some of them familiar, others strangers.

'The crowds have waited a long time for this. And what a marvellous sight it is!'

Cecil had found a vacant chair just inside the doorway and was reaching for a glass of champagne. He turned his head slightly towards her and his eyes began to widen, but by then she had pulled the trigger and fired one, two, three, four, five, six times.

It was loaded, then; the gun was loaded.

He was in my care, thought Harriet. Freddie was in my care.

Epilogue

The summer of '53 went on forever. It seemed like autumn would never come. In the end you wanted it to come. Prayed for it like you prayed for peace. Or for absolution.

Mrs Wallis appeared the following day at Bow Street Magistrates Court and was remanded in custody at Holloway Prison until her trial and, but for the presence of a single, disgruntled court reporter from the *Evening Standard*, her appearance might have gone unremarked. Instead, it was a bald and uncompromising headline that met Londoners as they left their offices and made their way home on that hot Wednesday afternoon in early June: 'Society Wife Arrested in Shocking Coronation Day Slaying!'

The Coronation Day slaying. It was like the title of some lurid paperback. After that, Athelstan Gardens was under siege. Crowds waited outside the house for a glimpse of the Wallises, for a comment from the police, for a chance to see inside the house. For a scent of blood. Would they have stared so much had the slaying taken place in a mean laneway in Limehouse or Shadwell? If the wife had been married to a coal man?

A lone police constable was stationed outside the front door.

The facts—and many facts that weren't facts at all—quickly came out: Mrs Wallis was a wealthy heiress; her husband was a wealthy shipping magnate; Mrs Wallis's brother worked at the Palace; Mrs Wallis had shot her husband during the Coronation in a bizarre revolutionary—possibly Communist!—act; Mr Wallis had been having an affair—two affairs; he had been pushing for a divorce; he had dealings in shady off-shore companies; he had an impeccable war record; he had no war record at all; he was a millionaire; he was secretly bankrupt; he was an American; he was a Communist.

There was an inquest, and at the inquest the police evidence showed that Mr Wallis had been struck four times by bullets fired by a single gun. His own gun. And the gun had been held by his wife. Of that fact there appeared little dispute. The headlines became more lurid: 'Society Slaying Latest! Husband Shot With Own Gun! Wife In Custody!'

It was a sensation. The people of Britain were agog.

You couldn't escape it that summer. Harriet Wallis: so stylish, so wealthy, so glamorous, such lovely children, such an attentive and successful husband. The woman who had it all. What could Mr Wallis have done, they wondered, to warrant this execution-style murder? Was Mrs Wallis to be pitied or hated?

The newspapers reported that Mrs Wallis had been wearing a Norman Hartnell dress on the day of the Coronation.

The trial commenced on the 22nd of September at the Old Bailey's Number Three Court before Mr Justice Winthrop. Mrs Wallis, according to *The Times*, wore a smart suit in charcoal grey, her hair was neatly arranged, she wore little make-up and she appeared calm and expressionless as the charge of murder was read out. She entered a plea of not guilty. Yet there was little doubt who had pulled the trigger—ten witnesses gave testimony—but the reasons behind the act, the events leading up to it, were in dispute. If it could be shown that she had been driven to it, had acted in a fit of temporary insanity, it was the defence's duty to show it. A woman's life was at stake.

Counsel for the defence, Mr Wellesley Hammond QC, asserted that Mrs Wallis had been greatly upset by the death of her younger brother on the morning of the murder. The brother had killed himself. A police inspector and a WPC from Paddington Green police station were called to the stand and related in detail the actions of Mrs Wallis on the morning of the murder.

Mr Simon Paget, Mrs Wallis's brother, was asked to testify on her behalf. According to Mr Paget, Mrs Wallis had been devoted to her younger brother. His death, he explained, would have upset her greatly.

But to the point that she was driven to murder her husband?

This Mr Paget was at a loss to explain.

Could the deceased be held accountable in any way for the demise of Mrs Wallis's brother?

Again, Mr Paget was at a loss.

It had been alleged, said Mr Hammond, that the murdered man, Mr Cecil Wallis, was having an affair with the nanny. Could the discovery of her husband's infidelity account for it?

Mr Paget could not imagine his brother-in-law forming such an attachment, but if it were proved to be so, well then, yes, it was possible that this accounted in part for what had happened.

Mr and Mrs Leo Mumford, the murdered man's sister and brother-in-law, were called to testify, as were Mr Archibald Longhurst, Mr Mumford's nephew, and a Miss Mavis Dinsley of Coventry; so, too, Mr and Mrs Vincento and Mr and Mrs Paxton, neighbours of the Wallises, and the celebrated industrialist Mr David Swanbridge and his wife, all of whom had been present at the shooting. Six bullets had been fired. Mrs Wallis had fired them.

The housekeeper, Mrs Thompson, along with Mr Oleksiy Gregorov and Mr Stanley Ferris, both employees of a small Chelsea catering establishment who had been on duty at the Wallis household that day, were also called to the witness box. Mr Gregorov and Mr Ferris claimed to have been in the rear of the house taking a cigarette break at the time of the shooting. Mrs Thompson had been serving a crab soufflé in the kitchen. When questioned, Mrs Thompson stated that Mr Wallis, who had left his guests to request more champagne be brought up from the cellar, had not, in fact, spoken to her at all.

What had Mr Wallis done in the crucial ten minutes before his murder?

The nanny, Miss Jean Corbett, was called to the stand. She had not been present at the shooting and could not account for her actions immediately prior to the arrival of Mrs Wallis.

This, declared Mr Hammond QC, was significant. What had the nanny been doing? Why couldn't the nanny account for her movements? 'Wallis Nanny Implicated! Why Won't She Tell All?' screamed the headlines in the newspapers but the nanny remained silent.

The trial took three days. The jury retired on the afternoon of the third day to deliberate its decision, and ordered a large plate of sandwiches from the hotel next door. It took them just 45 minutes to find Mrs Wallis guilty of murder, and much of that time was taken up with the eating of the sandwiches.

Mr Justice Winthrop passed a sentence of death by hanging at Holloway Prison.

The summer finally drew to a close. An armistice was signed in Korea. The Russians tested another hydrogen bomb. A British man, one-time employee of a well-known shipping firm, was arrested and extradited from South Africa on charges of theft and embezzlement. And after fourteen years sugar was de-rationed.

On the day before the execution the Home Secretary dismissed any final appeals for a reprieve.

At a few minutes to seven on the morning of Monday the 9th of November, Harriet Wallis was taken the short distance from the condemned cell to the execution room. The execution took place at precisely seven o'clock. At four minutes past seven, the execution notice was posted outside the prison gates. After death, the corpse was inspected by the prison doctor. It was then left to hang for an hour, as was the custom. There was no room for error in a judiciary hanging.

Dawn came and the day began. It was a cold Monday morning in November and people went to work by bus and by train as normal. Yes, a woman had died, but sugar had been de-rationed. Mrs Wallis was buried the following day in an unmarked grave in West London. No members of the family were present.

The children did not attend the trial, nor the execution. They were taken abroad to Canada, it was reported, by their uncle and aunt. What happened to them after that, whether they ever returned to England, was unknown. Mr Simon Paget left the Palace soon after his sister's arrest and, according to the newspapers, took up an advisory position in the Middle East with a civil aviation firm. The house in Athelstan Gardens was vacated soon after the murder, and boarded up. It was sold a year or so later; purchased, like most of the houses in the street, by the Royal Brompton Hospital and turned into flats for the nurses, which was just as well, for who wanted to buy a house where a murder had been committed?

And the nanny, Miss Jean Corbett, who had not been able to account for her movements that day, disappeared from the public eye and was soon, like Harriet Wallis herself, forgotten.

READ ON
FOR AUTHOR Q&A
AND FURTHER POINTS FOR
READING GROUP DISCUSSION ...

MAGGIE JOEL

ON WRITING

The Second-Last Woman in England

WHAT WAS YOUR INSPIRATION FOR THIS STORY AND HOW DID YOU DEVELOP IT?

The story is not inspired by any real person or event but I do remember coming across some reference to a murderess being hanged in Britain in the mid-1950s, and the idea of this – of the state exacting such a punishment – really struck me. It seemed so barbaric, so archaic. If you grew up in Britain in the 1960s or 70s you are likely to have heard of the case of Ruth Ellis who, in 1955, was the last woman to be hanged, for the murder of her lover. It's a famous case – they made at least two movies about it – not simply because she was the last, but because she was a glamorous young woman who lived, what appeared to be, an exciting and enviable lifestyle. The idea that the state could put her to death shocked a lot of people at the time, and probably went some way towards ending capital punishment for women in the United Kingdom. I had no interest in retelling her story but I thought, 'How shocking would it be if our murderer was a very respectable, very well-to-do society wife and mother?' And there was my opening scene.

SO THE IDEA FOR A STORY STARTS WITH A SINGLE IMAGE?

For me, yes. If that image is strong enough, interesting enough, it will nag away at me until I write it down. At that point I will have no idea of a story, but if the image that I'm describing, and if my writing down of that image, seems to work, I keep going with it until a scene has been written, perhaps two or three scenes. At this point it's time to stop and sit back and review what I've done. It's here that the characters, the subsequent plot, and the setting for the story start to appear – hopefully!

WHAT DO YOU SEE AS THE BOOK'S MAIN THEME?

It's hard to put my finger on one primary theme as there were a number of concurrent themes that appeared as I wrote. Perhaps the most obvious is the constraints imposed on the individual by both middle-class family life, and life in early 1950s Britain. Both ideas seemed ripe for narrative exploitation. I'm fascinated by the contrast between the self we show to others and the real self, seen only by ourselves. I was also interested in exploring how events from way back in a person's past can impact on the present, and, following on from that, how the veneer of civilised life can, in an instant, be stripped away.

BOTH THIS BOOK AND YOUR PREVIOUS NOVEL, THE PAST AND OTHER LIES, BEGIN WITH A HANGING – ALBEIT IN VERY DIFFERENT CIRCUMSTANCES. COINCIDENCE, OR IS THERE SOMETHING MORE SINISTER AT PLAY HERE?

Definitely coincidence! In *The Past and Other Lies*, we have a teenage suicide; in this book it's a state-endorsed execution. The two situations are so poles apart it wasn't until both books were written that I even noticed it. I'm relieved to be able to report that the book I'm currently writing starts with a young woman picking flowers in a garden and I trust that will reassure readers I don't harbour any kind of hanging fixation!

THE STORY OF THE SECOND-LAST WOMAN IN ENGLAND IS VERY FIRMLY PLACED IN POST-WAR BRITAIN. HOW IMPORTANT WAS THIS HISTORIC SETTING TO THE BOOK AND WHY THAT PERIOD?

When I was growing up in 1970s England there was a great deal of 1950s nostalgia but, looking back at that time now, I realise that that nostalgia was focused purely on the late 1950s. It's as though there was no recognition of popular culture existing prior to 1955. Those years, 1950 to 1954 were a cultural blank for me and a historic blank too, come to think of it. I wanted to know what happened. How did people get from the end of the war to rock'n'roll in ten years? What came between? And the more I studied the period the more fascinating I found it. The world before 1939 had been swept aside. At one point in the book, Cecil observes: '*One did one's bit for the war effort, endured it so that things would remain the same, could return to how they were. But now the war had been over for seven years and nothing was the same.*'

That must have been a terrific shock for people of Cecil's generation, of their upbringing. They retained the values of that previous era but nothing was ever the same again. And in the book, that is ultimately the cause of Cecil's demise.

THIS BOOK, LIKE *THE PAST AND OTHER LIES*, IS A STUDY OF FAMILY RELATIONSHIPS. WHAT IS THE ATTRACTION TO YOU OF THE FAMILY AS SUBJECT MATTER?

It seems to me that the family, and the family home, is a microcosm of the society you live in, a tangible representation of the moral values, the ideas, the beliefs of that society. That's intriguing to me; it offers so many possibilities. In *The Second-Last Woman in England*, the setting is a family home in early 1950s England, a period with a morality and a set of conventions that seem almost alien to us in the twenty-first century. The Wallises reflect those ideas and conventions and at the same time struggle against them – much as any family would in any place and setting in history.

WE ARE ALWAYS FASCINATED BY THE IDEA OF A WOMAN COMMITTING MURDER – WHY DID YOU CHOOSE THIS SUBJECT?

I think when a woman murders, we look for a reason – how could she have done this, what drove her to it? – in a way that perhaps we don't do so much for a man. It seems to be me that something exceptional must occur for a woman to commit murder. And add to that a woman of a certain class living a certain, perhaps very privileged, lifestyle, and there is a basis for a captivating story. My story began with the single image, as I mentioned earlier – a woman waiting in the condemned cell, the walk to the execution room, the crowds standing silently outside the prison, the death notice stuck on the prison gates. Then juxtapose that with the same woman a year earlier at a cocktail party in Chelsea, and all I had to do was get her from point A to point B.

SUGGESTED POINTS FOR DISCUSSION

1

Do we feel any sympathy for Harriet? Did she get what she deserved or is she a victim of a cruel set of circumstances?

2

To what extent does Cecil Wallis contribute to his own death? Are his actions justified or do we hold him in any way responsible for what occurs?

3

Is Jean's hatred of Cecil justified? In the end she does not go through with her plan but is Jean any less to blame for Cecil's death than Harriet?

4

The Wallis children, Julius and Anne, appear to be the innocent victims of the tragedy that unfolds – but is this really so? Do their actions play a part in the events leading up to their father's murder?

5

To what extent does the location of the novel, set as it is in austere post-war London, impact on the story? Could the events described in the novel have happened at some other time in history or in a contemporary setting?

6

Cecil's life appears to be ruled by a set of standards and principles that seem out of step with the world he now finds himself in. He is driven by a need to 'do the right thing' and yet he makes two critical decisions during the course of the book that ultimately cost him dearly. What were those decisions and do we agree with, or condemn, his choices?

7

The war has been over for seven years and yet its impact is felt in almost every chapter. To what extent do events from the past affect the actions of the characters?

8

So many incidents, some large, others seemingly minor, contribute to the final tragic act. Could things have turned out differently for Harriet and Cecil, or was it always going to end this way?